Shinjū

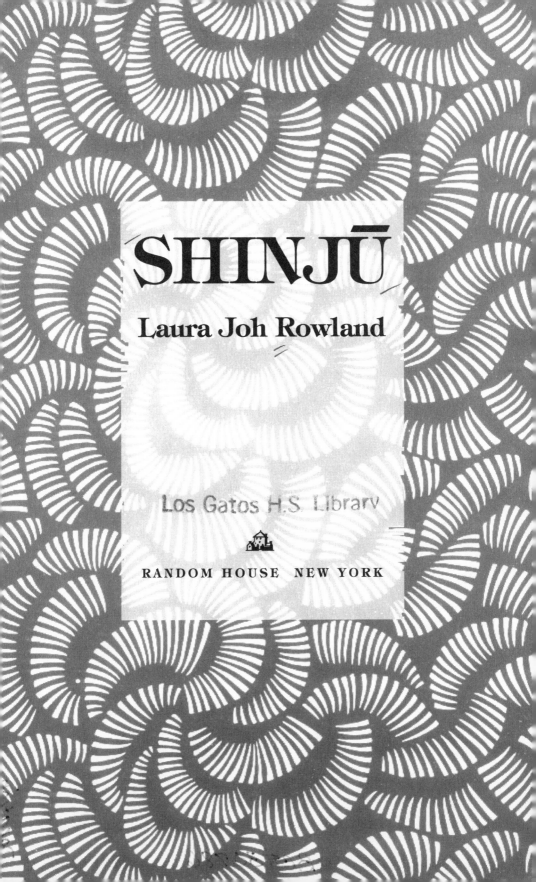

SHINJŪ

Laura Joh Rowland

RANDOM HOUSE NEW YORK

Library of Congress Cataloging-in-Publication Data
Rowland, Laura Joh.
Shinjū / Laura Joh Rowland.
p.   cm.
ISBN 0-679-43422-4
1. Japan—History—1333–1600—Fiction.   2. Tokyo (Japan)—History—
Fiction.   3. Police—Japan—Tokyo—Fiction.   I. Title.
PS3568.O934S55   1993
813′.54—dc20   94-10181

Manufactured in the United States of America
2 4 6 8 9 7 5 3
First Edition

BOOK DESIGN BY LILLY LANGOTSKY

To my parents,
Lena and Raymond Joh

Shinjū

Edo

Genroku Period, Year 1, Month 12

(Tokyo, January 1689)

Prologue

The horseman halted his mount on a narrow path that led to the Sumida River, listening to the night. Had he heard a footstep somewhere in the dark forest that surrounded him? Was someone watching him? Fear set his heart racing.

But he heard only the icy wind rattling the bare winter branches and the faint chuffing of his mare as she stirred restlessly beneath him. High above the horizon, the last full moon of the Old Year shone brightly, silvering the path and the forest with a chill radiance. He peered into the shadows, but saw no one.

Then he smiled grimly: guilt and imagination had deceived him. This path in the remote northern outskirts of Edo saw little enough traffic by day. Now, at just past midnight, it was deserted.

As he'd foreseen.

He urged the mare forward through a thicket of branches that caught on his hooded cloak and on the long, bulky bundle slung over the horse's back behind him. The mare faltered, whinnying softly, unaccustomed to the extra weight. He tried to calm her, but she refused to go on. As she stamped her hooves, the bundle wobbled dangerously. He flung a hand back to steady it. Cold fear licked at him. What if it fell? Strong as he was, he would never be able to lift it back on—not here. And he couldn't carry it the rest of the way to the river. It would take an hour by foot; impossible with a burden nearly as long as and even heavier than he. Besides, dragging it would tear the fine rice straw of the tatami mats with which he'd wrapped it, damaging the contents.

The horse, after one more stamp, suddenly continued down the path. The bundle held firm. Fear receded. His eyes watered and his face grew numb from the cold; his gloved hands seemed frozen to the reins. What sustained him was the knowledge that each misery-laden step brought him closer to the completion of his mission.

Finally, the woods thinned and the path sloped steeply toward the river. He could smell the water and hear it lapping at the shore. Dismounting, he tied the horse to a tree and stepped off the path.

The boat was right where he'd left it yesterday, hidden among the lower branches of a huge pine. With his cold-stiffened hands, he grasped its prow. Carefully, so that the rocky ground wouldn't damage its flat wooden bottom, he dragged it onto the path beside the horse. Then he untied the ropes that bound the bundle to the horse's back. When the last knot opened, the bundle dropped into the boat with a loud thud.

He began to push the boat down the slope to the water. The slope, though not more than forty paces long, did not provide an easy launch. Soon he was panting with the effort of alternately pushing, lifting, and dragging the boat toward the river. At last he reached the shoreline, and the boat slid in with a *whoosh*. He waded into the freezing water, pulling the boat with him until it cleared bottom and floated free of the rushes. Then he climbed inside.

The boat rocked precariously under the combined weight of him and the bundle. Water sloshed over the sides. For one dreadful moment he feared the boat would sink, but it abruptly stabilized with its gunwales just above the water. Sighing his relief, he lifted the oar, stood in the stern, and began to row south toward the city.

The river spread before him like an immense length of oiled black silk stippled with moonlight. The splash of his oar made a rhythmic counterpoint to the keening wind. On the near shore to his right, pinpoints of flame winked on dark land that rose gradually toward the hills: lanterns lighting the Yoshiwara pleasure quarter; torches flaring in Asakusa's temple gardens. On the distant eastern shore he could discern nothing of marshy Honjo. No pleasure craft decorated the scene, as in summer. Tonight he had the river to himself. He could almost enjoy the solitude and the eerie beauty of the night.

But soon his arms grew tired. His breath came in painful gasps. Sweat drenched his garments, letting the frigid wind penetrate them. He longed to simply drift with the river's current as it flowed toward Edo Bay and the sea. Only his desperate need for haste enabled him to push on. Just a few short hours now remained until dawn, and he needed the cover of darkness. If only he could have made the journey by land, on horseback! But Edo's many guarded gates closed before midnight, sealing off each sector to prohibit exit or entry. The river was the only way.

So he felt immense relief when the city's familiar sights began to appear. First the pavilions of the daimyo, powerful provincial lords who owned much of the land along the upper stretches of the river, as well as most of Japan. Then the whitewashed walls of the city's rice warehouses. Piers and wharves crowded with boats jutted out into the river, now turned foul and fishy, stinking from the waste dumped into it every day. At last the Ryōgoku Bridge arched above him, the interlocked pillars and struts of its wooden structure an intricate pattern cut out of the sky.

Exhausted, he stopped at the end of a pier downstream from the bridge, but still within sight of it. He set aside his oar and tied the boat to a piling. Once again, fear gripped him, stronger this time. The whole great city of Edo lay beyond the blank facades of the warehouses. He could sense the million souls that lived there—not asleep, but watching him. Choking back his panic, he knelt before the bundle. Gently, so as not to unbalance the boat, he unwound the stiff straw wrappings. A glance at the sky told him that the moon had long set; dawn's first rosy light tinted the eastern horizon. He could make out the docks of the lumberyards in Fukagawa on the opposite bank.

He fought the impulse to jerk at the last mat, instead folding it carefully away.

The two bodies, joined in death and by ropes that bound them at wrists and ankles, lay facing each other, heads positioned cheek to cheek. The man wore the short kimono and cotton trousers of a commoner. His cropped hair framed a blunt, coarse face. Puffy eyes and a sensual mouth bespoke a life of dissipation, carnality, and avarice. He'd deserved killing. How easy it had been to lure him to his death with a promise of riches! But the woman . . .

Her innocent young face, covered with rice-flour makeup, glowed a translucent white. High on her forehead, the fine dark lines drawn above her shaved brows took wing over the long-lashed crescents of her closed eyes. Her lips had parted slightly to reveal two perfect teeth: Darkened with ink according to the fashion for ladies of high birth, they gleamed like black pearls. Long black hair spilled nearly to her feet over a silk kimono that twisted around her slender body.

Sighing, he reminded himself that her death was as necessary as the man's. But he could not look at her beauty without a spasm of grief—

A sharp clacking noise made him start. Was someone walking toward him along the pier? Then the clacking repeated: two long beats followed by three short. He relaxed. It was only a night-watchman, somewhere inland, striking his wooden clappers to signal the time. The water had carried the sound.

From his cloak he took a small, flat lacquer case, which he tucked into the woman's sash. Then he put his arms under both bodies and heaved. They tumbled over the side of the boat. There was a muffled splash as they hit the dark water. Before they could sink, he caught the end of the rope that bound their wrists and wrapped it around the piling, wedging it firmly into a crack in the slimy wood. He took one last look at the corpses that now floated just beneath the water's surface in an undulating tangle of the woman's hair. Then he looked back toward the bridge.

And nodded in satisfaction. When they were found—as they soon would be—everyone would surmise that they'd jumped from the bridge together and drifted downstream until the piling caught them. The letter sealed in the watertight case would confirm that impression. He watched to make sure the rope was secure. Then he untied his boat and began the long, cold journey back upstream.

*Y*oriki Sano Ichirō, Edo's newest senior police commander,
made his way slowly on horseback across Nihonbashi Bridge. Early
on this sunny, clear winter morning, throngs of people streamed
around him: porters carrying baskets of vegetables to and from
market; water vendors with buckets suspended from poles on their
shoulders; shoppers and tradesmen bent low under the packages
on their backs. The planks thundered with the steps of wood-soled
feet; the air was bright with shouts, laughter, and chatter. Even the
hallmarks of Sano's samurai status couldn't speed his passage. His
mount, a bay mare, merely raised him above the bobbing heads.
The two swords he wore—one a long, curved saber, the other a
shorter dirk—elicited no more than an occasional mumbled ''A
thousand pardons, honorable master.''

But Sano enjoyed his leisurely progress, and his freedom. He'd
escaped from the tedium that had marked his first month as a *yoriki*.
A former tutor and history scholar, he'd quickly found the administration of his small section of the police department far less
satisfying than teaching young boys and studying ancient texts. He
missed his old profession; the thought of never again chasing down
a lost or obscure fact left a sad, empty ache at the center of his
spirit. Still, although family circumstances and connections, rather
than choice or talent, had thrown him into the unfamiliar world
of law enforcement, he'd sworn to make the best of the situation.

Today he had decided to explore his new domain more fully than he could by sitting in his office and affixing his seal to his staff's reports. Exhilarated, he peered over the bridge's railings at the panorama of Edo.

The wide canal, lined with whitewashed warehouses, was jammed with barges and fishing boats. Smoke from countless charcoal braziers and stoves formed a haze over the low tiled and thatched rooftops that extended over the plain in all directions. Through it he could see Edo Castle perched on its hill at the end of the canal. There Ieyasu, first of the Tokugawa shoguns, had established the seat of his military dictatorship seventy-four years ago, fifteen years after defeating his rival warlords in the Battle of Sekigahara. The upturned eaves of the keep's many roofs made it look like a pyramid of white birds ready to take flight: a fitting symbol of the peace that had followed that battle, the longest peace Japan had known in five centuries. Beyond the castle, the western hills were a soft shadow, only slightly less blue than the sky. Mount Fuji's distant snow-capped cone rose above them. Temple bells tolled faintly, adding to the panoply of sounds.

At the foot of the bridge, Sano passed the noisy, malodorous fish market. He edged his horse through the narrow winding streets of Nihonbashi, the peasants' and merchants' quarter named after the bridge. In the open wooden storefronts of one street, sake sellers bartered with their customers. Around the next corner, men labored over steaming vats in a row of dyers' shops. Mud and refuse squished under the horses' hooves and pedestrians' shoes. Sano turned another corner.

And emerged into a vast open space where last night's fire had leveled three entire blocks. The charred remains of perhaps fifty houses—ash, blackened rafters and beams, soaked debris, fallen roof tiles—littered the ground. The bitter smell of burnt cypress wood hung in the air. Forlorn residents picked their way through the mess, hunting for salvageable items.

"Aiiya," an old woman keened. "My home, all my things, gone! Oh, what will I do?" Others took up her cry.

Sano sighed and shook his head. Thirty-two years ago—two years before his birth—the Great Fire had destroyed most of the city and taken a hundred thousand lives. And still the "blossoms of Edo," as the fires were known, bloomed almost every week among the wooden buildings where a strong wind could quickly fan a single spark into a ferocious blaze. From their rickety wooden towers high above the rooftops, the firewatchers rang bells at the first sight of a flame. Edo's citizens slept uneasily, listening for the alarm. Most fires were accidents, caused by innocent mistakes such as a lamp placed too near a paper screen, but arson wasn't uncommon.

He'd come to learn whether this fire had resulted from arson. But one look at the ruins told him he could not expect to find evidence. He would have to rely on witnesses' stories. Dismounting, he approached a man who was dragging an iron chest from the rubble.

"Did you see the fire start?" he called.

He never heard the answer. Just then, running footsteps and cries of "Stop, stop!" sounded behind him. Sano turned. A thin man dressed in rags streaked past, panting and sobbing. A pack of ruffians brandishing clubs stampeded after him. The man's bare feet slipped in the mud, and he went sprawling about ten paces from Sano. Immediately the pursuers set upon their quarry, clubs flailing.

"You'll die for this, you miserable animal!" one of them shouted.

The ragged man's sobs turned to screams of pain and terror as he threw up his arms to shield his head from the blows.

Sano hurried over and grabbed the arm of one of the attackers. "Stop, you'll kill him! What do you think you're doing?"

"Who's asking?"

At the sound of the gruff voice beside him, Sano turned. A burly man with small, mean eyes stood at his elbow. He wore a short kimono over cotton leggings; his cropped hair and the single short sword fastened at the waist of his gray cloak marked him as a samurai of low rank. Then Sano caught sight of the object in the man's right hand, a strong steel wand with two curved prongs above the hilt for catching the blade of an attacker's sword. It was a *jitte,* a parrying weapon, standard equipment of the *doshin,* the law enforcement officers who patrolled the city and maintained order.

Comprehension flashed through Sano. This man was one of his hundred-odd subordinates, one of the long line of bowed heads he'd passed during the formal ceremony at which his staff was presented to him. The armed ruffians, who had ceased torturing their victim to look at him, were the *doshin*'s civilian assistants. Privately employed by their superior—and responsible only to him—they performed the dirty work of policing, such as capturing criminals, under his direction. Now three of them moved menacingly in on Sano.

"Who are you?" the *doshin* demanded again.

Sano said, "I am *Yoriki* Sano Ichirō. Now explain to me why your men are beating this citizen."

Although he kept his voice calm and stern, his heartbeat quickened. He'd had little chance to exercise his new authority.

The *doshin*'s mouth gaped. He passed a hand over his jutting jaw in obvious confusion. Then he bowed obsequiously.

"*Yoriki* Sano-*san,*" he muttered. "Didn't recognize you."

He jerked his head at his assistants, who formed a hasty line and bowed, hands on their knees. "My sincerest apologies."

His sullen tone belied the respectful words. Sano could sense the *doshin*'s veiled contempt. The mean little eyes narrowed still more as they traveled over his freshly shaved crown and his oiled hair drawn into a neat looped knot at the back. They registered disgust at the sight of Sano's best outer garment, the black-and-brown-striped *haori,* and his new black *hakama,* the wide trousers he wore beneath it. Sano bristled at such open rudeness, but he could understand the man's contempt. The reputation of *yoriki* for vanity was well known. He himself cared little for fashion, but his superior, Magistrate Ogyu, had stressed the importance of proper dress and appearance.

"Your apologies are accepted," Sano said, deciding to address the matter at hand instead of making an issue over his subordinate's manners. "Now answer my question: what has this man done for which you must punish him?"

Now Sano could see bewilderment on the *doshin's* face. *Yoriki* seldom ventured into the streets, preferring to keep their distance from the rough-and-tumble of everyday police work. They appeared only for very serious incidents, and then as field commanders dressed in full armor with helmet and lance. Sano supposed he was the first to ever investigate a common fire.

"He did this," the *doshin* answered, gesturing at the ruins. "Set the fire. Killed fifteen people." He spat at the man, who still lay facedown in the mud, shoulders trembling with muffled sobs.

"How do you know?"

The *doshin's* prominent jaw thrust out even further, in anger and resentment. "The townspeople saw a man fleeing the street just after the fire started, *Yoriki* Sano-*san.* And he confessed."

Sano walked past the assistants and over to the fallen man. "It's all right," he said gently. "Get up now."

Clumsily the man hunched at the waist, then rose to his knees. Sitting back on his heels, he wiped the mud from his face. Then, to Sano's surprise, his mouth opened in a wide, toothless smile.

"Yes, master." His head bobbed, and his eyes twinkled. Despite the wrinkles that creased his cheeks and forehead, he looked as innocent as a child.

"What's your name?" Sano asked.

"Yes, master."

Sano repeated the question. Getting the same response, he tried another. "Where do you live?"

"Yes, master."

"Did you start the fire?" Sano asked, beginning to understand.

"Yes, master, yes master!" Then, seeing Sano's frown, the man lost his smile. He got to his feet, but fell back as the *doshin*'s assistants surrounded him again. "No hurt, master!" he pleaded.

"No one will harm you." Furious, Sano turned to the *doshin*. "This man is a simpleton. He doesn't understand you, or what he's saying. You cannot accept his confession."

The *doshin*'s face flushed, and he squared his shoulders. The *jitte* shook in his clenched fist. "I asked him if he started the fire. He said yes. How was I to know he was an idiot?"

A voice from the swelling crowd of spectators cried, "If you'd taken the time to talk to him, you would have found out!" Someone else shouted, "He's just a harmless old beggar!" Mutters of agreement followed.

"Shut up!" The *doshin* turned on the crowd, and the mutters faded. Then he faced Sano. "Arson is a serious crime," he said with exaggerated patience and not a little self-righteousness. "Someone must pay."

For a moment, Sano was too appalled to speak. This law officer—and many others, if the rumors he'd heard were correct—cared more about finding a scapegoat than about uncovering the truth. He wanted to chastise the man for shirking his duty. Then he saw the *doshin*'s free hand stray toward the short sword. He knew that only his rank kept the man from challenging him on the spot. He'd made the *doshin* lose face before the assistants and the townspeople. And, on his first day in the field, he had made an enemy.

To make peace, he contented himself with saying, "Then we must find the real arsonist. You and your men and I will question the witnesses."

Sano watched the *doshin* and his men move off to mingle with the crowd. A curious elation came over him. He'd corrected an injustice and probably saved a man's life. For the first time, he realized that being a *yoriki* offered many opportunities for seeking the truth, and just as many rewards for finding it. More, perhaps, than his work as a scholar, poring over old documents. But he wondered uneasily how many more enemies he would make.

It was early afternoon by the time Sano returned to the administrative district, located in Hibiya, southeast of Edo Castle. There the city's high officials had their office-mansions, where they both lived and worked. Messengers bearing rolled documents passed Sano as he rode along the narrow lanes between earthen walls that shielded the tile-roofed, half-timbered houses. Dignitaries dressed in bright, flowing silk garments walked in pairs or groups; fragments of conversation dealing with affairs of state and the latest political gossip reached Sano's ears. Servants scurried in and out of the gates, carrying trays stacked high with lacquer lunchboxes. The thought of those delicacies made Sano regret the greasy noodles he'd eaten at a food stall on his way back. But the arson investigation had taken longer than he'd anticipated, and the quick though unpleasant meal he'd had would let him return to his other duties without further delay. Turning the corner, he headed toward police headquarters.

"*Yoriki* Sano-*san!*" A breathless messenger ran up to him, ducking in a hasty bow. "Please, sir, Magistrate Ogyu would like to see you at once. In the Court of Justice, sir." He raised questioning eyes for Sano's response.

"Very well. You're dismissed."

A summons from the magistrate could not go ignored. Sano changed course.

Magistrate Ogyu's mansion was one of the largest in the district. At the roofed portals of its gate, Sano identified himself to a pair of guards dressed in leather armor and headgear. He left his horse with them, then entered the mansion's grounds and threaded his way through a small crowd of townspeople gathered in the courtyard. Some were waiting to bring their disputes before the magistrate; others, accompanied by *doshin* and with their hands bound by ropes, were obviously prisoners awaiting trial.

Sano paused at the main entrance of the long, low building. Barred wooden lattices covered the windows. The roof's projecting eaves cast deep shadows over the veranda. Seeing the mansion for the first time, he had imagined its dark, brooding appearance symbolic of the often harsh sentences pronounced inside. The surrounding garden, with its unlit stone lanterns and skeletal winter trees, reminded him of a graveyard. Shaking off his fancy, he climbed the wooden steps. At a nod from the two guards stationed there, he opened the massive carved door.

"Blacksmith Goro." Magistrate Ogyu's reedy voice echoed across the long hall as Sano paused in the entryway. "I have considered all the evidence brought before me regarding the crime with which you are charged."

Sano went to wait at the back of the hall with the samurai courtroom attendants. At the far end, Magistrate Ogyu knelt upon the dais. A thin, stoop-shouldered old man, he seemed lost in his voluminous red and black silk robes. Lamps on either side of his black lacquer desk lit him like a figure on stage. The rest of the room was dim; sunlight filtering through the latticed rice-paper windows provided the only other illumination. Directly before the dais was the *shirasu,* an area of floor covered with white sand, symbol of truth. There the accused man, bound at wrists and ankles, knelt on a mat. Two *doshin* knelt on either side of the *shirasu.* A small audience—witnesses, the accused's family, and the headman of his neighborhood—formed a row toward the back of the hall.

"That evidence indicates beyond all doubt that you are guilty of the murder of your father-in-law," Ogyu continued.

"No!" The scream burst from the accused man. He writhed on the mat, straining at his bonds.

Several of the spectators cried out. A woman collapsed weeping onto the floor.

Ogyu raised his voice above the din, saying, "I sentence you to death. So that they may share in your disgrace, your family is to be banished from the province." He nodded to the *doshin,* who leaped up and bore the screaming, struggling prisoner out the back door. The attendants hurried forward and escorted the spectators from the room, one dragging the weeping woman by her armpits. Then Ogyu called, "Sano Ichirō. Come forward."

Sano walked to the front of the room and knelt behind the *shirasu,* a little shaken. Ogyu had just sentenced a man to death and his family to exile, but he was as calm as could be. Sano reminded himself that Ogyu had served as one of Edo's two magistrates for thirty years. He'd handled so many trials that he had grown inured to sights that would disturb others. He bowed deeply to Ogyu and said, "How may I serve you, Honorable Magistrate?"

Ogyu's pale, spidery hands toyed with his magisterial seal, an oblong chunk of alabaster that bore the characters of his name and rank. His pinched face with its drooping eyelids gleamed sallow and sickly in the flickering lamplight, and his age-spotted bald pate looked like a diseased melon.

"Arson is a serious crime," Ogyu murmured, studying the seal with elaborate concern. He paused, then added, "Though not an uncommon one."

"Yes, Honorable Magistrate," Sano answered, wondering why Ogyu had summoned him. Surely not to exchange trivialities. But Ogyu, like many other members of the refined upper classes, never came directly to the point. Kneeling in the Court of Justice, Sano felt as though he—or rather his powers of comprehension—were on trial.

"Such important but distasteful matters are best left to the devices of the lower classes. And one's actions have a most unfortunate way of reflecting unfavorably on others.'' Ogyu turned his head to gaze toward the north windows, in the direction of the castle.

Then Sano understood. Spies and informers abounded in Edo; they were part of an intelligence network that helped the shogun maintain the Tokugawas' unchallenged control over the nation. Someone had undoubtedly begun reporting to Ogyu on Sano's activities the day he assumed his position as *yoriki*. That someone must have been in the crowd at the site of the fire. And Ogyu had just told him that for a man of his rank to do *doshin*'s work shamed the entire government, all the way up to the shogun. Although he didn't want to contradict his superior, Sano felt compelled to defend himself.

"Honorable Magistrate, the *doshin* and his men would have arrested an innocent man if I hadn't stopped them,'' he said. "By questioning the witnesses, we got a description of the real arsonist, and—''

Ogyu lifted a finger, silencing Sano. The gesture came as close to an open rebuke as Sano had ever seen him make. But instead of speaking about the investigation, Ogyu changed the subject. "I had the privilege of taking tea with Katsuragawa Shundai yesterday.''

The syllables of the name fell over Sano like an iron blanket. All further protests died on his lips. Katsuragawa Shundai was his patron, the man who had gotten him this position.

During the civil wars of the last century, Sano's great-grandfather, a vassal in the service of Lord Kii, had saved the life of a fellow soldier, head of the Katsuragawa family. The Katsuragawa fortunes had risen while the Sanos' declined, but that act had bound the two families inextricably. Sano remembered the day when his father had called in that old debt. . . .

His father had taken him to see Katsuragawa Shundai at the city treasury. Kneeling in Katsuragawa's sumptuous office, they had accepted bowls of tea.

"I do not have much longer to live, Katsuragawa-*san*," his father said. "That is why I must request your assistance in the matter of my son. I have no fortune to leave him, and he is a mere tutor with no prospects and no special talents. But surely, with your influence . . . ?"

Katsuragawa did not reply at once to the unspoken question. He lit his pipe, then cast a measuring glance at Sano. Finally he said, "I will see what I can do."

Sano kept his eyes on his bowl. He hoped that Katsuragawa would do nothing, because he knew that his duty to his father required that he accept whatever was offered. However, he could live with the idea of benefiting from Katsuragawa's patronage. In peacetime, samurai no longer made their fortunes by the sword. Their hope for success lay in getting a position in the government bureaucracy, through some combination of ability and connections. But he hated the thought of leaving his beloved profession for another that would suit him as little as he suited it.

Ogyu's voice recalled Sano to the present. "I trust that we understand each other?"

"Yes, Honorable Magistrate," Sano said heavily. Ogyu had reminded him of his obligation to his father and to Katsuragawa. To fulfill that obligation, he'd agreed to serve as a senior police commander when Ogyu, at Katsuragawa's request, had offered him the post. It left no room for argument, independent action, or unconventional behavior. Duty, loyalty, and filial piety were the cardinal principles of Bushido—the Way of the Warrior—the strict code that governed a samurai's conduct. His honor, highest and most important of all virtues, depended on his adherence to the code. And the military government Sano served valued conformity and obedience more than it did the pursuit of truth and justice, which were, by comparison, fluid and negotiable. Sano must defer to his superior's desires at the expense of his own. He also felt deeply disgraced by Ogyu's implied criticism. Never again would he venture out of the administrative district to investigate firsthand the cases that crossed his desk. From now on, those cases would remain words on paper. He bowed again, expecting Ogyu to dismiss him.

But Ogyu had not finished. "A small matter has come to my attention," he said, "one that must be handled with the utmost discretion. You will do exactly as I say."

His uncharacteristic directness piqued Sano's curiosity.

"A fisherman pulled two bodies, a man and a woman, from the river this morning," Ogyu continued. His small mouth pursed in disgust. "A *shinjū.*"

Sano's curiosity grew. Double love suicides were almost as common as, and surely even more distasteful than, the fires that Ogyu had told him to leave to the *doshin.* Often lovers who couldn't marry due to family opposition chose to die together in the hope that they might spend eternity in the Buddhist paradise. Why did Ogyu want to involve him in a petty *shinjū?*

Ogyu gave him the answer to his unspoken question. "This was found on the woman's body," he said, taking a folded letter from his desk and offering it to Sano.

Rising, Sano crossed the *shirasu* and accepted the letter. The delicate rice paper crackled in his hands as he opened it and read the characters inked in a fine feminine hand.

> Farewell to this world and to the night farewell
> We who walk the path that leads to death—
> To what should it be compared?
> To the frost by the road that leads to the graveyard
> Vanishing with each step we take:
> How sad is this dream of a dream!
>
> Noriyoshi (artist)
> Niu Yukiko

Sano recognized the passage from a popular Kabuki play about a pair of doomed lovers. This was their final song before their death. Now he knew why Ogyu wanted him to handle the matter with discretion. The man, Noriyoshi, was a peasant, as the lack of a surname and the appendage of his profession made clear. A nobody. But Yukiko was daughter to Niu Masamune, lord of Satsuma and Osumi Provinces and one of the wealthiest, most powerful daimyo.

"I can see that you appreciate the delicacy of this situation," Ogyu said. "Since the cause of death is obvious, you will dispense with the matter as quickly and quietly as possible. You will have Niu Yukiko's body returned to her family, and inform your staff that anyone who publicizes her name or the circumstances of her death will meet with the most severe punishment.

"The man Noriyoshi, however . . ." Ogyu picked up a brush and dipped it into his inkwell. "Noriyoshi shall suffer the full penalty dictated by the laws of the land. That will be all, *Yoriki* Sano."

Conflicting emotions warred within Sano. Ogyu wanted him to close the case without investigation. To keep Yukiko's identity confidential, and to disgrace Noriyoshi's family by exposing his corpse in public—customary treatment for love suicides. But Ogyu's overemphasis on discretion aroused his suspicion. Every instinct told him to probe for the truth about the *shinjū*. But he had made a pledge to behave correctly and play by the rules.

"Yes, Honorable Magistrate," he said, bowing. "I obey."

Police headquarters occupied a site in the southernmost corner of the administrative district, far from the office-mansions and as remote from the castle as possible. According to the tenets of the Shinto religion, any contact with death conferred a ritual impurity, a spiritual pollution. Even the police's indirect administration of executions made other officials shun them. The appearance of their headquarters reflected this isolation: completely surrounded by a high wall, with not even its rooftops visible from the street.

Sano gained admittance from the guards stationed at the gate and turned his horse over to a stableboy. Crossing a yard lined with *doshin* barracks, he entered the rambling wooden main building. He walked through the reception room, a large, open space broken by square pillars. There chaos reigned. Four clerks seated at desks on a raised platform in the room's center dispatched messengers and dealt with the many visitors lined up before them. *Doshin* waited to sign on or off duty, or to give their reports. Servants streamed through the side entrances, bearing tea trays to and from the inner rooms where the *yoriki* had their private offices. Muted daylight came in through the windows, falling in shafts through the tobacco smoke from many pipes. The sound level remained at a constant civilized hum with only an occasional raised voice. But Sano found the inner reception room quiet, empty except for two men. Both wore formal dress—full, flowing silk trousers and wide-shouldered surcoats belted with wide sashes—of the most fashionable cut and pattern. The scent of wintergreen oil emanated from their meticulously arranged hair. They were the epitome of the proud, style-conscious *yoriki*.

"Yamaga-*san*. Hayashi-*san*." Sano bowed. "Good day."

Yamaga, the taller and elder, inclined his head slightly in acknowledgment. Face radiating hostility, he did not reply to Sano's greeting. Hayashi, a man of Sano's age, twisted his thin lips in a sarcastic smile.

"Good day, newcomer," he said. "I trust that your work goes well with you. Or at least as well as could be expected, for one not born to the responsibility." His mocking air made the solicitous words an insult.

Saddened, Sano watched them go. He'd seen at once that he would not easily make friends with them or his forty-seven other colleagues. Unlike himself, they were true *yoriki* who had inherited their positions from their fathers. That an unqualified outsider could slip so easily into their ranks was an affront to their family and professional pride. Now their chill disapproval followed him as he walked down the long corridor and entered his own suite of offices, nodding a greeting to the clerks under his supervision.

When Sano slid open the door to his private office, he found another source of unhappiness awaiting him. Hamada Tsunehiko, his sixteen-year-old personal secretary, lolled on the mats near the charcoal brazier that heated the room, reading an illustrated story-book. The reports that Sano had given him to file lay disregarded upon his desk. His plump body strained the seams of a black cotton kimono patterned in white swirls and bordered with red checks. His shaved crown made him look less like a grown samurai than an enormous infant. When he saw Sano, his round, pudgy face took on an almost laughable expression of horror.

"*Yoriki* Sano-*san*!" he cried. "You're back!" Hastily he scrambled to his knees and bowed, first tucking the book out of sight beneath his buttocks. "I await your orders!"

Sano gazed at Tsunehiko with exasperated affection. The secretary's father, a powerful bureaucrat who wanted his idle, not-very-bright son to have an occupation, had prevailed upon Ogyu to find work for Tsunehiko. Ogyu had assigned him to Sano's office. So far he had proven himself lazy and incapable of getting even the simplest tasks right on the first try. He also breathed loud and hard through his chronically plugged nostrils, a further irritation. Still, Sano found it impossible to dislike Tsunehiko. The boy was cheerful, good-natured—and just as out of place as Sano felt.

"All right, Tsunehiko," Sano said. "Please take this report." He knelt before his desk while Tsunehiko took paper and writing supplies from the cabinet. After Tsunehiko had ground the ink and settled himself at his own smaller desk, Sano began. "The sixteenth day of the twelfth month, Genroku year one," he dictated. "Regarding the matter of the suicides of artist Noriyoshi and Lady Niu Yukiko—"

He paused when Tsunehiko gasped in dismay at the two characters he'd written, then crumpled the paper. A mistake, already: Tsunehiko's skills at calligraphy and taking dictation were minimal. Sano would have preferred to write the reports himself, but he must conform to the rules, even in so small a matter as using the incompetent secretary assigned to him. Just as he must issue a report in accordance with Magistrate Ogyu's orders, though it ran counter to his own instincts. Besides, he didn't want to hurt the boy's feelings. He waited for Tsunehiko to take a fresh sheet of paper from the cabinet. Then, together they slowly and tediously completed the report to the accompaniment of Tsunehiko's labored breathing. Sano read over the fourth and final draft, saw to his relief that it contained no errors, and affixed his seal to it.

"Take this to the chief clerk and have him convey the orders to the departments involved," he told Tsunehiko.

"Yes, *Yoriki* Sano-*san!*" Tsunehiko took the report, rolled it, and tied a silk ribbon around it. Still breathing hard, he rose and slid open the door.

Laughter sounded in the corridor outside. Yamaga and Hayashi swished past.

"We'll cut a swath through Yoshiwara tonight," Sano heard Yamaga say. "The women there will satisfy our every desire."

Hayashi replied, "Then let us not delay!"

Their laughter rang out again as they disappeared. Phrases of lewd conversation drifted back toward Sano: ". . . voluptuous buttocks . . . fragrant loins . . ." All at once a picture of the future flashed before him. He saw what would happen if he followed the path that Ogyu had laid out for him. His principles would lose their meaning for him. He would end up like Yamaga and Hayashi, who cared more about fashion and tradition than for their work. He would let his minions run his department while he left his post early to sport with prostitutes in the pleasure quarter. He would sacrifice truth for security, justice for the sake of comfort.

"Wait!" he ordered Tsunehiko.

Snatching the report from his surprised secretary's hand, he

tore it in two. Quickly he wrote another report classifying Noriyoshi's and Yukiko's deaths as suspicious and requiring further investigation. This he gave to Tsunehiko. Then he strode from the
room. He didn't want to coast along in his position, reaping the
certain rewards that unquestioning obedience would bring. Instead
he wanted to feel the excitement of pursuing the truth—as he had
when he'd been a scholar, then again during the arson investigation—and the elation of knowing that by finding it, he had done
some good. Somehow he must reconcile personal desire with the
Way of the Warrior and all its obligations to family and master.

He must discover the truth about the *shinjū*.

Edo Jail was a place of death and defilement to which no one
ever went voluntarily. Sano had never seen it before and wouldn't
have come now, except he knew that the bodies of Noriyoshi and
Yukiko had been taken to the morgue there. Now he surveyed the
jail with mingled curiosity and unease.

The Tokugawa prison sprawled along a narrow canal that
formed a moat before its entrance. Guard towers perched at each
corner of the high stone walls that rose straight up out of the
stagnant water. Dark liquid of an unidentified and probably unspeakable nature trickled from holes at the base of the walls down
to the canal. Above the walls, gabled roofs protruded. Signs of
neglect gave mute testimony to the city's repugnance toward the
jail and its inhabitants: weeds and moss growing between the
stones, missing roof tiles, and peeling plaster. A rickety wooden
bridge spanned the canal, ending at the guardhouse and the portals
of a massive, iron-banded wooden gate. All around the jail lay the
miserable shacks and drab, winding streets of Kodemma-cho.
Located near the river in the northeast sector of Nihonbashi,
Kodemma-cho provided an ideal site for the jail—as far from the
castle and the administrative district as convenience would allow.

Sano was thankful for the shrill shouts of the ragged children
playing in the streets, and for the greasy smell of food frying in
backyard kitchens. They masked whatever sounds and smells ema-

nated from the jail. A tremor ran down his spine as he remembered the stories he'd heard about what went on there. Taking a deep breath, he urged his horse onto the bridge.

A commotion began in the guardhouse as Sano arrived. When he dismounted and secured his horse to a post, the three guards nearly fell over one another trying to get out the door. He saw them exchange confused glances. Then they bowed low.

"We are at your service, master," the guards chorused.

Sano took in their unkempt appearance and cropped hair, the much-repaired leather armor and leggings, the single long sword that each wore. These were commoners—probably former small-time criminals—permitted to bear arms in order that samurai would not have to serve in such a degrading capacity.

"I am *Yoriki* Sano Ichirō," he said. "I wish to interview the men who handled the bodies of the double-suicide victims this morning."

The guards gaped at him. They'd probably never had a *yoriki* visitor before, Sano thought, let alone received such an unusual request from one; he was sure that his colleagues never set foot here. One of the guards let out a nervous titter. The large man next to him, presumably the leader, backhanded him a sharp blow.

"What are you waiting for?" he growled. "Take him to the warden at once!"

The guard slid back the thick wooden beams that barred the gate. Sano entered the jail compound, prepared for the worst.

His first impression of the compound was reassuring. In a simple courtyard of packed earth, five more guards patrolled. The odor of urine hung in the air, but no worse than near the backstreet privies of Edo. Thirty paces beyond rose a dingy wooden building with heavy bars over the windows. Entering through its plank door, he could see past the entryway to a room that might have been an office in the administrative district, except for the shabby appearance of the furnishings and workers. The guard led him down the outer corridor and knocked on a door.

"Enter!"

Bowing to someone within, the guard said, "Honorable Warden, I bring you a distinguished visitor." He moved over to let
Sano inside.

The warden, a stout man at a desk piled with papers, greeted
Sano's request with a look of bewilderment. Then he shrugged and
said to the guard, "Bring the *eta.*" He turned to Sano apologeti-
cally. "I must ask you to see them outside, *yoriki.* They aren't
allowed in this building."

"Of course."

Sano followed the guard back out to the courtyard, pondering
this bit of jail protocol. The *eta* were society's outcasts. Their
hereditary link with such death-related occupations as butchering
and leather tanning rendered them spiritually unclean. Consequently, other classes shunned them. They lived apart from the
rest of the population in slums on the outskirts of town. They
couldn't marry outside their class, or otherwise escape from it.
They performed the dirtiest and most menial of tasks: emptying
cesspools, collecting garbage, clearing away bodies after floods,
fires, and earthquakes—and staffing the jail and morgue. Sano had
known that the *eta* acted as corpse handlers here. But he hadn't
realized that even within the jail, certain areas were off limits to
them.

"Please wait here, sir." The guard disappeared around the
corner of the building. Presently he returned with three men, all
wearing identical short, unbleached muslin kimonos.

Two were still in their teens, the other a man of about fifty.
Eyes wary, like those of trapped animals, they immediately
dropped to their knees before him, foreheads touching the ground,
arms extended. The two young ones were trembling, and Sano
understood why: a samurai could kill them on a whim—to test a
new sword, if he so desired—without fear of reprisal. But he had
also heard horrifying stories about the suffering inflicted upon

prisoners by *eta* jailers, torturers, and executioners. Now he addressed them with a mixture of pity and revulsion.

"You handled the bodies from the *shinjū* this morning," he said. "Is that right?"

Silence. Then the older man said, "Yes, master." The others echoed him, faintly.

"Did you see any signs that they were not suicides? Any wounds? Bruises?"

"No, master," the older man said. The others, trembling violently now, didn't answer.

"Don't be afraid. Think. Tell me what the bodies looked like."

"I'm sorry, master, I don't know."

After several more attempts, Sano realized that he would get no useful information from these frightened, inarticulate men. "You may go now," he said, disappointed.

The two younger men hastily backed away, still kneeling, then rose and took off at a run. But the older one didn't move.

"Honorable master, I beg permission to try to help you," he said.

Sano's hope stirred. "Stand," he ordered, wanting a better look at this *eta* who had the courage to assert himself. "What is it you want to tell me?"

The *eta* stood. He had gray hair, intelligent eyes set deeply in a square, stern face, and a dignified bearing.

"I can say nothing myself, master," he said, looking Sano straight in the eye. "But I can take you to someone who knows all there is to know."

Intrigued, Sano said, "Very well."

He followed the *eta* along the same path the guard had taken, around the building then through another courtyard. There he saw a huge building of unpainted plaster, set on a high stone foundation: the jail proper. Tiny windows far above the ground gave it the look of a fortress. Five more guards let them through a door even thicker and more heavily reinforced than the main gate.

Noise and odor simultaneously attacked Sano's senses. Moans and sobs issued from behind the solid doors that lined the passage. A pair of jailers pushed past Sano. One banged loudly on each door, adding to the din.

"We're watching you, you stinking sons of whores!" he shouted. "Behave yourselves!"

The other shoved trays into each cell through slots at the bottoms of the doors. In the weak daylight that shone through the windows at either end of the passage, Sano saw that the rations were rotten vegetables and moldy rice. Flies buzzed thickly, alighting on his face and hands. Furiously he brushed them away. A powerful stench of urine, feces, and vomit filled his nostrils; he tried not to breathe. Rivulets of filthy water ran out of the cells and onto the stone floor. Sano gasped as a huge rat scurried across his path. Quickly the *eta* led him around a corner and down another passage. Here the noise diminished, although the smell didn't. Sano began to relax, when suddenly a door flew open. Two jailers hurried toward him, dragging between them a naked, unconscious man. Blood poured from the man's nose; fresh cuts covered his torso. The jailers opened a cell and threw the man inside. As Sano passed, he caught a glimpse of five emaciated men lying in a pool of filth in the cramped space. He looked away, horrified. Could anyone possibly deserve such treatment? Couldn't the government control its subjects some other way than by torturing and starving those who broke the law? That most sentences were short seemed a dubious blessing: many prisoners were executed after their trials. That the government he served would do such things frightened him. He tried not to think of it.

Then, mercifully, the *eta* led him outside into the cold, fresh air. They were in another courtyard, this one surrounded by a high bamboo fence. Sano inhaled gratefully.

"The morgue, master." The *eta* opened the door of a thatch-roofed building and gestured for him to enter.

Sano hesitated. He feared that whatever awaited him in the

morgue would be worse than anything he'd seen yet. But when he stepped inside, there was only a wooden-floored room with cabinets and stone troughs lining the walls, and in the center two waist-high tables with raised sides. A man stood at the open window, his profile to Sano, reading a book by the fading afternoon light. He wore a long dark blue coat, the physician's traditional uniform, with a gray quilt over his shoulders to ward off the room's damp chill. He turned. One look at his face sent a shock of recognition through Sano.

The man was perhaps seventy years of age, with a high, bony forehead and prominent cheekbones. A deep furrow ran from either side of his long, ascetic nose to the narrow line of his mouth. He had short white hair that receded at the temples but grew abundantly over the rest of his scalp. His shrewd eyes regarded Sano with displeasure, and he glanced down at his book as if annoyed at the interruption. Sano, following his gaze, also looked at the book. As he moved closer, he saw a drawing of the human body, covered with foreign words.

The foreign book and the man's distinctive features and uniform identified him to Sano immediately. Ten years ago he had seen this man paraded through Edo's streets in disgrace. He had seen that face on the town notice boards and on broadsheets distributed by the news sellers.

"Dr. Ito Genboku!" Sano blurted out. "But I thought——" He stopped, not wanting to offend the doctor with personal remarks.

Fifty years ago, the government had instituted a policy of strict isolation from the outside world. Iemitsu, the third Tokugawa shogun, had wanted to stabilize the country after years of civil war. Fearing that foreign weapons and military aid would allow various daimyo to overthrow his regime, he'd expelled the Portuguese merchants and missionaries and all other foreigners from Japan, and purged the country of all foreign influence. Only the Dutch were allowed trading privileges. Confined to the island of Deshima in Nagasaki Bay, the merchants were guarded day and night, their contact with the Japanese limited to the shogun's most trusted retainers. To this day, foreign books were banned; anyone caught practicing foreign science faced harsh punishment.

But a clandestine movement had sprung up among intellectuals. Japanese *rangakusha*—scholars of Dutch learning—procured foreign books on medicine, astronomy, math, physics, botany, geography, and military science through illicit channels. They pursued their forbidden knowledge in secret. Now Sano marveled at finding himself in the presence of the most famous *rangakusha,* a man whose courage he'd secretly admired, and never forgotten. Dr. Ito Genboku, once physician to the imperial family. Exiled to Enoshima for practicing Dutch medicine and carrying out scientific experiments. What was he doing here?

"Yes, I am Ito Genboku, and no, I never did go to Enoshima," Dr. Ito said, echoing Sano's thoughts. He had a dry but pleasant voice. Humor and irony colored it as he added, "Although some would consider my position as custodian of Edo Morgue much worse than exile. No doubt the Tokugawas thought so when they changed the terms of my sentence. However, it has its compensations." He held up his book. "I can pursue my studies in peace here. No one cares, as long as the morgue operates smoothly." Then, abruptly: "Who are you, and what do you want?"

As Sano introduced himself and explained why he'd come, he realized that he had not offered the proper greetings to Dr. Ito. Something about Ito made formality seem unnecessary. Perhaps it was Ito's unusually direct manner, or the fact that his status as a physician placed him outside the rigid class system that defined relations between other men.

"The *eta* couldn't tell me anything, so this one brought me to you," he finished. "Did you see anything to indicate that the deaths were anything but suicide?"

"I've not seen the bodies. Regrettably I have been occupied with those who perished in last night's fire." Dr. Ito bent a challenging gaze upon Sano. "Perhaps the best way for you to gain

knowledge about the deaths would be to exercise your own powers of observation instead of relying on mine. However, Niu
Yukiko has already been returned to her family for burial.''

So Magistrate Ogyu hadn't trusted him entirely after all, Sano
thought. He'd issued the return order himself, leaving no room for
mistakes or negligence.

''But we still have Noriyoshi's body,'' Ito continued. ''Would
you like to examine it with me?''

Sano felt trapped. The Shinto tradition in which he'd been
raised taught that any contact with death conferred a spiritual
pollution. But to admit his fear of defilement to this man would
be shameful. His small independent quest for truth and knowledge
seemed insignificant beside Ito's sacrifice.

''Yes, Ito-*san,*'' he answered.

Dr. Ito turned to the *eta.* ''Mura-*san,*'' he said, using the
respectful form of address as he would to any other man, ''fetch
Noriyoshi's body.''

Mura left the room. When he returned, the two other *eta* that
Sano had met were with him. Mura held a bundle of cloth, which
he gave to Dr. Ito. The others carried a long form shrouded in
white cotton; they placed it on one of the tables and began to
unwrap it.

''Noriyoshi's effects,'' Ito said, offering the cloth bundle to
Sano.

Sano spread the contents on the other table, delaying his first
look at the body emerging from the shroud. Wrapped inside the
blue trousers and kimono he found one straw sandal.

''A poor man,'' Sano remarked, fingering the coarse, cheap
material of the clothes. The sandal, heavily worn on the inner heel,
could have belonged to any commoner. He sighed. ''The Nius
would have opposed a marriage between him and Yukiko for that
reason alone.'' Had he risked Ogyu's wrath and braved the jail's
horrors for nothing? ''Maybe it was a love suicide after all.''

''Perhaps Noriyoshi himself will tell us.'' Dr. Ito laid aside his book and walked toward the now-exposed body. Although his posture was upright and authoritative, he moved gingerly. A spasm of pain crossed his face. "You may go now," he said to the *eta* who had brought the body. "Mura-*san*, I'd like you to stay."

Unable to postpone seeing the body any longer, Sano looked toward the table.

His first sensation was relief. The rigidity that held Noriyoshi's limbs stiff, his toes pointed straight at the ceiling, and his mouth agape made him resemble a somewhat grotesque doll instead of a man who had once lived and breathed. He bore no resemblance to the mutilated corpses Sano had seen at the public execution grounds, or to the bloated carcasses pulled from the canals after a flood. Dirt and shreds of seaweed clung to his bare skin and his loincloth, but there was no blood and no sign of decay. Curious now, Sano approached the table for a closer look. The deep red bruises circling Noriyoshi's wrists and ankles caught his attention.

"Burns from the ropes that bound him to Yukiko," Dr. Ito explained.

Otherwise, Noriyoshi was unmarked. His stomach was paunchy and his face puffy, but his arms and legs were wiry and he had most of his teeth. Before his death, he'd apparently enjoyed at least fair health for a man of forty-odd years. If he had died by any means other than drowning himself, it didn't show.

"I've seen enough," Sano said. "Thank you for—"

But Dr. Ito didn't seem to hear. Frowning at Noriyoshi, he said, "Mura-*san*. Turn him."

The *eta* obligingly rolled the body onto its side. Dr. Ito bent over it, scrutinizing the head and neck.

Sano moved closer. Then he caught the body's odor: a sweet, sickly butcher-shop scent, mixed with the fishy taint of the river. He moved back toward the open window. Ito gestured for the *eta* to turn Noriyoshi facedown.

"What caused this?" Sano asked, pointing to what looked like a large reddish bruise discoloring Noriyoshi's back, buttocks, arms, and legs.

"The blood settling after death." Taking a cloth from inside his coat, Ito covered his hand with it. Then he began to probe Noriyoshi's head. Despite being a doctor of progressive outlook, he apparently hadn't overcome his own aversion to the dead.

"Mura-*san*, a knife and razor," Ito ordered. Then, to Sano: "There is a flattened spot here at the base of the skull. We shall have a better look at it."

Sano looked, but saw nothing. He didn't want to touch the head himself. He waited while Mura cut away a patch of hair and shaved the scalp bare where Ito had pointed. Then he saw the livid purple indentation. He shifted his gaze to Ito's face and kept it there.

"What caused it? A blow that killed him before he was thrown into the river?"

"Or perhaps a rock or piling that struck him—when he jumped into the river." Dr. Ito emphasized the last words. "Or during the first hour after death, when a blow could still produce a bruise. It is impossible for me to say. But there is a way to tell if he did drown."

Sano's pulse quickened. Instinct told him that a murderer had inflicted Noriyoshi's wound. He must know for certain. "How?" he asked eagerly.

"If he drowned, he will have water inside him," Ito answered. "But in order to know that, we must cut him open."

Sano stared at Ito, appalled. Dissection of a human body, as well as any other procedure even remotely associated with foreign science, was just as illegal as it had been at the time of Ito's arrest. Perhaps the authorities no longer cared if Ito broke the law, but what about him? If the wrong people found out, he would not only lose his position, he would be banished, never to see his home or family again. He started to protest. But Dr. Ito's gaze locked with his, freezing him into silence. *I risked everything to seek forbidden truths,* the shrewd eyes seemed to say. *How far are you willing to go?* Sano's mind recoiled from the unspoken challenge. He tried to conjure up images of his father, of Magistrate Ogyu. He reminded himself of his obligation to them. But instead he saw the *doshin's* assistants beating a helpless beggar. He felt again the elation of the moment when he'd corrected an injustice and set an investigation back on the road to truth.

"All right," he said.

As soon as the words left his mouth, he realized that he had committed himself to this when he'd agreed to view the body. He'd taken the first step, and there had never been any choice about the second.

At a nod from Ito, Mura went to the cabinet. From it he took a wooden tray of tools—steel saws, long razors, and a collection of knives and instruments such as Sano had never seen before. They must have been Dutch in origin. Mura set the tray on the table beside the body, then went to the cabinet again and brought out a white cloth. This he tied over the lower half of his face.

His practiced movements told Sano that this was not the first dissection ever performed here. As did a bamboo pipe running from a hole in the table down to a drain in the floor. The room had been prepared for Dr. Ito's experiments.

Mura turned Noriyoshi's body onto its back. He picked up a slender knife and held it over Noriyoshi's chest. Apparently he, not Ito, would do the actual cutting. Despite his unconventional views, Ito followed the tradition of letting the *eta* handle the dead.

Sano watched with horrified fascination as the blade sliced cleanly into Noriyoshi's skin and moved down the center from the base of the collarbone to the navel.

"No blood?" he asked, relieved to be spared the sight of it. The raw, pink edges of the cut looked bad enough. His heart was racing; his hands went cold and clammy.

"The dead do not bleed," Dr. Ito replied.

Now Mura made several cuts perpendicular to the first. He inserted a flat-bladed instrument into one of them.

Sano looked at the glistening red tissue that appeared as Mura folded the skin back from Noriyoshi's rib cage, and at Mura's slimy hands wielding the instrument to slice it away. He swallowed hard. Nausea spread through his stomach. Sweat trickled down his face despite the cold air coming through the window. His skin crawled. He fought the sickness by trying to concentrate on something else. He couldn't have Noriyoshi's corpse exposed to the public; signs of the dissection would show. When he returned to his office, he must issue a cremation order. But the distraction failed. Not wanting to see, yet unable to look away, he watched as Noriyoshi's innards were revealed. The pale, gleaming ribs with twin pinkish-gray spongy lobes and a red, meaty object beneath. The coiled tubes of viscera showing at the lower edge of the cut. Like a flayed animal, he thought dizzily. And the smell rising from the open cavity was the same, too: sweet, strong, and rotten.

Like other men his age, he'd never gone to war. He knew about its atrocities, of course: men decapitated with a single sword slash, or shot with guns bought from foreign barbarians. Limbs severed. Bodies hacked to bits. He'd read accounts in the history texts and heard the stories handed down from generation to generation. Somehow he'd always imagined the carnage of battle as noble, necessary, and part of a samurai's domain. This—this cold, deliberate mutilation of a human body—seemed obscene. It was defilement in its worst form. He could feel the pollution staining his skin, seeping into his nostrils, coating his eyeballs. His stomach lurched. Even his sweat seemed contaminated; he couldn't bring himself to touch it. He pressed his lips together to keep it from running into his mouth.

"Mura-*san,* the lower two ribs on the right side," Ito said.

Sano watched as Mura took one rib between the jaws of a sturdy pair of grips. He closed his eyes at the sickening crack of bone—

once, twice. When he opened them again, he saw why Mura had covered his face. Bits of red tissue flecked the white cloth just over the *eta*'s mouth.

"Good." Ito nodded. "Now cut . . . there." He sketched a line in the air above the place where the ribs had been, over the section of spongy lobe now exposed. To Sano he said, "If there is water, it will be in the breathing sacs."

Sano nodded quickly, afraid that he would vomit if he tried to speak. He watched the thin knife slice the breathing sac and braced himself for the gush of fluid.

It never came. Instead the sac merely shrank a little, like the punctured swim bladder of a fish.

"No water." A grim satisfaction suffused Dr. Ito's face. "This man did not drown. He died before he entered the water. He was murdered, then thrown into the river."

Sano's vision darkened, and his legs wobbled beneath him. Then he retched.

"*Yoriki* Sano-*san*. Are you ill?"

Sano tried to answer, but bile seared his throat. Without making a proper farewell, he stumbled from the room. He had to get out. Fast.

The jail corridors seemed endless; the prisoners' cries were the sounds of demons in hell. Somehow Sano made it to the door. He managed to climb onto his horse and get halfway across the bridge. Then his stomach heaved again. Dismounting, he vomited into the canal. But the end to his sickness brought little relief. He felt horribly soiled by his experience. Conscious only of a desire to put as much distance between himself and Edo Jail as possible, he rode blindly through the twilight at a furious gallop.

Then, looming before him like a blessing from the gods, there appeared a building with a dark blue curtain hanging out front. The curtain displayed the character *yu:* hot water. A bathhouse. Sano jerked on the reins and fell off his horse. Dashing inside, he threw some coins on the counter.

"Sir, the price is only eight *zeni*!" the attendant cried, holding out Sano's change.

Sano ignored him. He snatched a bag of rice-bran soap from the counter and shoved his swords at the attendant for safekeeping. Then he stumbled into the bathing area. In the dim, steamy room, men in loincloths and women in thin under-kimonos scrubbed and rinsed themselves, or soaked in the deep tub. Oblivious to their curious glances, he ripped off his clothes, throwing them on the floor in an untidy heap. He scoured his skin with the soap until it hurt. He sloshed a bucket of water over himself. Then he plunged into the tub, completely immersing himself again and again. The water was scalding hot and scummy with soap residue, but he forced himself to keep his eyes and mouth open so that it could cleanse him inside as well as out.

Finally a sense of peace came over him. He no longer felt contaminated. Gasping, he dragged himself out of the tub and went to sit on a bench in the steam room. Then he closed his eyes and groaned as realization struck him.

Noriyoshi had been murdered. Logic told him that Yukiko had, too. But since he couldn't tell anyone about the illegal dissection, he must find some other way to prove what no one was supposed to know.

3

Sano awoke to the sound of footsteps outside his bedchamber in the *yoriki* barracks. Stirring beneath thick quilts, he lifted his head from his wooden neck rest. A slit of light widened as the door slid open, and the maid entered on her knees, bearing a bucket of hot coals.

"Good morning, *yoriki-san,*" she said cheerfully, bending to dump some coals into a brazier near his futon.

Through the thin walls came other sounds of morning in the barracks. The veranda that ran past the doors of his and ten other adjoining apartments creaked and shuddered under hurrying feet. Sano's colleagues called greetings to one another. It had taken him a while to get used to the noise, so different from the quiet of the house where he'd lived with only his parents and one maid-of-all-work. Grimacing at a loud crash from the other side of the wall, he rose cautiously.

To his relief, the queasiness that had continued all yesterday evening after the dissection had passed. He felt refreshed, hungry, and even confident that he could discover who had killed Noriyoshi and Yukiko. Only the lingering fear of disobeying Magistrate Ogyu and concern for his reputation clouded his thoughts.

Hurriedly Sano pulled on his heavy winter robe and went to the entryway for his shoes. Shivering in the chill gray morning, he followed the veranda to the privies attached to the building. He saw none of his colleagues, for which he was glad: the camaraderie they shared didn't include him.

When Sano returned to his rooms, his manservant helped him wash, then dress in fresh black *hakama,* white under-robe, dark blue kimono printed with black squares, and a black sash. The maid had stored his bedding in the closet, removed yesterday's clothes for washing, and swept the mats. As the manservant oiled and arranged his hair, Sano reflected that his position had its benefits. This apartment, located within the police compound, was bigger and better than he'd ever imagined having. A whole family could sleep in the bedchamber. The sitting room, equally large, had a desk alcove with built-in shelves, like one in a rich man's house. His income was two hundred *koku* a year, the cash equivalent of enough rice to feed two hundred men for that long. Even after deductions for room, board, stable fees, and servants' wages, he made many times as much as he had tutoring.

Sano sighed inwardly as he dismissed his manservant and headed for the barracks dining room. He couldn't really enjoy these pleasures because his peers were anything but welcoming.

Although it was late, six men still knelt in the dining room, finishing their morning meal: Yamaga, Hayashi, and four others, all immaculately groomed and dressed, manicured hands holding their tea bowls. Their heads turned toward Sano as he paused in the entrance. The conversation ceased.

Then Hachiya Akira, senior *yoriki,* a heavy man of fifty with a soft-jowled face, spoke. "We thought you were not coming." He took another sip of tea from his bowl. "Many thanks for giving us the honor of your company." Murmurs from the others echoed the mild disapproval in his tone.

"My apologies," Sano said as he took his place beside Hayashi. As little as they welcomed his presence, the other *yoriki* still expected him at meals and in their rooms when they gathered at night to drink and talk. Otherwise he would have eaten in his own apartment and spent his free time reading or with old friends. This endurance of slights, baiting, and loneliness was a duty he couldn't shirk.

"Very well." Releasing him, Hachiya turned to the others and resumed their conversation, which, as usual, dealt with politics.

"Whatever one thinks of the government," he said, "it does maintain order throughout our nation. There has not been a significant disturbance since the Shimabara peasant uprising was quelled more than fifty years ago. Because the Tokugawa military force far exceeds that of any daimyo clan that might challenge the regime, we are free from the threat of war."

But throughout history, ambitious men had successfully faced great challenges to win power for themselves, Sano remembered. Five hundred years ago, Minamoto Yoritomo—a Tokugawa ancestor—had defeated the imperial forces to become shogun. The Ashikaga clan had supplanted the Minamoto. More recently, great warlords had waged almost a hundred years of civil war in their quest to dominate. Despite the apparent permanence of the Tokugawa supremacy, no regime lasts forever. That the government was quick to detect and crush budding insurrections showed that it recognized this fact. Still, a majority of samurai considered the Tokugawas invincible and such precautions superfluous.

"However, I must admit that things have changed since the assassination of that superb statesman, the Great Elder Hotta Masatoshi," Hachiya continued. "Without his guidance, Shogun Tokugawa Tsunayoshi seems to have lost his taste for government affairs. Why, I remember when he conducted proceedings against the corruption in Takata just eight years ago. The daimyo was stripped of his fief, his second-in-command was ordered to commit *seppuku,* and the rest of the partisans were banished. Now Tsunayoshi occupies himself with other pursuits. Lecturing his officials on Chinese philosophy and classics. Reviving the old Shinto festivals. Acting as patron to the theater and endowing Confucian academies."

Hachiya's neutral tone implied no dissatisfaction. With spies everywhere, no one dared criticize the shogun openly. But Sano had gotten the message and knew the others had, too. Tokugawa Tsunayoshi had his detractors, both here in this room and at every level of society.

Yamaga's thin nostrils flared in distaste as he said, "His Excellency's chief chamberlain—the clever and charming Yanagisawa—wields much power now." He set down his bowl. Then, in a lighter manner, as if to change the subject: "The incidence of certain physical practices seems to be on the rise. One can observe the consequences. His Excellency . . . many individuals . . . the treasury . . ." He let the words hang.

"Ah." Noncommittal sounds came from the others as they nodded and lowered their eyes.

Sano hid a smile as he accepted an *ozen*—an individual meal tray containing rice, fish, pickled radish, and tea—from the maid. Yamaga's gift for circumspect communication nearly matched Ogyu's. He'd just told them, although not in so many words, that the rumormongers said Chamberlain Yanagisawa preferred men to women and had had an affair with the shogun, whose protégé he'd been since his youth. From that affair sprang Yanagisawa's influence over the nation. And the shogun's own appetite for men wasn't satisfied by Yanagisawa. Evidently he used government funds to lavish gifts upon many lovers, including a harem of boys. This had caused resentment within the ranks of the shogun's retainers, as well as among the great daimyo, although not because they disapproved of his sexual preference. Many samurai practiced manly love; they considered it an expression of the Way of the Warrior. Rather they objected to the shogun's blatant favoritism.

The conversation turned to general matters. Talking during meals was considered rude, but the other men had finished eating and apparently saw nothing wrong with gossiping around Sano as he ate. Excluded from the conversation, as he had been every morning, Sano mentally stepped back to look at himself and his companions. How different they were from the warriors of old!

Instead of gathering outdoors in the morning to discuss strategy before a battle, they dined in comfort while chatting about politics. Hachiya, now holding forth on his problems with a certain treasury official, was hardly General Hōjō Masamura, who had successfully defended the country against invading Mongols four hundred years before. Although Sano was grateful for the peace that had brought prosperity and stability to the country, he regretted the lost simplicity of those bygone days.

The Way of the Warrior had undergone a subtle alteration in response to the changed times. Samurai still upheld honor, bravery, and loyalty as the highest virtues. They still carried swords and were responsible for keeping their fighting skills up to standard in the event of war. But in addition to swearing allegiance to a lord, they owed sometimes conflicting loyalties to a whole network of superiors, allies, and patrons, in addition to shogun and emperor. And while most samurai practiced the martial arts at academies such as the one Sano's father operated, many didn't. Like Yamaga and Hayashi, they'd gone soft. True, Tokugawa Ieyasu's Ordinances for the Military Houses called on samurai to engage in polite learning as well as military training. In peacetime, their energy must be directed into civilian channels; both their education and the dwindling value of their stipends made them ideal candidates for service in the government bureaucracy. But Sano couldn't help thinking that the samurai soul had lost much of its steel.

And, along with it, the certainty born of knowing that your life is to be spent in preparation for battle to the death in your lord's service. Nothing in Sano's life had prepared him for the task of investigating a murder and finding a killer. How should he go about it?

Pondering his dilemma, Sano realized belatedly that Hayashi was asking him a question in an impatient tone that indicated he'd already repeated it once.

"I'm sorry, Hayashi-*san*. I wasn't paying attention. What did you say?"

Looking straight into Sano's eyes, Hayashi said pointedly, "It is a commonly held opinion that they who teach do so because they have no other skills. Therefore, it is good that the government is so well organized that it virtually runs itself. This way it matters little how posts are filled. Nor the qualifications of the men who hold them. Would you not agree?"

The words hung ominously in the air. Silence fell as the others awaited his reaction. Sano could feel himself flushing as he saw them exchange glances, suppress smiles. He'd had all he could take of the constant baiting and veiled insults. Perhaps because he shared Hayashi's low opinion of his qualifications, a sudden fury boiled up inside him. The frustration of the past month spilled over. A bitter retort sprang to his lips. Only the knowledge that an open quarrel with Hayashi would earn him a reprimand from Ogyu made him bite it back. Ogyu expected the police department to run smoothly and unobtrusively.

"Some might think so," Sano forced himself to answer calmly. "Others perhaps not."

Hayashi's smirk made him even angrier. Out of anger came inspiration. No matter what these men thought, a tutor and history scholar had plenty of useful skills! Ones that could be applied to any task—even the investigation of a murder. When he wanted to learn about a historical event or person, he questioned people who had witnessed the event or known the person. As yet he had no witnesses to the murders. But he could talk to those who'd been close to Yukiko and Noriyoshi. Maybe that way he could discover their killer's motive and identity. Throwing down his chopsticks, he rose and bowed his farewells to the others.

Hachiya frowned. "Leaving us so soon?"

"Yes." Sano looked down at the six upturned faces. The hostility he saw there saddened and worried him. His inability to make comrades of his peers boded ill for the future. But he tried to convince himself that their enmity didn't matter. Finding the truth and bringing a killer to justice did. "I must go to my office and leave orders for my staff. Then I shall pay my respects to the families of the dead."

The *yashiki*—great fortified estates of the daimyo—occupied large tracts of land south and east of Edo Castle. Each was surrounded by a continuous line of barracks, where as many as two thousand of the lords' retainers lived. Decorated with black tiles set in geometric patterns, their white plaster walls were punctuated by heavily guarded gates. Smooth, straight thoroughfares, wide enough to accommodate huge military processions, divided the estates. Along them, multitudes of samurai moved on foot or on horseback.

Sano walked quickly through the avenues, checking each gate for the crest that would identify the Niu *yashiki*. The weather had turned colder; a cloudy sky pressed down upon the city, threatening snow. His breath frosted the air, and he bunched his gloved hands in the sleeves of his cloak for extra warmth. Under his arm he carried the obligatory funeral gift: a package of expensive cakes, wrapped in white paper and tied with black and white string. The castle loomed before him, an imposing conglomeration of stone walls and tile roofs set on a wooded hilltop.

He paused for a moment to look about. The sight of Edo Castle, the fortresses around it, and all the armed men reminded him forcibly that this city was first and foremost a military base. The thousands of townspeople, crammed into the meager remaining land between here and the river, existed only to serve it. Edo belonged to the shogun and the daimyo.

Niu Masamune, as befitting his wealth and power, would have one of the estates nearest the castle, Sano thought as he continued on his way. Ah, there it was: the Niu clan symbol, a dragonfly within a circle, painted in red on a white banner. Black mourning drapery hung in loops above the gate. Sano reflected that the dragonfly, symbol of victory, seemed an inappropriate crest for the Nius. They and their allies had, after all, suffered defeat at Sekigahara by the Tokugawa faction. After the battle, the Nius had been stripped of their ancestral fief. But Ieyasu, the first Tokugawa shogun, had realized that unless he somehow pacified his conquered foes, they wouldn't stay conquered for long. He'd granted them other fiefs—the Nius' in distant Satsuma, far from their traditional power base. He and his descendants had exacted a fortune in tributes from these daimyo clans, while allowing them to keep much of their wealth and to govern their provinces autonomously. Thus Niu Masamune maintained his status as one of the highest-ranking "outside lords"—those whose clans had sworn allegiance to Tokugawa Ieyasu after Sekigahara. The elaborate gate, with its red beams, twin guardhouses, massive double doors, and heavy tile roof, proclaimed its supremacy over the simpler gates of lesser daimyo.

Sano stopped a few paces from the Niu gate. Never had he imagined calling on a daimyo, for any reason. Now he wondered whether he had the audacity to elicit details of Yukiko's life while seemingly paying an official condolence call. Only his increasingly compelling need to seek the truth and find Yukiko's killer gave him the courage to approach the guardhouse.

He identified himself to one of the guards and explained, "I wish to pay my respects to the Niu family." Then, not wanting to tell a total lie about his reason for coming, he added, "And to settle a few matters regarding Miss Yukiko's death."

The guard said, "Please wait." Unlike the Edo Jail guards, he acted neither surprised nor servile. As retainer to a great lord, he no doubt encountered many visitors who ranked far higher than a *yoriki.* He left his guardhouse and crossed to the other, where he consulted his partner. Then he opened the gate, spoke to someone inside, and closed it again. "Wait," he repeated to Sano.

Sano waited. The damp chill seeped into him, and he paced

before the guardhouses to keep warm. Finally, when he was beginning to think he would never gain admittance to the *yashiki,* the gate opened again.

Another guard stood there. Bowing, he said, "Sir, Lord Niu is not presently in the city. But if you would be so obliging as to come with me, Lady Niu will see you."

Sano wasn't surprised to find Lord Niu absent, or Lady Niu at home in Edo. According to the law of alternate attendance, the daimyo spent four months of each year in the capital, and the rest on their provincial estates. When they returned to their estates, the shogun made them leave their wives and families in Edo as hostages. The daimyo were divided into two groups, one of which was in Edo while the other was in the country. These restrictions, which greatly humiliated the proud daimyo, effectively kept them from plotting and staging a rebellion. They also had to maintain two establishments, thereby draining their wealth into nonmilitary expenditures. Peace came with a high price, and the daimyo had paid it with their money, their pride, and their freedom. Still, Sano hadn't expected Lady Niu to receive him. Most ladies spent their days confined to the women's quarters of their mansions while the daimyo's retainers handled the households' official business. They seldom received strangers of the opposite sex. Even more curious now—and increasingly unsure of how he should act once inside— Sano followed the guard through the gate.

He saw immediately that the *yashiki* was laid out like a military camp, where soldiers' tents were arranged around the general's. Here the barracks bordered a vast courtyard where tens of samurai patrolled, protecting the estate's center where the Niu family lived. Other samurai tinkered with weapons in the guardrooms, or sat idly. More barracks, larger and more elaborate residences for higher-ranking officers, formed an inner wall. A paved walk led Sano and his escort through them and into a formal garden. Beyond this lay the daimyo's mansion, a large but deceptively simple-looking structure with half-timbered walls and a tile roof, set above the ground on a granite podium. Sano knew that such mansions were rambling complexes of many buildings, connected by long corridors or intersecting roofs, that housed hundreds. Awe, combined with a sense of his own inferiority, weakened Sano's resolve. Was he a fool, daring to confront such a rich and powerful family?

Just outside the house stood an open shed containing several palanquins decorated with elaborate carved lacquerwork. Sano followed the guard beneath the covered porch and into the spacious entryway, where he removed his shoes and donned a pair of guest slippers. He placed his swords on a shelf that held a large collection of bows, swords, and spears; etiquette dictated that samurai must always enter a private home unarmed. Then he followed his guide into the house proper.

The guard's quick pace allowed him only a glimpse of a vast empty reception room with a coffered ceiling, murals of green islands in a swirling blue sea, and a large dais at the far end where the daimyo sat during formal ceremonies. A maid was opening windows to air the room; through them, Sano saw the outdoor stage where Nō dramas were performed in summer. Everything was elegant and luxurious, but not ostentatiously so. The Tokugawa sumptuary laws forbade lavish home decoration, and no daimyo would risk seizure of his property.

A corridor led to another reception room. From it came the murmur of voices. When they entered, the guard knelt and bowed.

"*Yoriki* Sano Ichirō, from the Office of the North Magistrate," he announced, rising to stand beside the door.

Sano also knelt and bowed. When he raised his head, his eyes went immediately to the woman who knelt upon the dais, dominating the room and everyone in it.

Against the painted backdrop of misty gray mountains, Lady Niu was a striking figure in her aqua kimono printed with colorful landscapes. Her body was broad and straight, like a man's; the white throat that rose from the kimono's deep neckline formed a strong, thick column. From the neck up, she had an arresting classical beauty. Her face was an elongated oval with smooth, youthful skin, a slender nose, long, narrow eyes, and a delicate small mouth vivid with scarlet paint. Her black hair, swept back from her forehead into an elaborate chignon fastened with lacquer combs, showed no gray. But her erect posture and confident air suggested maturity. A silk quilt patterned in diamonds of aqua and black covered her lap and spread over the square frame of a charcoal brazier. Against it, her hands lay folded, their smallness and daintiness belying the aura of power she exuded. Lady Niu was a fascinating study in contrasts: a woman whose appearance combined beauty with strength, who radiated femininity but did not let convention shut her away from the world. Sano wanted to know more about her.

Bowing again, he recited the words appropriate to the occasion. "I offer you this humble token of my respect." With both hands, he extended the box of cakes. Funeral custom prohibited him from directly mentioning death during a condolence call. He would have to introduce the subject after the formalities were done.

"Your tribute is much appreciated." Lady Niu's voice was husky but melodious. If she felt any grief over Yukiko's death, she hid it behind her properly calm demeanor. She inclined her head. Then she turned toward the wall on her left. "Eii-*chan*?"

Now Sano took notice of the others in the room. The figure coming toward him was not a child, as the diminutive *chan* implied, but a large, hulking man with a lumpy, pock-marked face. His vacant expression at first made Sano think that this was a feebleminded servant kept on for some reason involving obligation or sentiment. However, the rich black silk robes and two elaborate swords identified Eii-*chan* as a high-ranking retainer in the daimyo's service. And Sano saw an unmistakable flash of intelligence—wary, measuring—in the tiny eyes that met his for an instant. Without speaking, Eii-*chan* held out a tray to receive Sano's gift and to offer the traditional return token, a decorated box of matches. Then he carried the tray to a table by the door, set the gift there among others, and resumed his place near Lady Niu.

"Lord Niu's daughters," Lady Niu said, nodding toward a standing screen on one side of the room, halfway between her and Sano.

Through its close-woven lattice, Sano discerned two shadowy figures. Otherwise he could see nothing of the women but a fold of red silk kimono lying on the floor beside the screen. As he watched, a hand snatched it out of sight. He noted that Lady Niu had said "Lord Niu's" and not "my" daughters. They must be the children of a concubine, placed in Lady Niu's charge.

"I understand that you have come on official business regarding Yukiko," Lady Niu said.

"Yes." Sano was glad that she'd brought it up first. "Regretfully I must trouble you with a few questions."

Lady Niu lowered her eyes, signifying resigned acceptance. Her expression was serene, like that of a royal beauty in an ancient painting.

Sano had planned his questions carefully. He must avoid giving any sign that he was investigating a murder, and avoid offending the Nius. And he was conscious of the listening daughters behind the screen, no doubt eager for forbidden knowledge. So instead of asking Lady Niu if she believed the deaths were suicide, he said, "Were you surprised by the manner of Miss Yukiko's demise?"

"Yes, of course," Lady Niu replied. She paused. "But in retrospect, I am forced to admit that it was sadly in keeping with Yukiko's character."

A small gasp issued from behind the screen, so faint that Sano barely heard it.

Evidently Lady Niu didn't. "Many young girls are influenced

too much by the theater, *Yoriki* Sano,'' she said. ''As you must have seen from the note that Magistrate Ogyu showed you. You are new to the police service, are you not?''

''Yes. I am.'' Her remark caught Sano off guard. He'd taken for granted that those who cared about such matters knew who he was and that he'd been assigned to handle the *shinjū,* but he hadn't realized that they included Lady Niu. Most women took no interest in government affairs. Once again he wondered what made Lady Niu different.

Just then a door at the side of the room slid open. A kneeling maid entered, carrying a tray laden with tea utensils and a plate of rice cakes. She rose and crossed the room. When she placed the tray before Sano and poured out the green tea, her hands shook, spilling it all over the tray. Sano saw her tense, pale face and red, swollen eyes.

''O-hisa! Take that tray away and bring another at once!'' Lady Niu's voice was sharp with impatience.

The maid burst into tears. Her sobs rent the quietness. She picked up the tray, but her fumbling hands tilted the cakes onto the floor. Sano reached over to help her, wondering at her extreme reaction to Lady Niu's scolding. Had something else— perhaps grief for Yukiko—caused it?

''Eii-*chan,* see to her,'' Lady Niu ordered.

For a large man, Eii-*chan* moved quickly, the instant before Lady Niu spoke, as if anticipating her order. In a flash, he was across the room. He put the cakes back on the tray, picked it up, and seized the weeping maid's arm with one fluid movement. He deposited both tray and maid outside the door, and returned to his position almost before Sano could blink, with a face as impassive as a carved No mask. Despite his doltish appearance, he was an efficient servant and probably more perceptive and capable of independent thought than his masters might suspect.

''I regret the inconvenience caused you by my clumsy maid,''

Lady Niu said. Then she tilted her head and frowned as if she heard something that displeased her.

Sano heard the muffled sobs, too. They came from the daughters behind the lattice screen. Were they also weeping for Yukiko? Sano thought he sensed a strange emotional undercurrent in the house. Comprised of what? Fear? Despair? Or did his knowledge that Yukiko had been murdered color his judgment?

"Midori. Keiko. Leave us." At Lady Niu's soft command the sobbing stopped. Then scuffles, footsteps; a door hidden by the screen opened and closed. The daughters had gone, without Sano's seeing them.

"It is best that we not discuss this matter any further in the presence of innocent young girls," Lady Niu said. "Now what else do you want to know?"

Just then the door O-hisa had come through slid open again. Sano, glad for the chance to collect his thoughts, turned to look at the young man who stood there.

"Forgive me for the interruption, Mother," the man said, "but the priest is here to see you about the arrangements for Yukiko's funeral."

For the first time, Lady Niu seemed uneasy. Her hands went up as if to push the man from the room. Then she folded them in her lap again and said woodenly, *"Yoriki* Sano, may I present my son, Niu Masahito, Lord Niu's youngest."

Sano bowed, acknowledging the introduction. He was struck by Lady and young Lord Niu's resemblance. They shared the same facial beauty and strong physique. Lord Niu's upper body showed signs of rigorous physical training: broad shoulders, clearly defined muscles in his neck and in the parts of his arms and chest not covered by his somber gray and black kimono. But Lord Niu's feverishly bright eyes gave his face an intensity that his mother's lacked. While Lady Niu appeared tall even when kneeling, her son was short. Although his carriage and the timbre of his voice put him in his early twenties, he stood no higher than a boy many years younger. Sano had heard Lord Niu Masamune called the "Little Daimyo" because of his size, so at odds with his status. His son took after him.

"Masahito, perhaps you would like to speak with the priest yourself." Lady Niu's voice held the merest hint of warning.

But Lord Niu didn't take the hint. He crossed the room to kneel at one side of the dais, facing Sano. He had a slightly stiff gait, and when he knelt he used both hands to position his right leg beside the other.

"*Yoriki* Sano is here to discuss some administrative matters regarding Yukiko's death," Lady Niu told her son. "They need not concern you."

"On the contrary, Mother. I can't think of anything that would interest me more." Lord Niu waved an imperious hand at Sano. "Continue. Please."

Lord Niu's presence worried Sano. It was a distraction that might render Lady Niu less cooperative, and himself more likely to make a misstep. Still, he was glad of a chance to meet another member of Yukiko's family.

"What was Miss Yukiko like?" he said, longing to ask whether she had had any enemies, but forced to disguise his intent with a polite query. "How did she get along with others?"

Lady Niu spoke quickly, as if to prevent her son from answering. "Yukiko was secretive. She kept her thoughts to herself. Still, she was a most gentle and accomplished girl. Everyone admired her."

"Everyone, Mother?" Lord Niu put in, emphasizing the first word.

He seemed to enjoy baiting her, but except for one pleading glance, she didn't react. She evidently indulged her son, tolerating behavior from him that would earn a daughter harsh punishment. Sano decided that Lord Niu's presence had an advantage after all. His remark clearly contradicted his mother's portrait of Yukiko.

"Who did not?" Sano asked Lord Niu directly.

Lady Niu intercepted the question. "Masahito is only joking. There was no one who did not hold Yukiko in the highest regard."

This time Lord Niu didn't interject. He kept his eyes on Sano, a smile playing at the corners of his mouth.

Sano tried a change of subject. Wanting to learn how Yukiko's murderer could have gotten an opportunity to kill her, he said, "Wouldn't it have been difficult for Miss Yukiko to get out of the house alone?" He would let them think he was merely asking how a sheltered young lady had managed to meet her lover.

"This is a large house, *Yoriki* Sano," Lady Niu answered. "Many people live here, and it is difficult to keep track of everyone. And we have learned that Yukiko bribed one of the guards to let her out the gate after dark on at least one occasion." Her lips tightened. "He has since been dismissed."

Sano's interest stirred. "Did anyone see her leave the night she died, or know where she went?"

"No." Lady Niu sighed. "Unfortunately, we all attended a musical entertainment given by Lord Kuroda." She tilted her head in the direction of the neighboring *yashiki*. "No one missed her." She added, "The event did not end until rather late."

Lord Niu emitted a sharp, ringing laugh. " 'Rather late'? That's putting it mildly, Mother." To Sano, he said, "We were up until almost dawn. Small wonder that no one bothered to check on who was where when we got home. Wouldn't you agree?"

"Yes." Sano was growing discouraged. The Nius had told him nothing he could take to Magistrate Ogyu as evidence of murder. And he was running out of questions.

Lord Niu leaned toward him, a speculative gleam in his feverish eyes. "From your questions, one would almost think Yukiko had been murdered. Because you seem to be trying to find out whether anyone would have, or could have killed her, and if we know who." He raised an eyebrow. "Yes? No?"

Sano, dismayed that Lord Niu had seen through him so easily, said nothing. He forced himself to hold the young man's penetrating gaze. Out of the corner of his eye, he saw Lady Niu shift restlessly, but she did not intervene.

"But Yukiko committed suicide," Lord Niu continued, his smile widening into a grin that revealed perfect teeth. "So there is no need for further questions, is there?" His tone conveyed dismissal.

Sano had no alternative but to make his farewells and follow the guard back through the corridor and main reception room. Disappointment weighed heavily on him as he reclaimed his shoes and swords in the entryway. He'd learned nothing much of value during this call, except that Lady Niu and her son apparently accepted Yukiko's death as suicide. Perhaps a bit too readily? Shouldn't they want to explore the possibility of murder, which endangered the entire family? Sano reined in his imagination. Although jealousy and rivalry could provoke murder within the best of families, he had no reason to believe that one of Yukiko's own relatives was involved in her death. The tensions he'd observed within the daimyo's household probably stemmed from another source. The crying maid, the daughter's gasp, and Lord Niu's hint at an enemy in Yukiko's past did not necessarily indicate otherwise.

Outside, the guard stopped to confer with another whom they met on the garden path. Sano waited, wondering if he would have better luck when he questioned Noriyoshi's family. Then a low whistle turned his head. Not birdsong, but a snatch of classical melody.

Sano looked around. Except for himself and the two guards, the garden was deserted. The shuttered windows of the surrounding barracks gazed back at him like blind eyes.

"Sir!" a voice whispered urgently. "Sir!"

Then he saw a face peering out of a doorway in the mansion, not far from the main entrance; a young girl's face, with long straight hair that fell around it from a center part and tossed in the wind.

"I have something to tell you," she hissed. "Come with me. Quickly!" She thrust out a hand to beckon him, and Sano caught sight of her kimono. It was red, like the fold he'd seen sticking out from behind the lattice screen. Then she vanished through the doorway.

Sano hesitated. What would happen to him if he followed her? Men had suffered demotion, maiming, or exile as punishment for even the hint of improper behavior toward a lord's daughter. He glanced at the two guards. Deep in conversation, they'd drifted down the path, their backs toward him. His desire to catch the killer gave him daring. The call of inescapable destiny beckoned. He took the risk.

Once through the doorway, he found himself in a long, narrow passage that ran between a high bamboo fence and the walls of the mansion's other wings. Following it, he saw no sign of the girl or anyone else, but he could hear voices coming from inside the house. He quickened his pace, looking over his shoulder and expecting someone to accost him at any moment.

The passage angled left and came to an abrupt end at an open gate. Sano peered cautiously through it. All clear. He tiptoed across the threshold and into a garden. There the gnarled limbs of a tall pine blocked the sky and made the dull winter day seem even gloomier. A bridge made of a single stone slab lay across a pond whose surface was littered with pine needles and dead leaves. Several boulders, their sides brown with lichen and moss, stood on the bank of the pond.

She stepped from behind the largest boulder so suddenly that he cried out in surprise.

"Shhh!" The girl put a finger to her lips, casting a furtive glance toward a veranda at one side of the garden.

Now that he stood face to face with her, Sano could see that she was no more than twelve or thirteen years old. She had plump cheeks, full lips, and a round chin. Eyes that must normally sparkle with merriment now regarded him solemnly.

"Can I trust you?" she asked.

Surprised by her ungirlish boldness, Sano answered her as he might have done one of his pupils. "I can't tell you who to trust and who not to trust," he said. "Miss . . . Midori?"

Apparently his honesty satisfied her, and he'd guessed right about her name. She nodded, threw another glance at the veranda, and whispered, "Yukiko didn't kill herself!"

"But your mother thinks she did." Sano fought down a surge of excitement, striving for objectivity. "And so does your brother." *And the magistrate, and everyone else but Dr. Ito and me.*

Midori stamped her foot, small fists clenched at her sides. "She's not my mother!" she cried. "Don't ever call her that." Her voice rose, and she clapped her hand over her mouth. Then, in a whisper nearly as loud, she hurried on. "She's my father's second wife. My mother—Yukiko's mother—was his concubine. She's dead. And I don't care what anyone thinks. Yukiko would never kill herself. Especially not that way, with a man. She didn't know any men. At least, not . . ." Blushing, she lowered her head so that her silky hair curtained her face.

Not as a lover, Sano thought, completing the sentence Midori was too embarrassed to finish.

"How do you know?" he asked. He reminded himself that she was a child, with a child's unwillingness to believe the worst about a beloved older sister.

Something of his skepticism must have entered his voice, because she flung her head up, eyes blazing. "I know!" she stormed. "I can prove it." She yanked on his sleeve so hard he thought the fabric would tear. "Someone killed Yukiko. Please believe me. You've got to—"

"Midori! What do you think you're doing?"

Sano jumped at the sound of the harsh voice. Turning, he saw

Lady Niu standing on the veranda, the open door framing her. Fury distorted her beautiful face. Beside Sano, Midori let out a little moan. The three of them stood in frozen silence for a moment.

Then Lady Niu said, "Go to your room at once, Midori." A deadly calm replaced the anger in her voice, but her expression did not alter.

Without looking at Sano, Midori scuttled off, head ducked, down a path leading out of the garden.

"As for you, *Yoriki* Sano," Lady Niu continued, "I advise you to leave at once. And never to return."

Sano heard footsteps behind him. He turned and saw his guard, looking angry and resentful.

"Take him away," Lady Niu told the guard.

Sano let the guard escort him to the gate, feeling relieved and very foolish. How ironic if, after all the other risks he'd taken, he had ruined his career to indulge a fanciful child!

Once safely back on the street, he regretted not hearing Midori's tale. It might have provided him with the evidence to convince Ogyu that more investigation was necessary. Maybe he would risk trying to question Midori again later, after he'd seen Noriyoshi's family.

Midori ran through the inner gate and garden, up the steps to the door of the section of the women's quarters that housed her bedchamber. But instead of going inside, she paused, shivering in the cold wind. Then, making an impulsive decision, she stepped out of her wooden-soled shoes. Carrying them by their thongs, she ran lightly along the veranda in her split-toed socks, past the row of doors beneath the roof's overhanging eaves.

An open window brought her up short. Through it she could hear the maids chattering as they swept the inner corridor. Midori ducked beneath the window so they wouldn't see her. As she turned the corner, more female voices filtered through the thin paper windows: her father's concubines gossiping with their attendants as they groomed themselves or sewed. A baby cried. Someone began to play a tune on the samisen, then stopped suddenly.

"No, no!" she heard her younger sisters' music teacher scold. "Too fast!"

The melody began again, slower this time. Midori slipped past the music room, thankful that the children were occupied and couldn't tag along after her.

Finally she reached her destination, a door at the north end of the women's quarters. She slid it open and peered cautiously inside. The corridor was empty. She darted across it and through another door that stood opposite—into Yukiko's bedchamber, where Lady Niu had forbidden everyone to go.

Midori closed the door behind her and looked around the chamber. All the windows were closed, allowing only a dim light from the corridor to filter in. She could barely make out the pattern of silver leaves on the white paper that covered the spaces between solid wooden doors leading to the adjacent rooms. Unlit charcoal braziers in the floor gave off no heat. A chill settled over Midori, one only partially due to physical cold. She hugged herself for warmth and comfort.

All Yukiko's things—her bedding, clothes, floor cushions, writing desk, calligraphy implements, and toilet articles—had been put away. The mats had been swept and the cabinets that covered one wall closed. The bare room offered no sign that Yukiko had once lived there, or even existed.

A sob caught in Midori's throat. The room's impersonal emptiness finally brought home to her the fact that Yukiko was really gone. Even the sight of Yukiko's shrouded body, laid out in the family chapel amid smoking incense burners and chanting priests, hadn't done that. Tears coursed down her face as she realized that Yukiko's death was not, after all, a nightmare from which she could awaken.

Dropping her shoes, she wiped her tears away with her sleeve. She must wait to mourn her sister. Now she had something else to do—something she'd been meaning to do for months. With Yukiko dead, it seemed more important than ever. She hurried over to the cabinets and flung the doors open. Then, frantic with her need to finish and escape before someone found her there, she began a wild search through the shelves of neatly folded clothing.

Her brave resolve almost crumbled. Touching Yukiko's kimonos, she could feel her sister's presence. She could smell the elusive flowery scent of her bath oil. Midori's eyes blurred again, and a tear dropped onto the clothing. But she forced herself to move on to a large chest that sat on the floor beneath the shelves.

There, under a stack of summer kimonos, she found what she'd been looking for: A pile of volumes, each a thick sheaf of cream-colored mulberry paper bound with a black silk cord.

Yukiko's diaries.

Midori snatched up the top volume. Carrying it over to the window where the light was best, she opened it, heart pounding. Now she would—or at least she hoped she would—learn why Yukiko had died. Despite her bold declaration to the handsome *yoriki*, she wasn't all that sure that Yukiko hadn't committed suicide. Lately her sunny, tranquil sister had seemed moody and withdrawn. All Midori did know was that Yukiko always recorded her thoughts, as well as her daily activities, in her diary. Now the diary would tell Midori whether Yukiko had really had a lover and grown desperate enough to take her own life—or whether something else had led to her death. Midori scrabbled impatiently through the soft pages, looking for the last entry. But halfway through, a passage caught her eye. With the tip of her tongue caught between her front teeth, she began to read.

> Yesterday we went firefly hunting at Lord Kuroda's villa in Ueno. In our gauzy summer kimonos, we flitted, ghostlike, over the dark fields, chasing the mysterious glimmering lights given off by the tiny creatures. The sweet scents of earth and fresh-cut grasses rose up from the ground. Crickets chanted a steady accompaniment to the children's shouts and laughter. We captured the fireflies in small wicker cages, where they continued to glow and flicker softly—living lanterns!

Midori smiled despite her grief. Yukiko's words brought back the enchantment of that evening. As long as she read, she felt as though her sister were still with her.

> On our way back to the house, Midori and Keiko, in an excess of high spirits, began to run and giggle and push each other. They dropped and trampled one of the Kurodas' firefly cages. As much

as I disliked seeing their woebegone faces, I instructed them to confess what they had done and apologize to Lady Kuroda. But they saw it was the right thing to do, I think, because they were not angry with me afterward.

No one could ever be angry with Yukiko, Midori thought, as grief seized her again. As eldest sister, she had disciplined Midori and the seven other girls firmly, but always with such love and gentleness that they were eager to obey, just to please her. . . .

Soft footsteps sounded in the corridor: stockinged feet making the thin wooden floor creak. Midori's head snapped up. Guiltily she clapped the diary shut and looked for a place to hide. She mustn't get caught here; her stepmother would punish her. The footsteps passed. Midori opened the diary at a different place, near the end. She began to read again, this time resisting the temptation to relive happy times, searching in earnest for clues.

The next passage she chose disappointed her. A description of an event that had taken place six years ago could have no bearing on Yukiko's death. Here Yukiko's tone grew troubled, her prose choppy as if she had written reluctantly, without her usual pleasure.

The seventh day of the eleventh month. A dark, rainy day. On such a day as this, my brother Masahito had his manhood ceremony. It was held in the main reception hall. Our father gave him his new adult name and special cap. Afterward, the *fundoshi iwai* ceremony. The whole family was present. Guests, too, in fine robes. Father's retainers stood in ranks at the back of the main hall. Lanterns burned. I was so proud and happy to see Masahito receive his new loincloth, the first clothes of manhood. Now I look back on that day and weep. Would that I could feel the same joy and pride for the man of twenty-one years as I did for the boy of fifteen!

Midori puzzled over this passage. Yukiko and Masahito had been very close for a half-sister and -brother, but lately she'd noticed a certain coldness between them. She turned the page, hoping to learn the cause of their estrangement. But the passage didn't continue. Instead she found a shopping list: embroidery thread, hairpins, face powder. Remembering that she had no time to lose, she hastily thumbed the remaining pages, looking for Noriyoshi's name. She almost laughed aloud in triumph when she didn't find it. Just as she'd thought: Yukiko hadn't known the man. She ignored the nagging suspicion that perhaps Yukiko had not written about her lover because she was afraid someone would read her diary. Midori turned to the last entry, written the day before Yukiko's death.

The time for decision has come. Except I do not know what to do. To act would destroy lives. But to do nothing—infinitely worse! To speak is to betray. To remain silent a sin.

Chewing her fingernail, Midori read the passage again. She ran her finger over the characters, which were shaky and irregular, unlike the beautiful calligraphy of the earlier entries. Yukiko's agitation had expressed itself in her writing. *Destroy . . . betray . . . sin.* Such extreme language convinced Midori that here was proof that someone had killed Yukiko, because of something she knew. But what? What decision had caused her such anguish on the last day of her life? Midori flipped to the previous page. She began to read with growing dismay and fascination. So absorbed was she that she didn't notice the door sliding open until it clicked to a stop.

Midori shrieked and dropped the diary. She spun around. Surprise turned to horror when she saw her stepmother silhouetted in the doorway. The light from the corridor left Lady Niu's face in shadow. Behind her loomed the unmistakable bulk of Eii-*chan,* whose silence and ugliness had always frightened Midori. Now she darted a frantic gaze around the room, desperately seeking a hiding place. The cabinet? The chest? But it was too late. Lady Niu was advancing on her. Whimpering, Midori waited for her step-mother's outburst and inevitable stinging slaps.

But Lady Niu stopped a few paces from her. Her serene gaze flickered over Midori, down to the diary on the floor, to the disarranged cabinets.

"You have entered this room against my orders." Although she didn't shout like she had in the garden, her hushed tone was somehow more frightening. "You have spoken to a police official without my permission, and no doubt told him foolish lies about our family. And now you have dishonored your sister's memory by abusing her possessions."

Midori began to tremble. Her lips moved in a soundless plea. "Please . . . no . . ." She sensed that what happened to her next would be far worse than a beating. She stepped backward and felt her elbow tear through the paper windowpane.

"For this you must be punished," Lady Niu went on in the same tone. She paused, her lovely eyes narrowing. Midori could almost hear her turning over the possibilities: no play, no company, no good food or favorite possessions for several days? She'd used all of these before. Then Lady Niu nodded, apparently reaching a decision.

"Go to your room until arrangements can be made," she ordered. To Eii-*chan,* who had come to stand at her side, she said, "See that Miss Midori gets to her room—and stays there."

Midori helplessly preceded Eii-*chan* to the door. Fear for herself drove from her mind all thought of what she had read in Yukiko's diary. Then a ripping noise made her look over her shoulder at her stepmother. She cried out in dismay.

Lady Niu had picked up Yukiko's diary. She was tearing the pages into little pieces and dropping them into the charcoal brazier.

5

Upon returning to his office, Sano found an uncharacteristically glum Tsunehiko waiting for him. The young secretary mumbled a reply to his greeting and barely looked up from his desk to bow.

"What's wrong, Tsunehiko?" Sano asked.

"Nothing," Tsunehiko replied, his eyes downcast, his lower lip outthrust.

Sighing, Sano knelt beside his secretary. Something was obviously troubling Tsunehiko; he'd had enough experience with young boys to read the signs. Resigned, he prepared to listen and sympathize.

Tsunehiko fidgeted with his sash, a bright blue one that matched the pattern of blue waves on his kimono, which gaped at the collar to show a section of plump chest. The chest heaved with each noisy breath. Just when Sano thought he would refuse to speak, he muttered, "The other *yoriki* take their secretaries with them when they go out on business. You never take me anywhere."

Now that his tongue had loosened, he rushed on, not giving Sano a chance to reply. "Yesterday you gave me a lot of orders, then walked out. Today you did the same thing. My father says I'm here to learn a profession. But how can I learn if you don't teach me anything?"

He lifted a pink, earnest face to Sano. His serious mood had caused his eyes to cross, giving him a comically dazed expression. Sano suppressed an urge to smile as Tsunehiko continued sadly:

"Besides, I get lonely by myself. I have no friends here. Nobody likes me."

Sano's mirth almost erupted into laughter at this mingling of adult and childish concerns. But he realized that he had so far proven a poor mentor for his secretary, offering little instruction and tolerating laziness and mistakes. The teacher in him still felt responsible for the nurturing of a young mind placed in his charge. He felt ashamed of neglecting that responsibility.

"From now on, we'll work more closely together, Tsunehiko," he said. "Whatever I can teach you, I will." At whatever aggravation to himself, he promised silently.

Tsunehiko bobbed his head, giving a wavery smile.

Sano returned it, both amused and irritated at the picture of the two of them—misfit *yoriki* and melodramatic young whiner— yoked together in ludicrous partnership. Then he changed the subject to the matter that had been foremost in his mind when he entered the office.

"Did you get the addresses I asked you for?" he said.

Before he'd left for the Niu estate this morning, he'd asked Tsunehiko to look up Noriyoshi's places of residence and work in the Temple Registry and Artists' Guild records. Now that he'd failed to learn anything about the murder from the Nius, interviewing Noriyoshi's associates was of prime importance. He fervently hoped that Tsunehiko had managed to perform this simple task.

"Yes, *Yoriki* Sano-*san*!" Tsunehiko beamed, completely restored to his usual cheerful self. Snatching up a paper from his desk, he presented it to Sano with a flourish.

Sano read the characters written in Tsunehiko's large, awkward script:

Noriyoshi, artist
Okubata Fine Arts Company
Gallery Street
Yoshiwara, Edo

"Yoshiwara." Sano lingered over the name of the district. Yoshiwara, the walled pleasure quarter near the river on Edo's northern outskirts, where prostitution of all kinds was legal. Where food, drink, and myriad entertainments—theater, music, gambling, shopping, and others less innocuous—were available in abundance for those with money to pay for them. The district had originally been called "reedy plain" after the land it occupied. Then some clever promoter had modified the characters of the name to mean "lucky plain," a euphemism that had endured. Still another name for it was the Nightless City: Yoshiwara never slept.

"He lived and worked at the same place," Tsunehiko added. "Both records gave the same address. Okubata was his employer."

"I see." In keeping with the rules that governed traditional teacher-pupil relationships, Sano did not praise Tsunehiko for work well done. But he could offer a reward. And there was no time like the present for keeping promises. Tsunehiko's participation would be a hindrance, but one he thought he could manage. . . . "How would you like to go with me to Yoshiwara and help investigate Noriyoshi?"

"Yes! Oh, yes! Thank you, *Yoriki* Sano-*san*!" Tsunehiko leaped eagerly to his feet. He toppled his desk, spilling papers, brushes, and ink all over the floor.

A short while later, they were on a slow, rocking ferry headed upriver toward Yoshiwara. The open boat, which could seat a row of five men along either side, would have been full in summer. But today, Sano and Tsunehiko were the only passengers. In their heavy cloaks and wide wicker hats, they huddled under the flapping canopy that provided scant shelter from the cold, damp river breeze. Behind them the two muscular boatmen sang in rhythm with their splashing oars, occasionally interrupting their song to shout greetings to men on passing fishing boats and cargo vessels. The brown water swirled around them, rank and murky, reflecting no light from the low gray sky.

Tsunehiko was opening the box lunch they'd brought to fortify themselves for the two-hour trip. "We should really be riding to Yoshiwara on white horses," he said. "That's the fashionable way. And in disguise, so no one will know we're samurai." He began to consume rice balls, pickles, and salted fish with great zest and speed.

Sano smiled. Laws forbade samurai to visit the pleasure quarter, but since the laws were seldom enforced, members of their class frequented Yoshiwara openly, in droves. Disguise was unnecessary, except to add a touch of intrigue to the fun.

"We're on official business, Tsunehiko," he said.

"Official business," Tsunehiko agreed. He grinned, showing a mouthful of partially chewed food.

Sano ate his own lunch more slowly. He'd chosen to travel by boat, sacrificing speed for the opportunity to study the river that had claimed the bodies of Noriyoshi and Yukiko. Now he gazed at the line of warehouses on his left. The pair could have been thrown into the river anywhere: From one of the piers or docks or boathouses at the foot of the stone embankment; from the Ryōgoku Bridge, under whose great arch the boat was carrying him now; or even from the marshes on the opposite bank. If he didn't learn anything in Yoshiwara, he would have to search up and down the river for witnesses, a task that might take days to finish.

At last the ferry drew up beside the dock. Sano paid the boatmen. Then he and Tsunehiko climbed out, stretching their cramped muscles as they mounted the steps that led up the embankment. They followed the road inland, past shops and restaurants that served the river trade. Servant girls smiled invitingly at them from the curtained doorways, then turned sullen when they didn't stop. Passing through the rice fields and marshes outside Asakusa, they could see the tiled roof of the Sensō Temple rising in the distance above the smaller houses and temples surrounding it. A gong tolled; the wind brought with it the faint smell of incense. A few priests, their heads shaved, called out from the roadside, extending their begging bowls for offerings.

A short walk brought them within sight of the moat and high earthen walls that encircled Yoshiwara. Two samurai clad in helmets and armor vests guarded the gate: the day shift of the continuous watch maintained over people passing through the gate's roofed and ornamented portals.

Questioning the guards, Sano experienced anew the difficulty of carrying out an unofficial murder investigation.

"Yes, we knew Noriyoshi," one of them said. But when Sano asked if he'd seen Noriyoshi the day of his death, the guard replied, "He went in and out all the time. How am I supposed to remember exactly when? Anyway, he's dead, so what does it matter?"

Having no ready answer to this, Sano asked, "Did anyone come out carrying a large box or package two nights ago?" One large enough to hold a dead body, he wished he could add. He was conscious of Tsunehiko wheezing beside him, hanging on every word. The secretary probably thought he was learning how a *yoriki* conducted business. Hopefully he wouldn't understand what was going on—or at least not enough for it to matter if he told anyone about this trip.

The other guard snorted. Unlike the Edo Jail guards, he and his partner, who wore the triple-hollyhock-leaf Tokugawa crest on their sleeves, evidently saw no need to act subservient toward a city official. "Probably." In a condescending voice, he added, "But we have plenty to do besides keeping track of all the porters, *yoriki*."

Like making sure no women escaped, Sano thought. Virtually all the *yūjo*—courtesans—had been sold into prostitution by impoverished families, or sentenced to Yoshiwara as punishment for crimes. While some reigned over the quarter like princesses, enjoying their luxurious surroundings while tolerating men's attentions, others, mistreated by cruel masters, led miserable lives. These often tried to flee through the gates disguised as servants or boys. The guards would naturally pay less attention to the comings and goings of porters, or of a man they knew.

"No disrespect intended," the guard went on in a tone that implied otherwise, "but you're blocking the gate. Are you going in or not?"

"Thank you for your assistance," Sano said. As he and Tsunehiko entered Naka-no-cho, the main street, he gazed around with interest. He'd seen Yoshiwara many times: during childhood summers, when he and his parents had joined other Edo families to watch the beautiful pageants of the *yūjo*. Later, as a student wandering the streets with his friends, gawking at the women. But years had passed since his last visit. The price of food, drink, and female companionship was far too high for him, and the necessity of earning a living left no time for the long trip there and back, or the hours of drunken revelry in between. Now he saw that while some things matched his memories, others did not.

The rows of wooden buildings were familiar, as were the bold signs advertising the teahouses—which sold not tea, but sake—shops, restaurants, and brothels, or pleasure houses. A familiar smell of stale wine and urine lingered in the air. But the quarter had grown. Although the walls limited outward expansion, new businesses had filled in the spaces between the older ones that Sano recognized. His last visit had taken place in evening, when glowing paper lanterns hung from the eaves and beautiful courtesans solicited customers from within the barred, cagelike windows that fronted the pleasure houses. Now, in the afternoon, the lanterns were unlit and the cages empty, with bamboo screens pulled down behind the bars to hide the interiors of the buildings, which showed the inevitable signs of age: yellowed plaster, worn stone

doorsteps, darkened wooden pillars. The season made a difference, too. The branches of the potted flowering cherry trees along
the street, pink with blossoms in spring or lushly green in summer,
were bare. Fun-seeking samurai and commoners, though numer-
ous, walked quickly instead of strolling, bundled against the cold
in their heavy garments. Even their laughter seemed subdued. The
glamour that Sano remembered had faded.

Yoshiwara's winter drabness didn't faze Tsunehiko. "Isn't this
terrific?" he enthused, goggling at the signs. "I don't understand
why Yoshiwara has to be way out here in the middle of nowhere.
If it weren't so far from town, we could come every day!"

"The government wanted it away from the city to protect
public morals," Sano answered, taking the opportunity to instruct
his protégé. "And it's easier for the police to control what goes
on in a centralized quarter than in a lot of scattered areas. They
can reduce the number of little girls kidnapped and sold to brothels
by procurers."

He would have added that the metsuke—government spies—
found Yoshiwara a convenient place to keep tabs on citizens of
dubious character. But Tsunehiko wasn't listening. He'd ducked
beneath the curtain covering the doorway of a teahouse. A sign
above it proclaimed, "WOMEN'S SUMO HERE! See the famous
wrestlers Holder-of-the-Balls, Big Boobs, Deep Crevice, and
Where-the-Clam-Lives compete!" On a smaller sign: "Tonight's
special: Blind search for a dark spot. Women wrestlers versus
blind samurai!" Guttural cries and loud cheers issued from inside
the teahouse, indicating that the matches, illegal elsewhere in the
city, had already begun.

Sano shook his head. Bringing Tsunehiko had been a mistake.
Now he would have to waste time keeping track of the boy. One
more worry, added to a puzzling murder case and the perils
associated with conducting a forbidden investigation.

"Come on, Tsunehiko," he said. "Let's find Gallery Street."

Then he found reason to be glad of Tsunehiko's company.

Backing out of the teahouse, Tsunehiko said, "Oh, I know where that is. Follow me, I know a shortcut."

He bounced off down Naka-no-cho, leading Sano around a corner and along a street where high walls hid the back gardens of the brothels from view. They plunged into a maze of narrow alleys lined with closed doors, barred windows, and overflowing wooden trash containers. Stray dogs rooted through the malador-ous debris. Sano was relieved when they emerged into the clean brightness of a wide street.

"Here we are," Tsunehiko announced proudly. "See?"

All up and down Gallery Street, open storefronts displayed racks and walls covered with colorful woodblock prints. Browsers strolled past, many of them samurai defying the laws that prohib-ited them from possessing these supposedly immoral works of art. Hawkers stood outside the galleries, chanting prices and extolling the quality of their merchandise. Inside, the proprietors haggled with their customers in strident tones. Sano studied the signs above the galleries. The Okubata Fine Arts Company lay halfway down the block. Now to get rid of Tsunehiko so that he could conduct the interview in private. . . .

To his delight, Tsunehiko's flightiness came to his aid. The secretary immediately wandered into one of the other shops and began pawing through a stack of pictures. Smiling, Sano headed down the street alone.

He'd no sooner reached the shop than the hawker accosted him, crying, "Good day, sir! Looking for fine prints at the best prices? Well, you've come to the right place!"

He was a man of quite astonishing ugliness. His most prominent feature, a large purplish-red birthmark, spilled across his upper lip, over his mouth, and down his chin. Hair sprouted from his nos-trils. Smallpox scars pitted his skin. Protuberant eyes gave him the appearance of an insect, perhaps a mantis. This resemblance was strengthened by his stooped shoulders and by the way he rubbed his bony hands together as he hovered close to Sano.

"Come in, come in," he urged, plucking at Sano's sleeve.

Sano stepped up onto the raised wooden floor of the shop and passed under the curtain that partially shielded it from the street. The shop was small, a single room with racks of prints crowding its floor and walls, which were hidden by more prints. It was also deserted.

"Now what can I show you?" the ugly man asked. Evidently he was both hawker and proprietor. "Some nice landscape scenes?"

He pointed to a set of pictures mounted on the wall: Mount Fuji during each of the four seasons. Sano could see why the shop had no customers. The prints were poorly drawn, with garish colors slightly out of register so that each picture was a blurred multiple image. He wondered how the shop managed to stay in business.

"Are you Okubata?" he asked the man.

"Yes, yes, that's me. But everyone calls me Cherry Eater." With a self-deprecating laugh, the proprietor touched his birthmark.

Sano thought the name had a second, lewder meaning, as the man's sly glance seemed to suggest.

Cherry Eater pulled a print from the nearest rack. "Perhaps you prefer classical art, sir?"

Sano winced when he saw the print, a crude copy of the ancient painting *He-gassen,* "Fart Battle." In it, two samurai on horseback blew farts at each other from bared buttocks. The artist had rendered the farts as huge, colored clouds of fumes.

"A fine tribute to your heroic ancestors," Cherry Eater suggested.

"No, thank you." Sano, nettled by the implied insult, eyed the proprietor for signs of irony or deliberate malice, but met with only a polite, bland gaze. "Actually, I've come to talk to you about your employee, Noriyoshi."

Before he could introduce himself, Cherry Eater exclaimed, "Ahhh! Why didn't you say so?" With a knowing nod, he ushered Sano to a display rack at the rear of the shop. "Sadly the great artist

Noriyoshi has departed from this world. But I have here his most recent work. His best work, I might add. You like it? Yes?''

Looking at the prints, Sano immediately understood how the Okubata Fine Arts Company made its money: by selling *shunga*—erotic art—to a select clientele. The other prints were nothing but window dressing. Noriyoshi's work showed amorous couples in every possible position and setting: In a bedchamber, with the man on top of the woman; in a garden, with the spread-legged woman seated in the fork of a tree and a standing man thrusting into her. Some pictures included third parties, such as maids assisting the couples, or voyeurs peeping through windows at them. Noriyoshi had depicted costumes, surroundings, and genitalia in great detail. A large print showed a reclining samurai, his swords on the floor next to him, his robes parted to expose a huge erection. With one hand he fondled the crotch of the nude maiden lying beside him; with the other, he drew her hand toward his organ. The caption read:

> Indeed, indeed
> With all their hearts
> Sharing love's bed:
> Caressing her Jeweled Gateway and taking
> The girl's hand, causing her to grasp his
> Jade Shaft: what girl's face will not
> Blush, her breath come faster?

All the prints were technically superior to the works at the front of the shop. The colors were clear and harmonious, the drawing masterful. In addition, they had a sensuous grace not usually found in common *shunga*. Sano felt himself growing aroused against his will.

''Perhaps Noriyoshi's pictures can assist you in your romantic endeavors,'' Cherry Eater said helpfully.

This jab at his sexual prowess, whether or not intentional, jolted Sano out of his reverie. The proprietor was either a very subtle wag, or too thoughtless to realize how his remarks might affect his customers. Turning away from the prints, Sano said sharply, "That's none of your business. And I'm not here to buy."

When he introduced himself, he watched with some satisfaction as Cherry Eater's face blanched so that the birthmark stood out like a fiery rash. The proprietor's eyes flew toward the pictures. The absence of round red censors' seals clearly identified them as contraband, their sale or possession illegal.

"I'm not concerned about your merchandise, either," Sano hastened to add. "I'd like you to answer some questions about Noriyoshi."

Color flooded back into Cherry Eater's face. "If I can, sir. Ask me anything at all." He grinned, expansive in his relief.

To put the man at ease and avoid provoking his suspicion, Sano began with an innocuous question. "How long did Noriyoshi work for you?"

"Oh, not long enough."

Despite Cherry Eater's innocent smile, Sano began to understand that the proprietor's jabs and wisecracks were indeed intentional, delivered in an apparent earnestness that would fool most people. Annoyed, he frowned a warning.

Mischief lit Cherry Eater's eyes as he counted on his fingers. "Noriyoshi was with me six . . . seven years."

Long enough for them to know each other well, Sano thought. "What kind of man was he?"

"Much like any other. He had two eyes, a nose . . ."

Sano's annoyance grew. He glared at Cherry Eater, touching his sword to underscore the threat.

Cherry Eater's insectile eyes goggled; his smile vanished. Obviously realizing that he'd gone too far, he amended quickly, "Oh, Noriyoshi was a very capable artist. Very prolific. His work sold well. I'll miss him."

Sano said patiently, "No, I mean what was he like as a person? Friendly? Popular?"

Cherry Eater grinned. "Oh, not very popular. But he did have many friends, I would say." He gestured toward the street. "All over the quarter."

"Tell me their names." Except for having to accommodate the proprietor's irritating nature, this was going better than Sano had expected.

Cherry Eater mentioned several, all men who worked as artists or in Yoshiwara's teahouses or restaurants.

Sano committed each name to memory. "No women?" he asked.

"No, sir, none that I know of. Except for the young lady who died with him."

A movement caught Sano's eye. He looked down. Although Cherry Eater's expression hadn't changed, he was shifting his weight from one foot to the other. This, along with the unexpected straight answer, told Sano that the art dealer was lying. His body and manner were betraying him.

To throw Cherry Eater off guard, Sano changed the subject. "Did Noriyoshi have any family in town?"

The feet stopped shifting. "No, sir. But plenty in the spirit world. He told me they all perished in the Great Fire."

"Who were Noriyoshi's enemies?"

"He had no enemies, *yoriki,*" Cherry Eater answered blandly. "He was very well liked."

Sano waited for a wisecrack; it never came. He watched the art dealer's shifting feet. "You may as well tell me," he said. "If you don't, I'll find out from someone else. Are you so sure you can trust your friends—" he recited the list of names Cherry Eater had given him "—not to talk?"

"I am most sorry to say that I don't know what you're talking about, sir." Shift, shift. The floorboards creaked under Cherry Eater.

"Who is Noriyoshi's woman friend?"

Cherry Eater folded his arms across his concave chest. "With all due respect, *yoriki,* I do not like the way you are addressing me. You're calling me a liar.'' Evidently his decision to bluff had calmed him; his feet stood firm. ''Either arrest me and take me before the magistrate, or else please leave my shop!''

Sano closed his eyes briefly. Self-disgust withered him. Inexperienced as he was, he'd mishandled the interview. Cherry Eater wouldn't tell him anything now. He could hardly arrest the man for refusing to answer questions about what was officially a suicide, and he didn't even dare arrest him for selling contraband artwork or insulting a police officer. Magistrate Ogyu had already made it clear that he didn't want his *yoriki* doing *doshin*'s work. Besides, he couldn't let Ogyu learn that he was investigating the deaths of Noriyoshi and Yukiko until he could prove they were murders.

''I didn't intend any offense,'' he said, hating to offer apologies in return for insults and teasing, but hoping to placate Cherry Eater enough to let him see where Noriyoshi had lived. He wanted to get some feeling for the man and an idea about what could have driven someone to kill him. ''I didn't come to arrest you or demean your character. I only want information for my records, and you've been most cooperative. Now I ask you to grant me a small request. May I see Noriyoshi's living quarters?''

''Of course, sir.'' Cherry Eater seemed glad for an excuse to stop talking about Noriyoshi's women and enemies. He slid open a section of the wall to reveal a dim passageway. ''This way.''

Sano followed him down the passage and out into a narrow dirt courtyard. One side was bounded by the wall of the shop next door. Along the other ran a flimsy shedlike building with a narrow veranda. At the back, a privy, a woodpile, and a row of ceramic storage urns stood against a bamboo fence. The bitter, acrid smell of ink overlaid the more familiar odors of sewage and sawdust. Cherry Eater led him past the shed. Through its open doors, Sano could see three identical cubicles. In each, an artist knelt at a sloping desk. One was cutting lines in a block of wood with a metal gouge. A second inked a finished block and pressed it against a sheet of white paper. The other was adding color to a finished print.

Cherry Eater stopped before the closed door of a fourth cubicle. "Noriyoshi's," he said, sliding it open.

Sano entered, stepping around the two pairs of wooden sandals on the veranda. His head grazed the low ceiling. Like the others, the room was very small; the desk against one wall took up much of the floor and left just enough space for a man to sleep. Frayed, sawdust-strewn mats covered the floor. Beside the desk a wooden toolbox lay open, revealing a collection of knives, picks, and gouges. A fresh block of wood sat on the desk. Next to it was an ink sketch, and a pot of crusty, dried wheat paste with a brush stuck in it. Noriyoshi had evidently been preparing to transfer the drawing to the woodblock for carving. Sano did a double take when he looked at the sketch. It was a *shunga* piece, in the same style as those in the shop, but featuring two men.

"A special edition for a special client, heh, heh." Cherry Eater hovered at Sano's elbow, grinning and rubbing his hands together. "Samurai often have an interest in such things, no?"

Sano ignored the hint. Although he had never practiced manly love, nor wanted to, he shared the prevailing opinion of this and other sexual matters: whatever people do in private is all right as long as it doesn't hurt anyone else. Besides, he was tired of the art dealer's innuendos and didn't much care what Cherry Eater thought of him or his class. He turned to a battered wooden cabinet that stood against the wall opposite the desk.

The mended garments, worn bedding, chipped crockery, and collection of inks, brushes, charcoal sticks, and sketches he found inside told him nothing he didn't already know: that Noriyoshi had been an artist of some talent and limited income. Sano was finishing a cursory inspection of some cotton kimonos when his hand touched something hard. He pulled out a small drawstring pouch. Its weight surprised him—until he opened it and saw the gold *koban* inside. There must have been at least thirty of the shiny oval coins, enough to keep a large family in comfort for a year. Surely too much for a poor artist to possess, or to earn by legitimate means.

"Do you know where this came from?" Sano asked Cherry Eater.

With amazing swiftness, Cherry Eater's hand flicked out and snatched the pouch. He tucked it into his coat, saying, "It's mine. Noriyoshi sometimes collected payments for me."

Sano looked from the proprietor's innocent face to his feet. Frustration mounted as he watched them shift: Cherry Eater was lying again. Sano resisted the impulse to beat the truth out of the man. His better instincts told him to have patience and seek another path to knowledge. If he didn't find it, he could always come back to the shop.

"Thank you for your kind cooperation," he said. "May I have a word with your employees now?" Maybe they could tell him more about Noriyoshi's activities.

A short time later, Sano walked back through the passage to the shopfront more frustrated than ever. The three artists, all at least twenty years younger than Noriyoshi, had not known their colleague well. They'd only worked there for a year since coming to Edo from the provinces, they said; he hadn't spent much time with them, and they didn't know where he went or with whom he associated during his leisure hours. Sano questioned each man alone, and he thought they were telling the truth. If Noriyoshi's friends proved as close-mouthed as Cherry Eater, he would have to canvass the whole quarter in search of someone who could and would give him more information. Maybe Tsunehiko could help, he thought without much hope. He wondered where the boy was.

When he reached the shop, he found Cherry Eater talking to a frail, bald man who stood outside in the street. The man carried a long staff in one hand and a wooden flute in the other. Their voices were low, urgent.

Cherry Eater, seeing Sano, abruptly stopped talking. He said to the man, "Go now. We'll talk again later."

But the man reached out a hand to Sano. "Master samurai! I am Healing Hands, the best blind masseur in Edo! Do you have pains, or nervous complaints? Allow me to relieve them for you! My skills are legendary, my price low." He cast his sightless eyes up at Sano. Cloudy and pale, they resembled those of a dead fish.

Sano wondered how the blind man knew he was a samurai. Cherry Eater must have told him, or maybe Healing Hands had smelled his hair oil. The blind did have sharp noses.

"I can entertain you with stories while I work, master," the masseur went on. "Would you like to hear an example?"

Without prompting, he launched into his narrative. " 'The Dog Shogun.' " His scratchy voice took on a sing-song quality. "Tokugawa Tsunayoshi, although an able ruler and a great man, has so far failed to produce an heir. His mother, the Lady Keisho-in, sought the advice of the Buddhist priest Ryuko. He told her that in order for Tsunayoshi to father a son, he must first atone for the sins of his ancestors. Together Lady Keisho-in and Ryuko persuaded Tsunayoshi that since he was born in the Year of the Dog, he should do this by issuing an edict protecting dogs.

"Now stray dogs must be fed and cared for. Fighting dogs are separated not with blows, but with a splash of cold water. Those who injure dogs are imprisoned; anyone who kills a dog is executed. And we must treat all dogs with respect. Like this!"

Healing Hands hurried over to a dog that was trotting along the street in front of the shop. He must have smelled the animal, or heard its nails clicking against the hard earth. Bowing low, he cried, "Greetings, O *Inu-sama*, Honorable Dog!" Then he turned to Sano. "I know many other tales, master. Would you like to hear them while you enjoy a most beneficial massage?"

Sano smiled, wondering if Healing Hands's massages were any better than his stories. The one about the Dog Shogun was old news; everyone had heard it when Tokugawa Tsunayoshi had issued his first Dog Protection Edict two years ago. The nation's shock and bewilderment had given way to unvoiced resentment of the money wasted on dog welfare, and the outrageous penalties inflicted on people who abused them.

"Not today," he said. Then, on impulse, he asked, "Did you know Noriyoshi?"

Cherry Eater broke in before Healing Hands could answer. "*Yoriki,* my friend here has an urgent appointment soon." To Healing Hands he said, "Had you not better hurry?" His feet began to shift, and his fluttering hands told Sano how anxious he was to have his friend gone.

Healing Hands ignored the hint and leaned comfortably on his staff. "Oh, yes, master," he said. "Noriyoshi was a kind man. He sent much business my way. He knew everyone, you see—great lords, wealthy merchants."

"Who was his lady friend?" Sano asked. Thanks to the masseur's garrulity, he might learn something today after all.

"Oh, you mean Wisteria? She works in the Palace of the Heavenly Garden, on Naka-no-cho. She—"

"Shut up, you fool! Say the wrong thing, and he'll have the *doshin* throw you in jail!"

At Cherry Eater's sharp outburst, the masseur fell silent. Sketching an apologetic gesture at Sano, he said uneasily, "I must go now, master." He turned and shuffled off down the street, tootling on his wooden flute to attract customers.

Sano took his leave of Cherry Eater and hurried after Healing Hands. He asked about Noriyoshi's enemies, and if any rumors about his death had reached the masseur's ears.

But Healing Hands had taken Cherry Eater's warning to heart. "Go and see Wisteria," was all he would say.

Sano gazed at the masseur's retreating back. This trip, while disappointing, hadn't been a total loss. He'd learned the names of Noriyoshi's associates and lady friend, that the artist had indeed had enemies and had somehow come by a large amount of money. Any of these facts could lead to Noriyoshi's murderer. Sano and Tsunehiko would have to stay in Yoshiwara until nightfall, when the Palace of the Heavenly Garden and the other pleasure houses opened. They could catch the late ferry back to Edo.

Then Sano remembered. Tonight was to be his first visit to his family since he'd left home. At once the burden of obligation crushed him with all its suffocating pressure. He couldn't bear to postpone his inquiry just when it seemed most promising. Neither did he relish the thought of facing his parents while knowing he was defying his master's orders and risking the secure future they desired for him. To disappoint his parents—especially his father—was to fail in his duty as a son.

Sighing, he headed down the street to find Tsunehiko and tell him it was time to return to the city.

6

A little before the dinner hour, Sano arrived in the district where his parents lived on the edge of Nihonbashi nearest the castle, among other samurai families who had gone into trade and merged with the townspeople.

He rode through the gate that led to their street, nodding a greeting to the two guards stationed there. A short bridge took him over the willow-edged canal. At its opposite side, the road ran through a strip of debris-strewn ground where a recent fire had destroyed two houses on either side of the road. Sano looked upon the sight with sorrow. His father's last letter had told him about the fire, which had killed members of all four families and destroyed their businesses. As he continued down the street, he wondered what other changes had come about since he'd moved away. He passed the grocer's, the stationer's and several food stalls, coming to a stop at the corner, outside the Sano Martial Arts Academy.

The academy occupied a long, low wooden building that stood flush with the street. Dingy brown tiles, the same color as the walls, covered the roof. Plain wooden bars screened the windows. A faded sign announced the academy's name. The place seemed both older and smaller than when he'd last seen it only a month ago. He dismounted in the gathering dusk, tied his horse's reins to the railing that bordered the narrow veranda, then entered. A wave of nostalgia swept over him.

In the practice room, oil lamps mounted on the wall lit the winter darkness. Two rows of young men dressed in loose cotton jackets and trousers faced each other in simulated combat. One row wielded wooden blades that substituted for actual steel swords, while the others parried the sword thrusts with a variety of weapons—staffs, spears, chains, iron fans. Their shouts and stamps echoed against the walls in a deafening roar. Sano breathed in the familiar combination of smells—sweat, hair oil, damp plaster, and old wood—feeling at once comforted and sad. He couldn't remember a time when the place had not been home to him. As a boy, he'd learned his fighting skills under his father's strict tutelage, beginning as soon as he was big enough to hold a child-sized sword. Later, as a young man, he'd instructed his own pupils. He'd planned to manage the school himself someday, in the way that any oldest or only son would take over the family business upon his father's retirement.

But the school had not prospered. This was partly because many samurai no longer bothered perfecting their military skills or having their sons trained. However, the main cause lay with the academy itself. Unaffiliated with a major clan, it received no stipend, and Sano's father had to pay the authorities for permission to operate. Lacking wealthy patrons and a prestigious location, and using teaching techniques learned from an obscure master with a small following, the academy attracted fewer pupils every year. Soon there weren't enough to occupy both Sano and his father. Sano had begun tutoring to earn his keep and contribute to his family's support. This year Sano's father had announced that upon his death the school would be turned over to his apprentice, Aoki Koemon—the *sensei* leading this class. Shortly afterward, he had taken Sano to see Katsuragawa Shundai about a government position.

"Sano-*san!*" Koemon came toward him, smiling. Bowing low, he said, "Good evening."

Sano greeted his old friend. They'd grown up together, but as adults Koemon always addressed Sano with the respect due him as the master's son. Now, seeing Koemon looking relaxed and confident in the world he himself had left behind, Sano experienced a twinge of envy. His past was closed to him; he couldn't go back. The present, with its greater financial rewards and troubling conflicts, was all he had.

"So what do you think?" Koemon asked, gesturing toward the class.

Contemplating the students, whose faces were familiar, and the array of weapons, which was not, Sano nodded. "Times have changed," he said.

He and his father and Koemon had debated for several years whether to include nontraditional weapons in the school's curriculum. His father, a strict devotee of *kenjutsu,* had wanted to limit instruction to the art of swordsmanship.

"Nowadays a samurai must be prepared to face opponents armed with a variety of weapons, and besides, the school must offer something new to attract pupils." Sano repeated the arguments that he and Koemon had used to counter the old man's opposition. But seeing that the change had been made in his absence gave him an inexplicable touch of uneasiness that he forgot when he noticed the weapon that Koemon held.

"You teach the art of the *jitte?*" he asked.

Koemon shrugged. "The basics. I'm no expert at it."

More out of curiosity than need, Sano had experimented with the *jitte* in the practice hall at the barracks. "Let's try it now," he said, shedding his cloak and hat and rolling up his sleeves.

With Koemon using a wooden sword in deliberate slow motion, Sano demonstrated how to deflect its blade, and how to deliver counterblows with the *jitte.*

"Parry like this," he said, raising the *jitte* to block a cut to

his shoulder. "Counterstrike before your opponent recovers—
quickly, because his reach is longer than yours."

He swung the weapon around to tap its slender shaft against
Koemon's arm. After blocking another cut, he thrust the blunt end
at his friend's neck.

"And when the time is right—" He arrested Koemon's next
slice by catching the blade in the *jitte*'s prongs. One sharp twist,
and he'd wrenched the weapon from his friend's hand. "With
enough force, you can break your opponent's sword in two."

Then they exchanged weapons so he could demonstrate how to
keep one's blade free of the *jitte*'s prongs and the footwork
necessary to avoid getting thrown or hit once the blade was caught.
Soon he was hot and sweaty, his energy flowing with the welcome
exercise. It felt good to be back in the familiar practice room. He
could almost believe he still belonged there.

When they'd finished, Koemon turned to the class, raising his
voice over the din:

"That's all for today!"

At his command, the pupils froze. Silence fell over the room.
They bowed to their opponents and to Sano and their *sensei,* then
filed toward the dressing-room door.

"Where is my father?" Sano asked when he and Koemon were
alone. "Out on business?"

Koemon hesitated. "He didn't come in today."

Sano's uneasiness returned. His father never missed a day of
work. "What's wrong?" he asked.

"I don't know." Koemon avoided Sano's eyes, indicating that
he did know what was wrong, but either didn't want to say or had
been told not to.

Sano bid a hasty good-bye to his friend. Now the change in the
school's curriculum took on an ominous significance. Why had his
father finally consented to it? With a knot of worry tightening in
his stomach, Sano left the practice room. He led his horse around
the corner, down the narrow side lane. There high fences shielded

the rear lots of the businesses, where the proprietors' living quarters were located. Through chinks in the fences, he could see the yellow flicker of lamps burning in gardens and hear the customary evening sounds: servants chattering, wooden buckets thunking their way up from wells, horses whinnying in stables behind the houses. The pungent odors of miso soup and garlic drifted from kitchens. But food was the farthest thing from Sano's mind as he pushed open his parents' gate.

He backed his horse into its space in the stable in the garden. Seeing the other stall empty increased his anxiety. His father had been predicting his own death for several years now. But the old man's failure to replace his horse when it died a few months ago was a more eloquent and sobering statement that his life was nearing its end.

Sano went into the house, leaving his shoes and swords in the entryway. In the large, earth-floored kitchen to his right, the elderly maid Hana knelt before the stove, stirring soup. Beside it, a pot of rice simmered. Vegetables lay on a wooden table beside the stone washbasin. Two black lacquer *ozen* stood near the wall, already set with bowls, chopsticks, and saucers. Sano nodded in response to Hana's smiling bow. She'd worked for the family since before his birth; normally he would have paused to chat with her, but a deep, barking cough sounded from inside the main room. Sano slid open the door.

His father sat huddled beneath a voluminous quilt. Bent over double, he coughed wrackingly into the cloth that Sano's mother held to his mouth. Then he drew a shallow, gasping breath and began to cough again. Sano's mother made soothing noises. With her free hand, she pulled the end of the quilt over the brazier, so that its warmth might reach her husband. An oil lamp on the floor beside them cast their shadows against the walls of the small room and highlighted the lines of suffering on the old man's emaciated face.

"*Otōsan!*" Sano cried in dismay.

For a long time now, his father's health had been poor without ever seeming to get worse. Now Sano was shocked to see how much his father had deteriorated in just one month.

Both parents turned simultaneously to look at him, his father's cough subsiding.

"*Otōsan,* why didn't you tell me you were ill?" Sano demanded, kneeling beside his father.

Spent, eyes closed, the old man shook his head. One thin hand came out from under the quilt and feebly waved away Sano's question.

Sano's mother answered for her husband. "He didn't want to worry you, Ichirō-*chan,*" she said. "And anyway, he's much better today. He'll be fine soon." Her voice and smile were bright, but her careworn face told the truth. She looked down at the cloth she held. Seeing the bloodstains, she hastily hid it in her lap.

"Has he seen the doctor?" Sano asked her, trying not to show impatience with her self-delusion. She had always denied the existence of problems, both because she hoped that to do so would make them go away, and because her upbringing had taught her to always present an untroubled facade to the world. He couldn't force her to confront the gravity of his father's illness; time and nature would do that. Pity for her nearly overshadowed his own grief.

"No doctor," Sano's father rasped. He coughed again—a mercifully short spell this time—then said, "It grows late. We will eat now. *Omae,* bring the food. Our son must not go hungry."

Sano's mother rose obediently and left the room.

With an aching heart, Sano noted another ominous change in his father. The old man had never liked to talk about his symptoms—the cough, the pains, the fever, the difficulty in breathing. Still, he'd willingly consulted doctors and tried their remedies; he'd visited fortune tellers to find out how long he had to live; he'd gone to both Shinto and Buddhist priests for prayers that might convince the gods to spare his life. Now, though, he was accepting his illness and its inevitable result with stoic resignation. Sano's eyes burned with unshed tears. Not wanting his parents to see them, he bent his head over the damp washcloth that his mother brought him. He could not meet her eyes as she gave his hand a brief caress.

Hana placed food-laden *ozen* before Sano and his father. They ate in silence, as usual strictly observing the custom of no conversation during meals. With nothing to distract him, Sano couldn't help noticing how little his father ate, and how slowly. A few spoonfuls of miso soup, a fragment of pickled white radish, and a sliver of fish, with tiny sips of tea between bites. His mother, who usually plied Sano with more food than he could eat, instead devoted her whole attention to constantly refilling her husband's dishes in a futile effort to make him eat more. Sano resolved to bring up the subject of doctors again when the meal ended.

But when the *ozen* were removed and the smoking tray brought, his father spoke first.

"I have found a prospective bride for you, Ichirō," he said. "She is Ikeda Akiko, nineteen years old, with a dowry of four hundred *ryō*."

Sano kept his face expressionless. His father persisted in making proposals on his behalf only to the daughters of wealthy samurai. This was why Sano remained unhappily single at the advanced age of thirty. He didn't want to contradict his father, but he hated to see him suffer yet another humiliation when, predictably, the proposal was rejected.

He said, "The Ikedas rank far above us, *Otōsan*. I don't think they would want me for a son-in-law."

"Nonsense!" His father's exclamation set off another coughing fit. "Our go-between will send gifts and contact them to arrange a *miai*. I am sure they will consent. Especially now that you are a *yoriki*."

Yoriki or not, the Ikedas would never agree to the *miai*—a formal meeting of him and Akiko and the two families—Sano knew. They would probably send the gifts back by return messenger.

"Yes, *Otōsan,*" he said, afraid his father would cough again if he disagreed. Surely that frail body could not stand much more strain.

Satisfied, his father changed the subject. "Does your work go well, my son?" he asked, lighting his pipe from the metal basket of embers on the tray. He took a puff, coughed, spat into a napkin, and set the pipe down.

Sano decided to say nothing about Magistrate Ogyu's reprimand or the illicit murder investigation. Instead he described his office, his duties, and his living quarters, presenting each in as favorable a light as possible without boasting. He didn't mention his colleagues' coldness or his own unhappiness.

The gleam of pride in his father's eyes was his reward. The old man sat straighter, and Sano could see the warrior who had once stood against entire classes of samurai in practice sword fights.

"Continue to serve well and faithfully in your position," he admonished, "and you will never lack a master. You must never become *rōnin.*"

His father had become a *rōnin*—a masterless samurai—when the third Tokugawa shogun, Iemitsu, had confiscated Lord Kii's lands forty years ago, turning the Sano family and the rest of the lord's retainers out to fend for themselves. His pride had never recovered from the blow of losing his master, his livelihood, and the hereditary position that had come down to him through many generations. But unlike other *rōnin,* he hadn't turned into an outlaw or rebel. Instead, he'd founded the academy and lived quietly, nursing his shame and sorrow. When Sano first heard as a child of the Great Conspiracy of four hundred *rōnin* who had tried to overthrow the government, he hadn't believed the story. As an adult, he was aware of the undercurrent of dissatisfaction that flowed beneath the country's peaceful surface, and of the Tokugawas' ongoing efforts to sniff out and contain the rebellions that arose among idle, unemployed samurai. But as a boy, he'd mistakenly assumed that all *rōnin* were strict, law-abiding men like his father, who directed their energy and ambition toward making their sons succeed where they had failed. Now he felt a surge of guilt as he wondered what his father would think if he knew how Sano had risked disgrace and possible dismissal by disobeying his new master's orders.

At the same time, a spark of irrational anger kindled in him. Hadn't his father, however unintentionally, fostered the searching, inquiring nature that now placed his future at risk? Hadn't his father sent him to the temple school to study literature, composition, math, law, history, political theory, and the Chinese classics to supplement the military skills he learned at home? The monks had educated him far beyond the usual scope of the common foot soldier, now virtually obsolete in a country without war. They'd taught him to think rather than to blindly follow orders, as he would have to do in the high-level government position his father had desired for him.

"Now that you are on the path to glory, I can leave this world willingly, with a peaceful mind," his father added softly, as if to himself.

Sano's anger died; guilt remained. He realized that his father had fought illness and held on to life just long enough to see him settled. Now the old man was giving up. How could Sano jeopardize the position that was supposed to secure the future his father wanted for him? How could he pursue a course that was bound to put him at odds with those who now controlled that future? The answer was simple enough: he couldn't. His father's spirit would never forgive him. The murder investigation wasn't worth that; truth and justice wouldn't bring Noriyoshi and Yukiko back to life. He wouldn't be able to live with himself if he failed in the obligation that his own name set out for him.

Ichirō. *First-born son.*

And, since he was an only child, the burden of filial duty rested on him alone.

7

"The eighteenth day of the twelfth month, Genroku year one," Sano dictated. "Record of the day's police activities." He proceeded to summarize the reports given him by the *doshin*. "Total arrests: forty-seven. Seventeen for disorderly conduct, twelve for theft, eight for mistreating or killing dogs, six for assault, three for adultery, one for prostitution outside the licensed quarter.

"Two samurai—one disorderly conduct, one assault—were placed under house arrest. The commoners were remanded to Edo Jail. The heads of all three adulteresses have been shaved, and their husbands granted divorces."

When Tsunehiko handed him the finished report, he affixed his seal to it. "Take this to Magistrate Ogyu's office. Then you may go home. That's all for today."

He suppressed a yawn, rubbing his eyes. They felt gritty and sore from lack of sleep. Last night he hadn't returned to the barracks. Instead he'd stayed at his parents' house, alternately sitting at his father's bedside, bathing the old man's face and administering herb tea to ease the pain, and lying awake listening to the coughs that shook the house.

Tsunehiko hovered in the doorway. "*Yoriki* Sano-*san,* we didn't do any investigating today," he said. "What about tomorrow?"

"I'm afraid we won't be doing any more, Tsunehiko." This

time the yawn escaped, and Sano covered his mouth. "Not tomorrow, or ever."

Tsunehiko's face mirrored Sano's own unhappiness. "Why not? It was so much fun!"

Having spent the entire night convincing himself of the rightness of dropping the investigation, Sano didn't want to think or talk about it. So he only said, "Because duty and obligation dictate otherwise," knowing that Tsunehiko, with his own samurai upbringing, would accept this explanation without question.

After Tsunehiko had left, Sano cleared his desk, then crossed the courtyard to the barracks. The weather had turned warmer, bringing the promise of spring. The late afternoon sun shone golden from a sky filled with puffy white clouds. In Yoshiwara, the nightlong festivities would have already begun. The *yūjo*—those exquisite, expensive prostitutes—would beckon customers from the windows of the pleasure houses. One, he knew, Wisteria of the Palace of the Heavenly Garden, held the key to Noriyoshi's and Yukiko's murders. . . .

Sano resolutely forced the thought away. He would go right to bed, without even eating dinner. When he entered his room, however, he hesitated before the cabinet that held his bedding. Tired as he was, he knew sleep would elude him while he wondered about Wisteria. Slowly he opened the cabinet and took out the futon and quilts, but stopped short of spreading them on the floor. He reminded himself of all the reasons he should not go to Yoshiwara. His father. His future. Duty, honor. But his desire for knowledge only grew stronger, until he could no longer deny it satisfaction. With a sudden recklessness, he dropped the bedding and went to the cabinet where his clothes were stored. He donned a long gray cloak and a wide, face-concealing straw hat. He gathered up all his cash—not only because spending time in Yoshiwara could get expensive, but because he might have to bribe someone for the information he wanted. Then he walked to the stables to get his horse. He would take the faster land route this time, instead of the slow ferry.

As he mounted his horse, he realized that, despite his firm resolutions, he'd meant to do this all along. Today he'd carried out his administrative duties without deviation from procedure or custom. But the one thing he hadn't done was complete the report that would close the investigation into Noriyoshi's and Yukiko's deaths.

"One last interview can't hurt," he rationalized aloud, surprising the grooms. "After this, I'll stop."

Still, he couldn't quite shake his guilt or his premonition of impending disaster.

Nighttime Yoshiwara more than lived up to Sano's memories. Beneath a fading crimson sunset, Naka-no-cho glittered with life and excitement. Lanterns blazed from the eaves. Restaurants, their doors thrown wide open, emitted the delicious smells of all possible foods—fried noodles, grilled fish and shrimp, and sweet cakes among them—to tempt the strolling crowds. Raucous laughter erupted from the teahouses; each window framed a tableau of joking, posturing men tossing back cups of sake. Beautiful yūjo in gaudy kimonos filled the window cages of the pleasure houses like so many exotic butterflies, with groups of hungry-eyed men loitering before them. The women flirted with the men in shrill voices. From the lighted rooms behind the women, samisen music issued: a few lucky men had already chosen their companions, and the parties had begun.

Sano found the Palace of the Heavenly Garden without difficulty: it was the largest house on the street. With its carved beams and pillars painted red and accented with yellow and green, it resembled a Chinese temple. Above the entrance, two resplendent dragons held between them a red banner that announced the house's name in gold characters. Sano pushed through the crowd that stood three deep in front of the window and saw that the women inside were even more beautiful than the others.

"Honorable lady, where can I find Wisteria?" he called to the nearest, a very young girl dressed in a red kimono printed with white, lucky characters. According to custom, *yūjo* were treated with the high respect usually accorded to noblewomen.

Red Kimono pouted daintily. "The Lady Wisteria, master? What can she offer you that I cannot?" Her stilted, formal style of speech was the same one all Yoshiwara prostitutes used to their customers. "Surely a warrior as masculine and discerning as yourself would prefer a delicate maiden who has just reached the flowering of her womanhood?"

She fluttered her fan, coyly shielding her face with it in a manner just as clichéd as her speech. The other women giggled, waiting for Sano's response.

Gathering his patience, Sano said, "I meant no insult to you, my lady." No matter how meaningless the courtesans' flattery or how brazen their invitations, one always replied with courtesy. To do otherwise ran counter to Yoshiwara tradition and invited the anger of their owners, who banned rude patrons from the pleasure houses. "But I need to talk to Wisteria."

"Talk? He comes here to talk?"

More giggles.

Sano decided that the best thing to do was identify himself and state his business. "I am *Yoriki* Sano Ichirō from the police department. I must speak to Wisteria about an official matter. Can you send word to her that I am here?"

Red Kimono was unimpressed, and obviously piqued at having wasted her effort on a noncustomer. Dropping her flirtatious manner, she said, "In your own sphere, others must do your bidding, *yoriki*. But I am not your servant." The other women giggled again. "Unless . . ."

Her disdainful gaze moved over him, taking in his simple cloak and hat. A haughty smile turned up the corners of her mouth.

Unless you have the money to pay, it implied, and I can see that you don't.

"Please," Sano said. "It's very important. I have to talk to her about Noriyoshi."

At the mention of Noriyoshi's name, Red Kimono's smile vanished. She nodded curtly. Turning to the room behind her, she beckoned. She whispered to a maid that appeared beside her. A moment later, the maid opened the door, bowing to Sano.

"Go with her," Red Kimono said.

Sano stepped into the entryway of the Palace of the Heavenly Garden, where he removed his shoes. As he placed his swords on the rack, he remembered that safety, as well as etiquette, dictated that they must not enter the house. An unhappy *yūjo* might try to escape her enforced servitude by committing suicide with an unattended weapon.

In the large salon, women and their customers reclined on bright silk cushions scattered over the floor, chatting and laughing. A samisen player performed a popular love song. Maids circulated with plates of delicacies and poured sake. Coins clinked as lavish tips passed from the customers—rich merchants, by the look of their opulent clothing—to the maids. Sano followed his escort through this room and out a sliding door onto the roofed veranda.

The veranda faced a garden that must have been the site of many parties in spring, when its cherry trees dropped blossoms over the lawn, upon the stone lanterns, and into the ornamental pond with a small temple on an island in the middle. Now, with winter not yet gone, it was deserted. But lanterns burned from the verandas of the buildings that surrounded it—one above every door. Lights glowed through the windows. Laughter issued faintly from a few of the rooms, where some *yūjo* had already begun entertaining their customers in private.

The maid pointed to a door at the back left corner. "There, sir."

Sano walked along the veranda to the door and knocked. He

waited. No laughter emanated from this room, only a listening silence. Then:

"Come in." It was a woman's voice, forced cheerfulness evident even in the short phrase.

Sano entered, bowing to the woman who knelt before a lacquer dressing table. "Good evening, Lady Wisteria."

She had turned a welcoming smile toward him; now it faded. "I was expecting someone else," she said. "Who are you?" Unlike Red Kimono's, her speech was plain, uninflected Edo—perhaps because he'd surprised her.

Sano bowed again and introduced himself, while covertly studying Wisteria. She didn't fit his preconceived picture of Noriyoshi's lady friend. He'd imagined a woman long past her prime, who played the role of mother to her clients. But Wisteria was no more than twenty, and clearly a *yūjo* of the first rank. She wore a lavish black-and-white-checked silk brocade kimono with a bold pattern of lavender wisteria blossoms and pale green leaves spilling diagonally from her left shoulder to the hem. It was obviously expensive. Her eyes, unusually round, made her piquant face exotic, provocative. The large, airy room reflected her status and set off her beauty. It was filled with luxurious furnishings: silk quilt and futon, carved lacquer chests and cabinets, painted lanterns. The alcove held a branch of dried winter berries in a creamy celadon vase that was surely the work of a master potter, and a scroll bearing classic Chinese verse in the unmistakable hand of a famous Kyoto calligrapher.

"I'm here about your friend, Noriyoshi," Sano said, turning from his examination of the room and back to her face.

Her eyes, liquid and luminous, seemed to darken. Turning abruptly to the round mirror on her dressing table, she picked up a comb and began to arrange her hair, drawing the long, shining black mass up at the sides into a complicated loop at the back. Her movements had a languid, sensuous quality that Sano found extremely erotic and arousing, despite his preoccupation with the murder case.

"I refuse to discuss Noriyoshi. And I'm expecting a guest." Her voice trembled. "So get out. Now."

The sadness and absence of animosity in her voice told Sano that grief, not anger, had provoked her rude dismissal. He hesitated, unwilling to cause her pain. But he didn't want to leave without learning what she knew.

Wisteria flung her comb to the floor and faced him. "Well? What are you waiting for?" Tears glistened in her eyes. "If you've come to tell me that Noriyoshi committed suicide for love of some silly little upper-class goose, and that his body will be put out on the riverbank for people to gawk at . . . well, I already know. The story is all over the quarter. So go. Leave me in peace."

Sano decided to tell her as much of the truth as possible. "Noriyoshi didn't commit suicide. He was murdered."

She stared at him. Sounds from the next room filled the silence: samisen music, with a male and a female voice singing softly. Her face registered first disbelief, then dawning hope.

"Murdered?" Her voice dropped to a whisper. "Can this be true? How do you know?"

"I can't tell you that," Sano said. He didn't know if he could trust her, and he didn't want the story of the dissection spread around Yoshiwara. "But it's true." He knelt beside her. "I want to find out why he was killed, and by whom. Will you help me?"

"How?"

"Tell me everything you know about Noriyoshi: his family background, what kind of man he was. Who his enemies were, and why one of them might have wanted to kill him."

Wisteria's eyes took on a faraway look. She began to run her fingers through her hair. Maybe the action was a nervous habit, but everything about her suggested sex—her luxurious room with the bed ready, her faint, flowery scent, her rosy mouth. Sano, watching her slender, soft hands, couldn't help imagining them caressing his body. He shifted nervously. The room seemed very warm.

"Everyone thinks Noriyoshi was a hustler who cared only for himself and his deals," she said. "Mention his name, and they do this."

Looking over her shoulder as if to make sure no one was watching, she smiled slyly and pretended to count money from an imaginary hand into her own. The vulgar pose looked incongruous on someone so elegant, but it gave Sano a vivid picture of what Noriyoshi must have looked like alive.

"But he was different with me." She paused, then went on in a lower voice. "I came to Edo from Dewa Province when I was ten. My father sold me to a brothel's procurer because his crops had failed that year and he couldn't afford to feed me as well as my mother and my four brothers. I started out as a maid here at the Heavenly Garden. Do you know what that was like?"

Sano nodded. Young girls, unless they showed extraordinary promise, were virtual slaves in the pleasure houses. They worked long, hard hours cleaning the rooms, helping in the kitchens, and running errands. All for inadequate food and shelter. Many died before they reached maturity; most of the others could hope to rise no higher than maid or second-class prostitute. Few became celebrated first-rank *yūjo,* and even fewer ever gained independence from the men who owned them.

"I met Noriyoshi a year later, when he came to the house to deliver some *shunga* for the ladies to show their customers. He stopped in the kitchen for some tea, and I was there peeling vegetables." A smile of reminiscence touched Wisteria's lips. "He asked me my name, where I was from. He must have known I was hungry; I was so thin my bones showed." She touched the smooth rich flesh at her collarbone. "And my hair had started to fall out.

"After that, he brought me food every day when no one was watching. I was afraid that he would stop, but he didn't. I got healthy again. My hair grew back. And Noriyoshi started to walk with me when I left the house on errands. He made me laugh at his jokes. And he started teaching me how to move, how to smile, how to talk to men. I must have learned my lessons well, because one day my owner said I didn't have to work in the kitchen anymore. He had the maids dress me up in fine clothes. And from then on . . .''

Her hand gestured toward her room and herself. "You know the rest of the story."

"Yes." Sano could guess how Noriyoshi, with his artist's eye, had spotted Wisteria's potential. He'd saved her from a harsh fate. But not unselfishly: he'd no doubt put her in his debt in order to avail himself of her favors. Sano's eyes went to the neckline of her kimono, where the swell of her breasts began. The blood surged to his loins. For a moment, he almost envied the dead man.

Wisteria's sharp glance rebuked him. "I know what you're thinking," she snapped. "But it wasn't like that. Noriyoshi was never my lover. He preferred men, you see."

That could explain the drawing on the artist's desk, Sano thought.

"When I heard how he died, I was angry," Wisteria said sadly. "Not because he'd fallen in love with that girl, or because she had managed to make him want her the way he never wanted me. But because he never told me. Never confided in me, the way he did about everything else. And now that you tell me he was murdered"—she swallowed—"I feel so ashamed of my anger."

Sano looked away tactfully as she struggled to control her tears. He was about to ask her again who Noriyoshi's enemies were, when someone rapped on the door.

Wisteria jumped to her feet. "Quick, quick!" She opened the cabinet door and gestured for Sano to get inside. "It's my client. He mustn't find you here."

From inside the dark cabinet, Sano heard her slide open the door. He heard a low male voice, and Wisteria making excuses. ". . . indisposed . . . sorry. Perhaps tomorrow night . . . many thanks.'' The rustle of silk as they embraced. What would it feel like to hold her himself? He was glad when the door slid shut again, interrupting his fantasy. He stepped out of the cabinet to see Wisteria unceremoniously toss her client's gift—a silk fan—on the dressing table.

"Noriyoshi's enemies?'' she said in response to Sano's question after they were settled again. "Which ones do you want to know about? All of them, or just the worst?''

"Start with the worst.''

Wisteria frowned, as if trying to decide who should head the list. "Kikunojo,'' she said finally.

"Kikunojo?'' Sano repeated in surprise. "Not the Kabuki actor? Why would he have killed Noriyoshi?''

She nodded, then shrugged. "Noriyoshi sometimes . . . accepted money from people in exchange for keeping their secrets.''

Blackmail. The ugly, unspoken word hung between them. Sano saw Wisteria flush and pitied her for having to expose her friend's flaws. But the flush reminded him of the way a woman looked when sensually excited, as did the way her breath quickened. His own excitement mounted. To add to his discomfort, the couple next door had abandoned their duet. A rhythmic thumping shook the thin walls. Sano looked away when Wisteria smiled briefly at him. She probably meant the smile as an apology for the noise, but to Sano, it said, "Wouldn't you like to do what they're doing?''

To cover his embarrassment, Sano asked quickly, "So Noriyoshi was paid for his silence. By who else besides Kikunojo?''

"One other that I know of. A sumo wrestler, but I don't know his name.''

Maybe one of Noriyoshi's other friends would know. "Did Noriyoshi collect a large payment shortly before his death?'' Sano asked, thinking of the gold he'd found in the artist's room.

Wisteria's eyes misted. "Maybe. He said he was about to come into enough money to pay off my debt to the Heavenly Garden, and to start his own gallery. We were going to run it together. He even had a building picked out. One with rooms behind it where we could live. But I don't know if he ever got the money.''

Sano decided not to tell her about the gold that Cherry Eater had taken. It would only hurt her. Besides, the sum he'd seen, while considerable, wasn't enough for such an enterprise. Noriyoshi must have been expecting much more. Maybe Kikunojo had killed him to avoid having to pay.

"Kikunojo might very well have murdered Noriyoshi," Wisteria said bitterly, echoing Sano's thoughts. "He threatened to do it. And Noriyoshi's other enemies——'' She reeled off a long list of people, both samurai and commoners, that Noriyoshi had owed money to, offended, or cheated. "I don't think they cared enough to kill him."

Here at last was some information he could take to Magistrate Ogyu. Bowing, Sano said, "My thanks, Lady Wisteria. I'll do everything in my power to bring Noriyoshi's murderer to justice.''

He rose to leave . . . and found himself unable to move away from Wisteria. Her eyes drew him into their dark depths; her body reached for him without moving. He gazed at her helplessly, longingly.

"Wait." Wisteria caught his sleeve. "Don't leave me alone." She tried to pull him back down to the floor. "Stay with me tonight.''

Sano pulled away. His manhood, already erect, now sprang to full, demanding life at the thought of lying with her. He saw now that for the whole time he'd spent with her, she'd been subtly, deliberately seducing him. His whole body ached for her. But there was no way he could afford her price.

"I'm sorry, my lady," he managed to say, removing his sleeve from her grasp. "Please." Please don't make me humiliate myself by admitting that I'm too poor to have you.

She stood, playing the fingers of one hand down the length of his arm. "No, you don't understand. I ask nothing of you." Her other hand stroked his chest. "Nothing except . . . you."

"Why?" Sano couldn't believe that a *yūjo* who kept company with the wealthiest, most powerful men in Edo would want him. Who cares why, his body asked as his skin tingled under her touch.

"Because with you, I don't have to hide my sorrow."

She stepped away from him. With a graceful gesture, she slipped the knot of her sash. Her kimono opened, then fell away from her body. Naked, she stood before him. Her breasts were small and round. Her arms and legs were slender, her skin a flawless golden ivory. At her shaven pubis, trademark of all *yūjo*, the delicate cleft of her womanhood showed. Beneath her perfume, Sano could smell her natural scent, pungent and intoxicating. She took his hands and lifted them to her breasts.

A moan escaped Sano when his fingers touched her nipples. Then he recoiled as she closed her mouth over his. Like other samurai, he'd experienced the pleasures of sex often enough—with his neighbors' maids, or with girls he met in the entertainment districts of Nihonbashi. But he'd never tried *seppun,* the exotic practice of touching mouths that had been introduced to Japan by the banished foreign barbarians.

"It won't hurt you," she murmured, her breath warm against his lips. Amusement shimmered in her voice.

At first the slippery wetness of her lips repelled him. Then his desire flared, and he opened his mouth to admit her probing tongue. Who would have thought that this outrageous exchange of breath and saliva could be so arousing? He pulled away just long enough to cast off his garments, hating to take his mouth from hers, his hands from their exploration of her breasts and buttocks.

They sank onto the futon together, and she pressed her body to his with an ardor that surprised Sano. He'd heard many stories about *yūjo:* their expertise, the elaborate games they played with costumes, toys, pillow talk, and aphrodisiacs, their false but flat-

tering cries of ecstasy. But unless he was much mistaken, her sighs
and arching back were not mere theatrics. He saw no cold mechan-
ical technique in the way she caressed his chest and loins and
grasped his erection—just a woman's simple and ancient desire for
a man. And she couldn't have simulated the ardor that his hands
read in her hard nipples, in the wetness between her legs. For a
moment he wondered why she differed from other *yūjo*. Was this
her special talent, her ability to want the men she bedded? Maybe
she was trying to bury her sorrow over Noriyoshi's death in
physical pleasure with someone whom she had no obligation to
entertain. The reason didn't matter. Her apparently real lust for
him brought Sano to the brink of climax. Almost swooning with
pleasure, he entered her.

And stopped thinking altogether.

Sano had slipped so easily from wakefulness into sleep that he'd
hardly been aware of the transition. Now he awoke with a jolt to
the sound of quiet sobbing. He sat upright, throwing off the quilts.
He looked toward the corner, where candle flame made a hollow
of light.

Wrapped in a white robe, Wisteria knelt, her profile toward
him, before a low table. On it she had arranged among the fruit,
flowers, and guttering candles a collection of small objects. She
bowed her head over them, lips moving as tears ran down her face.
Sano crawled off the futon and moved to her side. He saw a cotton
headband on the table, with a tobacco pipe and a hand of playing
cards. The cards, each with a miniature *shunga* on the back,
seemed hardly suitable for a Buddhist altar. Then he understood.
Noriyoshi had painted the cards; the headband and pipe were his.
Wisteria, in her white mourning clothes, was praying for Noriyoshi's spirit.

Both moved and embarrassed, Sano tried to think of something
to say. He wasn't used to seeing such an open display of grief; most
people kept their feelings hidden, even at funerals. Maybe he

should let her mourn in privacy. But he couldn't leave without somehow acknowledging what had happened between them. He laid a tentative hand on her shoulder.

"Go to your new home in peace, Noriyoshi," Wisteria murmured. "We will meet again someday." She turned to Sano. Her round eyes were wells of misery, her nose and mouth swollen from weeping.

Sano felt her pain echo inside his own chest. "I'm sorry," he said inadequately. He tried to take her in his arms, but she shrank from his touch.

"My only real friend is dead!" she cried, sudden anger sparkling through her tears. "And how have I honored him? By bedding a *yoriki*!" A choked sob burst from deep within her. "You, who care nothing for other people's pain!

"You come here asking questions and acting so concerned. But there is no justice for lowly peasants, who cannot pay or influence our rulers to provide it. You'll go back to your desk and write up a pretty little official version of what happened to Noriyoshi. *Shinjū*. Nice and neat and easy. No inquiry to make more work for you or your superiors, or to trouble the family of that girl, whoever she was. You'll stamp Noriyoshi's disgrace with your seal and your silence. While the one who killed him goes free!"

Although Sano knew that grief and self-disgust had prompted her attack on him, the words hurt. He knew how close he'd come—how close he still was—to doing exactly as she predicted.

"I do care," he said. "And I don't intend to let Noriyoshi's killer go free." As he spoke, the thought of Magistrate Ogyu, Katsuragawa Shundai, and his father made him wince inwardly.

Wisteria covered her face with both hands. "Leave me," she whispered.

Sano dressed quietly and let himself out the door. In the salon of the Palace of the Heavenly Garden, he found the party still in progress; outside, Naka-no-cho still pulsed with life, its crowds and gaiety undiminished beneath the night sky. But the main gate was closed. Sano, on his way to the public stables where he'd left his horse, gazed at it in dismay. He'd stayed with Wisteria much longer than he'd planned, and now he, along with everyone else in Yoshiwara, was locked in for the night.

He trudged toward the poorer section of the quarter and a modest inn that he remembered from his student days. There, for an exorbitant price that would use up all the money he'd brought, he could catch a few hours' rest while he waited for dawn and the opening of the gates.

Later, as he lay on a straw pallet listening to the boozy snores of nine other men who shared the room with him, he experienced a new uneasiness. He recognized it as guilt for having taken his pleasure from a lonely and bereaved woman. The memory of her grief made him wish he'd had the strength to refuse her. Their coupling hadn't brought her comfort. Now he felt as if he owed her compensation for the extra pain he'd caused.

That compensation could cost him his family's honor. But what had he to offer her except his best effort to bring Noriyoshi's killer to justice?

8

This time Sano's interview with Magistrate Ogyu took place not in the Court of Justice, but in Ogyu's private office. The morning sun streamed through the translucent windows, dispelling any resemblance to the courtroom's dim gloominess. No *doshin*, defendants, or witnesses were present, only Ogyu's elderly manservant, who shuffled about serving tea. Sano didn't have to face Ogyu across the white sand of truth like a condemned man awaiting his sentence. They knelt on silk cushions like any two officials engaged in a civilized meeting. But Sano still felt as if he were on trial.

"Honorable Magistrate, I respectfully request your permission to continue the investigation into the deaths of Niu Yukiko and Noriyoshi," he said.

He'd debated whether to approach Ogyu today, or wait until he had more facts to support his case. Guilt had finally prompted him to speak now: candor was the least he owed his superior.

Ogyu said nothing. Instead he cradled his tea bowl in both withered hands, sniffing the steam that rose from it. Today he wore his ceremonial clothes—a black *haori* with broad padded shoulders over a black kimono stamped with circular gold family crests. The stark garments made his skin seem especially pallid and desiccated. Against the wall mural's colorful landscape, he looked like an ancient pen-and-ink ancestor portrait.

"I am glad that you came to see me," he said finally. "It appears we have much to discuss."

Sano tried to draw hope from the neutral statement. "Yes, Honorable Magistrate?"

"There is the small matter of a report that you have written." Ogyu glanced down at an unfurled scroll on the desk before him.

With foreboding, Sano recognized his own writing and seal. It was the report classifying the deaths as suspicious.

"I am afraid this document does not reflect the understanding that we reached at our last meeting," Ogyu continued.

Sano's heart plummeted. Ogyu's displeasure with the report would make him unreceptive to any suggestion.

"Also, you have issued a cremation order for Noriyoshi in defiance of the law which states that *shinjū* participants must endure public exposure as punishment for their crime. What have you to say for yourself, *Yoriki* Sano?"

"Please let me explain," Sano said. He could almost feel the floor caving in under him. "When I heard of the deaths, I thought they required further investigation. That's why I wrote that report." Seeing Ogyu frown, he rushed on. He didn't mention the cremation order and fervently hoped Ogyu would drop the subject. "Forgive my presumptiousness; I should not have disobeyed your orders. But now that I've made some inquiries, I believe that Yukiko and Noriyoshi were murdered. I beg your permission to finish my investigation, to find their murderer and bring him to justice." He didn't think it necessary to remind the magistrate that while the murder of a peasant might not warrant much official concern, that of a daimyo's daughter couldn't go ignored.

The frown lines in Ogyu's forehead deepened, whether in surprise or irritation, Sano couldn't tell. "And how do you know this?" he asked.

Sano drank some tea to calm himself. "I've learned that Noriyoshi didn't like women, which means he probably would not have killed himself for the love of one. And he had enemies. At least one of them hated him enough to kill him.''

"And who might that be?'' Ogyu sipped from his own bowl, then motioned for the servant to refill both it and Sano's.

"Kikunojo, the Kabuki actor.''

"How did you learn of this . . . enemy?'' The pause before the word conveyed Ogyu's skepticism.

"I spoke with Noriyoshi's close friend, a woman named Wisteria,'' Sano answered. Giving Wisteria's name to lend credibility to his story, he nevertheless hoped he wouldn't have to explain what she did for a living.

But apparently Ogyu knew. Rumor said that he still frequented Yoshiwara's pleasure houses, despite his age. He sighed and quoted an old proverb. "Two rare things: square eggs, and a *yūjo*'s sincerity.''

"I think she was telling the truth,'' Sano said. Inadvertently he remembered last night. Wisteria's grief; her plea to him to arrest Kikunojo for her friend's murder; her passion. . . . Sano's blood stirred. He forced himself back to the present.

Ogyu was shaking his head. "*Yoriki* Sano.'' How can you be so gullible? his tone implied. How dare you waste my time with such nonsense?

"Magistrate, when I went to the morgue, I saw a large bruise on Noriyoshi's head, as if someone had struck him,'' Sano said with growing desperation. "And he—didn't look as though he'd drowned.'' This was dangerous ground. What if Ogyu wanted to know more about his visit to the morgue?

Fortunately Ogyu's refined sensibilities kept him from taking up the subject. He made a moue of distaste and said, "We will not talk of such things here.''

Having already presented his best arguments, Sano could think of nothing else to say. If Ogyu dismissed two and refused to discuss the other, what hope had he of succeeding?

Now Ogyu cleared his throat and signaled for another round of tea. Sano braced himself for a circumspect rebuke, perhaps an allusion to his patron, Katsuragawa Shundai. However, he soon found himself following the magistrate's convoluted thought trail down a completely different path.

"There are many lessons to be learned from the animal kingdom," Ogyu said. "When the tiger goes to the stream, the deer wait until he has drunk his fill and departed before they go to drink. When the hawk takes flight, small creatures hide until he has passed."

Sano nodded, waiting for him to get to the point.

"When the dragonfly spreads his splendid wings, other insects dare not approach, lest they arouse his wrath," Ogyu finished. He paused to let his meaning sink in.

This last scenario bore no resemblance to nature, but Sano got the message anyway.

"So you've heard of my visit to the Nius," he said. The Nius, with their dragonfly family crest and their overshadowing power.

Ogyu winced at such bluntness. "*Yoriki* Sano, do you really need to be reminded of the dangers of offending a great daimyo family? Lady Niu called on me personally to complain about your intrusion." His voice rose to its highest, most querulous pitch. "What stupidity, what foolhardiness could drive you to inflict yourself upon the Nius in such an impertinent manner, at such an unfortunate time?" A livid patch appeared on each of his sallow cheeks, and his eyes narrowed.

Sano accepted the insults stoically, although each one tore at his samurai spirit. His face burned with the shame of having angered his superior to the point of open fury. Through his misery he felt the cold, equally shameful touch of fear. What would Ogyu do to punish him? But the inquisitive, detached part of his mind wondered why Ogyu was so anxious to halt the investigation and placate the Nius.

"The Nius received me with all possible graciousness," he said bravely. In spite of Ogyu's displeasure, he still thought he'd done right to question them. He only regretted learning so little. "Lady Niu didn't appear at all offended. And why should she be? All I did was ask a few questions, which she and young Lord Niu seemed glad to answer. Furthermore, if Miss Yukiko was murdered, why should the Nius object to an investigation? Wouldn't they want to cooperate so that the murderer can be found? Wouldn't they want justice—vengeance—for their family honor?"

"*If* Yukiko was murdered, *Yoriki* Sano."

Ogyu's resistance reminded Sano of something Wisteria had said last night: "No inquiry . . . to trouble the family of that girl, whoever she was." Now he wondered if the Nius had some reason for not wanting Yukiko's death investigated. Could it be that they didn't want the murder discovered, or the murderer caught? Was Ogyu helping them to hide the truth? If so, why? Sano tried to close his mind against these thoughts. He wanted to believe that his superiors acted only on the highest moral principles. The Nius and Magistrate Ogyu just wanted to avoid the scandal that would arise if Yukiko's part in the *shinjū* became common knowledge. That was all. But suspicion lingered, a queasiness in his soul.

"Yukiko and Noriyoshi died by their own hands," Ogyu was saying. His voice was calm now, and his face had returned to its normal pallor. But he continued to speak with uncharacteristic directness, as if he didn't want to take the chance that Sano might misunderstand. "The manner of their deaths makes this evident, as does the suicide note. There will be no more discussion of the matter. And now I must extract your promise not to trouble the Nius again, or to waste your time pursuing fantasies."

Sano gathered his courage for one last try. Drawing a deep breath, he said, "Magistrate Ogyu, I am sure that Yukiko and Noriyoshi were murdered. I even have a suspect." He knew he was speaking too aggressively and with too much emotion, but he couldn't restrain himself. "I beg you to let me continue the investigation, and to let me explain to the Nius why it is necessary. The murderer is walking free, a danger to society. As a *yoriki,* I feel it's my duty to apprehend him before he harms anyone else. And your duty as a magistrate,'' he added recklessly.

He waited in an agony of suspense for Ogyu's answer. Surely Ogyu, a fellow samurai, could not resist the appeal to duty.

Instead of replying to Sano's impassioned speech, Ogyu changed the subject. "I am sorry to hear that your father is unwell,'' he said.

The courteous remark hit Sano like a fist to the stomach. Angry blood pounded in his ears and darkened his vision. Trust Ogyu to invoke the call of obligation in such a deliberately malicious way! Speechless with rage, Sano struggled to control himself.

Through his chaotic thoughts, Ogyu's voice went on, dryly, mercilessly. "A man of his age deserves a peaceful retirement and the respect of those closest to him. It would be a pity if a family disgrace were to worsen his illness.''

A wave of panic extinguished Sano's anger like a splash of icy water. Ogyu was threatening to dismiss him! For his father's sake, he couldn't let it happen. But he couldn't relinquish the investigation without one last plea.

"Magistrate Ogyu,'' he began.

Ogyu accepted more tea from the servant. He did not offer Sano any: the interview was over. Reluctantly Sano rose and bowed. He crossed the room on unsteady legs.

"*Yoriki* Sano?''

Hand on the door catch, Sano turned.

"Might I expect to see your final report on the *shinjū* this morning?'' Ogyu asked mildly. "When I see Lady Niu at Miss Yukiko's funeral in the afternoon, I should like to tell her that the matter has been resolved.''

Sano bowed again, opened the door, and walked out, letting Ogyu interpret his silence in any way he chose.

9

Keeping his gaze focused straight ahead, Sano hurried along the street toward police headquarters and the haven of his own rooms. Men passed him; he avoided their eyes. He couldn't stand the thought of talking to anyone or going to his office, where he would have to see Tsunehiko and the rest of his staff. Not with his body still trembling with impotent rage. He needed time alone to master his emotions.

"Good morning, *Yoriki Sano-san,*" someone called.

Sano sped past without replying. At last he reached headquarters. But when he got to the barracks, he saw floor mats and bedding hung out to air on the veranda railings. He heard women's voices. All the doors stood open; in his room, a maid was scrubbing the floor. He'd forgotten that the barracks were cleaned thoroughly once a week at this time. Frustration adding to his anger, he ran to the back garden. To his relief, it was deserted.

Solitude brought him no peace. Seeking to vent the anger he couldn't express to Magistrate Ogyu, Sano looked around and saw a fist-sized rock at his feet. He picked it up and hurled it into the pond with all his might.

It hit the water with a satisfying *splash!* Instantly he felt better. He chuckled wryly at himself. Such a childish gesture! Just like one of his young pupils having a temper tantrum. He squatted beside the pond, gazing at the pine needles floating on its surface as he pondered his next move.

Now that his rage had cooled, he could better understand Ogyu's position. Yukiko's and Noriyoshi's deaths had looked like suicide. The magistrate could hardly justify a murder investigation on the strength of a questionable bruise on Noriyoshi's head, or the fact that Noriyoshi hadn't liked women and had made enemies. Sano admitted the mistake he'd made by approaching Ogyu with such flimsy evidence. He couldn't blame Ogyu for resorting to extreme tactics to avert what he considered a potential disaster. What he needed was to find indisputable proof of the murders. Proof that neither Ogyu nor the Nius could brush aside, and which they would ultimately be grateful to have.

Sano rose with a sigh. To find proof, he would have to disobey Ogyu's orders again. And perhaps, while seeking it, he would find evidence of the Nius' involvement in the crime, and Ogyu's collusion in covering it up. The prospect dismayed him, with its promise of danger for him and his family. But somehow, almost without his noticing, his sense of personal duty toward finding the truth had burgeoned until it rivaled the obligation he owed to his father, his patron, and Ogyu. Added to it was a vague but strong feeling of indebtedness toward Wisteria and Dr. Ito. Wisteria's testimony and lovemaking and Ito's dissection had cost them each something; he couldn't let their actions count for nothing. With a shock, he realized that he would risk almost anything to fulfill his personal duty. His desire for the truth fueled an inner reserve of strength and daring he hadn't known he possessed. This frightened him more than the threat of losing his position. To depart from the Way of the Warrior, from its code of unswerving loyalty and obedience, must have consequences that he hadn't begun to imagine.

He headed for the stables, reassuring himself that this particular inquiry needn't cause him any ill consequences. Questioning

Kikunojo should put him in no danger. With luck, Magistrate Ogyu and Lady Niu wouldn't hear of his actions until he had some results.

He tried to ignore his suspicion that they would oppose an investigation no matter what proof he laid before them.

Sano's spirits rose considerably by the time he reached the Saru-waka-cho theater quarter near the city's Ginza district, named for the silver mint that the Tokugawas had built there. Yesterday's balmy weather was holding, and the pleasant ride reminded him of childhood holidays when the whole family, along with various friends and relatives, would spend a day at the theater. They'd arrive when the performances began at dawn and stay until the last one ended at sunset. His father, who, like many older samurai, preferred classical No drama, would complain about the melodramatic Kabuki plays, even while enjoying them. Sano also remembered more recent excursions, when the theater offered a chance for him and other young men to flirt with the young women who also attended. However, during the last five years, work had left him little time for such diversions. Now he studied the district with nostalgia.

Saru-waka-cho sparkled with familiar color and activity. Bright signs plastered over the walls of the four main theaters announced the current play schedules. An occasional burst of song or cheering from the open upper-story windows signaled a play in progress. In square towers perched high on the rooftops, drummers beat a steady bass rhythm to summon theatergoers from distant parts of the city. People of all classes and ages crowded the wide streets, lining up at the ticket booths, seeking refreshment at the many teahouses and restaurants that occupied the spaces between the theaters, or pausing to exchange greetings. Sano knew some of them had waited all night to get a good seat to see their favorite actors.

"Where is Kikunojo performing?" he asked the attendant at the public stable where he left his horse.

The attendant pointed in the direction of the largest theater. "The Nakamura-za," he said.

Sano made his way through the jostling crowds. When he reached the Nakamura-za, he saw signs posted across the front of the building: "*Narukami*, starring the great Kikunojo!" To his disappointment, there was no line outside. The performance had already started.

"Can I still get in?" he asked the ticket seller without much hope. *Narukami*—the story of a princess who saves Japan from a mad monk who has used magic to keep the rains from falling—was a popular attraction. And Kikunojo would fill the theater no matter what the play.

But the ticket seller nodded. He took Sano's money and handed over a ticket, saying, "There are seats left, sir. The play has been running for a month now; most everyone has seen it already."

Entering the theater, Sano paused for a moment to get his bearings. The vast room, lit only by windows in the roof and along the upper gallery, was dim because fire laws prohibited the use of indoor lighting. When his eyes grew accustomed to the darkness, he could make out the unlit lanterns hanging from the rafters, each bearing the crest of an actor who had performed in the Nakamura-za. Women and commoners occupied the less desirable seats along the walls. Raised dividers separated the space before the stage into square compartments, where the shaved crowns and upright sword hilts of the samurai predominated. Refreshment sellers ran up and down the dividers carrying trays of food and drink. The incessant chatter and restless movement of the audience almost drowned out the sound of the musicians' wooden clappers. Sano climbed the nearest divider and walked along it until he spotted a compartment near the front with an empty space. Kneeling on the mat with five other samurai, he turned his attention to the stage.

The play was nearing its end. Against a painted backdrop of mountains and clouds, the actor playing the mad monk Narukami sang about the havoc he would wreak upon the country by withholding the rains. Exaggerated black eyebrows and whiskers gave him a demonic appearance. The brilliant red and gold cleric's mantle that he wore over his brown monk's robe caught the dim light. He bellowed each word in a resounding voice designed to carry over the noise of the audience, stamping, pacing, and gesticulating to hold their attention. The musicians seated at the side of the stage played a cacophonous accompaniment on their clappers, flutes, and samisens.

The song ended, and the music with it. A hush fell over the theater. Heads turned toward the back of the room.

"He's coming," someone whispered.

The clappers sounded again, rapid, frantic. Sano felt a ripple of anticipation pass through the audience.

A woman was walking slowly and daintily down the gangway that extended from the back of the theater to the stage. Princess Taema, dressed in a magnificent purple satin kimono printed with white chrysanthemums, was coming to free the rains and save her people. Her face was strikingly beautiful with its stark white makeup and scarlet mouth. Long black hair, pulled back at the sides, hung down to her waist.

"Kikunojo." The name, spoken on a collective sigh, echoed through the room. "Kikunojo." Then the audience burst into wild cheers.

Princess Taema reached the stage. The audience quieted as she began to sing. Sano sat transfixed. Although he knew that Kikunojo was Edo's foremost *onnagata*—specialist in female roles—he couldn't believe that the figure onstage was not a real woman. Voice, posture, expression, and movements were all completely feminine. Not even the kerchief of purple cloth that covered the actor's shaved crown could detract from the illusion. Sano watched, fascinated, as Princess Taema began to seduce Narukami.

Any effeminate man could be dressed up to resemble a beautiful woman, but Kikunojo's genius lay in his ability to project emotion. Sano could feel the sexual current flowing from Princess Taema to Narukami, and he knew the rest of the audience could, too. How could Narukami resist her ploy?

He couldn't. With much song and gesture, he yielded. Princess Taema cut the magic rope that held back the rain. The musicians produced the sound of falling water. Japan was saved amid cheers, whistles, and clapping from the audience.

Sano remained in his seat until most of the crowd had left the theater. Then he headed down the divider and onto the stage, where Kikunojo held court before a group of female admirers.

The *onnagata* was bigger than he looked from a distance. He stood taller than Sano, head and shoulders above the women crowded around him. The actor who played Narukami must have worn high-platformed sandals to top him. As Sano moved closer, he spotted more signs of Kikunojo's true sex. The long, graceful hands, white with the same powder that covered the *onnagata*'s face, had large knuckles and bony wrists. His features, though delicate, lacked the softness of a woman's. The tricks he used to disguise his masculinity were obvious: the long, trailing ends of the special sash that made him seem shorter, the way he kept his chin lowered to hide his adam's apple.

But none of this bothered Kikunojo's admirers. In fact, the spectacle of male sexuality hidden beneath a woman's hairstyle and clothing excited them to a fever pitch. They flushed and giggled as they shyly advanced one at a time to offer tributes to him: a prettily wrapped package, a stammered compliment. Each of these Kikunojo accepted with an ethereal smile and a graceful bow. He placed the gifts on a small table evidently intended for that purpose.

"Go on! I dare you!" The woman next to Sano nudged her companion, a grandmotherly matron.

Grandmother darted forward and stood on tiptoe to touch

Kikunojo's purple kerchief. Her wrinkled face full of glee at her own audacity, she scurried back to her place. The other women howled with laughter.

Sano smiled. The government had tried to reduce the sexual appeal of *onnagata* by requiring them to shave their crowns, but many women found the kerchiefs just as erotic as a full head of hair.

He waited until the last admirer had departed, then introduced himself. "Kikunojo-*san,* may I have a word with you in private?"

Kikunojo produced a silk fan from the folds of his kimono. Hiding the lower half of his face with it, he murmured, "Honorable master . . . my duties . . . errands . . . another performance soon . . . many apologies, but I have no time now . . . perhaps another day . . . ?" The gesture, the high, sweet voice, and the vague, trailing speech perfectly mimicked those of a noble lady.

"It's about Noriyoshi," Sano said. "We can either talk here, in public, or somewhere else. Your choice." Impressive though the act was, he didn't intend to let Kikunojo get away.

Awareness widened Kikunojo's eyes before his lids slipped down again. He nodded demurely and said from behind the fan, "Come with me."

Sano followed Kikunojo's stately figure through a door near the stage and down a dim passage to the *onnagata*'s dressing room. They left their shoes outside the curtained doorway, and Sano noted with amusement that Kikunojo's were bigger than his own. In the tiny cubicle, bright kimonos hung from standing racks. Five wigs on wooden heads occupied one shelf, while others held fans, hair ornaments, shoes, and folded undergarments. Brushes, powder puffs, and makeup jars littered the dressing table; silk scarves were draped over the large mirror. A table held packages similar to the ones Sano had just seen Kikunojo receive, probably gifts from other admirers. Had Niu Yukiko been one of them? The suicide note suggested a connection between her and the Kabuki theater, even if she hadn't written it. And Lady Niu had commented upon the theater's bad influence on young girls.

Kikunojo knelt before the dressing table. Sano knelt, too, feeling awkward. True *onnagata* like Kikunojo never stepped out of their female personae, even offstage. They claimed that this allowed them to perform their roles more convincingly. Was he supposed to join in the charade by addressing Kikunojo as a woman? He couldn't forget that Kikunojo was a man. The actor's very male odor of sweat, easily discernible in such close quarters, served as a vivid reminder.

To his relief, Kikunojo dropped his act, either because he sensed Sano's discomfort or because he saw no need to waste his efforts on a *yoriki*.

"Whatever you have to say, please make it quick," he said. He tossed aside his fan, lifted his head, and straightened his drooping posture. But his voice remained high and girlish, as if playing women onstage had somehow feminized him. "I have another performance this afternoon, and some very important business to conduct before then."

"Such as paying someone like Noriyoshi to keep your secrets?" Sano asked, hoping to catch the actor off guard.

Kikunojo just shrugged. "So you've heard he was blackmailing me," he said. "I hope you won't mind if I undress? I'm in a bit of a hurry."

"Not at all." Sano watched, intrigued, as Kikunojo removed his purple kerchief to reveal his bare crown. The actor undid a complicated system of pins and knots that anchored the long black wig to his own hair, which was slicked back and tied in a tight knot at the nape of his neck. Then he picked up a cloth, dipped it into a jar of oil, and scrubbed the makeup from his face. In a startling transformation, the beautiful young Princess Taema became a man of regular but unremarkable features, long past his thirtieth birthday.

"Noriyoshi won't be troubling me or anyone else now," Kikunojo went on. "He's dead, and I must say I'm not sorry. The little weasel!"

You wouldn't be so outspoken about your feelings if you knew you were a murder suspect, Sano thought. Kikunojo had just made his motive clear.

"What was he blackmailing you for?" he asked.

Kikunojo stood and untied his sash. He shed his outer- and under-kimonos. Beneath them he wore cotton pads over his chest, hips, and buttocks. These he removed to expose a slender but well-muscled body. Sano decided that Kikunojo would definitely have had the strength to kill Noriyoshi and Yukiko and throw their bodies into the river.

"There's an odd story making the rounds," Kikunojo said. "People are saying that Noriyoshi didn't really commit suicide. That he was murdered. Have you heard?"

"I may have." Even as Sano decided that Wisteria must have spread the story, he could appreciate Kikunojo's trick. The actor had neatly avoided answering the question by throwing out an interesting fact. Such quick thinking bespoke a man intelligent enough to plan and execute an elaborate murder. "What was he blackmailing you for?" he repeated, refusing to fall for the trick.

Kikunojo took a man's black silk kimono decorated with gold cartwheels and blue waves from the rack. This he put on over a blue under-kimono, tying it with a plain black sash. "I hardly think that's any of your business," he said.

He looked with feigned interest toward the door. Through a gap in the curtain, a portion of the stage was visible. The intermission entertainment had begun for those members of the audience who hadn't left the theater. An actor dressed as a samurai performed the *yariodori,* a comic dance that poked fun at the retainers of daimyo. He waved and flicked his plumed war staff in the manner of a woman doing her spring housecleaning. The cheers presumably came from the commoners in the audience; the hisses and catcalls from the samurai.

"It is if Noriyoshi was murdered," Sano said.

Kikunojo gave an exasperated sigh as he pulled a black cloak over his kimono. "I didn't kill him, if that's what you've come here to find out." When Sano didn't reply, he said, "Oh, all right. Noriyoshi found out that I was seeing a married lady. Her husband would kill us both if he found out. You know how it is."

Sano did. Kabuki theater had been founded about a hundred years before by a Shinto priestess from Izumo Shrine. But Kabuki had soon lost its religious associations. Courtesans took up the theatrics, and their lewd performances overstepped the bounds of propriety. Male admirers vied for their favors, often creating public disturbances. The government responded by banning female performers from the theater. Since then, all female roles had been played by men. But the troubles hadn't ended. *Onnagata* proved just as adept at creating scandal as the courtesans. They attracted both women who found their masquerade titillating and men who simply liked men. Kikunojo, with his clandestine affair, was part of a tradition.

"The shogun can do as he pleases—with the wives and daughters of his ministers, yet," Kikunojo continued. "But we ordinary adulterers get punished, if not by irate spouses, then by the authorities. What do you think of that, *yoriki?*"

Sano thought that Kikunojo had once again tried to divert the conversation. "Rank commands privileges, Kikunojo-*san*. Now, about Noriyoshi?"

Kikunojo shot him a look of grudging respect. "Noriyoshi kept asking for more and more money," he said. "He bled me dry. Finally, about a month ago, I got to thinking: if he talked, who would believe him? It would be his word against mine, and who was he? So I took the chance. I said I wasn't going to pay anymore, and I told him why." Kikunojo took a white bridal kimono and red under-kimono from the rack and laid them on a square cloth with fresh socks and purple kerchief, the wig he'd removed, and a selection of makeup. "I should have done it a long time ago. Because he never talked, and he never asked for any more money."

If Kikunojo had really stopped paying, where had the money in Noriyoshi's room come from, Sano wondered. He saw a way to take advantage of the opening Kikunojo had given him.

"Suppose Noriyoshi was murdered," he said. "Could you prove you were somewhere else when it happened?"

Kikunojo laughed as he tied the ends of the cloth around his possessions. "My good man, even if I'd wanted to kill Noriyoshi, I wouldn't have had the time. The night he died, I had a rehearsal until well after midnight. We're starting a new play tomorrow. After that . . ." His smile eerily evoked the lovely Princess Taema. "After that, I was with my lady."

"Would she corroborate that?"

The *onnagata* bent a pitying look on Sano. "Of course not. Didn't I say she's married? And don't bother asking me her name, because I won't tell you."

Sano clenched his teeth together in annoyance. Getting facts from people during an unofficial murder investigation was proving difficult indeed. He had no legal means of forcing them to tell him anything, and any illegal methods he used would undoubtedly attract Magistrate Ogyu's attention.

"Any more questions?" Kikunojo asked.

"One. Are you acquainted with Lord Niu's daughter, Yukiko?"

Although Sano watched Kikunojo's face closely, he saw no hint of uneasiness, only mild surprise at an apparently irrelevant question.

"Yukiko," the actor said, narrowing his eyes thoughtfully. "Yes, I think I've seen her. The whole Niu family attends the theater often."

If Kikunojo had killed Noriyoshi and Yukiko, his admission

could be a clever way of implying that he had nothing to hide. Besides, Sano could easily have learned that the Nius were Kabuki enthusiasts, and a lie would have aroused his suspicion. Sano tried to imagine how and why the murders might have taken place. Maybe Kikunojo had killed Yukiko because she'd somehow witnessed Noriyoshi's murder.

"If you'll excuse me, I have to go now," Kikunojo said. "I'm late already." Then, very casually, as if the thought had just occurred to him, he added, "If you think that Noriyoshi got killed by someone he was blackmailing, then perhaps you should talk to a certain sumo wrestler named Raiden."

Again Sano admired Kikunojo's quick intelligence. What better way to divert suspicion than to direct it toward someone else?

"What did Noriyoshi have on him?" he asked.

Kikunojo shrugged. "You'll have to ask Raiden." He slid open the dressing room's outer door, letting in a gust of cool wind from the street.

The prospect of seeing an *onnagata* walk casually out the door in male attire drew Sano's interest momentarily from the investigation. "I thought you always appeared in public dressed as a woman," he said.

"Sometimes I have to sacrifice my art for the sake of privacy," Kikunojo explained. "If I were to venture outside in those"—he waved toward his kimonos and wigs—"people would recognize me. Some of my more persistent and adoring admirers might follow me. And I can't have that. Not today—I have a very personal matter to attend to. A pity, though. I'll have to get dressed all over again when I get there." He slung the bundle over his shoulder.

Kikunojo was going to see his lady, Sano realized belatedly. Although why the actor needed to take along a bridal kimono was more than he cared to think about.

Lowering his eyes demurely, the *onnagata* smiled. "*Sayōnara, yoriki,*" he murmured, bowing low. Without makeup or costume, he became a woman before Sano's eyes. Then the great Kikunojo turned and dashed into the street, a nondescript man quickly lost in the crowd.

On impulse, Sano followed him. Kikunojo had a motive for Noriyoshi's murder and a connection with the Nius. He also had the intelligence to plan and the strength to carry out the murders. In male dress, he could move freely about the city without attracting attention. His presence at the rehearsal could be verified by the other actors, but had he really spent the rest of the night with a lady? Sano had to find out who she was. To do that, he could spend hours questioning the theater gossips—or let the *onnagata* lead him straight there.

10

Although Sano's military education had included no training in the art of stealth, he found it surprisingly easy to follow Kikunojo. The *onnagata* walked briskly, threading his way through the street with agility, but his height made him easy to keep in view in a crowd comprised mostly of women and children. Sano hung back about twenty paces as they proceeded down Saru-waka-cho, ready to take cover behind a cluster of pedestrians or inside a teahouse should Kikunojo look over his shoulder.

Kikunojo didn't. He seemed unaware of Sano's presence. Sano didn't have to worry that Kikunojo might suddenly jump on a horse and ride off, either. He'd heard that the shogun, an enthusiastic arts patron, meant to grant Kikunojo samurai status in recognition for his theatrical achievements, but for now Kikunojo was still a commoner, and commoners did not ride. Sano began to enjoy his secret pursuit.

Then, just as Kikunojo passed the Yuki-za, the puppet theater's door opened and a horde of men poured out: samurai leaving the choice floor seats after the play. Kikunojo was lost in their midst. Sano hurried forward, frantically trying to locate his quarry.

"Hey, watch where you're going, brother," someone said. The other men jostled Sano, carrying him back in the direction from which he'd come.

Sano fought his way back to the Yuki-za. When he reached it, he saw no sign of Kikunojo. He peered up the street and down the nearest alley. No Kikunojo there, either. Then he saw three pairs of palanquin bearers hoist the poles of their sedan chairs onto their shoulders and trot away from the theater entrance. Immediately he guessed that the *onnagata* was inside one of the curtained vehicles. But which? For lack of any idea, Sano picked one at random. He followed it out of the theater district to a quiet nearby street where the weighty tile roofs and trim half-timbered walls of wealthy merchants' houses rose above wooden fences. Hiding behind a public notice board, he watched the bearers stop and set the palanquin down before a gate. Was this Kikunojo's lady's residence? Sano peered at the shuttered windows, hoping for a glimpse of her.

The palanquin's curtain lifted. To Sano's intense disappointment, the passenger who stepped out was not Kikunojo, but a very old, very drunk man who swayed and dropped his money when he tried to pay the bearers. Sano cursed his luck as he headed back to the theater district for his horse. Now he would have to consult the gossips after all. But after the excitement of the chase, such a tedious prospect didn't appeal to him. He was beginning to enjoy detective work. The novel idea that deceit could serve an honorable purpose held a strong attraction for him. He thought of Kikunojo's reference to Noriyoshi's other blackmail victim and remembered that Wisteria, too, had mentioned a sumo wrestler. First he would look for Raiden.

He found the wrestler in a cheap entertainment district near the Nihonbashi Bridge, where commoners congregated. The proprietor at one of the teahouses that sold tickets to the big matches had given him the detailed directions necessary for locating anything in Nihonbashi's maze of nameless streets.

"Turn left off the Great North-South Road at the big furniture store," the proprietor had said. "Then keep going past the streets with the silversmiths and the basket makers, past some houses where the women take in laundry and dry it on racks on the roofs. Turn right. Go past the noodle restaurant, the barber shop, and three teahouses. You'll find Raiden on the street in front of the storyteller's hall. That's his place. He's always there.''

Sano rode past the silversmiths and the basket makers. He found the laundries and the noodle restaurant, the barber shop and the teahouses. A noisy crowd had gathered in front of the storyteller's hall, but apparently not to hear the old man who was entertaining a group of mothers and children inside. Intent on some action taking place in their midst, they yelled encouragement to the unseen participants.

Dismounting, Sano tied his horse outside one of the teahouses and elbowed his way through the crowd until he could see what was happening.

In place of the straw rice bales that usually defined a wrestling ring, pebbles marked a lopsided circle that had already become trampled and disarranged. A ragged little boy beating on a block of wood with a stick substituted for the drummers who paraded through the city to announce the official matches. At one side of the ring paced a man who could only be Raiden.

The wrestler was about Sano's age and height, but there the similarity ended. He wore a bright yellow kimono printed on the back with one of the rebus designs currently popular: a cherry branch, sword, and oar, which, when named aloud, sounded like ''I Love a Fight.'' It hung open to reveal a huge flabby belly girdled with a fringed black loincloth. Putting his hands on his hips, Raiden bent at the waist, exposing massive naked buttocks. He canted sideways, raising one bent-kneed leg high, then lowering it so that his dirty bare foot struck the earth with a mighty stomp. Dust rose in puffs. He stomped again: both to show his strength and to drive away evil spirits. His fierce scowl made a demon mask of his round, pudgy face.

The audience cheered. ''Raiden!'' The name, a colorful pseudonym like many assumed by professional wrestlers, meant ''Thunder and Lightning.'' And Raiden's excited spectators certainly acted as though they expected from him all the power and drama of a violent storm. ''Raiden! Raiden!'' A few men set up the chant, tossing coins at their champion's feet.

''No contest,'' the man beside Sano remarked.

Sano looked at Raiden's opponent and privately agreed. The man disrobing on the other side of the circle was as big and fat as Raiden, but clearly no professional wrestler. The good clothes and the absence of swords marked him as a merchant. When he took off his kimono, Sano caught a glimpse of its opulent lining: the wealthy commoner's secret protest against the government's laws forbidding him to wear silk. Shivering in the cold, the man clumsily imitated Raiden's stomps. His moonlike face wore an expression of confused glee, as if he didn't quite understand how he'd got himself into this but was tickled at his own daring. The men who held his clothes, presumably his friends, cheered him on.

Raiden took a pouch out of his kimono. He poured a white substance from it into his hand. Most of it he scattered into the makeshift ring; the rest he tongued. Salt—to purify himself and the ground according to ancient tradition. Then he shrugged off his kimono and threw it to the boy with the wooden drum.

The two competitors faced off, crouched at opposite sides of the circle. Fists to the ground, they stared into each other's eyes. The audience fell silent. Sano's heart began to pound as the tension mounted. Instinctively he took a step backward, away from the ring.

This was not the ancient Shinto fertility ritual of fourteen hundred years ago, in which wrestlers from neighboring villages competed for the blessings of the gods at rice-planting time. Neither was it the legendary match of some five hundred years later that had determined which of two imperial princes would succeed to the emperor's throne. And it bore no resemblance to today's great tournaments, where professionals retained by the daimyo performed in formal style before huge audiences on the grounds of Edo's important temples. This was street-corner sumo at its worst: wild, dirty, and unpredictable. Anything could happen. Sano wondered if he should try to stop the match. Although the government issued periodic edicts against street-corner sumo, it wasn't currently illegal. He saw two *doshin* he recognized as his subordinates on the other side of the ring. The match even had tacit official sanction.

With loud roars, Raiden and his opponent charged simultaneously. Fat met fat with a tremendous smack. The impact sent both men staggering apart. The spectators jumped back and recovered their voices.

"Kill him! Kill him!" The shouts thundered in Sano's ears.

Raiden rushed the merchant with a speed amazing for such a large man. Using *tsuppari*—slapping technique—he delivered a series of rapid, open-handed blows to the merchant's chest, throat, and face. The merchant grunted, more out of confusion than from pain, Sano thought. He tried to slap back, but Raiden advanced, forcing him to the edge of the ring. Just when it seemed the match would end with Raiden's victory, the wrestler stepped back. He grinned and beckoned his panting opponent to attack him. Sano understood that Raiden didn't want an easy win. He was pulling his punches and giving the merchant another chance in order to bring in more spectators and more money.

Gamely the merchant threw himself at Raiden. The two grappled, Raiden standing his ground almost without effort as the merchant shoved and gasped. Raiden broke the merchant's hold. He fell back two paces, whether or not on purpose, Sano couldn't tell. Maybe he'd lost his balance; maybe he was still baiting the merchant.

"That's the way!" shouted the merchant's friends.

Buoyed by their support, the merchant launched a fresh charge. Sano winced, anticipating another crash. But Raiden sidestepped at the last minute. Seizing the sides of the merchant's loincloth in both hands, he used the man's own momentum to cast him out of the ring: the outer-arm throw, one of sumo's classic forty-eight "hands."

The merchant went hurtling into the crowd. His friends caught him as he fell. Raiden's supporters cheered; the merchant's cried out in disappointment. Then the cheers and cries turned to uneasy mutters.

Sano's heart lurched when he saw why. The wrestler's teasing grin had become a murderous grimace. His face purpled with a strange fury. Without warning, he lunged at his fallen opponent. He pummeled the helpless merchant with his fists, all the while bellowing like a mad bear.

"Stop!" the merchant screamed. Blood spurted from his nose. "You win! I surrender!"

The merchant's friends tried to fend off Raiden's assault, but the wrestler turned on them. Suddenly the crowd became a turbulent mass of flying fists, kicking legs, and thrashing bodies. Men yelled insults, uttered cries of pain.

"Stop!" Sano shouted. The crowd's noise drowned his voice. He tried to draw his sword, but bodies pressed against him, making movement impossible. If only he'd stopped the match when he'd had the chance!

This was the real danger of street-corner sumo. Not that a wrestler would get hurt in the unrefereed matches—although many did—but that violence would break out among the audience. A crowd could quickly become a mindless killing tool, a sword flying free of any controlling hand. Now the spectators ran for safety. Sano saw the drummer go down and get trampled under the pounding feet.

Fortunately the two *doshin* chose that moment to remember their duty. "Break it up!" they shouted. "Everybody go home. Fun's over!"

Poking and prodding with their *jitte,* they dispersed the crowd. One of them called his assistants to pick up the wounded men. Sano, standing in the shelter of a teahouse doorway to avoid being driven off with the rest of the crowd, watched the other *doshin* stroll over to Raiden, who stood in the center of the ring.

The wrestler's mysterious rage seemed to have passed as quickly as it had come. Now his face wore a dazed frown. Blinking in apparent befuddlement at his departing audience, he called half-heartedly, "Any more challengers? Who among you is brave enough to face the mighty Raiden?"

No one was. The *doshin* extended his hand to Raiden, palm up. Raiden sighed, then bent to pick up the coins from the ring. He counted half the money into the *doshin*'s hand. The *doshin* smirked and walked away, jingling the coins. He didn't notice Sano, but then he would hardly expect to see his superior in a place like this.

So Raiden paid the *doshin* to tolerate his matches and keep order at them. Sano shook his head, knowing he must reprimand his subordinates during the next report session. The outcome of the fight could have been much worse: Men had died during such matches and the riots they provoked. Cautiously he walked over to Raiden, who now stood alone in the ring, scratching his crotch with one hand as he examined the coins he held in the other. The wrestler looked harmless enough now, but would his rage resurface?

"Not even enough to eat on," Raiden complained. "Why did those *doshin* have to go and break up my match?"

Had he forgotten that he'd attacked a helpless man and started a riot? Confused and wary, Sano nevertheless decided to take advantage of the situation.

"Let me buy you a meal," he said. Raiden might be more amenable to answering questions—and less likely to erupt again—if plied with food and drink.

Raiden's pout dissolved into a sunny smile. "All right," he agreed with an alacrity that told Sano he was used to accepting handouts from strangers. Probably he lived on them. That he performed on the street meant he had no daimyo sponsor or other source of steady income.

Sano waited while Raiden donned his kimono, along with the shoes, cloak, and swords that had been lying in a heap outside the ring. Then the two of them walked down the street to the noodle restaurant.

The place was little more than a roadside food stall. Its sliding doors stood wide open; only a short blue curtain hanging from the eaves protected it from the outdoors. Inside, along the left wall, a strip of earth floor led through the small dining room to the kitchen, where two women toiled amid steam and smoke over a charcoal stove. Their huge cauldrons sent forth the enticing odor of broth made with garlic, soy sauce, miso, and scallions. An old man dressed in a blue cotton kimono and headband stood behind the counter that partially divided the dining room from the kitchen. A few lucky diners knelt on the raised plank floor in front of the counter with their bowls and chopsticks, but the rest sat on the floor's edge, with their feet either in the kitchen corridor or the street. Sano and Raiden went inside and approached the counter.

"Two house specials." Raiden, who, from the bows and nods he got from the proprietor and customers, seemed to be a regular, gave their order. "And plenty of sake."

The special turned out to be *kitsune udon,* "fox noodles," named for the mischievous fox spirit whom everyone blamed for their troubles. The thick white noodles bathed in rich brown broth and topped with a crusty golden square of fried tofu were the spirit's favorite food. Sano noticed that Raiden's bowl was twice as large as his own, and the bottle of sake enormous. He handed over his money, thinking that detective work was getting expensive. The Nius' funeral gift, the trips to Yoshiwara, the theater ticket, and now feeding a wrestler added up to as much as he'd formerly made in a week of tutoring.

With some difficulty, Sano and Raiden cleared a space for themselves on the edge of the floor. Sano found himself jammed between the counter and Raiden's massive bulk. But at least the heat from the kitchen and from the sweaty wrestler kept him warm.

Raiden shoveled noodles and tofu from bowl to mouth with his chopsticks, pausing between bites to deliver bits of monologue.

"It's a shame that a great wrestler like me has to fight for *zeni* in the street, don't you think?" *Slurp, gulp.* "Living hand to mouth like a common beggar! Well, let me tell you, stranger, it wasn't always this way for Raiden."

Sano couldn't help staring at Raiden's hands. They seemed oddly jointless, like the hands of people in wood-block prints. The fingertips, which ended in tiny, spatulate nails, bent almost all the way back with each movement. Sano wondered how such weak-looking hands could have the strength necessary for sumo. Or for killing two people and carrying their bodies to the river?

Raiden paused to fill his cup with sake and drain it with one swallow. "Two springs ago, I was the top wrestler in Lord Torii's stable. I had fine living quarters in his estate, ten apprentices to serve me, and all the women I wanted. The best food, and as much of it as I could eat. I fought the best men and defeated them all. The shogun himself praised my skill."

Surely an exaggeration. If Raiden had been a top wrestler, Sano would have heard of him, but he hadn't. And Lord Torii was one of the lesser daimyo. His wealth amounted to a fraction of the Nius', hardly enough to maintain a luxurious sumo stable. Besides, the shogun's interests tended toward Confucianism and the arts, not popular sport.

"A great life, don't you think?" Raiden said, downing another cup of sake. A certain wistfulness in his voice told Sano that the wrestler was bragging just as much to bolster his ego as to impress. Sano could pity him, even as he remembered Raiden assaulting the merchant.

Raiden emptied his bowl and signaled the proprietor to bring him another. Sano reached in his cash pouch for more money. "But Lord Torii dismissed me because I picked up the master-of-arms and threw him against the wall. Unfair, don't you think? After all, I didn't really hurt the man. He lived. And I didn't mean to do it. Ever since I hurt my head in a match a while back, there's been a demon living inside it, making me do awful things.'' He touched his temple and added sadly, ''That's how I got my name: 'Thunder and Lightning.' I strike anywhere, anytime, and when I do, everybody had better get out of the way.''

Raiden, apparently a man used to dominating the conversation, showed no interest in Sano. Other than his habitual ''don't you think?'' he asked no questions. Sano ate in silence and let him ramble on. Identifying himself would only inhibit the careless flow of confidences, and Raiden was telling him plenty without the least urging. Already he'd learned that the wrestler was short on funds and had a consistently volatile temper. Both these qualities would make him dangerous prey for a blackmailer like Noriyoshi.

Now Raiden launched a tirade about the hardships of his life: poor food, greedy landlord, disrespect from other wrestlers. Sano decided it was time to guide the conversation to a more relevant subject.

''Did you hear about the artist who committed *shinjū*?'' he asked. ''Noriyoshi, I think his name was.''

Raiden stopped eating long enough to give Sano a wary glance. ''Maybe,'' he said casually. He sucked a noodle into his mouth and wiped his lips on his sleeve. But a sudden jerk of his body at the mention of Noriyoshi had already belied his nonchalance.

''You knew him?'' Sano prodded.

''Maybe.'' Raiden's tone remained casual, but he began to chew with a savage intensity.

''You didn't like him?''

Raiden said nothing. Sano waited. He didn't think the garrulous wrestler could remain quiet for long. And he was right. Raiden hurled his empty bowl out the door and shouted, ''I hated the miserable scum!''

His body tensed, and his flaccid hands balled into fists. His face darkened the way it had just before he'd attacked the merchant.

Sano saw the other diners staring at them. A few got up and ran out of the restaurant. Surreptiously moving his hand to his sword, he said, "Easy now, it's all right," in what he hoped was a soothing tone. Even after such a brief acquaintance, he could recognize the signs of an impending rampage. Could he stop the wrestler before he hurt someone?

Then, to Sano's amazement, the tension left Raiden's body, and his face went blank. He blinked, shaking his head as if to clear it, and gaped at Sano without apparent recognition.

"I'm sorry," he said in a fuzzy voice. "Were we talking? Did you just ask me something?" He looked down. "Where's my bowl?"

Sano allowed himself to relax tentatively, relieved that Raiden's dangerous mood had passed. "We were talking about Noriyoshi," he said, hoping the name wouldn't provoke another outburst. "Why did you hate him?"

Raiden frowned in bewilderment. "Did I hate him? Oh, yes, I guess I did. Because he got me thrown out of Lord Torii's stable. The master-of-arms wouldn't have told Lord Torii that I broke discipline and almost killed him. He didn't want to lose face. But Noriyoshi was there that day, delivering some paintings. He saw the whole thing. Told me that if I didn't pay him a thousand *zeni* a week, he would tell Lord Torii. I didn't have the money. He talked; Lord Torii dismissed me. Terrible, don't you think?"

Sano felt less satisfaction at learning Raiden's motive than he'd anticipated. Raiden seemed to have no control over his demon. He was capable of killing on a moment's impulse during one of his sudden rages, but had he the wits to arrange a double murder that looked like suicide?

Both Kikunojo and Raiden had readily admitted that they'd been Noriyoshi's blackmail victims. But if Kikunojo's link with Niu Yukiko seemed weak, Raiden's was weaker still. Upper-class samurai women never attended public sumo tournaments, let alone the street-corner matches. Even if social events had brought Yukiko into contact with the Toriis, Raiden's association with them had ended almost two years ago. What circumstance could have linked Noriyoshi and Yukiko and united them with Raiden the night of the murder? Intuition told Sano that a direct connection between Noriyoshi and the Niu clan must exist, that it provided the motive for the murders. So far, however, he saw nothing.

"Have you ever fought a match against Lord Niu's men?" he asked.

The proprietor had brought Raiden a third bowl of noodles without being asked, perhaps to forestall another violent episode. "Sure," Raiden said as he dug into it. "The tournament at Muen-ji." The Temple of Helplessness, built on the burial site of the Great Fire's victims, was a popular site for public spectacles. "Three years ago."

"Have you met his daughters? The eldest one, in particular— Yukiko?"

"Heh, heh, heh." Raiden ground his huge elbow into Sano's side. "Know what you're thinking. But no. The daimyo never let us near their women. They don't trust us. A pity, because some of them . . ." He began describing the charms of the women, whom he'd only seen from a distance.

Sano thought he was telling the truth. He had none of Kikunojo's intelligence or acting talent to help him lie easily and convincingly. That he did have a careless mouth and little instinct for self-preservation was obvious. He hadn't bothered to find out who Sano was or why he was asking questions, and his lewd remarks about Lord Torii's women would earn him a harsh punishment if they reached the wrong ears. Sano finally had to interrupt his rambling discourse.

"Are you glad Noriyoshi is dead?" he asked.

Raiden emptied the last of the sake into his cup. "I'm not sorry. But there's at least one person even less sorry than I. I wasn't the only one he blackmailed, and from what I hear, he got a lot more money out of the other fellow."

"You mean Kikunojo, the Kabuki actor?" Sano asked.

The wrestler gave him a puzzled look. "Him, too? Didn't know that. No, I was thinking of someone else."

"And who is that?"

"A member of a very powerful clan," Raiden answered. For the first time, he looked around furtively and lowered his voice. "I don't know which member, and I won't say the family name, but—"

Bending over, he drew on the dusty ground with his chopstick. He produced a picture far less skillful than any of Noriyoshi's, but Sano easily recognized its subject.

It was a dragonfly crest, insignia of the Niu clan. Here at last was the connection between Noriyoshi and the Nius.

11

Lady Niu hesitated outside her son's door, holding a tray that contained a lacquer box, matches, a few long wood splinters, and a bay-bark candle. Anxious to see Masahito, yet dreading their encounter, she balanced the tray on her hip and knocked. No answer came. She heard only the distant chanting from the family Buddhist chapel, where the priests were holding a vigil over Yukiko's body. But Lady Niu could sense Masahito's presence, as strongly as if she could see him through the translucent paper windows set in the wall. She slid the door open and entered.

An icy gust of wind assaulted her, and she uttered an exclamation of dismay.

Masahito knelt, his back to her, facing the open window. Although the chamber was almost as cold as the garden outside, he wore only a thin white silk kimono. His feet were bare. When Lady Niu crossed the floor to stand beside him, she saw that his face wore the rapt expression of deep meditation—eyes half closed, lips parted, he seemed unaware of his shivering body, or that the cold had raised bumps on his bare arms. His chamber reflected the austerity and lack of comfort he preferred in his surroundings. Plain white plaster covered the walls; a frayed tatami with its edges bound in common black cotton lay on the floor. He wouldn't allow her to supply him with furnishings more in keeping with the rest of the house. He slept on the same worn and flattened futon he'd had for years, and he used charcoal braziers only in the coldest weather. Despite his father's wealth, Masahito lived like a monk, as if he wanted to see how much suffering he could withstand. Fearful for his health, Lady Niu walked over to the window and closed it.

"Mother!"

She whirled at the sound of his voice, almost dropping the tray. "Masahito. I've come to give you your moxa treatment. We'll have to hurry; it's almost time for Yukiko's funeral." She and the other women had already put on their white mourning kimonos for the procession to the temple, but he still needed to change into his black ceremonial robes. She added, "I wish you wouldn't leave the window open. The draft will give you a chill."

He regarded her with an unsmiling stare as frigid as the room. "I told you never to enter my chamber without my permission, Mother," he said.

His disapproval gripped Lady Niu's heart like a physical pain. Masahito—her precious only son—had been born after years of hoping and praying for a child. She loved him more than she'd ever loved anyone else, showering gifts and attention upon him throughout his life. But more often than not, he repaid her with hostility. She'd heard the servants whispering that she'd spoiled him because he'd been born with a crippled leg, and now his soul was crippled as well. Yet how else could she compensate him for being the youngest son—and child of a daimyo's second wife— excluded from the succession by birth and from his father's favor by his deformity? Even her position as a Tokugawa cousin and member of the Fujiwara family that had dominated the imperial court in ancient times couldn't give him the status he deserved. She suppressed the urge to fuss over him, to wrap him in warm clothes. To do so would provoke more harsh words.

She said cautiously, "I am sorry. Does your leg pain you?"

As soon as the words passed her lips, she regretted them. His leg did hurt. She, who knew him so well, should have seen the signs invisible to anyone else: the tension around his mouth, the faint shadows under his eyes. Even the room's icy discomfort should have told her. She remembered how, as a child, he would hold his hand dangerously close to a candle flame. When she snatched the hand away and demanded why he would do such a foolish thing, he said, "It makes me forget my leg." Today other worries pressed in on her, and she hadn't observed him with her customary care.

Now Masahito sighed impatiently. "I'm fine, Mother," he said. But he carefully unfolded his legs and extended them straight before him in preparation for the treatment. Although she knew the effort hurt him, his expression didn't change. He never betrayed his pain, making himself walk without a limp and without using a cane even when he thought he was alone. He drew his kimono back as far as his groin. The left leg was sturdy and muscular, its flesh smooth and unmarked. The right was brittle and weak-looking, with healed scars and raw sores marring the withered thigh.

As usual, the sight of her son's bad leg caused a surge of tender anguish to engulf Lady Niu. She wanted to caress and coddle him, to ease his pain with maternal care. But Masahito's response to affection had always been unpredictable. During his childhood, he had sometimes returned her embraces, sometimes hit or kicked her. He'd hated to acknowledge his pain or accept comfort. Now he might tolerate her love or rebuke her with his sharp tongue. So instead she knelt, opened the lacquer box, and began to take out the eleven small gray moxa cones. Made of mugwort leaves gathered on the fifth day of the fifth month, ground in a pestle and rolled into shape, they were soft and flaky to the touch. She wet the base of each one with the tip of her tongue, then arranged them on Masahito's thigh, careful to avoid the unhealed sores left by previous treatments. Unable to resist the temptation, she let her fingertips brush his skin as if by accident. Touching him gave her the most exquisite, heart-breaking pleasure. . . . She lit the candle and used a wood splinter to transfer flame to the cones. Soon a thin smoke began to rise from them, and the mildly bitter scent of burning leaves mingled with the candle's fragrance. The priests' chanting droned on as they prepared Yukiko's coffin for transport to the temple, lending a mystical atmosphere to the treatment. Masahito seemed a living Buddha and she a worshipper burning incense before him.

Lady Niu watched her son's face for a sign that the treatment was draining away the distemperous vapors that caused his pain. She had much to discuss with him, but she didn't want to speak until relief made him more receptive to advice. The cones smoldered. The smoke thickened. Finally his face relaxed—though whether because the moxa was healing him or because the pain caused by the burning cones distracted him, she couldn't tell.

"This is a critical time for our family, Masahito," she said. "It demands discreet behavior from all of us. Even sacrifices." She paused, hoping she wouldn't have to continue. To say exactly what she expected from him would be to voice the unspeakable. The unthinkable.

He regarded her in silence, his feverish eyes glowing in his handsome face. A faint, malicious smile played at his lips.

Faltering, she said, "Perhaps . . . perhaps it would be better for you to . . . refrain from certain activities." Her mind recoiled from the thought of those activities.

Masahito's smile widened, but not with humor or warmth. He shook his head. "Oh, Mother. For once in your life, why not say what you mean?" he said. "There's no one here but us. So come. Tell me what you want me to do." He folded his arms, waiting in exaggerated anticipation. "Well?"

He was bullying her, Lady Niu thought miserably, just as he'd once bullied his brothers and sisters and playmates. Whether larger or smaller than he, it hadn't mattered; he could always drive them to tears or rage. The sheer force of his personality kept them from striking back and made them work harder to please him. A sudden vivid memory surfaced: Masahito, aged nine, pitting his sisters, two of his older brothers, and all the retainers' children against each other in a violent reenactment of the Battle of Dan-no-ura, which had taken place five hundred years ago, and which had ended the emperors' effective reign and ushered in the era of military rule. The game had resulted in many injuries, some serious, and the destruction of a garden pavilion. Of all the children, only Yukiko had resisted him and tried to stop the debacle.

Lady Niu could still remember the horror she'd felt when she'd found her small general gloating over the burning pavilion and his sobbing, bloodied troops.

"Why, Masahito?" she'd cried. "Why?"

He'd looked straight at her, his face radiant with triumph beneath the cuts and bruises. "I wanted to change history, Mother," he said, "and I did." His complete lack of remorse had chilled her. "Tell Father that today the Taira clan have defeated the Minamoto."

Tell Father. Those two words had given her the real reason for what he'd done. Her fierce, angry son didn't care about history. Unloved and ignored by his father since birth, he courted punishment because it was better than no attention at all.

Loath to discipline him herself, Lady Niu had swallowed her grief and sent him to live with her husband in their provincial castle. Maybe now that Masahito was older and beginning to excel in swordsmanship in spite of his deformity, they could be father and son. Maybe, with masculine guidance, he would grow into an honorable, decent man. But her husband, still repulsed and shamed by his crippled child, didn't educate or reform Masahito. A loyal servant sent word to her that Lord Niu had simply locked Masahito in a remote chamber to live like a caged animal—alone, unwashed, fed on scraps of garbage. Sick with guilt, Lady Niu had him returned to Edo, where she struggled valiantly to tame his wild spirit. She would never again subject him to his father's cruelty, despite his excesses, which grew worse over the years. She'd managed to hush up all of them, often at outrageous cost.

Now Lady Niu whispered, "Please, Masahito." All her love and money and scheming couldn't save him this time, if he didn't help himself.

"What you want, Mother, is that I should forsake my pleasures and my ambitions because Yukiko is dead and the police are nosing around. You think they'll learn things about me, even if they can't prove I killed anyone."

"Masahito—"

His sarcastic voice lashed her mercilessly. "You want me to stay away from the summer villa in Ueno. You want me to—"

"Stop!" Lady Niu shrieked. She clapped her hand over her mouth to stifle more screams. How she hated him when he tormented her like this! And how she loved him. His face seemed even more beautiful suffused with evil mischief than when he was in one of his infrequent kind moods. At times like this, she wished she loved him less. That way she could control herself as she did with everyone else, could prevail as she did in every other situation. Now she prayed for detachment and serenity. Only by putting aside her feelings for him could she bend him to her strong will, which he had inherited.

Having gotten the desired reaction from her, Masahito relented. He caressed her cheek with the back of his hand and said gently, "Mother, you worry too much. There's nothing to be afraid of. The police will find plenty of other suspicious individuals in Yukiko's background. That actor she admired. The suitors whose marriage proposals were rejected. And anyway, with Noriyoshi dead, the danger is gone. In fact, our lives will soon be better than you ever thought possible. Believe me."

Lady Niu savored her son's rare affectionate gesture. She took his hand in both of hers and held it tight. She wanted to beg him to cease his dangerous activities. To do it for her, if not for himself, because her fear for him was tearing her apart. But she knew he would only grow angry at her interference and begin tormenting her again.

She contented herself with saying, "Sano Ichirō's visit disturbed me. I received him because I wanted to meet the *yoriki* who is officiating in the matter of Yukiko's death, but now I'm sorry I did. He is an intelligent, unconventional, and persistent man. You shouldn't have spoken to him the way you did—you only whetted his interest. Who knows what he might discover if he keeps prying into our affairs?"

"Sano? Who is Sano Ichirō, anyway? Just an insignificant creature, not worth a moment's thought."

Masahito freed his hand from her grasp and let out a hoot of maniacal laughter. He'd slipped into the grandiose, reckless mood she feared most. His already bright eyes began to blaze; his body seemed to exude power. Now he would never heed caution or recognize his own vulnerability. He would court death as he had once courted punishment. He would subject himself to agonizing pain and fear, recover, then seek more agony.

"I've already taken steps to keep him away from us," Lady Niu said, fighting to remain calm against her rising terror. What if he should die? Her own life would be empty without him. "Magistrate Ogyu has agreed to restrict his interference. But there are limits to what I can do. I don't want to arouse suspicion by asking for too many favors, not when it would be so easy for you to maintain a low profile." She tried to keep the pleading note out of her voice, knowing it would only invite mockery. "Just for a while."

Masahito sighed. "Mother, I don't need you to protect me. I know what I'm doing, and I can take care of myself. If *Yoriki* Sano continues to be a problem—"

He picked up a burning moxa cone. Ignoring her cry of protest, he crushed it between his fingers. He laughed again as it crumbled into ash and fell to the floor in a thin trail of smoke.

12

Niu Yukiko's funeral procession filed through the streets of Edo, slowly making its way east from the Zōjō Temple toward the river.

First came black-clad samurai bearing white lanterns on long poles, followed by more men carrying clusters of sacred lotus made of gold paper. Then the high priest in his gorgeous silk mantle, borne on a litter by orange-robed priests. More priests held smoking incense burners, tinkled bells, beat drums, or scattered rose petals upon the ground. After them strode Lord Niu. He carried the funeral tablet, his gait stiff, his face somber. Then came the coffin, a little white house with a tile roof. Its bearers wore the Niu dragonfly crest on their black garments. More bearers followed with a huge bamboo cage full of twittering birds; then more priests, chanting sutras. Behind them walked the family, with their retainers and attendants, the men in black, the women in pure white.

And the other mourners: rank after rank, hundreds of them, all come to pay their last respects to the daughter of a great lord.

Sano marched with these last. After leaving Raiden, he'd gone back to the barracks to don his ceremonial robes—white silk under-robe, black silk kimono with his family crest of four interlocked flying cranes embroidered in gold at the back, breast, and hem, flowing black trousers, and black *haori* with padded shoulders. His swords were muffled in black cloth as a gesture of courtesy to the deceased. Now he hoped his costume would let him blend with the mourners and avoid Lady Niu's notice.

After her warning and Magistrate Ogyu's reprimand, the thought of approaching the Nius again filled Sano with dread. But since learning of Noriyoshi's connection with them, he felt he must see Yukiko's sister Midori again. Perhaps the "proof" she'd claimed to have would lead him to the identity of the blackmail victim and murderer. As a tutor, he'd learned that children often invented tales; caution told him to take anything she said with a healthy dose of skepticism. Still, the possibility that she held the key to the murders was too strong to overlook.

There were more reasons Sano had to risk stealing a moment with her. Making this effort would discharge his obligation to Wisteria, proving to both her and himself that he wasn't going to deny Noriyoshi justice because of class considerations. And he'd begun to wonder if the Nius had indeed been involved in the murders and were playing Ogyu for a fool, using the unsuspecting magistrate to cover up their crime. Much as Sano disliked Ogyu, he came from a long line of men who would give their lives to protect their masters. He couldn't let the Nius involve Ogyu in shady business that might erupt into scandal. For once his personal desires and his professional obligations coincided. Sano peered through the ranks of mourners ahead of him, searching for Midori.

He'd spotted young Lord Niu, the chief mourner, when he caught up with the procession outside the temple, and Magistrate Ogyu among the men toward the front of the line. He'd seen Lady Niu leading the women, her large sturdy frame easily recognizable. But the other women all looked alike in their white kimonos and caps. How would he ever find Midori among them? Even if he did, when and how could he speak to her alone?

The procession passed beneath the arch of a torii gate, descended a flight of stone steps, and halted on the riverbank. There, in the middle of a huge tree-bordered square, under a thatched roof supported by pillars, waited a pit filled with wood. Beside it, tables held offerings of food and drink; braziers sent up fragrant smoke to mingle with the incense and the fresh river breeze. The mourners arranged themselves around the pit. Sano took advantage of the general shift to work his way forward, toward the Niu women grouped near the edge of the pit.

The men with the birds set down the cage and opened it. In a flurry of wings and song, the birds soared skyward, their flight symbolizing the soul's release from earthly life and ascent to the spirit realm. Sano saw a girl who looked like Midori. As he tried to catch her eye, the crowd shifted again, and he found himself almost within touching distance of Magistrate Ogyu. Hastily he moved back again.

The high priest began to chant to the accompaniment of the bells and drums. The mourners listened in silence. Hemmed in by the men around him, Sano surreptitiously rose to his toes, pretending to watch the priest as he darted glances at the women. He found the girl he'd taken for Midori: she wasn't. He waited, hoping the funeral would end soon and knowing it wouldn't.

Finally, after more than an hour, the pallbearers placed Yukiko's coffin on top of the wood in the pit. Lord Niu stepped forward, holding a torch. He lit it at the brazier, then cast it onto the pyre.

The wood caught fire with a sound like a loud gasp of horror. Instantly a sheet of crackling, thundering flame engulfed the coffin. Black smoke rose from it. In no time at all, coffin and shroud burned away to reveal Yukiko's naked body—small, delicate, seated upright, head shaven. The flames blistered and darkened her flesh. Her face became a grotesque black mask as her features dissolved against her skull. Bodily fluids hissed and sputtered as the heat evaporated them. The smell of burning meat filled the air. Ashes wafted toward the river.

Sano watched with some of the same feelings he always experienced at funerals: sorrow over a life prematurely ended; instinctive revulsion at the horrible sight of a burning body; and a growing relief as the purifying fire did its work. Since he hadn't known Niu Yukiko, he felt no grief. Instead, an acute sense of duty toward the dead girl's spirit stirred in him. For as life ends with death, so do love and hate, happiness and sorrow, pain and pleasure. But Sano believed that truth and justice could transcend death as other worldly concerns do not.

I will find your killer, he promised Yukiko silently.

As he waited for the flames to consume Yukiko's body, Sano covertly studied the faces of the mourners. Maybe he would see guilt or glee or some other inappropriate emotion on one of them. Something that would identify its owner as a murderer. But he was disappointed. In accordance with funeral custom, no one displayed the slightest emotion. Lady Niu wore her usual serenity like part of her costume. Sano thought he detected restlessness in Lord Niu, but it might have been the product of his imagination, or of the way the flames cast shifting patterns of light across the young man's face.

With a sudden loud crash, the roof sheltering the pyre collapsed in a mass of flame and smoke. The mourners drew back. Sano moved with them and managed to extricate himself from the men surrounding him. He worked his way around the perimeter of the circle of mourners until he was directly behind the family group, with six or seven rows of people between him and the Niu women. He still couldn't find Midori. But standing beside him was someone familiar.

She wore a plain cotton kimono that identified her as a servant. Her face was unremarkable, with a rather flat nose and small mouth. Except for her red and swollen eyes, he would not have recognized her as O-hisa, the weeping maid he'd seen at the Nius' mansion.

"O-hisa," he whispered, touching her sleeve to get her attention. "Where is Miss Midori?"

The maid looked at him, her face blank and uncomprehending.

Ahead of him, Sano could see Lady Niu's back, uncomfortably close. "We met two days ago at the house," he explained hastily. "I'm *Yoriki* Sano—do you remember me? I must speak to Miss Midori. It's very important. Can you show me where she is?"

Now recognition spread across O-hisa's face. Her eyes and mouth rounded into circles of fear. "No . . . I'm very sorry . . . I . . . ."

Stammering more barely intelligible words, she made a move as if to run toward the gate.

Sano blocked her path. "Please," he began.

O-hisa turned and plunged into the crowd of mourners. They stirred, uttering murmurs of surprise and annoyance.

Sano stared in dismay at the turmoil she'd left in her wake: women beating her dusty footprints from their hems, the old man she'd knocked to the ground. Appalled by the spectacle he'd created, he wondered if he should try to resume his place among the men, or leave before Lady Niu or Magistrate Ogyu saw him. He hesitated too long. A heavy hand came down on his shoulder. He turned and found himself face to face with Lady Niu's manservant. Eii-*chan*'s homely visage remained rigidly impassive, except for the warning glint in his small eyes. *Offend my masters and die by my hand,* they seemed to say.

"What is the meaning of this?" Lady Niu herself was advancing on him, regal and furious. Three of her husband's retainers accompanied her, stern and hostile in their black garments. The crowd parted to let them pass. The priest's chanting trailed off; the bells and drums stopped. Only the fire's crackle continued unabated.

Panic clutched Sano. What would she do to him? He flung a wild glance toward the male mourners and saw heads turning his way, Ogyu's among them. And what would his superior do upon learning that Sano had not only disobeyed orders but disrupted Yukiko's funeral as well? Eii-*chan* and the other samurai surrounded him. He stood his ground, hoping Lady Niu wouldn't reveal his presence to Ogyu by saying his name.

She didn't, maybe because she didn't remember it, or because she didn't want her friends to know that a police commander had crashed her stepdaughter's funeral. When she reached him, all she said was, "I warned you once, and I won't warn you again," in a low tone meant only for him. Her lovely eyes flashed in anger—and, strangely, fear. She turned to her manservant. "Eii-*chan*, see this man to the gate."

Before she'd finished speaking, Eii-*chan* had already taken the initiative, moving with that odd swiftness he had. He stepped around Sano. Fierce pain streaked up Sano's arm to his shoulder as Eii-*chan* seized it, bent it behind him, and wrenched it upward. Only his instinctive self-control enabled him to turn a scream into a gasp. Only his desire to keep Ogyu from seeing him—if the magistrate hadn't already—made him bow his head instead of struggling to free himself. Nearly fainting from the pain, he stumbled out of the murmuring crowd with Eii-*chan* propelling him forward. He was dimly aware of Lady Niu offering apologies to the mourners, and the priests resuming the service. Shame increased his distress as he sensed the hundreds of curious onlookers witnessing his humiliation.

As soon as they reached the steps—too far for anyone to recognize him—Sano began to fight. He trod hard on Eii-*chan*'s insteps and jabbed his free elbow into the manservant's stomach. Eii-*chan* didn't react or make a sound. Although Sano suspected that a man of feeling and spirit lived within Eii-*chan*, he seemed made of stone: hard, numb, silent. Was he mute, or did he simply choose not to speak? He half-pushed, half-lifted Sano up the steps, twisting his arm. This time Sano cried out in spite of himself.

"Wait, Eii-*chan*." It was a man's voice, behind them.

Eii-*chan* paused at the gate and turned, swinging Sano around with him, but not releasing Sano's arm. Through a haze of pain, Sano saw young Lord Niu standing at the top of the steps, small but proud in his black robes.

"You can't stay away from us, can you, *Yoriki* Sano?" Lord Niu said. He came forward and leaned against the gatepost. "Now I think you can see that interfering in our affairs can result in very unpleasant consequences. Yes? No?"

Sano, biting back another cry of pain, couldn't reply.

Then, almost as an afterthought, Lord Niu said, "Oh, Eii-*chan*. You can let him go now."

Eii-*chan* released Sano. Sano gingerly flexed his shoulder and arm. Nothing seemed broken, but his muscles ached. Anger flared inside him—not at Eii-*chan,* whom he regarded more as an animated tool than as a man, but at Lord Niu, who could have ended his misery sooner, but had deliberately chosen to let him suffer. The malicious glint in his eyes confirmed this. Sano wanted to rail against the insult, to hurl accusations and threats at Lord Niu: "Someone in your household killed Noriyoshi and your sister, and I'll prove it!" But he held his peace, reminding himself of Tokugawa Ieyasu's words: "Look upon wrath as thine enemy." He couldn't let anger make him careless.

"What is it you want with us now?" Lord Niu asked.

Swallowing his rage, Sano forced himself to lie courteously. "I only wanted to pay my respects to your family," he said.

Lord Niu let out a burst of scornful laughter. "Do you mean to tell me that you have ceased your ridiculous investigation into our private tragedy?"

"Unless I find evidence indicating that it isn't so ridiculous after all." Sano couldn't resist making a verbal counterattack. "Maybe you could give it to me?"

A momentary frown creased Lord Niu's forehead—dismay, or simple irritation? "You can't be serious. There is no such evidence, and even if there were, why would I have it?"

Was the emphatic denial a stall to buy Lord Niu time to recover his wits? Sano thought perhaps he could goad the daimyo's son into an unguarded revelation.

"Noriyoshi had ties to another member of your family besides Yukiko," he said.

But Lord Niu had regained his poise. Instead of acknowledging the question, he said to Eii-*chan*, "Return to the funeral. I think *Yoriki* Sano can find his own way home."

Eii-*chan* turned and walked down the steps without a word. To Sano, Lord Niu said, "If you come near our estate or near any member of our clan again, I cannot guarantee your safety. Eii-*chan* and our other retainers take an unfavorable view of those who trespass on our property or persons."

He delivered the words casually, but with a malevolent glow in his feverish eyes. Sano recognized the tacit threat: if he approached the Nius again, he would be killed.

"I see that you understand my meaning," Lord Niu said. "Perhaps you're not as stupid as I thought. Just foolhardy, but decidedly capable of learning your lesson." A contemptuous smile twisted his mouth as his gaze held Sano's. "Farewell, *yoriki*. I trust we won't be seeing each other again." He pushed himself away from the post and started slowly down the steps, his head high and his body rigid.

That's what you think, Sano silently told Lord Niu's retreating back. Resentment and humiliation burned dully in his blood like bad wine. His hand moved to his sword, gripping its hilt with all the force of his anger against Lord Niu, who had given him even more reason to investigate the Nius' role in the murders.

Then Lord Niu turned. "Oh, by the way," he called. "I wouldn't bother trying to see Midori, if I were you. My mother has sent her to the nunnery at the Temple of Kannon in Hakone." His laugh rang out as he continued on his way.

Sano watched Lord Niu rejoin the mourners at the funeral pyre. The flames had died down, although smoke continued to rise from the smoldering embers. As he started back toward the city center, a heady excitement stirred beneath his initial disappointment. Attending the funeral had endangered him, but not, perhaps, to no avail. Midori was in Hakone, a long, arduous journey west along the Tōkaido—the Eastern Sea Road that linked Edo with the imperial capital in Kyoto. This was bad news, but at least he knew where to find her. It wouldn't be easy to justify a five-day leave of absence to Magistrate Ogyu; still, he could operate more freely once outside Ogyu's domain.

Besides, the Nius' continuing resistance to his investigation confirmed his suspicion that they wanted the mystery of Noriyoshi's and Yukiko's murders to remain unsolved. And their abrupt removal of Midori from Edo meant they were afraid that she might tell him why.

13

Sano had departed from the Tōkaido's starting point at the
Nihonbashi Bridge at daybreak. Dressed in his winter traveling
clothes—a wide, circular wicker hat, heavy robes, trousers, shoes
and socks, and his warmest hooded cloak—he'd ridden southwest
out of the awakening city. Now, as the sun burned the last of the
dawn's shimmering pink radiance from the sky, he approached
Shinagawa, second of the fifty-three stations that marked the highway between Edo and Kyoto.

The wide, sandy road, banked in the middle and bordered on
each side by regularly spaced tall firs, narrowed and began to
climb. Sano could see ahead of him the many bent figures of
pedestrians toiling toward Shinagawa. To his right, the land rose
steeply toward the forested hills. On his left it dropped sharply
away below a line of fishermen's shacks to the sea. Small boats
crowded the harbor. The faint shapes of larger ships floated on
distant deeper water, against a hazy horizon. Seabirds wheeled and
soared, filling the sky's high blue bowl with darting wings and the
air with their sharp, plaintive cries. The sibilant lap of the waves
made a constant, gentler music. The clean, fresh salt breeze invig-
orated Sano, renewing his optimism and confidence. His journey
was going to be a success. When he got to Hakone, Midori would
give him proof that Noriyoshi and Yukiko had been murdered, and
maybe even tell him the identity of the killer.

"Wait, *Yoriki* Sano-*san!* I have to stop!"

The shout that came from twenty paces behind him shattered Sano's mood. With a sigh of irritation, he reined in his horse and looked over his shoulder. He watched as a smiling, wheezing Tsunehiko, mounted on a huge black steed, bounced up to him. For one blessed moment, he'd completely forgotten his traveling companion.

Tsunehiko scrambled off his horse. "I'll be quick, I promise." He hurried to the roadside, hiking up his cloak.

Shaking his head, Sano leaned over to grasp the reins of Tsunehiko's horse before it could wander away. He watched his secretary urinate against a tree, wishing he were traveling alone and blaming himself for the fact that he wasn't.

After Yukiko's funeral yesterday, he had gone straight to Magistrate Ogyu's mansion. He'd wondered whether he should wait awhile to ask for a leave of absence. If Ogyu had seen him at the funeral, it would be better to allow the magistrate's anger time to cool. But a growing sense of urgency made Sano reluctant to postpone his journey. If he didn't solve the mystery soon, he feared he might never do so.

He'd waited until after dark. At last two bearers rounded the corner with a palanquin. Magistrate Ogyu stepped out at the gate.

Sano greeted his superior, who, to his relief, didn't mention the funeral. Then he said, "Honorable Magistrate, I must beg you to allow me a five-day leave of absence. As you know, my father is not well. His doctor has advised me to make a pilgrimage to the shrine at Mishima to pray for his recovery."

Fabricating an excuse had presented him with a moral dilemma. He hated lies and subterfuge, but for the past few days, he'd dealt constantly in both. Now he'd come to realize that his investigation was compromising not only his career, but also his principles. He tried to justify the lies by telling himself that small truths must fall sacrifice to his pursuit of a larger one. Justice—for the murder victims, as well as for Wisteria and Midori and others who had loved them—must take priority. Still, he felt a deep unhappiness that he couldn't deny. His personal quest was carrying him into a disturbing and unfamiliar world, away from the radiant path of duty, obedience, filial piety, and integrity defined by the Way of the Warrior. Finally he'd settled on the pilgrimage story after discarding several others, because it was plausible and contained elements of truth. He would go to Mishima, which was the station just after Hakone. If spies at the highway checkpoints reported his movements to Ogyu, he would at least appear to be doing exactly as he'd proposed. A doctor *had* recommended the pilgrimage, and Ogyu, always a champion of duty, couldn't refuse to let him go.

Ogyu stroked his chin thoughtfully. "A pilgrimage on your father's behalf. Such an admirable expression of filial piety. Of course you may have your leave of absence, *Yoriki* Sano. When do you propose to begin your journey?"

"Thank you, Honorable Magistrate. Tomorrow morning, if I may." Sano bowed, surprised that Ogyu had conceded so easily. Did the magistrate really believe his story? Maybe Ogyu was just ready to seize any chance to get rid of him for a while. He wondered whether Ogyu knew about Midori and saw that his sudden need for a pilgrimage coincided with her departure from Edo. If so, did Ogyu not care if he visited the nunnery? Perhaps he'd wrongly imagined a criminal collusion between the magistrate and the Nius.

"I am much obliged for your kindness," he added, telling himself he was lucky to get a leave of absence at all, whatever the reason.

Then Ogyu said, "You will, of course, take your secretary with you." His tone made it not only an order, but a condition of Sano's leave.

Sano felt his mouth drop open in dismay. Tsunehiko! What a terrible encumbrance! The secretary was no horseman; he would make the journey last even longer. And how could Sano afford to feed him for five days? There would be other expenses, too:

lodging, stable fees, tolls at each of the ten checkpoints between Edo and Hakone.

"I value your advice, Honorable Magistrate," Sano faltered, "but I shan't require a secretary's services."

Ogyu dismissed his objection with a shake of his head. "A traveling companion is necessary for a man in your position," he said sternly. "Do not worry about the cost."

Then Sano understood. Ogyu was sending Tsunehiko along to spy. Now his suspicions about the magistrate's motives returned, and he regretted revealing his travel plans. But it was too late for regrets.

"Please come inside, Sano-*san*," Ogyu said with a benign smile. "I will write up two official travel passes and distribute to you the funds to cover your secretary's expenses. Then you had better go directly to his home and tell him to prepare for the journey."

Now Sano controlled his annoyance as Tsunehiko remounted the black steed. The secretary put his foot in the stirrup and heaved himself up, wheezing as he arrived, belly down, on the saddle.

"Easy." Sano calmed the horse as it began to buck. He held the reins firmly until Tsunehiko could sit up. To Tsunehiko, he said, "If you didn't drink so much, you wouldn't have to stop so often."

The reproach didn't bother Tsunehiko. Beaming, he said, "But *Yoriki* Sano-*san,* riding makes me thirsty. And hungry, too." He took another swig of water from his flask, then pulled a parcel of dried plums from his overloaded saddlebag. He began to munch, his cheeks bulging around his smile. "This is so much fun. Many, many thanks for taking me with you!"

Sano hid a smile as they resumed their journey. He couldn't stay angry with his secretary, not when the day seemed so bright with promise. His qualms about the lies he'd told Ogyu bothered him less. He was doing the right thing. Soon his superior would realize it and appreciate his efforts—if, of course, Ogyu was not deliberately concealing a crime but merely trying to spare the Nius what he deemed undeserved pain. The memory of his confrontation with Lord Niu lost some of its power to disturb Sano. He began to enjoy Tsunehiko's lighthearted company; he even joined in when the boy began to sing. This wasn't so bad after all. He had no doubt that he could manage to keep Tsunehiko from finding out the real purpose of the journey and from accompanying him to the Temple of Kannon.

Although the Tōkaido boasted less traffic now than in spring or summer, he and Tsunehiko had plenty of company. They passed two heavy ox-drawn carts full of lumber, property of the government, the only wheeled vehicles allowed on the highway because the Tokugawas wanted to discourage the transport of arms, ammunition, and other war supplies. Peasants scurried about collecting leaves, branches, and horse dung for fuel. An occasional wealthy passenger swayed and bobbed in a *kago,* a basketlike chair borne on the shoulders of brawny louts whose kimonos hung open to display magnificently tattooed chests and legs. Peddlers, their merchandise heaped on their backs, plodded doggedly along. A group of religious pilgrims sang and clapped as they marched toward some shrine or temple. Beggars played their wooden flutes to entice donors. Several times Sano and Tsunehiko exchanged greetings with other samurai, who either rode as they did at the moderate pace that a long journey required, or galloped past on some shorter mission.

In Shinagawa, the roadside inns, teahouses, and restaurants were doing a brisk business. Cooking odors drifted from behind curtains into the street. Tsunehiko greeted the sights and smells with a cry of rapture.

"Please, can we get something to eat, *Yoriki* Sano-*san?*" he begged.

"Later." Sano, having watched the secretary eat almost nonstop since the onset of their journey, knew he was in no danger of starving. They could have a meal at the next station, while the horses rested and fed. He wanted to cover as much ground as possible before dark. He led the way to the checkpoint, where the low plaster post house stood well back from the road.

In front of the post house, a line snaked toward the window where station officials registered the travelers, checked their documents, and either granted or denied further passage. A nearby stable offered packhorses for hire. As Sano dismounted and took his place in line beside Tsunehiko, he heard drunken laughter coming from beyond the stable. There the local *kago* bearers sat around a fire in their encampment of flimsy shacks, drinking sake while they waited for customers.

After a few moments, Tsunehiko said impatiently, "What's taking so long?"

Sano stepped out of line to look. A gray-haired woman and her two male escorts stood at the window. The official was sorting through a pile of papers, pausing now and then to question the woman.

"I don't see why they have to bother about some old lady," Tsunehiko complained when told. "They shouldn't make us wait. We're in a hurry!"

Sano resisted the impulse to tell him that they would have made better time if he hadn't stopped so often. Tsunehiko's obvious pleasure in the trip and his pride at traveling with his superior were rather endearing.

"The government can't afford to let the daimyo smuggle their women out of Edo," Sano said, taking the opportunity to teach his ignorant secretary. "With the hostages safe in the provinces, they would be free to express their anger toward the shogun's taxes and restrictions on their freedom by launching a rebellion."

Finally the woman followed a female official into the post house to be examined for the identifying scars and marks specified on her travel pass. Sano wondered how the Nius had arranged a pass for Midori so quickly. Those prized documents required many signatures and could take months to get. The Nius must have paid a fortune in bribes. Although they could well afford the expense, surely this meant they had strong reason to want Midori away from Edo.

When he reached the head of the line, Sano presented their passes and paid their tolls. He and Tsunehiko helped the searchers turn out their saddlebags to check for smuggled gold, foreign goods, and firearms. As government officials, they passed the inspection without difficulty. But as he prepared to depart, Sano experienced an uneasy, prickling sensation.

Someone was watching him. He could feel eyes trained on him, boring into his back with malicious intent.

He pretended to recheck the fastenings of his bags. Then he turned quickly. Several more travelers, including some mounted samurai, a few peasants, and a religious pilgrimage, had arrived since he'd last noticed. The few faces that looked back at him showed no more than ordinary interest. He saw no one he recognized.

"What are we waiting for, *Yoriki* Sano-*san?*" Tsunehiko sat astride his horse. "Is something wrong?"

"No, nothing." Sano didn't want to alarm Tsunehiko. He mounted his own horse, taking one last glance around as he led the way back to the road. The *metsuke*—government spies—kept a watch on all comings and goings along the Tōkaido. Probably one of them, disguised to blend with the crowd, had chosen that moment to observe him. That was all.

But Sano's uneasiness persisted. As they continued toward the next station at Kawasaki, he caught himself looking backward with increasing frequency. Were those three samurai or that peddler following them? The highway curved through a patch of woodland, and for a moment he and Tsunehiko had it to themselves. Tsunehiko stopped to urinate again. While he waited, Sano gazed into the pine trees that met overhead to form a canopy through which patches of blue sky showed. An excellent spot for soldiers to take cover from enemy arrows and bullets during war, he thought. And an equally excellent place for evildoers to hide. Every year, countless travelers were robbed and murdered on the Tōkaido.

Horses' hooves clopped on the road behind Sano. He peered back toward the curve, waiting for the rider to pass. Then the hoofbeats stopped. The morning was still, except for the twitter of birds and the rustle of the boughs overhead. Its silence, made ominous by that watching presence, unnerved Sano. His hand went to his sword. Did he dare shout, "Who goes there?" or ride around the curve to look? He had no desire to face an unknown assailant in this deserted place.

"Hurry up, Tsunehiko," he called instead.

He was relieved when they emerged from the woods into open space. Then, to his frustration, he saw a serious obstacle to a quick escape: the Tama River. Several swimmers were fording horses across the smooth, sparkling water; others waited on the rocky bank. Ferrymen were helping passengers into flat wooden boats. The Tokugawas and their efficient peacekeeping tactics! To restrict troop movement along the Tōkaido, they'd destroyed most of the bridges.

In his haste to be gone, Sano didn't bother to negotiate fares with the river men. He paid the high prices they asked and helped Tsunehiko unload the horses. He hurried his secretary into one of the boats, threw their bags in, and jumped inside after them. The ferryman began to row them across the river with infuriating slowness, while two pairs of swimmers guided the horses carefully between hidden underwater rocks and logs.

Tsunehiko stuck his hand in the water and immediately pulled it out again. "Oh, it's cold!" he exclaimed. To the swimmers, he called, "How can you bear it?"

The swimmers laughed, their tanned, grinning faces bobbing in the water beside the horses. "We're tough!" one of them answered.

Sano listened with half his attention. He squinted across the water to the receding shore. Although he could see no one lurking among the trees, his sense of impending danger did not diminish.

From his hiding place behind a clump of firs, the watcher stood and gazed toward the river as the ferryboat carried Sano Ichirō to the opposite bank. The *yoriki* kept turning around to peer at the woods. He obviously knew he was being followed. Maybe he'd guessed as far back as the post house, but certainly when the watcher had almost come upon him on that deserted stretch of road.

But the watcher kept his position, unworried. He could tell by the way Sano's puzzled gaze had darted from one person to another on the road—and the way it now swept the woods—that Sano didn't know who was watching him, or from where. The watcher knew that he was a superb spy. He'd had plenty of experience with disguises and hiding. His drab hat and cloak had allowed him to blend first with the other travelers, and now with the landscape. And he knew how to conceal his thoughts and intentions so that no one noticed, let alone suspected him. People—Sano included—looked straight through him as if he wasn't there. He hadn't had to take to the fields yet, as he might when they got farther from Edo and the traffic thinned. And he didn't much care that the *yoriki* was on guard. Anxiety would eat away at him. It would reduce him to helplessness by the time the watcher was ready to make his move.

Still, one thing disturbed the watcher. Not the smells of woods and water or his need for secrecy, which all vividly reminded him of the night he'd dumped the bodies in the river. The brilliant sunlight did much to banish any similarity between then and now. And the passage of time had allowed him to recover from the worst of his fear. His nightmares had stopped. He no longer awoke, sweating, heart pounding, from dreams of his own arrest, torture, and execution.

No—it was the young samurai traveling with Sano that bothered him. He'd expected Sano to be alone, and he didn't like surprises. Then he told himself that the boy's presence had its advantages. Sano made slower progress than he would have otherwise. Two men were easier to track than one. The watcher could lag far behind and still keep them in view, still catch up with them at every station. And the boy would distract Sano, making him less observant, less cautious.

The ferryboat reached the opposite bank. Sano and his companion stepped out and began unloading their bags. Their horses splashed ashore. Anxiously the watcher waited as his quarries dried, loaded, and mounted their horses and disappeared over the wooded bluff beyond the river. His eagerness nearly sent him rushing after them, but he fought it. Patience, he told himself. They couldn't escape.

He made himself wait a few more heartbeats. Then he whistled softly to his horse. She'd been waiting obediently down the road and now trotted up to meet him. The two of them descended the slope to the river, where the ferrymen and swimmers waited to convey them to the opposite shore.

He had plenty of time to choose his moment, and night would offer better opportunities than day.

14

Sunset had turned the western sky to a clear, lavender-streaked gold by the time Sano and Tsunehiko reached the inland village of Totsuka. Although Totsuka was the sixth Tōkaido station and the usual stopping place for travelers who had left Edo in early morning, Sano had hoped to push on farther. He wanted to shake their still-unseen pursuer, if indeed one existed. But night was fast approaching, wrapping the land in its chill darkness. He and Tsunehiko were cold, tired, and hungry; the horses, too, needed warmth, rest, and food.

"We'll spend the night here," Sano said after they'd cleared the checkpoint at the entrance to Totsuka.

Tsunehiko, who had turned glum and silent from fatigue, smiled again. "Oh, good, *Yoriki* Sano-*san,*" he said with a heartfelt sigh of relief.

Totsuka's thatch-roofed inns, restaurants, and teahouses stood side by side along the Tōkaido. Lanterns burned cheerily against the encroaching night. From the doorway of each establishment, pretty "waitresses"—the illegal and officially nonexistent village prostitutes—beckoned to the travelers. Earlier arrivals carried baggage into inns and drank in the teahouses. Medicine sellers hawked their salves and potions. A band of pilgrims peered into a religious-supply shop. Snatches of song and music burst from fenced courtyards, where the inns' customers had already begun their parties. Surrounding the commercial district, the villagers' houses nestled cozily among the trees.

Sano and Tsunehiko rode up the street in search of lodgings. They bypassed the stately, templelike edifices reserved for daimyo and court nobles. Near the middle of town, they found a small, modest inn whose front door opened directly onto the street. Its cylindrical orange lanterns bore the name Ryokan Gorobei. Signs advertised low prices for room and board; but the building seemed tidy and in good repair. The floor of its entranceway was swept clean, and its back wall was decorated with a shrine to Jizo, patron god of travelers and children. The fat little god sat on his shelf, surrounded by rice cakes, cups of sake, and burning oil lamps.

"This will do," Sano said, dismounting.

Before he led the way inside, he looked backward. Was it just his imagination that made him think the watcher pursued them? He saw the familiar faces of travelers they'd met on the road, but none with whom he could associate that malignant presence. Trying to shed his anxiety, he told himself that soon he and Tsunehiko would be safe within four walls.

"Welcome to the Ryokan Gorobei, welcome!" The smiling innkeeper rushed out of his living quarters in back of the entrance- way to greet them. Short, bald, and rotund, he looked a bit like Jizo himself. He bowed and said, "Thank you for choosing my humble inn. I am Gorobei, and I will do everything in my power to make your stay a pleasant one."

He brought them a register to sign, then called to the stable boy, who ran out to take charge of the horses. Then he picked up one of Jizo's lamps and led Sano and Tsunehiko into the storage room. They left most of their baggage there, keeping with them only the things they would need that night. Tsunehiko hung his swords on the rack with those of the other guests, but Sano hesitated, his hand on the scabbard of his long sword. What if the watcher should make an appearance tonight?

"You need not worry about leaving your weapons, master,"

said the innkeeper. "Very, very safe here. Ryokan Gorobei has its own nightwatchman."

"No reflection on your establishment, but I'd rather keep them with me," Sano told him.

Gorobei led them across a small but pretty garden to the guest quarters. Climbing the steps of a narrow veranda, he slid open a door. The room, just large enough to sleep two men, was bare and clean. Its only furnishings were the tatami mats, a charcoal brazier, and a wall cabinet to hold bedding and the guests' personal items. Gorobei lit the brazier and the lamps that stood beside it. Then he smiled and bowed.

"I hope these poor lodgings will serve, masters. The bathhouse and privy are that way." He pointed. "Please let me know if there is anything you need." With another bow, he bustled off toward the entranceway, where voices indicated that another party had arrived.

Once bathed, dressed in a comfortable robe, and enclosed in the warm, bright little room, Sano felt his tension melt away. Physical comfort made all threats seem distant and unreal.

"I'm starving," Tsunehiko announced, wheezing as he knelt beside the brazier. "When do we eat?"

As if in answer to his question, the door slid open. A maid entered on her knees. She bowed, then gave them two trays that held generous portions of fish, rice, vegetables, and soup. Sano, weary of scrutinizing every face he saw, was glad that inns had no public dining rooms and guests ate in their own quarters. The maid poured the tea and sake, then withdrew.

"Good stuff," Tsunehiko mumbled, his mouth full.

Sano nodded in agreement. The rice was fragrant, the vegetables and soup well seasoned and savory. Ryokan Gorobei offered good value for its prices. He must remember to leave a generous tip. The knot of worry in his stomach loosened, releasing a voracious hunger. He ate almost as much as Tsunehiko, leaving only a portion of untouched radish pickle for his disappointed secretary to finish.

"My, it's noisy," Tsunehiko remarked as they finished their last cups of sake. "What are they doing over there?"

He leaned over and started to slide back the window panel.

"Don't—" Sano flung out a hand to stop him.

Tsunehiko looked around in surprise. "Why not?"

Sano dropped his hand. "Never mind," he said. He didn't want to reveal their whereabouts, but he couldn't resist looking outside. Maybe this time he would see the watcher. "Go ahead."

Tsunehiko opened the window. The laughter and music that had grown steadily louder during their meal rushed in on a cold gust of wind. Sano looked across the garden toward the other guest rooms. Through the open window of one, he saw a group of samurai. A woman in bright kimono, probably the inn's "waitress," knelt in their midst, playing the samisen. One of the samurai struck a clownish pose and began to sing in an off-key voice. The others roared with laughter. In another room, two priests chanted sutras. Sano turned his gaze to another wing that stood a little apart from the rest. Was the watcher one of those shadowy forms silhouetted in flickering lamplight against the translucent windows? Or was he staying at another inn, ready to pick up their trail in the morning? Maybe he lurked somewhere in the darkness beyond the village. Safe within his own cozy room, listening to the ordinary noises, Sano could almost believe that the watcher posed no danger to them.

Almost.

Tsunehiko yawned. "I'm so tired," he said.

Sano yawned, too. His body's need for sleep was fast overcoming his mind's desire to stay alert. When the maid returned to fetch the trays, he asked her to set out their bedding. Then he put on his cloak and swords.

"I'm going out for some fresh air," he told Tsunehiko. He

didn't want to frighten his secretary, but he wanted to take one last look for the watcher, and assure himself that they would be safe for the night.

Outside, he made a circuit of the courtyard, which had grown quiet as the parties wound down and the guests prepared for bed. He looked out onto the deserted street. A few lanterns still burned outside the teahouses and inns. On the way back to his own door, Sano greeted the nightwatchman, a younger version of Gorobei who must be the innkeeper's son. Otherwise he saw no one. He no longer felt the watcher's presence. Was his own fatigue making him less sensitive to it?

Back inside the room, he locked the windows and doors, frowning at the flimsy wooden catches designed more to ensure privacy than security. Tsunehiko already lay asleep on the floor, his fat body hidden under the quilt with only the top of his head showing. His daytime wheezes had turned into soft, phlegmy snores. Sano shed his cloak and swords and extinguished the lamps. He lay down on his futon, drawing the quilt over himself. As drowsiness descended upon him, he heard the rhythmic beat of the night-watchman's wooden clappers signaling "All is well." But his hand reached out from under the quilt, toward the weapons that lay beside him. With his last conscious effort, he grasped the hilt of his long sword and unsheathed it.

Sano slept.

In the garden of the Ryokan Gorobei, the watcher waited behind a spreading pine tree. As midnight drew near, lamps no longer burned in the guest quarters. The inn's grounds lay in almost total darkness, illuminated only by a diffuse glow from the star-pricked sky. Shrubs and buildings loomed blackly over gravel paths that gave back a dim reflection of the starlight. Only the wind's restless movement animated the night, rattling the darkened paper lanterns and the trees' bare branches.

Then footsteps crunched on the path. A yellow light rounded one wing of the guest quarters. The nightwatchman appeared, lantern slung over one arm, clappers in his hands, and a sturdy wooden club hanging from his sash. He was making his rounds, as he had done without pause since sundown. He strolled past the buildings, stopping beside each door.

In the lantern's light, the watcher could see the man's round, cheerful face beneath his straw hat, see his breath clouding the cold air. He held his own breath, willing himself to become part of the tree that hid him. But he had no real fear of discovery yet. He knew from long observation that the man came into the garden every third round and only as far as its edge during the others. He exhaled when, just as he'd expected, the man turned and passed through the gate that led to the street. A moment later, the footsteps sounded again, the light came around the building, and the whole routine repeated itself.

But now the sight of the man filled the watcher with impotent rage. How would he get inside Sano's room—and out again— without the miserable fool seeing him? He could approach the door while the nightwatchman was out in the street, but what if he was unable to force it open quickly enough? The nightwatchman would return and sound the alarm on his clappers. The whole village would awaken and descend upon the grounds like a swarm of demons.

The watcher tried to persuade himself to give up and wait for another chance, along the road tomorrow or at the next night's rest stop. But a consuming urge to finish his deed now, tonight, kept him in his place. This time, when the man finished inspecting the garden and turned toward the gate, the watcher moved out from behind the tree.

His hands grasped the man's neck. He squeezed, crushing the soft, warm flesh and rigid sinew.

The man let out a choked cry. He stiffened and dropped his

lantern and clappers. His body thrashed; his legs flailed. He gasped and wheezed, fighting for air. His fingers clawed the watcher's, trying frantically to break their grip.

The watcher held fast, clenching his teeth with the effort. He barely felt the pain as those scratching nails tore at his knuckles. Soon the man's struggles weakened. His gasps ceased; his hands dropped. He twitched for a moment more, then went limp. The watcher eased the lifeless body to the ground and dragged it into the shrubbery. He snuffed out the fallen lantern. Darkness enveloped him in its protective cloak. A sense of absolute power swelled inside him. No one stood in his way now.

He moved across the garden toward Sano's door.

Screams and moans echoed in Sano's ears as he walked again through the foul-smelling corridors of Edo Jail. This time his guide was not Mura the *eta* but Magistrate Ogyu, his black ceremonial robes sweeping the filthy floor.

Ogyu stopped at the end of the corridor and threw open a door. "Come, *Yoriki* Sano," he called, his high, reedy voice nearly drowned out by the cries of the prisoners. "Come and experience the fate of those who disobey orders and leave their obligations unfulfilled!"

Sano didn't want to go. He didn't want to know what lay beyond that door. But an unseen force propelled him down the corridor. Almost sobbing with terror, he fell to his knees, seizing the magistrate's robes.

"Please . . . no . . ."

Ogyu laughed. "Where is your samurai courage now, *Yoriki* Sano?" he mocked.

With a mighty kick, he sent Sano flying through the door to land inside the room on hands and knees. Sano cried out, once in surprise, then again in shock at the sight that met his eyes.

Inside the morgue, Mura and Dr. Ito stood on either side of a dissection table. Mura held a long razor and had a white cloth tied over the lower half of his face. As Dr. Ito raised a beckoning hand, Sano noticed something that turned him sick with fear.

The table was empty. Waiting. For him.

"No!" Sano screamed.

The watcher stealthily mounted the stairs of the veranda outside Sano's door. His straw sandals made no noise, but each footfall produced a soft creak as his weight bore down on the wooden planks. He tried the door.

Locked. He unsheathed his dagger. Sliding it between door and frame, he pushed on the catch. It gave way with a crack that almost startled him into dropping the dagger. He froze, listening.

Only muffled snores came from inside the room. The noise hadn't awakened them. Slowly, carefully, the watcher slid back the door. Dagger in hand, he squinted into the darkness of the room. There he could barely make out the two sleeping forms.

Now . . .

A loud gurgling sound awoke Sano. Suddenly Ogyu, Mura, Dr. Ito, and the morgue vanished. Sano gave a hoarse yell of surprise as he sat bolt upright in the darkness. Through the clinging haze of sleep, he saw a shadowy figure moving toward him. He cried out again, this time in sheer terror, as he instinctively lashed out at it with the sword that he still gripped in his hand. The figure leaped backward, turned, disappeared. Sano's blade sliced empty air. Running footsteps shook the floor, then faded into the distance.

Sano struggled free of the tangled bedcovers and jumped to his feet, sword ready. Fully awake now, he strained to see his surroundings and remember where he was. His heart still pounded; the lurid dream images of Edo Jail and the menacing intruder were still vivid in his memory. In his confusion, it took him a moment to recognize the dim confines of his room at the inn. All was quiet and peaceful. His fear should have subsided, yet he experienced the frightening conviction that something was very wrong. Every fiber of his being vibrated in alarm.

The room felt oddly cold. An icy draft stirred the air, but didn't obliterate the strong metallic odor that made Sano's nostrils flare. Another peculiar scent—fainter, and musty, like dried herbs— prickled his throat and forced a sneeze from him. And there was something else different about the room, something missing.

Tsunehiko's snores. Sano no longer heard them—or any sound at all from the inert form next to him.

"Tsunehiko?" he called.

Bending over, he touched his secretary. And gasped, jerking his hand away. Something warm, wet, and faintly sticky coated the quilt. Filled with dread, he dropped his sword and groped around on the floor for the lamp and matches. It took his shaking hands three tries to light the wick. The lamp guttered, then flared into brightness. Sano looked at Tsunehiko.

Shock stopped his heart, froze the words on his tongue. His lungs sucked in breath with a long, sharp hiss.

Tsunehiko lay face up on the futon, the quilt pulled back to expose his neck and shoulders. Blood from the cruel gash in his throat, red and lustrous in the lamplight, stained his bedding and nightclothes. His sightless eyes gazed at the ceiling. He did not move, or speak, or make a sound.

15

"**N**o!" Sano cried.

Moaning, he knelt beside Tsunehiko. He ripped off his robe and pressed it to the terrible wound, trying to stanch the flow of blood that had already ceased. He slapped the boy's cheeks in a desperate effort to revive him. But he knew in his heart that Tsunehiko was dead. That first horrifying look had told him.

Now he understood the significance of the intruder, the strange gurgle, and the departing footsteps. He hadn't dreamed them after all. Half asleep, oblivious to the danger, he'd heard Tsunehiko cry out as his throat was cut, and let the murderer escape afterward.

"No!"

Grief and rage exploded in Sano's chest as he thought of Tsunehiko's youthful innocence and cheerfulness. Not bothering to dress, he seized his sword. He registered the open door and splintered catch in the moment it took to hurl himself outside. The murderer—was it the mysterious watcher?—had entered and killed without difficulty. But he wouldn't get away! A monstrous craving for vengeance howled inside Sano, one for which he hadn't known he possessed the capacity. He wanted blood for blood. He wanted to call down the wrath of the gods. Barefoot, clad only in his loincloth, he stumbled into the freezing darkness of the garden. He thrashed his way blindly around the guest quarters, sword raised.

"Stop! Murderer!" he shouted.

As if in reply, rapid hoofbeats pounded away from the village and into the night.

"Stop! Murderer!"

Lights began to appear in the inn's windows as Sano charged past them. He heard the guests stirring inside their rooms, and heard excited voices asking, "What is it? Who's shouting?" But where was the nightwatchman? Having failed to keep the intruder away, he should now be summoning the checkpoint guards and village police with his clappers.

Sano found no one lurking outside the guest quarters. Then, as he ran through the garden, his foot struck something. He tripped and went sprawling facedown. He gasped as his body hit not cold, hard ground, but something warmer and more yielding. Someone rushed up with a lantern and began to scream. Righting himself, Sano saw an old woman standing over him, her face stricken.

"Jihei!" she screamed. "My son!" She burst into sobs.

Sano looked at the thing he'd tripped over, and understood why the nightwatchman hadn't sounded the alarm. Gorobei's son lay motionless on his back. His terror-filled but lifeless eyes bulged; his tongue, protruding from between clenched teeth, oozed blood. Dark bruises encircled his throat. He was dead; strangled—probably by the same man who had killed Tsunehiko. Sano closed his eyes as the dizzying horror washed over him again. The woman's sobs echoed his own anguish. He heard running footsteps and men's voices. He opened his eyes to see his fellow guests, the samurai and priests, gathered around him.

"Stay with her," he ordered the priests, pointing at the distraught woman. To the dazed, bleary-eyed samurai: "Come with me! We have to catch the killer!"

Without waiting for a response, he ran for the stables. The samurai, pudgy from easy living and the worse for tonight's drinking, nevertheless rose to the challenge. In various states of undress, they panted after Sano, clutching their swords, bellies jiggling.

But although Sano and his helpers searched up and down the road and all through the sleeping village, they found no one. The killer had simply vanished into the night.

The next few hours passed in a blur. Sano endured them with every bit of the self-control and stoicism he possessed. He informed the grieving innkeeper that in addition to his son, a guest had been murdered. He reported the murders to the guards, who summoned the village police, elders, and headman. Everyone trooped over to the Ryokan Gorobei to see the bodies.

"Are you sure he's dead?" the headman kept asking anxiously as he hovered over Tsunehiko's corpse.

Sano knew that the death of an upper-class traveler meant much trouble and expense for a post town. It meant sending reports to the central highway administration in Edo, holding an inquest, notifying the next of kin, arranging for cremation of the body or its transportation home. But the headman's idiotic question made Sano's precarious self-control snap.

"Yes, of course he's dead, you fool!" he shouted, throwing on his cloak over his shivering body. "So just forget about putting him in a *kago* and sending him on to the next town so he can die on someone else's hands!"

The headman gaped at him. Then he frowned. "How do we know you didn't kill him yourself?"

"This wasn't robbery-murder," one of the elders chimed in helpfully as he opened the cabinet and pawed through its contents. "Look, the money's still here." He held up Sano's and Tsunehiko's cash pouches.

It had occurred to Sano that the officials might suspect him of committing the murders. Now he said, "Look at my weapons—there's no blood on them. Even if I'd wanted to kill my companion, I wouldn't have done it in our room. But if I had, I would have sneaked away instead of raising the alarm. I wouldn't have needed to kill the nightwatchman, or to force the door.

"If we're to catch the killer, we must send a search party up and down the highway and out into the countryside. Now. Before he gets away.''

Fortunately no one else took up the headman's argument—due, Sano guessed, more to his status as a *yoriki* than to his explanation. But they hesitated so long over the decision to send the search party that Sano despaired of ever catching the killer. Three of the elders wanted to wait until daybreak; it was so dark, they said, that a search would be useless. The others thought it best to begin immediately—but they didn't want to risk disturbing important guests at the inns. The headman threw up his hands in confusion. A young man who had only recently inherited his job from his father, he'd obviously never dealt with murder before. At last he announced that they would postpone the decision itself until he'd had more time to think about it.

"Then let me organize the search," Sano pleaded. "I'll take full responsibility for any disturbance."

But the headman and elders refused. As an Edo official, Sano had no authority in Totsuka. He must remain at the inn; a guard would see that he did. He must dictate a statement and sign many documents, just like anyone else whose companion had died on the highway. In addition, he must attend the inquest in the morning, arrange for the cremation of Tsunehiko's body, and promise to convey the ashes to the boy's family on his return trip.

Finally they left Sano alone, in a spare guest room hastily prepared for him by Gorobei's weeping maid. Exhausted though he was, Sano didn't sleep. Instead he knelt on the floor and watched the windows gradually brighten with the coming dawn. The emotions he'd suppressed came flooding back. Grief, anger, and horror sickened him. Although the room was warm, a violent tremor seized him, one that had nothing to do with physical cold. He clenched his jaws and tightened his muscles against it. The floor shuddered with his uncontrollable spasms. After what seemed an eternity, they subsided, leaving his body weak and drained but his mind sharply lucid.

He knew without proof, but also beyond doubt, that the man who had been watching him had killed both Tsunehiko and the innkeeper's son. But why? The answer came to Sano from some still, quiet place deep inside him.

He, not Tsunehiko, had been the intended victim. Only his fortunate awakening and quick reflexes had saved him from a killer who, unable to tell them apart in the darkness, had meant to kill them both as a precaution and begun with the wrong one. As to why, he knew the answer to that, too. He was getting close to the truth about Noriyoshi's and Yukiko's murders, and someone wanted to stop him. Who, then? Young Lord Niu or one of the countless Niu clan retainers, who would kill at their master's bidding? Kikunojo, with his intelligence and flair for disguise? Raiden, of the great strength and violent tendencies? Sano could not dismiss them as suspects. Or perhaps the spy who had reported on his activities to Magistrate Ogyu and Lady Niu had had orders to kill him.

With a kind of desolate satisfaction, Sano pondered these questions. He'd wanted proof that Noriyoshi and Yukiko had been murdered. What better than an attempt on his life? But any pleasure he might have taken from realizing his goal fell before his guilt over Tsunehiko.

He shouldn't have exposed Tsunehiko to danger. He should have at least told him the real purpose of the journey. He should have recognized the threat posed by the watcher and warned Tsunehiko, protected him somehow. More to the point, he should never have undertaken the journey at all. Magistrate Ogyu had ordered him to abandon the investigation, and he should have obeyed. He couldn't shift the blame to Ogyu for sending Tsunehiko with him. The boy's blood was on his hands.

Sano realized that he'd never seriously considered giving up the investigation, not even when his obligations to his father and Ogyu had held him back temporarily. The part of him that yearned after the truth had always known he would continue. Now he did consider the alternative. The cost of truth was too high. He couldn't pay it with more human lives.

Then his desire to bring the killer to justice rose anew. His craving for vengeance came surging back. He couldn't let Tsunehiko's murderer go unpunished. His honor demanded satisfaction, his spirit a relief from sorrow and guilt.

Sano's hand moved to his waist. He slowly unsheathed the long sword and held it before him in both hands.

He stayed like that, unmoving, for what remained of the night.

16

Fujisawa, Hiratsuka, Oiso, Odawara. The names of the post
stations ran together in Sano's mind, as did his memories of the
journey through towns and woods, over hills and plains, along
seashore and across rivers, past houses and temples. Pushing himself beyond exhaustion, he neared Hakone in the gray early afternoon two days after leaving Totsuka.

The approach to Hakone was the most difficult and dangerous
section of the Tōkaido. Here the land turned mountainous; the
road narrowed to a steep, rough trail that twisted upward through
stands of tall cedar trees. Sano dismounted and continued on foot,
leading his horse. Soon he was panting from the effort of climbing,
sweating despite the moist, bone-chilling cold. The altitude made
him light-headed, and he couldn't get enough of the thin air into
his lungs. Every breath seemed poisoned with the resinous fragrance of the cedars.

And the landscape overhelmed his troubled mind. In its surreal
splendor, it seemed like something out of an ancient legend. Every
step sent small rocks skittering dizzily over the sides of sheer cliffs.
Roaring waterfalls tumbled over boulders and precipices toward
the sea, which Sano occasionally glimpsed in the east. Fissures in
the ground leaked steam: the breath of dragons, who lived beneath
Mount Fuji, hidden in the clouds to the northwest. Far below, a

swirling river appeared and disappeared. High, fragile wooden bridges crossed it, leading Sano through tiny mountain villages.

An eerie enchantment shrouded the villages like a magic spell. The peasants Sano met there greeted him with polite bows, but they seemed illusory. He passed few other travelers. Those who flocked to Hakone in summer to enjoy the medicinal benefits of its fresh air and hot springs avoided it in winter, when the climate was considered unhealthy. Sano faced the dangers of the road alone: robber gangs; the old demons who lived in caves and played evil tricks on the unwary. And the watcher—now murderer—whose presence Sano no longer sensed but took for granted. He walked with his sword drawn, his eyes constantly searching.

Once he stopped and shouted, "Here I am! Come and get me, I dare you!"

Hearing his voice echo through the mountains, he wondered whether he was going mad. When he at last saw Hakone Village below him in the distance, he welcomed his escape from solitude and return to the normal, everyday world.

Hakone Village's hundred-some houses clustered around a segment of the Tōkaido that ran along the southeast shore of Lake Ashi. The lake, dotted with fishing boats, reflected the leaden sky. High, wooded mountains, some with almost vertical sides, surrounded it. Mount Fuji towered above the others, a faint white peak wearing a fainter hat of white clouds.

Sano felt a vast relief as he completed his descent. He'd almost reached his destination. Soon he could rest in a clean, cozy inn, with food for his stomach and a hot bath for his aching muscles. Then he reached the checkpoint, where he encountered an obstacle he should have expected. Hakone was famous for the strength and severity of its guard. The village's location, with mountains on one side and lake on the other, made it a natural trap for the shogun's men to detain suspicious-looking travelers—especially samurai who were not trusted Tokugawa allies. Twenty guards in full armor manned the fortified gates barring the way into the village, and they would not let Sano pass.

"Come with me," said one guard.

In a small bare room in the post house, Sano spent an hour answering the rapid-fire questions of three officials who wore the Tokugawa crest on their kimonos.

"Who is your family? Where are you from? What is your destination, and what is the purpose of your journey? Who is your lord? What is your occupation, and who is your immediate superior?"

Sano wanted desperately to be on his way, but he couldn't afford to antagonize the officials, who might hold him for hours— or days—longer.

"Sano Ichirō of Edo, son of Sano Shutarō, martial arts instructor, who was formerly in the service of Lord Kii of Takamatsu Province," he answered politely.

Through the open door he could see other officials turning out the contents of his saddlebags onto the floor in the next room. One searched his clothing, while another examined his travel pass.

"I am a *yoriki* under the supervision of Ogyu Banzan, the north magistrate of Edo. I am on a pilgrimage to Mishima."

He waited for the officials to ask if he was meeting anyone in Mishima, and whom. Their job was to sniff out secret assignations related to plots against the government. Instead they seized upon his name, losing interest in the purpose of his journey.

"*Yoriki* Sano Ichirō of Edo," the leader said. "Were you not involved in the murders that took place in Totsuka the day before yesterday?"

Sano was amazed at how fast their spy network passed news along the Tōkaido. He responded to their questions about the murders, suspecting that they already knew most of the answers. Finally, after a thorough reprise of the Totsuka inquest, they let him go.

Since the Temple of Kannon lay high in the mountains behind Hakone Village, Sano left his horse and baggage at an inn and set out on foot. The steep path curved and twisted. Cedars pressed in closely on each side, their heavy dark green boughs blocking Sano's view at every turn as he climbed. Snow and ice whitened the ground in great slippery patches. Sano found a dead branch and used it as a staff as he struggled from one precarious foothold to the next. The Nius would have sent servants to ease Midori's way, but still the trip must have been hard for her. The higher he climbed, the more the cold, wind, and dampness intensified. Droplets of icy water struck his face. He felt as though he'd reached the clouds. His heart pounded from the exertion; his lungs heaved.

But his determination to catch the murderer and avenge Tsunehiko's death kept him going. He only hoped that what awaited him at the Temple of Kannon would make his journey worthwhile. When he finally paused to rest, he saw that he was high above Hakone, with village, lake, and mountains spread below him under a thin veil of mist. Vertigo made him sway. He leaned on his staff for support. Then he turned and once more began the perilous climb upward.

Suddenly, just when he'd almost depleted his last reserves of strength, he emerged into a level, open clearing. Here the surrounding cedars obscured the sky and created a premature twilight. When Sano's eyes adjusted to the dimness, he saw a temple that perhaps dated back more than a thousand years, to when Buddhism had first come to Japan.

A great free-standing gate with tiled double roofs supported on eight strong pillars marked its entrance. Sano passed through this gate and a smaller inner one, into an earthen courtyard dotted with unlit stone lanterns. To his right stood the main hall, square and forbidding on its high stone podium. On his left he saw the pagoda and the wooden cage that housed the temple bell. A few stone mon-

uments comprised the graveyard. The lecture hall, sutra reposi-
tory, and storehouses occupied ledges cut into the slope that rose
behind the courtyard. Above these, a steep path led to what Sano
guessed was the nunnery, a long, low building cantilevered over
the mountainside on a support of interlocking wooden beams.

Although the temple must have undergone periodic repair over
the years, only the five-story pagoda had been restored to its
original condition. Its freshly plastered white walls shone; new
blue-gray tiles covered its roofs. Gleaming paint accented the
woodwork in traditional Chinese colors: green for window mullions, red and yellow for the roofs' intricate structural members.
The bells encircling the pagoda's tall bronze spire rang softly in the
wind. But the other buildings showed signs of advanced deteriora-
tion. Moss and lichen crusted their peeling plaster; wooden beams,
doors, and window lattices had warped and split. Broken tiles
marred the roofs' clean lines. Sano saw no priests or nuns or
pilgrims. If the watcher had followed, he did not appear. The
temple seemed deserted, suspended in a timeless hush.

He climbed the stairs to the main hall. The massive door
creaked open at his touch. He paused in the entryway to slip off
his shoes, then entered the hall. Against the far wall, a huge
Buddha sat enthroned upon a lotus flower. Time had turned the
many-armed bronze statue a deep greenish black. All around it
stood smaller painted wood images of guardian kings: fierce warriors with clenched fists and raised spears. Hundreds of burning oil
lamps and smoldering incense burners animated the deities with a
hazy, flickering glow. Years of flame and smoke had blackened the
hall's exposed rafters and suffused it with a musty, ancient fragrance. Faded murals showed ghostly sepia images of the Buddha
surrounded by palaces and hills. Tucked in the far left corner,
almost as an afterthought, was a woman-sized gilded wooden
figure of Kannon—Kuan Yin, Chinese goddess of mercy, bodhi-

sattva who forswore emancipation from the wheel of continual rebirth in order to save the souls of others. She wore a jeweled crown and a flaming halo.

Sano dropped a coin into the offertory box that stood on a post near the altar. He closed his eyes and bent his head over his clasped hands, offering silent prayers for his father's health, Tsunehiko's spirit, an end to Wisteria's grief, and the success of his mission.

The whisper of robes dragging on the floor startled Sano out of his prayers. He turned to see a tall, slender nun in a long black robe and veil standing before him. She could have been any age between thirty and sixty, with pale, stern features and a high forehead. Her long fingers toyed with the rosary at her sash, automatically counting prayers.

"Welcome, honorable pilgrim," she said, bowing. "I am the abbess of the Temple of Kannon, and I would be delighted to tell you about the temple's history. The temple was built during the Heian Period, approximately eight hundred years ago."

The practiced quality of her voice indicated that she had recited this speech many times before. Its unctuous tone told Sano that she, like other religious leaders, was anxious to curry favor with members of the warrior class, who supported their temples.

"Now the Temple of Kannon is sanctuary to twenty nuns who have forsaken earthly life to seek spiritual enlightenment. If you accompany me, I will tell you about the images that you see here."

Sano bowed. "Forgive me, Abbess, but I am not here on a pilgrimage. I've come to see one of your nuns, Miss Niu Midori." He identified himself, saying, "I apologize for the intrusion, but this is a matter of utmost importance."

"I am afraid that is impossible." The abbess's voice lost its unctuousness, turning cold. "As I have already said, our nuns have forsaken the world and its concerns. They shun contact with those from the outside. Our novices, in particular, are subject to the strictest seclusion. You cannot see Miss Midori now, or ever. I regret that you have come all this way for nothing."

It was a dismissal, delivered with finality. Sano's already flagging spirits sagged lower.

"Please, Abbess," he said. "I promise I will not stay long with her, or interfere with her faith." Had she received orders from Lady Niu to shield Midori from all visitors, or him in particular? He'd seen no recognition on her face when he'd given his name. "I just want to speak with her alone for a few moments. Nothing more.

"And afterward," he added, "I would like to make a small gift to the Temple of Kannon." The clergy, he knew, were always eager for donations.

Instead of replying, the abbess turned from him and clapped her hands twice. The door flew open. Two orange-robed priests entered the hall: tall, muscular men carrying long, curved spears.

"Good day, master," the abbess said. "May the Buddha in all his divine mercy grant you a safe journey home."

Sano had no choice but to let the priests escort him outside. He was familiar with the legendary fighting skills of the mountain priests, who had warred against each other and the ruling clans for hundreds of years. When he tried to bribe them into letting him see Midori, they remained mute and unresponsive to his pleas, their faces stony. They saw him as far as the gate, then stood watching as he descended the path.

Once out of their sight, Sano flung down his staff. He dropped to his knees, staring down over the treetops at the village and lake. He tried to summon the strength to descend the mountainside. Soon night would fall; the air had already grown chillier with the dying day. If he waited too long, he might get hurt trying to negotiate the treacherous path in darkness, or lose his way and freeze to death. But despair, combined with exhaustion, held him immobile. This journey had come to nothing; Tsunehiko had died for nothing. He was no closer to unraveling the mystery of Noriyoshi's and Yukiko's deaths than when he'd left Edo. How could he live with his failure and the tragic consequences of his actions?

Stand up, Sano told himself. Pick up your staff, put one foot in front of the other, and . . .

His head whipped around at the sound of running footsteps coming from the temple grounds above him. The priests. Hand on his sword, he leaped to his feet, driven by the samurai instinct to stand and fight. Then common sense reminded him that there were at least two priests and only one of him. If he wanted to live, he'd best leave now, before they found him. Seizing his staff, he hurried down the path.

"*Yoriki!* Wait!"

The high female voice stopped Sano in his tracks. He turned and saw a small figure skidding down the path toward him. Reaching him, she stumbled and would have fallen had he not caught her. He stared at her in shock.

It was Midori, although he barely recognized her. Instead of a bright silk kimono, she wore a coarse, shapeless hemp robe. Bare feet peeped out from beneath its hem. She seemed smaller, as if she'd lost weight. Her face was thin, pale, and peaked, her lips chapped. Most shocking of all, her head had been shaved. Only a bluish tinge on her bare scalp remained of her long black hair.

Between gasps, she said, ". . . saw you from the nuns' dormitory . . ." One hand went to her heaving breast. ". . . climbed out the window . . . couldn't let you go without telling you . . ."

"Calm down, it's all right," Sano said. He drew her off the path and seated her on a fallen log. She was shivering in her thin robe, so he took off his cloak and draped it over her shoulders. Then he waited with rising anticipation for her to catch her breath. At last he would possess the information for which he'd traveled so far and paid so dearly.

But when she spoke, it wasn't about her sister or Noriyoshi. "I hate this place!" she cried passionately, beating her fists against the log. "Cooking and scrubbing floors and praying from dawn till sunset. Then a few hours' sleep on a hard straw bed before that awful bell wakes me up and the whole thing starts all over again."

Tears brightened her eyes. "If I have to stay here any longer, I'll die. Please, take me away with you!"

Pity welled inside Sano as he shook his head. "I can't do that," he said. Although his refusal might turn her against him, he had to tell her the truth.

Midori sighed, accepting his words with averted head and slumped shoulders. "I know you can't," she said sorrowfully. Her hand went up as if to stroke her hair, then jerked back as it touched bare scalp. "My father's men would hunt us down. They would cut off your head and bring me back here. I shouldn't have asked. Forgive me."

"Can you tell me how you happened to come here?" Sano asked. He didn't want to set off another outburst by mentioning her sister's death right away, and he wanted the story in her own words, uninfluenced by his own expectations.

"My stepmother is punishing me." Now Midori's eyes glittered with anger. "I hate her! If I ever see her again, I'll kill her. I'll get a sword and cut her a hundred times. Like this!" Wielding an imaginary sword, she slashed at the air. "I don't want to be a nun. I want to live in Edo and go to parties and the theater. I want my sisters, and my pretty clothes, and my dolls, and, oh . . . !" She burst into wild sobs, hiding her face in her hands.

"Has your father no say in the matter?" Sano asked. He knew that many men cared little about their daughters' happiness, but he wouldn't have expected Lord Niu to give one up to the clergy so easily. He had more to gain from marrying Midori off to a son of another important clan. This way he lost the chance to cement a political alliance and had to pay a dowry to the temple.

Midori raised her head, wiping her eyes with the back of her hand. "I hardly ever see my father. Besides, he lets my stepmother run the household as she pleases. Just like he lets my older brothers run his province. The servants say he can't think for himself anymore. His mind isn't right, and it gets worse every year, they say."

Sano suddenly remembered the Little Daimyo's other nickname: the Crazy Little Daimyo. He'd heard rumors of bizarre happenings in Satsuma Province: Lord Niu's wild parties, and his howling rages, when he would gallop his horse around the castle grounds, hacking viciously with his sword at anyone unfortunate enough to get in his way. If, as Midori said, Lord Niu's authority had passed to his wife, it would explain Lady Niu's unusual power. Sano wondered if anyone else in the family shared Lord Niu's violent disposition. Perhaps the young Masahito, who resembled him physically? But Yukiko's, Noriyoshi's, and Tsunehiko's murders bespoke a different kind of mentality: sane and calculating.

"What are you being punished for?" he prompted Midori, guiding the conversation away from this interesting but secondary subject.

"For disobeying my stepmother's orders by going into Yukiko's room. For talking to you—and to make sure I never talked to you again."

So he'd guessed correctly.

"She doesn't want me to tell anyone what I read in Yukiko's diary," Midori continued.

Sano leaned toward her eagerly. Here came the evidence he sought, from Yukiko herself, or as nearly as possible. "And what was that?" he asked, keeping his voice calm so as not to frighten Midori.

Midori wrapped his cloak more tightly around her. "Well . . . Yukiko wrote about firefly hunting. And about our brother Masahito's manhood ceremony."

She went on to describe both, obviously enjoying Sano's attention and wanting to keep it by drawing out the story. Sano let her talk, although he was uncomfortably conscious of the cold and of the rapidly fading daylight. He knew that valuable information comes, sometimes unexpectedly, to those who listen well. But he kept part of his mind on the path, watching for the guards.

"I didn't see that man Noriyoshi's name in the diary," Midori said. "Not once! And I know Yukiko wasn't in any hurry to marry; she always said a girl should be willing to wait until a suitable match can be made for her. Besides, how could she have met that man? She never went out without a chaperone, and never at night." A frown wrinkled Midori's forehead. "Except—"

Now Sano was glad he'd let her ramble. "You saw her go out the night she died? Did the diary say where, or why?"

Midori's answer disappointed him. "No. It wasn't then, it was last month. On the night of the full moon. I didn't see her leave, but I saw her come home very early the next morning. And I didn't have time to read that part of the diary—my stepmother stopped me. So I don't know where she went."

Last month. The wrong time entirely. Sano lost interest. He suspected that Yukiko had been killed right there at the Niu estate, anyway, and her body moved afterward. Increasingly eager to extract the relevant information and leave the mountainside, he said, "When we spoke in Edo, you said you had proof that Yukiko was murdered. Was it something you read in the diary? Will you show it to me?"

To his dismay, Midori just stared at him blankly. "I can't," she said. "My stepmother tore it up. And why do you need to see it, anyway? I just told you that it proved Yukiko didn't know that man. So she couldn't have committed *shinjū* with him. Isn't that enough? Can't you look for the person who killed her now?"

It was far from enough. Sano took two abrupt steps down the path, turning his face away from Midori so that she wouldn't see the devastation there. What a tragic waste this journey had been! All he'd learned was that, according to a little girl, Yukiko hadn't mentioned Noriyoshi's name in a diary that no longer existed. Anger swelled in his chest, directed not at Midori for misleading him, but at himself for hoping for too much. He had to force himself to turn back to her and say, gently, "Did the diary say anything else?"

For the first time since they'd met, Midori showed less than complete candor. Hunching her shoulders, she looked at the ground and mumbled, "No. Nothing."

To Sano it was obvious that she was lying. There was something else. Something crucial to his investigation. He wanted to demand, "What was it? Tell me!" Instead he knelt beside her.

"Even something that doesn't seem important could turn out to be helpful later," he said. "If you want me to find out who killed your sister, you must tell me everything."

No answer.

"Look at me, Miss Midori."

She sighed and met his gaze defiantly. "It didn't have anything to do with Yukiko dying," she protested. "It was about our family."

Evidently it hadn't occurred to her that one of her own relatives might have killed Yukiko. Now Sano watched sudden comprehension register on her face. She recoiled visibly, her small body scooting backward on the log. Her eyes beseeched him to banish her fears.

Sano hesitated. He hated to see her suffer more than she already had. But he understood the loyalty that bound her to keep her family's secrets and knew he had to break through its armor to learn the truth.

"Your family's affairs could have everything to do with Yukiko's death," he said as gently as possible.

Midori's teeth gnawed her chapped lips, drawing blood. At last she began to speak in a dull monotone.

"The day before she died, Yukiko wrote that she couldn't decide whether to tell what she knew about someone. 'To speak is to betray,' she said. 'To remain silent a sin.' After I read that, I looked back to see who she was talking about." Midori paused. "It was our brother, Masahito."

Young Lord Niu. Noriyoshi's blackmail victim, also in the power of a sister with a strong sense of right or wrong. Would she have pressured him to confess a misdeed, as she had the little girls who had broken a firefly cage? He was cunning enough to plan the false *shinjū,* and had access to plenty of loyal helpers. Crazy like his father, perhaps. Son of a powerful woman who would use her influence to protect him from the law. And, in the end, desperate enough to kill again to avoid exposure? The puzzle arranged itself into a picture whose logic and rightness Sano found immensely satisfying. Only one piece was missing.

With an effort, Sano controlled his rising excitement. "What did Yukiko know about Masahito, Miss Midori?"

Midori shook her head with the conviction that her earlier denial had lacked. "I don't know. All Yukiko said was—"

She frowned and pursed her lips in an effort to remember. Then she said, "For what Masahito did, the penalty is execution, maybe not just for himself, either, but for the whole family, who must share his awful punishment because it's the law. Yukiko said that the thought of death filled her heart with dread. But she was willing to die rather than live in shame and dishonor, because it's a samurai woman's duty. And she thought duty was more impor- tant than her loyalty to our family, even if she would condemn us to the same cruel fate as his by exposing Masahito.

"My stepmother came in then, and I didn't get to read any further," Midori finished. "I don't know what Masahito did, but it must be very bad."

Sano tried to imagine what Lord Niu might have done to merit such extreme punishment. Samurai were not subject to the same laws that bound commoners. Usually they were allowed to com- mit *seppuku*—ritual suicide—instead of being executed for their crimes. Only for very serious offenses involving disgrace to their honor were they stripped of their status and treated as common- ers. Arson and treason came to mind; sometimes murder, depend- ing on the circumstances, could also mean execution for both the criminal and any relatives who had collaborated in or even known of the crime. Without more information, Sano could only guess which Lord Niu might have committed. But he had no doubt that the need to keep it a secret had provided Lord Niu's motive for the murder of not only his sister, but of Noriyoshi and Tsunehiko as well.

"He killed her, didn't he?" Midori asked. "Because he didn't want her to tell?"

Wanting to spare Midori's feelings, Sano said, "Maybe not. After all, we have only Yukiko's word for what happened. Perhaps she misunderstood, or wasn't telling the truth in her diary." Objectivity forced him to consider both possibilities.

Hope kindled in Midori's eyes. Then she shook her head, fingering her shaven scalp. "No," she said mournfully. "Yukiko wouldn't lie. And she must have been sure. I know she was upset before she died."

Midori hugged her knees to her chest as if for comfort as well as warmth. Sano's heart ached for the pampered daimyo's daughter, sent against her will to a place she hated, to live a life of deprivation and servitude. It was the fate of many girls, but with a terrible difference. Other girls, sold into prostitution or given in marriage to cruel husbands, could find solace in believing they'd made a noble sacrifice, and in idealizing the families they'd left behind. Midori had to face the worst about hers. Sano hated his part in her anguish. He wished things could have turned out any other way. But whatever the outcome, innocent people would suffer when his investigation bore fruit. He realized that now, even if he hadn't when he'd impulsively begun.

"I'm sorry," he began, then fell silent. He couldn't think of any words of sympathy that wouldn't sound trite or insincere.

Midori didn't answer. She was gazing down at the village, her face pinched with misery.

The sudden ringing of the temple bell broke the silence and made them both jump. Its deep, resounding peals echoed across the mountains and lake, signaling the evening rites.

Midori cast a nervous glance uphill. "I'd better go back now, before anyone misses me," she said. "When the nuns catch me disobeying, they make me go without supper.'' Reluctantly she rose, handing back Sano's cloak. "Good-bye, *yoriki-san*."

She took a few steps, then turned and said, in a voice newly adult in its seriousness, "I want Yukiko's death avenged. I want her killer punished.'' Her face, too, had sharpened, giving Sano a disconcerting glimpse of the woman she would become: as formidable in her own way as Lady Niu. "If it's Masahito"—she swallowed hard, but continued bravely—"then so be it.''

Sano watched her small, forlorn figure climb the path toward the temple. Then he started down the mountainside. Tonight he could rest. But tomorrow he must begin the journey back to Edo, where he faced the onerous tasks of notifying Tsunehiko's parents of their son's death, and proving Lord Niu Masahito guilty of three murders.

17

Magistrate Ogyu bent to examine the stone bench that stood outside his tea ceremony cottage. Although the morning sunlight revealed no dirt, he ran his finger over its surface. He held the finger close to his eyes, frowning at the almost invisible film of dust on his skin.

"Clean this bench immediately," he said to the servant who hovered at his elbow. "Lady Niu will be arriving soon. Everything must be perfect."

"Yes, master." The servant began to sweep the bench with a small broom.

Ogyu turned to inspect the garden. He needed to make sure the gardeners had cleared away the dead branches from the flagstone path and arranged leaves in an attractive pattern on the pond. But his movement crackled the paper tucked into his sash. Unwillingly, but also unable to stop himself, he drew out Lady Niu's letter, which he'd received yesterday. He read it for what must be the twentieth time, skipping over the formal salutations to the heart of her message:

In view of recent events, I feel it is imperative that we meet and plan our strategy for dealing with their ramifications.

The "events" she referred to could only be Sano Ichirō's secret visit to the Temple of Kannon and the murder of the boy Tsunehiko. Ogyu's spies had reported both to him, the only out-of-the-ordinary things to happen over the past three days. He wondered why Sano had told the seemingly pointless lie about Mishima. But whatever the reason, it was a matter between superior and subordinate, best handled privately. Tsunehiko's death was an unfortunate but all too common highway tragedy. What had these incidents to do with Lady Niu?

Ogyu could only guess. His uncertainty had kept him awake last night and soured his stomach; he still felt nauseated despite the infusion of bamboo ash he'd taken. Added to his worries was the disturbing news that one of his Edo informers had brought just this morning: Sano had not stopped investigating the *shinjū*. The day before he left, he'd interviewed both the actor and a wrestler. Ogyu didn't think Lady Niu had found out yet; his informers in those quarters were better than anyone's except the shogun's. But he knew she soon would, and that she would blame him for not seeing that Sano followed orders. The thought of her displeasure worsened Ogyu's sickness. Hot, acrid bile rose in his throat as he remembered how she could ruin him if she chose. A curse on Sano Ichirō, that stubborn, disobedient fool! Would that he'd never seen the man!

Cramming the letter back into his sash, Ogyu tried to dismiss his worries. He could handle Lady Niu. He need only practice the skills he'd honed to perfection over the years. Manipulation. Verbal swordplay. Spotting the advantage and seizing it before his adversary had even noticed. Using the adversary's own strengths and weaknesses as weapons. And he could favor his triumph over Lady Niu by making sure the stage was properly set for their confrontation. He turned his attention to the tea ceremony cottage.

The small, boxy hut, with its thatched roof, rough earth walls, and bamboo mullions, looked like a farmhouse uprooted and transported to Edo. Ogyu usually enjoyed the contrast between it and his urban mansion. He enjoyed the effect of rustic simplicity, which he'd spared no expense to create. Money, he often thought, could buy even peace and serenity.

But today, his apprehension wouldn't let him regard the cottage with his usual complacence. The leafless garden seemed bare and unappealing. He'd planted cherry trees for spring, annuals for summer, and maples for autumn, but he'd neglected to include evergreens for winter. The ancient stone lanterns looked dingy and worn instead of picturesque. He'd spent hours placing the stepping stones that led to the cottage in an artistically irregular line. Now he had a sudden urge to rearrange them. The cottage's design didn't meet his approval, either. The kneeling entrance was too high, the windows too small. As the threat of Lady Niu's impending visit eroded his confidence, he saw the tea cottage for what it was: the second-rate creation of a dilettante who fancied himself a tea master.

Ogyu felt a spurt of impotent rage toward Lady Niu and Sano Ichirō, both of whom had so seriously disturbed his tranquillity of late. He sought an outlet for his rage.

"Come here, you!" he shouted to his servant. "See this spot you missed." He pointed to a tiny streak of dirt on one of the otherwise immaculate stepping stones. "Attend to it at once, and if your work is not perfect from now on, I will dismiss you!"

"Yes, master. Right away, master." The servant hurried to obey.

The fear in the man's eyes restored Ogyu's sense of power. Now he could picture himself emerging victorious from his clash with Lady Niu, just as he had from every difficult situation that had arisen in his long life. Smiling, he followed the stepping stones—which looked fine now—to the cottage. He slipped off his shoes and slid open the door to the kneeling entrance that stood at thigh height above the ground, designed to induce humility in tea ceremony guests. Ordinarily he would enter the cottage through the server's door in the rear, which led to the kitchen. But he wanted to view the cottage from Lady Niu's perspective. As he climbed inside, his smile widened. Today this entrance would serve another purpose. Lady Niu must kneel when she approached him, as she never would on any other occasion. The opening advantage would be his.

Inside the cottage, Ogyu cast an approving eye around the room. Flecks of straw gleamed in walls made of red-ochre earth. The central pillar was a slender tree trunk, irregularly shaped but polished to a subtle gloss. Rich woodgrain veined the unpainted rafters and columns. In the alcove, a scroll bearing a winter haiku hung above a crude black vase made by a primitive Korean potter. Yes, everything about the room met the highest standards of tea culture.

Ogyu had added one special touch, though, which he considered an improvement over traditional tea cottage design. Hidden beneath wooden grills, three sunken charcoal braziers burned. Ogyu saw no reason to sacrifice comfort for rusticity. In winter, the heat from the hearth, a square burner set in the floor by the host's place, was hardly adequate.

He went into the tiny kitchen and took from the cabinet a tea whisk and bowl, a box of the finest powdered green tea, ladle, napkins, slop jar, and water vessel. He filled the water vessel from an urn that held his water supply, then carried it into the main room and set it on the hearth to boil. The other items he arranged on a lacquer tray on the serving mat by the hearth. Then he knelt to wait for Lady Niu. As he often did before a tea ceremony, he relived his odyssey from his parents' country home to this cottage, just as rustic but far more costly.

He had been born Asashio Banzan, son of a minor vassal of a minor Tokugawa ally. In a province ravaged by civil war, he and his family had lived like peasants. As a precocious eight-year-old, he'd won the favor of his teacher at the fief's samurai school, and ultimately of the lord, with his scholarly aptitude. The prize: a job as page at Edo Castle.

At Edo Castle, he'd been physically the weakest and smallest of the hundred-odd pages, but by far the cleverest. His natural instinct for exploiting the weaknesses and desires of both his elders and his peers served him well. He traded help with work for protection against bullies. He lent money, arranged liaisons with women, procured drink and drugs, and covered up his colleagues' mistakes and misbehavior. In return, the other pages did his drudge work, and castle officials rewarded him with bonuses and choice assignments. He gave friendship in exchange for information he could use against his enemies. In this way, he'd perfected the political skills for which he was now famous. The years had seen him rise quickly to chief page, then clerk, secretary, administrator. But a man of his low origin could go no further.

Then came his marriage to the only child of one of the shogun's chief retainers, achieved partly by flattering his prospective father-in-law, partly by conducting covert smear campaigns against his rivals. He'd taken his wife's family name, Ogyu, and become his father-in-law's adopted son and heir. He'd risen to the rank of councillor. When his father-in-law died, the family wealth came to Ogyu, along with the old man's position: north magistrate of Edo.

With his spy network for eyes and ears, he'd run the city for thirty years, exercising an iron control that he hid under a guise of elegant nonchalance. Never had a hint of scandal stuck to him; he had always managed to hide the small acts of corruption he considered perquisites of his position.

Until recently, when one moment of carelessness and greed had brought him under Lady Niu's power.

Two years ago, the shogun had issued the first Dog Protection Edicts. Violators had begun appearing in Ogyu's courtroom. Most were poor peasants whose sentences he'd pronounced without a second thought. Then one day a well-dressed young man had come to see him.

"Magistrate Ogyu, I am the son of Kuheiji, the oil merchant," the man said, bowing as he knelt on the floor of Ogyu's office. "My father has been arrested for killing a dog. Tomorrow he will be brought before you for judgment and sentencing. I'm prepared to offer you a large sum in exchange for his release."

Ogyu studied the merchant's son, noting the signs of fear that the man's businesslike manner couldn't hide: restless shifting one moment, followed by unnatural stillness the next. "And what makes you think I would be open to such an offer?" he asked.

He'd accepted bribes before, but only when an offense was minor and the offender's guilt questionable. The shogun had informed him—in person, yet—that the Dog Protection Edicts were to be enforced rigorously, with no exceptions. Ogyu could lose his position, or even his life for doing otherwise.

"I meant no insult, Magistrate." The merchant's son was trembling visibly now. "As a dutiful son, I am pleading with you for my father's life and freedom. Here—I give you three hundred *koban*. And I swear on my own life that I will tell no one."

Ogyu had started to wave his hand in dismissal. The hand stopped in midair as he stared at the gold coins the man spilled out of a bag and onto the floor. With this much money, he could build a summer villa in the hills. But woe on him if the shogun learned of the bargain! Then he thought: how would His Excellency ever know? The glitter of the coins helped him think of more reasons why he should accept the bribe. He began to rationalize. The dog was already dead; punishing the merchant wouldn't bring it back to life. One small infraction of the law on Ogyu's part wouldn't jeopardize Tokugawa Tsunayoshi's chances of producing an heir.

"Very well," Ogyu said, gathering up the coins.

He'd freed the merchant, built his villa, and almost forgotten the matter. Then, last spring, he'd called on Lord Niu. Lady Niu waylaid him in the corridor as he was leaving.

After an exchange of pleasantries, she said, "A fine oil adds much to the taste of food. Even the dogs whom the shogun protects would agree, I think. Would you not pay three hundred *koban* for the best oil a merchant has to offer?''

To anyone else, her comment would have sounded idiotic. But Ogyu realized with horror that it meant she knew about the bribe. He'd lived in fear ever since. Now that fear prevented him from enjoying the memory of all his achievements. He couldn't think of his spectacular rise to power without fearing that he'd reached the pinnacle of a mountain, only to find himself poised to tumble down its other side. Was this the day Lady Niu would finally use her dangerous knowledge?

The sound of voices outside interrupted his thoughts. Lady Niu had arrived; the servant was ushering her into the tea garden. His mouth dry with anxiety, Ogyu went to meet her. He reassured himself that Lady Niu simply wanted a discussion, as her letter had said. He would talk her out of making trouble for him. Everything would be fine.

When he saw her sitting on the bench, he experienced another qualm. She was dressed with impeccable correctness for the cere-mony, as if she, too, saw an advantage in coming prepared to this meeting. Her black outer garment, worn fashionably off the shoul-ders, covered a black silk kimono patterned with the traditional winter combination of plum blossoms, pine boughs, and bamboo. Regal and beautiful as always, she rose when she saw him.

Ogyu greeted her in the prescribed manner, fighting uneasiness as he bowed. "My lady, welcome to my humble residence. Your acceptance of my invitation to take tea does me a great honor.''

Lady Niu bowed, too. Although she, as a daimyo's wife, out-ranked Ogyu, he was a man, a magistrate, and some twenty years her senior. Their bows reflected these considerations, with neither bending lower than the other. They'd begun their sparring as approximate equals, a fact that pleased Ogyu.

"On the contrary, Ogyu-*san*. It is your hospitality that does me the honor." Lady Niu's greeting also followed the conventional pattern. "The tea ceremony offers us a haven from worldly cares.

But havens can be temporary, or even illusory. Is this not so?'' Her lips curved in a smile. The cosmetically blackened teeth, meant to enhance her beauty, made her mouth look like a fount of death.

''Uh, yes. Quite.''

Her remark had no special significance, Ogyu decided as he left her at the cottage's kneeling entrance and went around to the server's door. She wasn't warning him that this peaceful moment must give way to conflict, if it hadn't already. With increasing trepidation, he passed through the kitchen and knelt in his place at the hearth.

He heard the splash of water as Lady Niu rinsed her hands and mouth at the basin outside, and a rustle of silk as she removed her shoes. Then the door slid open, and she entered on her knees. The humble posture failed to detract from her dignity, as Ogyu had hoped. Nor did her next comment relieve his nervousness.

'' 'Mountains and plains, all are taken by the snow—nothing remains,' '' she recited, reading the haiku on the scroll. She bowed to the alcove and took the seat of honor in front of it. ''Ah, such poetry refreshes me. I feel a great sense of leisure, as though I need not hurry back to the bustle of the world.'' She tucked her robes comfortably around herself, as if indeed preparing to stay a good while.

The purpose of the tea ceremony was the ritual Zen purification of body and mind, in surroundings that affirmed man's oneness with nature. But Ogyu had had another aim in mind when he'd invited Lady Niu. He'd hoped that the ceremony's rigid confines would somehow defuse a volatile situation. Lady Niu, with her refined manners, wouldn't speak of unpleasant matters within the sanctuary of the tea cottage. Now he realized that she was fully capable of using the ceremony for her own purposes. She'd already managed to gain an advantage over him by letting him know his scheme had backfired. Caught in a trap of his own making, he was now unable to get rid of her without rushing the ceremony and appearing an ungracious host.

Ogyu's hands shook as he wiped the inside of the tea bowl with a napkin. "A very astute observation, my lady," he said weakly.

Please, he thought, let something happen to end this farce of a tea ceremony! Ordinarily he would have taken his time wiping the bowl, enjoying its shape and texture; now, he gave it a few hasty swabs, barely conscious of his actions. Let an earthquake bring down the roof!

The roof didn't fall. Instead Lady Niu said, "The poem reminds me of a scene from a play that featured Edo's foremost *onnagata*." She paused, letting him absorb her words. "The play may have also had a line about thunder and lightning. I expect you know it? If not, a certain member of your staff might."

"Onnagata": Kikunojo. "Thunder and lightning": Raiden, the wrestler. "Member of your staff": Sano Ichirō. Ogyu felt faint as he translated Lady Niu's oblique references, automatically scooping tea into the bowl. She was telling him she knew that Sano had persisted in investigating the *shinjū,* and even the identities of those he'd interrogated.

"Yes. I mean no." Ogyu ladled water from the simmering urn onto the tea, wondering how in heaven her spies had managed to glean that information. His only hope now was to placate her— fast. "Please accept my sincerest apologies for . . ."

For what? She hadn't actually accused him of anything. He couldn't come right out and say, "For failing to stop Sano like you asked me to." Not with Lady Niu maintaining the pretense that this was an ordinary tea ceremony. Such a gauche and vulgar violation of tea convention would lose him whatever advantage he still had.

"For my miserable performance as a host," he finished, hoping she would understand.

Lady Niu did not acknowledge his apology. She was watching the stream of water splash into the tea bowl. "Good water is crucial to preparation of good tea," she remarked. "Do you get yours from the springs of Hakone?"

"No, no, from Mount Hiei," Ogyu stammered. Was it sheer coincidence that she should mention Sano's destination? Picking up the wooden whisk, he began to beat the tea and water into a green froth. He could feel nervous perspiration sticking his clothes to his skin. Now he wished he hadn't had the braziers lit.

"My stepdaughter Midori recently entered the nunnery at the Temple of Kannon in Hakone," Lady Niu continued. Then she shook her head, frowning. "Forgive me. Of course you—and at least one member of your staff—know this already." Pause. "Why else make such a long journey, in spite of a tragedy at Totsuka?"

Bowl and whisk fell from Ogyu's hands as he grasped Lady Niu's meaning. Foamy green tea spattered the floor. Moaning, Ogyu dabbed at it with his napkin. Midori was at the Temple of Kannon. That was why Sano had gone there: to question her. His lie made sense now, ideal as it was for disguising the real purpose of his journey. Such outrageous insubordination! Not even Tsunehiko's murder had stopped him. And how humiliating for Ogyu to learn of it this way. Why hadn't his spies found out and told him? For what did he pay them?

"I didn't know your stepdaughter had become a nun," Ogyu babbled, clutching the fallen bowl. "Forgive me, I didn't know she was in Hakone. My apologies for my clumsiness."

Somehow he managed to clean up the mess. Under Lady Niu's bland stare, he prepared a fresh bowl of tea. She was angry, although she didn't show it. A fresh wave of nausea lapped at Ogyu's stomach. She would destroy him. Clinging to the tea ceremony's false semblance of normalcy, he passed Lady Niu the tea bowl.

She turned it in her hands as she examined it in accordance with the ritual. "What a beautiful bowl," she said, stroking the rough glaze with a fingertip. "When I drink, I shall think of the potter who made it and those illustrious persons who have drunk from it before me."

Hearing her meaningless, conventional words, Ogyu went limp

with relief. She'd finished what she'd come to say. She was satisfied with conveying her displeasure and wouldn't harm him.

"You are too kind, my lady," he said gratefully.

Released from fear and uncertainty, he began to enjoy the ceremony. Lady Niu drank and complimented the tea. She wiped the bowl where her lips had touched and passed it back to him, reciting a poem she had written. Ogyu drank and capped her poem with one of his own. He poured the dregs into the slop jar, and they repeated the process again, then again. Ogyu's giddy relief raised him to new heights of eloquence. His conversation had never sparkled so. Surely he'd never before hosted the ceremony with such elegance. And Lady Niu was the perfect companion: beautiful, literate, her manners unimpeachably proper. Ogyu could almost like her.

Seeing her out the gate, he gushed, "Thank you, my lady, for honoring my poor cottage with your exalted presence. It would be more than I could hope for to have you come again. How can I secure your promise? Just name your request."

"The pleasure and honor are all mine," Lady Niu answered, inclining her head. "There is one thing you can do for me. If you will permit me to speak plainly?"

A pang of fear hit Ogyu's stomach. "Of course," he said, involuntarily hunching his shoulders and trying to smile. Nausea returned as he realized that she'd merely postponed the real purpose of her visit to avoid spoiling the tea ceremony. What a fool he must have seemed to her, exuberant in his false sense of security! And now he'd played right into her hands.

Lady Niu's gaze turned cold and hard. All pretense at graciousness fell away as she said, "Sano Ichirō's inquiries have aroused the interest of the *metsuke*." The last word issued from her mouth like a drop of poison.

"The shogun's spies?" Ogyu blurted, aghast. The last thing he wanted was to draw attention to the workings of his department. Who knew what might come to light? "Are you sure?"

"I have it from a very reliable source," Lady Niu said. "What is more, they are entertaining the thought that my stepdaughter Yukiko and that man Noriyoshi were murdered, as your *yoriki* so obviously believes."

"Then it was murder," Ogyu whispered, clasping his hands to still their trembling. How awful if the shogun should think he'd tried to cover up such an important crime! It would mean a reprimand at best; demotion at worst. Now he wished he had listened to Sano. But he had truly believed the deaths a *shinjū*. Who could blame him for agreeing to spare the Nius the trouble of an inquiry? No one knew the hold Lady Niu had upon him.

Lady Niu shook her head impatiently. "Do not be ridiculous," she said. "It was suicide. The *metsuke,* those despicable schemers, allow themselves to be carried away by the idea of a scandal in Lord Niu's house, and all the opportunities such a scandal would create. Why, imagine the wealth that would pour into the Tokugawa coffers if they could strip my husband of his fief!" Her voice harshened with passion. "But they are about to begin their own investigation. This we must prevent."

"Prevent," Ogyu repeated, amazed that a mere woman should presume to match wits with the shogun's men. "But how?"

Lady Niu gave a flat, humorless laugh. "That is for you to decide, Magistrate Ogyu-*san,*" she said, emphasizing his title.

"Me? Why? How?" Ogyu's queasy stomach churned at the thought of entering such a dangerous conspiracy. Imagining the ruin of his career and possibly even exile or death, he feared he would complete his disgrace by vomiting in front of her.

"Why should be obvious." Lady Niu opened the gate. "And how is for you to decide." She stepped outside. A maid came forward to help her into her waiting palanquin. Over her shoulder, she said, "Just remember the oil merchant, and I am sure you will think of something." Then she was gone.

Ogyu closed the gate and leaned against it, eyes shut, as sour waves of panic and sickness weakened him. He took deep breaths through his mouth, fighting for control of his body and emotions. Remember who you are, he told himself. You have triumphed before; you will again. He remembered his rival for the position of chief page all those years ago; he'd framed the boy for thievery and secured the job himself. During his tenure as magistrate, he'd survived periodic attempts to unseat him; he'd used his connections and influence to have his detractors transferred to posts far from Edo. Now he tried to deny that Lady Niu's was a more serious threat than any other he'd faced.

Gradually strength returned. Ogyu opened his eyes and staggered toward the door. He wondered why Lady Niu was so anxious for him to prevent the investigation and so willing to take extreme measures to see that he did. Then concern for himself overrode his curiosity. He must act now to avoid ruin. Miraculously, though, he felt less fear than he had before the meeting. The threat, its size and shape now defined, began to seem more manageable. He actually smiled as he entered his mansion. He was no fool, but a cunning and powerful magistrate. He always knew when a situation required a bold stroke instead of circumspect maneuvering. This instinctive knowledge was another of the talents that had enabled him to rise to his present position. However, as a man of refinement and fastidious tastes, he wouldn't dirty his own hands.

To the servant who met him in the entranceway, Ogyu said, "Send for *Yoriki* Yamaga and Hayashi at once."

He must give the orders. But others would act to prevent the *metsuke* investigation and to end Sano Ichirō's interference in the Nius' affairs once and for all.

18

A sudden pounding of hoofbeats scattered the crowd in front of the noodle restaurant where Raiden sat finishing his midday meal. The sumo wrestler looked up from his bowl to see two horsemen in full battle regalia: richly decorated leather armor, metal helmets and face masks. Swords drawn, they brought their galloping mounts to a halt in front of him.

"You, there!" one of them called.

Raiden uttered a cry of dismay at the dust that the horse's hooves had thrown onto his food. He glared up at the riders. Flinging the bowl aside, he stood, arms folded, legs apart.

"You mean me?" he growled at the lead rider.

"Yes. You." The rider's mask distorted his voice but did not disguise its implicit threat. Two cold eyes returned Raiden's glare. "Are you Raiden, the wrestler?"

Raiden fell back a step. His anger subsided as the first prickings of fear started within him. He recognized the crests on the riders' armor and the winged ornaments on their helmets. These were *yoriki,* whose rare appearances in the streets always meant big trouble for someone.

"What if I am?" Raiden said, trying to sound brave. But his voice quavered, and his heart began to thud.

Instead of answering, both *yoriki* jerked their horses' reins. The horses pranced backward, clearing the street in front of Raiden. The *yoriki* who had spoken gave a piercing yell:

"Take him!"

At once a pack of men descended on Raiden. Two grabbed his arms and pulled him away from the restaurant. The others surrounded him, clubs raised. Beyond them, Raiden saw three *doshin* with *jitte* in hand, four other men who each carried a stout ladder, and a crowd of avid onlookers.

Raiden's confusion and panic increased. He struggled to free himself. "Hey, let me go. What are you doing? What do you want with me?"

"You're under arrest for the murders of Noriyoshi, artist, and Yukiko, daughter of Lord Niu," the lead *yoriki* shouted from astride his rearing horse. To the others: "Take him to jail."

"You're making a mistake," Raiden protested. "I didn't kill anyone."

But even as he spoke, he experienced an uncomfortable, familiar, and queasy sensation of doubt. The demon that lived in his mind sometimes affected his memory; people often told him he'd done things of which he had no recollection. He might have killed those people, then forgotten—he'd certainly hated Noriyoshi enough. But the thought of jail alarmed him. He must convince the police of his innocence.

"You've got the wrong man," he said.

Suddenly a blinding rage boiled up inside Raiden, just as it had at frequent, unpredictable intervals since he'd injured his head. His demon surfaced. With a roar of fury, Raiden threw his massive weight right, then left. The men holding his arms let go. He heard one of them crash into the restaurant amid the excited cries of the diners. Raiden charged at his other attackers. He swept one aside with his arm and downed another with a punch in the jaw. He plowed over the fallen men, kicking and trampling. But the *doshin*'s men outnumbered him. Their clubs began to rain blows upon him. Still Raiden fought. Possessed by the demon, he felt no pain and cared not whether he lived or died.

Then, as suddenly as it had come, the demon departed. Fear and panic returned. "No!" Raiden screamed.

He flung his hands up to protect his face—too late. Pain flared on his cheeks and mouth. He tasted blood, spat out one of his teeth. The clubs cracked against his arms, ribs, and back. He went down, sobbing in terror now. Pinioned beneath the *doshin*'s men, he lay gasping and whimpering like a wounded animal. The shouts of the crowd rang in his ears. Someone bound his wrists. The rope cut into his flesh. Hands dragged him to his feet. The ladders interlocked around him, forming a cage. A *jitte* prodded his back.

"Walk," its owner shouted in his ear.

Still whimpering in pain and terror, Raiden staggered forward. He ducked his head to hide his shame. He knew what he would see if he raised his eyes.

He'd seen parades like this before. The proud mounted *yoriki* in the lead; the *doshin* marching behind them; and last, the assistants with their bound and corralled prisoner. He'd joined the crowds who flocked to see the spectacle; he'd jeered and hurled rocks at the prisoners. Now he was the victim of those taunts. The rocks were aimed at him.

"This is a mistake," he cried as a rock struck his brow. He cowered within his ladder-cage, but more rocks flew between the rungs to pound his chest and back. "I'm not a murderer." He must make everyone listen and believe, before they reached the jail. Then it would be too late. "Please, let me explain."

He lifted pleading eyes to his tormenters. His spirits sank at the sight of the angry mob. The leering faces, merciless stares, flailing arms. The mouths crying out for his blood. "Please . . ."

Again the jab in the back. "Shut up and keep moving!"

After a while, Raiden's awareness of the crowd, his captors, and even his predicament faded. The simple act of walking required all

his thought and energy. Finally the procession halted, and Raiden
found himself outside the gate of Edo Jail with no clear memory
of the route they'd taken. Fresh terror restored his wits.

"Please, no, don't take me in there, I don't want to go," he
babbled as his captors disassembled the ladder-cage. Like everyone
else, he knew what went on in the jail. Once inside, he could
forget about convincing the authorities of his innocence.

No one spoke to him. They dragged and pushed him down a
foul-smelling corridor. He heard his own screams mingle with the
inhuman howls of the other prisoners. Someone opened a door. A
hard shove sent him stumbling into a dim room. He fell facedown
in the corner. Rough hands bound his ankles. The door slammed.

Raiden rolled over. He was alone in a tiny cell with high, barred
windows. Frantically he writhed on the floor, straining at his
bonds.

"Let me out!" he shouted.

No answer came. At last, weakened to exhaustion, he gave up.
He lay panting, bathed in sweat that soon turned icy in the draft
that poured through the windows. He forced himself to think.
Could he bribe the jailers? Failing that, his only hope of survival
lay in enduring the torture that he knew would follow. No matter
what they did to him, he must not confess to murder. Now he
called upon all the self-discipline his twenty years of sumo training
had instilled in him. With relief, he felt his mind grow quieter as
fear receded. Courage flowed through him, the way it did when
he stepped into the ring.

The door swung open. Two jailers entered the room. Each
carried a long staff; each wore a spear and a whip at his waist.
Raiden kept his eyes off the men and their weapons and concentrated his attention inward. Let them do their worst.

The shorter jailer closed the door and stood beside it, leaning
on his staff. The other, a huge brute with one eye sealed shut by
shriveled scar tissue, towered over Raiden.

"Ah, Raiden, the mighty warrior," he mocked. "Lying on the

floor like a trussed pig. Now tell me the truth: did you kill Niu Yukiko?''

"No. I did not. And if you leave me unharmed, I will reward you handsomely.''

One-Eye laughed. "With what?'' He leaned over, and with one vicious yank tore off Raiden's threadbare kimono. He found the money pouch and emptied three *zeni* from it onto the floor. "This?'' To his companion, he called, "Shall I prove that the great Raiden lies?'' He flung aside his staff and drew his whip.

The whip whined through the air. It lashed against Raiden's chest with a crack of fiery agony. Raiden gasped, but managed not to scream.

"I didn't kill her,'' he whispered.

"Yes, you did,'' One-Eye said. "You killed her, and you killed Noriyoshi, and then you threw them both into the river. Admit it!''

"No.''

The whip whined again. "You killed them.''

"No.''

"Yes. Say it: I killed Niu Yukiko. I killed Noriyoshi.''

Over and over came the whip and the accusations. Raiden's world shrank to a space that contained only his anguish and the jailer's ugly face. He imagined that he was being punished for all the things his demon had done. Mauling other wrestlers, tearing up the practice room, wrecking teahouses and brothels. But none of it was his fault. He wasn't a bad man, just an unfortunate one.

"No. . . . wasn't me . . . don't deserve this. Good man . . . good samurai. No. No.'' The words blubbered from his bloody, swollen mouth.

Then One-Eye went to work with his spear. Tears ran down Raiden's face as it gouged his flesh. His muscles shrieked their agony; his bladder and bowels loosened. The floor beneath him grew slick with his blood, urine, and feces. Still he managed to repeat:

"No. I didn't kill anyone."

Finally One-Eye stepped back. "He's a tough one," he said to his companion. "Maybe he's telling the truth."

Raiden's battered body untensed, savoring the respite from torture. Cautious hope stirred in his pain-befogged mind. Were they going to give up?

The short jailer mumbled something Raiden couldn't understand. Then they both left the cell, slamming the door behind them.

"Merciful Buddha," Raiden whispered thankfully.

Now his tears flowed in relief as he waited for someone to come and free him. But he grew uneasy as time passed and no one came. What was taking them so long? The ropes had numbed his hands and feet; he wanted them untied, now. He wanted to leave this terrible place. He wanted a bath, a drink, and medicine for his wounds.

"Hey," he rasped. "Come back. Let me out."

The door opened. Through it came his two torturers. One-Eye's evil smile sent a thrill of fear through Raiden. A smoky metallic smell made his nostrils quiver. It came from the stone ewer that Short Man carried. Then Raiden understood.

"No!" he screamed. "Not *neto-zeme*! No!"

One-Eye was turning him onto his stomach. Without the strength to resist, Raiden pleaded for mercy. Facedown, he wept and slobbered against the filthy floor.

"No," he gasped as a spear sliced a long cut down his back. Gritting his teeth against the blade's sting, he said, "Please, I'll pay you anything, I don't have much, but I'll get the money somehow—*Oww*!"

He stiffened as One-Eye's hands stretched open the flesh on either side of the cut. He felt Short Man bending over him, tipping the ewer.

"*Aiiiii!*"

The molten copper trickled into Raiden's wound. Pain seared

his back, driving him to the brink of madness. As he screamed and sobbed, he could hear his flesh sizzle as it cooked. He imagined the wound's edges curling and blackening.

"Did you kill Niu Yukiko and Noriyoshi?" One-Eye's voice sounded distant, indistinct.

Still gripped by agony, Raiden couldn't answer. He screamed again as more copper poured into him.

"Answer me, pig. Did you kill them?"

With the part of his mind that could still reason, Raiden knew that if he confessed, he was finished. But he couldn't take any more *neto-zeme*. The suffering was unbearable, like nothing he'd ever experienced before, or wished to experience again.

"I don't remember," he wailed, hoping the truth would satisfy his torturers.

But One-Eye's derisive laughter assaulted his pain-dazzled senses. "You killed them. Confess!"

Suddenly a flood of liquid fire cascaded onto Raiden's back. His scream rose so high it caught in his throat. Short Man had dumped the ewer's entire contents on him. The copper spread across his skin, burning as it went. Raiden's arms and legs jerked in wild spasms. Involuntary sobs convulsed him. His courage and resolve dwindled to nothing.

He gulped and managed to choke out, "Yes. I killed them."

Afterward, Raiden was barely conscious of being carried from the jail and transported to the Court of Justice on a litter. Through a cloud of pain and confusion, he heard the old, bald magistrate say in a reedy voice, "Raiden, you have confessed to the murders of Niu Yukiko and Noriyoshi. I sentence you to death."

Then a cold, nightmarish journey by litter, during which he slipped in and out of delirium. He dreamed of wrestling a faceless opponent in a match that wouldn't end. Somehow he knew that the opponent was his demon, the other self he'd fought and hated for the past three years. The audience jeered and stamped their feet. He was stumbling backward out of the ring . . .

Raiden awoke. He was lying on the ground, looking up at a pale, colorless sky. Wisps of fog swirled around him; the sun's ghostly white globe floated near the horizon. Somewhere nearby, water lapped at the shore. The ring and his opponent had vanished, but Raiden still heard the audience stamping and jeering. He turned his head, wincing at the pain that his effort caused. Horror shocked him into alertness.

"Oh, no," he murmured.

The jeering audience was a flock of ravens. They fluttered and squawked as their beaks tore at two rotting, headless corpses that lay on the ground near Raiden. Beyond them, men were assembling a rough wooden cross. Their hammers produced the stamping sounds he'd heard in his dream. This was the execution ground by the river. What a disgraceful place for a samurai to die!

Shame combined with his sorrow over losing his life, forming a huge, wordless ache that consumed Raiden. A sob rose in his throat; he swallowed it. As a last gesture to the samurai code of bravery, he waited with stoic resignation for an end to his suffering. At least the evil demon would die with him.

The men lifted him from the litter and bound him to the cross. Grunting with the effort, they raised it in a series of dizzying jerks.

Raiden found himself upright, facing the river. Severed heads on tall pikes dotted the bank. Corpses dangled from the two crosses beside his. Mist hung over the brown water, where a few fishermen watched silently from their boats. Raiden took one last look at the world. He closed his eyes and waited.

The executioner's ear-shattering yell.

A spear thrust into his chest.

A wave of agony to end all agony.

Raiden screamed as it swept him away. He heard his blood pounding in his head, a great red pulse that quickly began to fade.

He saw the wrestling ring that had formed the boundaries of his life, and the faceless opponent. He was falling, falling out of the ring. At the last moment, he seized the demon and dragged it with him. He felt a burst of victorious joy.

Then nothing.

19

Sano returned to Edo only five days after he'd left, but to him it seemed as though an eternity had passed.

As he rode, sad and travel-weary, through the bright afternoon streets, he saw with surprise that the New Year season had arrived. Housewives and merchants swept dirt out their doors, cleaning their houses and shops in preparation for New Year's Day, just three days away.

"Devils out! Fortune in!" they chanted.

Bedding aired on balconies and clotheslines. Moneylenders' shops did a brisk business as customers paid off the Old Year's debts. Pine boughs, bamboo stalks, and plaited paper ropes decorated every entrance. Rice cakes balanced on the lintels of doors and windows, placed there to bribe evil spirits to go elsewhere. In the marketplace, shoppers crowded around the stalls, buying holiday foods that they must prepare before New Year's Day, when no cooking was permitted. *Mochi* vendors pounded glutinous rice into the dense, pasty cakes that everyone would give and receive in great numbers. A cheery exuberance pervaded the city as its inhabitants anticipated the biggest festival of the year: *Setsubun,* New Year's Eve.

The holiday atmosphere didn't penetrate Sano's leaden misery. Never had his favorite festival meant so little to him. His solitary journey had given him too much time to brood. The urn containing Tsunehiko's ashes, which he'd picked up on his way back through Totsuka, made a bulky lump in his pack that served as a constant reminder of all he must do. He had to catch a murderer and avenge his friend's death without sullying his family's honor. And he must solve the mystery behind Lady Niu's efforts to stop his inquiries, while avoiding further attacks by the mysterious watcher. Now, more than ever, he needed to persuade Magistrate Ogyu to let him continue the investigation—and allow him to question young Lord Niu.

Sano's mouth twisted in a bitter grimace. What chance had he of succeeding? Ogyu, who had so zealously protected the Nius, wouldn't rejoice when he learned of Sano's visit to Midori. But without her statement, Sano had no case against Lord Niu. He would have to tell Ogyu about Hakone.

As soon as he entered the outer office of the magistrate's mansion, he knew something was wrong. All the clerks, messengers, and servants abruptly stopped working to stare at him. Sano paused in the doorway. Embarrassment spread a hot flush over his face. His ears rang in the silence. Then, just as quickly, everyone bent to their tasks, their voices lower than before, eyes averted.

The chief clerk spoke from his desk without looking up from his ledgers. "You are wanted in Magistrate Ogyu's reception chamber, *Yoriki* Sano-*san*."

With apprehension tensing his muscles, Sano walked through the corridor to the reception chamber's door. He hesitated there, hearing low conversation within cease at his approach. He took a deep breath and knocked.

"Enter," Ogyu's voice called.

His mouth dry and his hands clammy, Sano opened the door. He swallowed hard when he saw the three men kneeling, two to the right and one to the left of Ogyu's desk.

Bowing, he said, "Good day, Honorable Magistrate. Hayashi-

san. Yamaga-*san.*" And to the broad man with bold features who sat by himself on Ogyu's left, the last person in the world he wanted to see right now: "Good day, Katsuragawa-*san.*"

What did the presence of the two *yoriki* mean? And, more important, what was his patron doing here? He hadn't seen Katsuragawa Shundai since the visit he'd paid with his father.

The men returned his greeting with solemn formality. Ogyu motioned for Sano to kneel. Sano did, trying to read the four carefully expressionless faces.

"After much consideration," Ogyu said, "I have decided that you were correct about Niu Yukiko and Noriyoshi."

Sano blinked in surprise. "You have?"

"Yes. They did not commit *shinjū.* They were murdered."

In his relief and elation, Sano didn't think to ask why Ogyu had changed his mind. He thought only of the ease and joy of conducting an official investigation instead of an unofficial one. He imagined all the city's doors opening to him. With Ogyu's capitulation, the largest obstacle in his path to the truth had vanished. Already bursting with plans, he started to thank his superior.

"Honorable Magistrate, I—"

Ogyu raised a hand, silencing him. "Because you were absent from your post, I had no choice but to turn the investigation over to Yamaga-*san* and Hayashi-*san.* They will explain to you what has transpired."

It was all Sano could do to keep his composure as he turned to face his colleagues. The investigation for which he'd risked and suffered so much, turned over to someone else! A terrible sense of loss burgeoned inside him.

"After making the appropriate inquiries, we had the wrestler, Raiden, arrested," Yamaga said. "Yesterday he was convicted of murdering Niu Yukiko and Noriyoshi. Early this morning, he was executed."

"No." Horrified, Sano turned an incredulous stare on Ogyu and Katsuragawa. Ogyu's expression remained impassive; Katsuragawa's watchful. "This can't be. What inquiries? What makes you think Raiden killed them? What's going on here?"

Hayashi cleared his throat. "Raiden confessed," he said.

Sano laughed, a loud, harsh sound that made his colleague flinch. "Well, of course he did!" he shouted, remembering the tortured prisoner he'd seen at Edo Jail. "But I want to know what proof you had that he murdered anyone. Come, tell me about these so-called inquiries!"

"You dare insult me?" Hayashi's face reddened. He started to rise, reaching for his sword.

Sano rose, too. Much as he abhorred useless violence, he would gladly have taken out his anger on Hayashi if Ogyu hadn't interceded.

"Please, please." The magistrate shook his head. "Let us not squabble like children." To Sano he said, "Did you yourself not identify Raiden as a suspect?"

Sano, sinking to his knees again, understood now. Ogyu was still protecting the Nius; he'd merely switched tactics. How better to close the investigation than by arresting, convicting, and executing a scapegoat? And Sano had delivered that scapegoat straight into Ogyu's hands. Yamaga and Hayashi had probably chosen Raiden over Kikunojo out of reluctance to offend the actor's high-ranking patrons. The lowly Raiden had had no such protection. With growing despair, Sano felt the blood of another death upon his hands.

"I never believed Raiden was the killer," he protested. His defense could no longer help the wrestler, except to clear his name, but he couldn't let Ogyu close the investigation with the real killer still at large.

"Raiden told his jailers he didn't remember committing the murders," Hayashi said coolly, his anger under control now. "Which only means that the madness that prompted his crime also allowed him to conveniently forget it."

The words gave Sano pause. Maybe Raiden's "demon" *had*

222 / Laura Joh Rowland

made Raiden kill, then forget. Could he have been so wrong? Had Tsunehiko died because he'd failed to see Raiden's guilt and arrest him before the fatal trip?

"Raiden wasn't the only one Noriyoshi blackmailed," Sano said, fighting doubt and guilt by stubbornly sticking to his theory. "He had no reason to kill Niu Yukiko. And I think I know who did."

"Mere supposition," Yamaga scoffed. Hayashi murmured in agreement.

Although Sano was reluctant to reveal more of his findings after seeing how they'd just used his earlier ones, he needed the magistrate's official sanction. Quickly he explained what he'd learned in Hakone. "I believe young Lord Niu merits scrutiny," he finished. "And I should start by determining whether he or one of his men followed me to Totsuka and killed my secretary."

Prudence kept Sano from accusing Ogyu outright of covering up for the Nius. To give in to the angry urge to demand explanations, to vent his fury in an outburst, would only offend his superior. He would have to be satisfied with laying out his guilty secrets and dangerous theory. With forced resignation, he waited for the reprimand he knew would come.

But Ogyu just sighed and shook his head. "The fantasies of a girl-child. And I am not sure that you are any less prone to fantasy yourself, if you attribute your secretary's unfortunate demise to anything but a common highway murder. As to inflicting any more trouble on the Nius, that is out of the question. The true murderer has been . . . dealt with."

"But—"

"The matter is closed." As if to underscore his statement, Ogyu nodded to Yamaga and Hayashi. "You may go now."

With a swish of silk robes, the two *yoriki* rose and made their bows. Sano could feel their contemptuous stares on him as they left the room.

"I wish to continue the investigation," Sano said, although he knew that such open defiance could only worsen his position.

Ogyu exchanged an oblique glance with Katsuragawa before replying. "I am afraid you will not be investigating this or any other matter any longer, Sano-*san*. As of this moment, you are relieved of your post as *yoriki* of the city of Edo, and all its attendant duties and privileges."

The words hit Sano like a physical blow. He actually swayed under its impact. Such a disgrace, both for him and his family! Ogyu's face wavered before him. Sounds echoed; the room dimmed. Of the magistrate's words he registered only a few disjointed phrases.

". . . insubordination . . . incompetence . . . disloyalty . . . mistake to appoint you in the first place . . . character unsuitable . . . If you would please vacate your office and your quarters at once . . ."

He almost forgot the investigation that had seemed so important a moment ago. How would this affect his father?

"Sano-*san*. Do you understand why I am dismissing you?" Ogyu asked.

Sano opened his mouth, but no words came out.

Ogyu must have thought he intended to argue or plead, because he said, "My decision is final. There will be no appeals. Do you understand?"

"Yes, Honorable Magistrate," Sano managed to whisper.

"And, if you would be so good as to leave Hamada Tsunehiko's ashes with my clerk, an official representative will deliver them to his parents and offer condolences on behalf of the city."

Sano felt no relief at being spared the task. How could Ogyu deprive him of the chance to fulfill even this responsibility? But the numbing paralysis of shock kept him from speaking. He nodded, obedient when it no longer mattered.

"Then you may go." Ogyu paused, then added, "I hope you will find success in your future endeavors."

Like a sleepwalker, Sano rose.

Katsuragawa spoke for the first time. "I'll go with you."

Sano looked at his patron in dismay. He didn't want to talk to anyone. He wanted to clear out his office and rooms in the barracks and leave as quickly as possible. He needed time to plan what he would say to his father. But Katsuragawa stood beside him, a hand on his shoulder.

"We need to talk, Sano-*san,*" he said.

He firmly guided Sano to the entryway where they both retrieved their shoes. Once outside, he led the way down a quiet lane that ran between the mansion's wall and its neighbor's.

They walked in silence for a while. Sano glanced sideways at his patron, noticing again the features that had impressed him at their first meeting. The heavy shoulders that almost swallowed Katsuragawa's short, thick neck. The distinctive profile, with its full lips, large-nostrilled nose, and wary, unblinking eyes. The great curve of his generous but firm belly. Katsuragawa's posture exuded confidence; his controlled movements and slow, deliberate pace suggested power held in check. Beside him, Sano felt small and diminished, although he was taller than Katsuragawa.

"As your patron, I accept some degree of responsibility for what has happened to you," Katsuragawa said, looking straight ahead. "Perhaps, in my eagerness to discharge a long-standing obligation, I acted too hastily. I should not have directed you into a position for which you are so unsuited. But the ultimate blame lies with you, does it not?"

He turned to face Sano. "Did you even try to conform to your superior's requirements? Did you even try to make up for your lack of qualifications and aptitude with loyalty and obedience?"

Jolted out of numbness by Katsuragawa's reproach, Sano retorted, "What have my shortcomings got to do with anything? I was dismissed not because I performed badly, but because I performed too well. I uncovered a murder that Magistrate Ogyu wanted to keep hidden." He flung out his hands. "How can you expect me to give my loyalty to a man so corrupt that he would sentence an innocent man to death in order to perpetuate this cover-up?" He was shouting now, but he didn't care who heard or if he offended Katsuragawa. His urge to defend himself—against his own as well as everyone else's accusations—was too strong. "Do you deny that there is a cover-up?"

"Sano-*san*." Katsuragawa stopped walking and folded his thick arms across his chest. In a condescending tone he said, "This is exactly what I mean by your lack of aptitude. Of course there's a cover-up! And if you'd been the right man for your job, you would have immediately understood why it was necessary."

Ignoring Sano's shocked exclamation, he demanded, "What do you think would happen if it became known that someone in Lord Niu's household had murdered Yukiko? And what if you proved that the 'someone' was another member of the family? What if the shogun saw fit to put the entire clan to death and confiscate its lands as punishment? Imagine the effect this would have on the country!"

Katsuragawa lifted his hands skyward. "Thousands and thousands of *rōnin*, eager to avenge their master's death. The Niu allies and other daimyo, restless after ninety years of Tokugawa rule, looking for a reason to start a rebellion. Put these together and what do you get?"

He leaned so close that Sano could see the pores in his swarthy skin. "Bloodshed. Another five centuries of war. You would have this? Just to satisfy your curiosity about the deaths of a common peasant and one insignificant woman? You would not sacrifice the life of a wrestler—a cretin who injures because he cannot control his temper—for peace?"

Sano hadn't considered the larger implications of the murders, and Katsuragawa's explanation had a certain terrifying logic. But something about it rang false. In the first place, Sano couldn't believe that national peace alone had motivated Ogyu.

"Why didn't Magistrate Ogyu explain this to me?" he asked.

"He probably assumed you understood." Katsuragawa turned and resumed his slow walk.

Sano followed. "Do you really believe what you told me? Does Magistrate Ogyu? Wouldn't the murderer, if he is a Niu, be allowed to commit *seppuku?* The family wouldn't be punished, like commoners would. And the Tokugawas are strong. The daimyo wouldn't risk a revolt. They have more to gain by holding on to their lands, their wealth—and their heads."

When Katsuragawa didn't respond at once, Sano said, "Please, at least consider what I've said. And if you decide I'm right, will you use your influence to reopen the murder investigation?"

Instead of answering, Katsuragawa bent a glance on Sano that simultaneously pitied him for his naïveté and expressed outrage at his effrontery. Sano saw the futility of asking for Katsuragawa's help. Even if Katsuragawa didn't believe in the disaster scenario, he and Ogyu and the other officials were bound by their own complex web of obligation, which Sano couldn't hope to unravel.

Katsuragawa said, "Sano-*san,* I am prepared to help you find a new position. Perhaps a better one than you've just lost. I have many contacts." His shrug indicated that he had only to wave a hand, and a new place would open for Sano. "There is also the matter of your marriage, which I understand your father would like arranged as soon as possible. I would be glad to offer my services as a go-between, and to act as guarantor to the extent that I am able."

A new position, possibly a higher one with a larger stipend. And, with Katsuragawa negotiating for him and ensuring his financial security, a chance to marry into a high-ranking family. Sano could reclaim his social standing and some part of his honor. Such prospects would greatly ease his father's disappointment. Katsuragawa's offer was generous, and Sano had to consider it. But he knew a bribe when he saw one. And the ghosts of Tsunehiko and Raiden stood between him and his acceptance of it.

"You'll help me—if I stop investigating the murders?" he said, naming the obvious catch.

Katsuragawa's mouth twisted with distaste at Sano's bluntness. "All right, then: yes."

"I can't do that."

Katsuragawa halted in his tracks. "Are you a fool, Sano Ichirō?" he demanded. He grabbed Sano by the shoulders and shook him. "Can you not see what you're doing to yourself, to your father? Besides, you can do nothing about the murders now. You're not a *yoriki* anymore. No one is obliged to answer your questions or follow your orders. If you attempt to conduct a private inquiry, you will be arrested and severely punished for interfering with government affairs. It's over, Sano-*san*. Give up!"

"No." As he pulled free of Katsuragawa's grasp, Sano realized that with one word, he'd severed his relationship with his patron. An exhilarating sense of liberation came over him, tempered by fear. An influential patron who could provide introductions to the right people was an absolute necessity for a samurai who wanted to rise in the world. Without one, Sano could relinquish any hope of advancement. What had he done?

"Then you are a fool." Katsuragawa brushed his hands together as if dusting off the last vestiges of his obligation to Sano and his family. He started away down the lane. Before he'd gone ten paces, he turned.

"Do you know why Magistrate Ogyu and I decided you would make a good *yoriki*?" he said. "Because we thought your inexperience would render you so incompetent as to be harmless. Because your indebtedness would make you easy to control." Katsuragawa laughed in derision. "We were wrong about you then, but not now. If you pursue this ridiculous course, you are as good as dead."

. . .

Twilight was falling by the time Sano reached his parents' home, his horse still laden with the baggage from his trip, except for Tsunehiko's ashes, which he'd reluctantly left with Ogyu's clerk. Behind him trailed the two porters he'd hired to carry his possessions from the barracks. Dismounting, he helped them unload the bundles outside the gate, paid them, and sent them on their way. Then he stood alone in the gathering gloom, contemplating a thought just as dark.

As a samurai, he'd always known there might come a time when he must commit *seppuku* to avoid disgrace, or to atone for it. His training told him that time had come. After what had happened, only his ritual suicide could restore honor to his name and family. But although his warrior's spirit welcomed the release and purification of death, he must forswear it. His life was not his to take until he had avenged Tsunehiko's death, cleared Raiden's name, and achieved justice for Yukiko, Noriyoshi, and Wisteria.

Sano roused himself to stable his horse and put his bundles in the entryway of the house. He slid open the door to the main room. To drive a dagger into his own stomach would have been easier. He dreaded facing his father, dreaded also seeing again the mark of death on the old man. So at first he was relieved to find the room empty. Then he saw something that disturbed him far more.

The door that connected the main room with the bedchamber stood open. Through it he saw his mother standing by the window, her back to him, despair evident in the slump of her shoulders. His father lay on the futon. His eyes were closed. Low, rumbling coughs shook his body almost continuously. Fear shot through Sano. He'd never seen his father take to bed so early. And the amount of sickroom paraphernalia arranged by the bed—tea bowls, washbasin, crumpled cloths, medicine jars—indicated that he'd been there all day, or longer.

"*Otōsan?*" Sano said.

His father stirred. Slowly he opened his eyes. A frown crossed his sunken face. Then the frown disappeared, as though the slight movement of facial muscles had exhausted him.

"Ichirō," his mother said, turning with a strained smile. "What a surprise. We were not expecting you."

Sano walked over to his mother and embraced her. Always a sturdy, robust woman, she now seemed smaller and more frail, as if weakened by her husband's illness. Then he knelt beside his father.

"My son," his father whispered. "Why have you come? Shouldn't you be at your post? Even if your work is done for the day, the others will want you in the barracks."

Should he make up some excuse, Sano wondered, and tell his father that he'd lost his position and his patron only when—or if—the old man grew stronger? Surely it would be an act of mercy.

His father's emaciated hand emerged from under the quilt to touch Sano's. "Go," he said, making a feeble pushing motion. A cough shuddered through his body. "Do not shirk your duty."

"*Otōsan.*" Sano swallowed against the dry lump in his throat. He couldn't lie. His father's own uncompromising honesty had always demanded the same from him. "I'm sorry, but I have something bad to tell you."

He explained all that had happened, from the start of his investigation of the *shinjū* to his parting with Katsuragawa Shundai. When he finished, he braced himself for his father's recriminations.

But his father said nothing. Instead he blinked once, slowly. Before he turned his face away, Sano saw the weak light in his eyes grow dimmer still.

"*Otōsan,* I'm sorry," Sano said, less alarmed by the wordless rejection than by the knowledge that he might have just destroyed his father's last chance for recovery. "Please forgive me. Don't give up!"

He put his hand over his father's. It shrank from his touch. For

the old man, he no longer existed. Now he wished he had committed *seppuku*. His father would prefer a son dead than in this terrible
disgrace which would speed him to his own grave.

"*Otōsan!*"

His mother was beside him, tugging gently on his arm, urging
him to his feet. "Let your father rest," she entreated him.
"Wouldn't you like to put your things away and have a bath before
dinner?"

Sano turned away from her pleading eyes and anxious smile that
begged him to act as though disaster hadn't just shattered their
world. He walked to the door.

"Where are you going?" his mother called, hurrying after him.
"When will you be back?"

"I don't know."

A steady rain began to fall, drenching Sano's clothes as he
roamed the streets. It pattered onto the tile rooftops and dripped
off eaves into puddles that splashed under his feet. Lamplight made
hazy yellow squares of the windows he passed. The tops of the fire
towers disappeared in mist and darkness. An occasional pedestrian
hurried past him, hidden beneath an umbrella. From the alleys
behind the houses, Sano could hear the rumble of wooden wheels
and the clatter of buckets and dippers as night-soil collectors made
their rounds. The night soil's odor mingled with the clean scents
of wet earth and wood, charcoal smoke and cooking.

Sano had been walking for hours; he'd lost track of how many.
His legs ached, but his mind would not let him rest. All the
thinking he'd done hadn't reconciled him to either of only two
possible courses of action: to somehow mend the rift between him
and Katsuragawa Shundai and salvage his career, or to commit
seppuku. Either way, he must relinquish the murder investigation
that could only result in more disgrace and a dishonorable death
for both himself and his father. But that was what he could not
accept. His desire for truth and justice forbade such passive sub-

mission to defeat, even as the Way of the Warrior dictated filial piety and obedience.

So he wandered aimlessly through the city, turning corners at random—or so he thought, until he saw the moat and walls of Edo Jail looming before him. Torches flared on the ramparts; the guards at the gate wore rain cloaks over their armor. The whole edifice shimmered in the mist like a haunted castle. Sano had never imagined returning to the loathsome place, but he marched across the bridge and up to the guards without hesitation.

"I am *Yoriki* Sano Ichirō," he said, hoping they hadn't heard otherwise yet. "I wish to see Dr. Ito Genboku." Conscious thought hadn't provoked his desire to see Ito again, but now he saw the rightness of it. The doctor had made sacrifices for his own ideals. Sano could talk to him. Ito would understand his dilemma.

The guards hadn't heard, and they admitted him. Instead of escorting him through the prison, one of them led him around the buildings, through a series of courtyards and passages, to a hut near the far wall. Its one window shone weakly; smoke rose from the skylight.

The guard opened the door without knocking. "Ito. Someone here to see you." He bowed to Sano and left.

Since there was no veranda or entryway, Sano left his shoes on the ground beside the door, where the thatched roof's overhang provided inadequate shelter from the rain. It didn't matter; they were soaked anyway. He ducked his head to avoid hitting the low door frame.

He was standing at the threshold of a single room that occupied the entire hut. Ito knelt in the middle of the floor beside a small charcoal brazier, lamp and book in front of him. In the corner, Mura the *eta* was washing clothes in a bucket. The doctor regarded Sano without surprise.

"Somehow I always thought you would return," he said. "Don't just stand there shivering, come and warm yourself. Mura-*san*? Sake for our guest, please. And a bowl of rice gruel."

232 / Laura Joh Rowland

Mura went to a makeshift kitchen composed of a one-burner stove and a few crowded shelves. Sano knelt by the brazier, grateful for its heat. He hadn't realized how cold he was. Great shudders racked his body and rattled his teeth. He couldn't hold his trembling hands still over the coals.

Without speaking, Ito rose. From the cabinet he took a quilt and brought it to Sano.

"No, thank you," Sano said. The cabinet had held just the one quilt, his host's own.

Ito continued to hold out the quilt. "Take off those wet clothes and put this around you, or you'll be sick." He added, "Please oblige me. I get few chances to offer hospitality."

Sano did as he was told. He drank the heated sake and ate the steaming gruel that Mura brought him. When warmth returned to his body, he told Dr. Ito everything that had happened since they last met.

Ito listened without comment. When Sano finished, he said, "What will you do now?"

"I don't know," Sano admitted. "I thought you might help me decide."

"I see. And why do you wish my advice?"

"Because you understand what it's like to be in this situation. And because I value your opinion."

Ito studied him in silence for a moment, his gaze stern but not without sympathy. Finally he said, "Sano-*san*, when I was convicted, I lost my home, my wife, my family, my wealth, my position, my servants, the respect of my peers, my health. My freedom. This room and the morgue are my entire world.

"I still have my studies"—he gestured toward the book—"and one friend, Mura, who helps me because he chooses to. But everything else is gone. I live in disgrace; I will die in disgrace. Often my pain and shame are almost unbearable. So I am the last person who would advise you to throw away your future prospects for the sake of your ideals."

Sano felt like a man who has opened a secret treasure box only to find nothing inside. Somehow he'd expected more from Ito than the same conventional words he could have heard from anyone else.

Then Dr. Ito said, "But I will not tell you to forsake your ideals, either. You would not be able to live with yourself if you did." He paused, gazing at Sano with a strange mixture of pity and approval. "I know this because I see much of myself in you.

"Giri, ninjō," he finished with a sigh. *"Tatemae, honne."*

"Yes." Sano nodded, thinking how well his situation illustrated the two classic conflicts Ito had cited: duty versus desire, conformity versus self-expression. Eternal and unresolvable.

"Each man must decide for himself what matters most," Ito began.

Sano waited. The flickering lamp made a hollow of brightness that contained only him and Ito. For now, the outside world didn't exist.

"Each man must know when he has decided, and know what his decision is. I think you do, Sano-*san.*"

Sitting perfectly still as he absorbed Dr. Ito's words, Sano gazed with unfocused eyes into the lamp's flame. Images began to form in his mind. His dying father, symbol of the duty set out for him in the Way of the Warrior. Katsuragawa Shundai, who represented the status and rewards he could attain if he fulfilled that duty. But other images superseded these: Yukiko's body burning on its pyre; the weeping Wisteria; Raiden's bewildered face; Tsunehiko laughing as he rode along the Tōkaido. These images burned brighter than the others, lit as they were by the fire of Sano's need for truth and justice. Time passed. The fire consumed the tangle of his uncertainty, leaving his mind clear and his head light. His breath escaped in a short laugh directed at his own self-delusion. He realized that Dr. Ito was right. He had decided, and he would continue his hunt for the murderer. Even if it meant sacrificing security and prosperity, and even his life. Honor must return to him as a result of following his own path, or not at all. And his father's life depended upon his self-redemption. All his walking and thinking had been nothing but an attempt to avoid acknowledging these facts.

"Thank you for your hospitality and your insight, Ito-*san*," he said. "Both have helped me beyond measure. But I mustn't impose upon you any longer."

He started to rise, feeling strengthened by the doctor's solicitude but no more at peace than he had been when he'd arrived. With no authority and nothing but his own inadequate skills to rely upon, how would he bring a powerful, seemingly invincible murderer to justice?

"It is late," Ito said. "The city gates will have already closed. You cannot return home tonight. Mura will make a bed for you here. Sleep, and in the morning you will have the strength and wisdom to do whatever you must."

20

The next morning found Sano back in the daimyo district. Dressed in a peasant's shaggy straw rain cape and wide straw hat, he walked up and down the wide boulevard in front of the Niu's *yashiki,* ostensibly collecting litter, but in reality watching their gate. Every so often he skewered some trash with his pointed stick and put it in his basket, hoping he could convince the guards that he was a street cleaner with every right to loiter outside their lords' houses. He couldn't let them identify him as ex-*yoriki* Sano Ichirō, barred from the Niu estate and keeping secret surveillance on young Lord Niu. If the Nius or Magistrate Ogyu found out what he was doing, he would be arrested, if not killed on the spot.

Sano pretended to scan the street for debris, while watching for Lord Niu to make an appearance. Subterfuge didn't come naturally to him, but he had no choice except to wait and hope Lord Niu would lead him to evidence that he'd committed the murders. He had no authority or help, as Katsuragawa had reminded him, not enough money to buy answers, and no other way to avoid the ubiquitous Edo spies. The memory of what Midori had told him about Yukiko's diary flashed through his mind. He had no other way of learning what Lord Niu had done that he would kill to hide.

Despite his minimal chance of success, Sano experienced a curious buoyancy of spirit. He was now free to use unconventional means of detection, and he had unlimited time at his disposal. He had no responsibilities to anyone but himself. He could pursue truth and justice as he chose, and somehow save his father's life. A true *rōnin,* he could live—or die—by his own wits. Although he yearned for the security of a master, his new freedom filled him with a terrifying exhilaration. The future had opened up before him, blank, yet hinting at unknown possibilities.

But his necessary disguise anchored Sano to the grimness of here and now. The cape, though it protected him from the chill drizzle, chafed his neck and wrists. Cold mud oozed through his straw sandals and into his socks; every step squished. And how humiliating for a samurai to dress like a common farmer! He also felt naked and vulnerable on foot, with his only weapon the short sword tucked into his sash under the cape. Missing his horse and his long sword, which he'd left behind because they marked his rank, he hoped he wouldn't need them. He was glad to discover, though, that his costume made him virtually invisible; people hurried past without glancing down from their horses or out from under their umbrellas at him.

Thirty-seven paces brought him to Lord Niu's gate. He took his time scooping horse droppings into his basket. No one entered or left the *yashiki.* Finally, not wanting to attract attention by staying too long in one place, Sano moved on. He left a few droppings as an excuse to return.

He looked casually over his shoulder whenever he picked up a scrap of debris. Reaching the end of the street, he turned and worked his way back again. This time three samurai wearing the Niu dragonfly crest entered the gate. Two more passes later, they came out. Still Lord Niu didn't appear. Sano began to feel increasingly conspicuous. The street was free of litter now, and he wished someone would drop something so he would have a legitimate reason to stay. He lingered outside the Nius' *yashiki* for as long as he dared, then started on another tour.

"Hey, you!"

At first, Sano didn't respond. People didn't address a samurai that way. Then he remembered his disguise and turned toward the voice.

"The street is clean enough," called one of the guards from the Niu gatehouse, "and I'm sick of looking at you. Get lost, you dirty beast!"

Dirty beast! All thirty years of Sano's samurai upbringing rebelled against the insult. Furious, he stared at the guard. An angry retort sprang to his lips. He dropped his stick, and his hand reached automatically for the sword that wasn't there.

"Well, what are you waiting for?" The guard came out of the gatehouse and started toward Sano, brandishing a small object.

It was a lighted match.

Laughing, the guard called to his comrades, "Shall I make him dance?" To Sano: "If you want to keep your filthy rain cape and your filthy life, you'd better run!"

"Yes, master!"

Shaken, Sano bowed low in accordance with his humble status. He picked up his stick and made a hasty retreat around the corner. There he stood, struggling to control his anger and shock. That guard, fearing no harsher punishment than a reprimand, might have set him on fire, killing him the way Lord Matsukura of Shimabara had once killed peasants who'd failed to meet their rice production quota! Finally his body stopped trembling. His breathing slowed and evened. He inspected his surroundings and tried to think of a way to maintain his watch for Lord Niu.

The side street, half the width of the boulevard he'd just left, ran between the wall of the Niu *yashiki* and that of its neighboring estate. Pairs of guards stood sentry at plainer secondary gates through which continuous streams of porters and servants passed. Here Sano worried less that someone might challenge him. The guards were occupied, the foot traffic heavy, the trash plentiful. But he had little chance of seeing Lord Niu here. A daimyo's son would use the main gate.

Disconsolate, Sano paced the side street, wondering what to do now that his plan had failed. He could search for witnesses who had seen a man throw a large bundle into the river. He could go back to Yoshiwara and question the rest of Noriyoshi's friends in the hope that one had seen him with Lord Niu the night of the murders. Sano shook his head. How far could he get before someone penetrated his disguise and reported him to Ogyu?

Then, as Sano passed the Nius' gate for the third time, it opened to discharge four samurai carrying a black palanquin. Neither the palanquin nor the bearers' cloaks displayed identifying crests, but they bore the unmistakable stamp of quality. What Niu family member or distinguished guest chose to leave through the side gate? Sano peered at the palanquin, his curiosity frustrated by its sealed shutters.

Suddenly the shutters opened. The passenger spoke to the bearers, then quickly closed the shutters again. His face, partially hidden by a wicker hat, had appeared for a mere instant. But Sano recognized him at once.

It was young Lord Niu.

Although mystified by Lord Niu's stealthy departure, Sano had no trouble following the palanquin. Nihonbashi's crowded streets offered many hiding places and kept the bearers' pace slow.

Lord Niu visited a swordmaker's shop, talked briefly to the other customers, and left without buying anything. He went to a seedy martial arts academy frequented by *rōnin,* where he practiced his swordsmanship. Sano strolled back and forth in front of the open door, watching. Lord Niu fought with a steel blade instead of a wooden practice sword. Unhindered by his bad leg, he executed each thrust and parry brilliantly, his reflexes lightning fast. Match after match ended with his blade against his opponent's throat. His skill left Sano breathless with admiration. Would that he need never face Lord Niu in combat!

Afterward, Lord Niu and three fellow students went to a

restaurant near the academy. Sano followed the bearers' example and used the time to buy lunch from street vendors. Although he risked eating at the stall next to theirs, he overheard nothing useful. They were taciturn men who gave their orders and then ate in silence. Sano wished he dared eavesdrop on Lord Niu and his friends instead. At this rate, he might never see or hear Lord Niu incriminate himself. But he stayed, ready to pursue Lord Niu for the rest of his life if necessary.

His quarry had begun to exert a powerful magnetism on him. He was gradually coming to believe that Lord Niu had killed a blackmailer, his own sister, and Tsunehiko, all in an attempt to cover some earlier dreadful crime. Sano couldn't let the creature out of his sight. Hatred and fascination whetted his appetite for vengeance, and he accepted whatever hardships awaited him. He bought two *mochi* cakes in case the pursuit took him someplace where food wasn't available. He endured sore legs, frozen feet, and the ever-present threat of death, watching with a fierce sense of anticipation as Lord Niu came out of the restaurant and climbed into the palanquin.

To Sano's disappointment, the bearers began to retrace their steps home. Then, bypassing the daimyo district, they followed a circuitous path down winding streets, across the Nihonbashi Bridge, along canals, and through rich and poor neighborhoods, gradually heading north. Finally they left the city's outskirts and continued into open country.

Sano felt safe enough following Lord Niu through the Kanda district, where undulating wooded hills lay brown and gray beneath low, swollen clouds that continued to send down a thin, cold rain. Although the crowds had vanished, there was still plenty of traffic on the Okushudo highway leading into Ueno, including peasants dressed like himself. Then the bearers turned onto a deserted road that climbed a steep hill into the woods. Sano dropped farther and farther behind so they wouldn't see him.

Finally, fearing he might lose them if they turned onto one of the trails that branched off the main road, he sped up and took to the woods.

Firewood gatherers had cleared the ground of dead branches that might have slowed his progress, but Sano had to contend with other hazards. Rocks thrust their sharp points against his already sore feet. Puddles soaked him to his knees. An arrow stuck into a tree told him that he was in some lord's hunting ground. As he hurried to keep Lord Niu's palanquin in sight, he expected a party of mounted hunters to descend on him at any moment. To his relief, the trail ended a short distance ahead, at a wall with a roofed gate bearing the Niu crest. The bearers set down the palanquin while two samurai came out of the guardhouses and opened the gate.

Sano watched from the woods as the gate closed behind the bearers and the palanquin, and the guards returned to their houses. This must be the Nius' summer villa. With the daimyo in his province and the rest of the family spending the winter in town, Sano didn't expect to find the villa heavily guarded. He approached it at an angle, moving deeper into the woods, away from the road and gate. Then, as he neared the wall, he heard the squelch of footsteps on the damp ground. Quickly he crouched behind a bush to peer through it at the pair of armored samurai carrying bows and arrows. As they marched past, snatches of their conversation reached him:

"I'll be glad to get back to Edo. Too quiet here."

"Not tonight, though." Laughter.

What did that mean? Sano waited until he heard them talking with the guards at the gate. Then he hurried in the direction from which they'd come. Additional patrols, if any, would be spread out around the estate. He followed the wall's curve until he could no longer see the road or gate. He paused to watch and listen. No one was inside the observation towers mounted at intervals along the wall. The forest seemed deserted, its gloom deepening with the fading sky, quiet except for the steady drip of water from the trees. Sano stole up to the wall.

Made of earth and faced with flat stones fitted together without mortar, it rose high above Sano's head. He began to climb, his fingers and toes finding precarious holds in the cracks between the stones. His straw cape rustled loudly, and he winced at the noise. He pulled himself on top of the wall and lay there, looking down at the other side. There he saw more forest, similar to the one he'd just left—a natural-looking mixture of evergreen and deciduous trees and shrubs. It, too, seemed deserted. Sano waited a moment more. Seeing no one, he dropped over the edge of the wall. His cape rustled again as he landed. He hastily tore it off, burying it under a pile of dead leaves. The rain had almost stopped, and his dark cloak and trousers would make better camouflage in the coming twilight.

He stood up and began moving in the direction of the gate. A trail led through the woods, probably cleared to make a scenic walk for the daimyo's ladies. It curved and wound, then ended at the edge of a clearing. Ahead Sano saw a wide gravel path leading from the gate. His eyes followed it to the distant house at his left. Immediately he felt as though he'd gone back in time.

Built in a style popular some eight hundred years ago, the Nius' tree-shaded summer villa crowned a small rise in the land. The large main house, or *shinden,* a boxy shingle-roofed wooden structure raised on stilts, faced south. At the foot of its steep staircase rested Lord Niu's deserted palanquin. Two more guards stood watch over a door fronted by a wide veranda and sheltered by a pillared roof. Covered corridors led from each side of the *shinden* to similar but smaller houses. Diamonds of light glowed behind the window lattices of all three buildings. From each side house, Sano guessed, another covered corridor extended backward, enclosing a rear garden and ending in open pavilions. Behind this compound, more interconnected buildings would house family apartments, servants' and retainers' quarters, kitchens, and stables. He'd seen such dwellings in old paintings. Female authors of the Heian imperial court, such as Murasaki Shikibu and Sei Shōnagon, had written their poems, stories, and diaries in them. Prince Genji had carried out his romantic intrigues in the chambers, pavilions, and gardens. Lord Niu's coming here out of season, in an unmarked conveyance, suggested some more sinister purpose for the elegant villa.

Moving from tree to tree, Sano approached the rear of the house. The clearing paralleled the covered corridor he'd expected to find. He stopped just short of the rambling wooden family quarters and crawled under the raised floor of the pavilion at the end of the corridor. Reaching the opposite side, he peered cautiously out toward the *shinden*. The back garden contained a small lake with an island in the middle. Arched bridges connected the island with the shore. Sano jerked his head back when he saw two more guards standing on the rear veranda. His curiosity, piqued by the other guards' conversation, increased. Did all the daimyo keep such tight off-season security on their summer estates, or were these men here for a special reason? Were there more inside the house? He wouldn't get anywhere near Lord Niu with them around. Frustrated and exhausted, Sano squatted under the pavilion, wondering what to do next. He leaned against the curved wooden surface of a large object beside him.

Maybe its half-familiar contours sparked a sense of recognition in him; maybe his samurai training made him wary of things encountered in dark places where he shouldn't be. Whatever, Sano examined the object. As his eyes grew accustomed to the dimness, he saw that it was a boat. Not a flimsy craft for carrying ladies about the lake, but a sturdy wooden punt with an equally stout oar laid across it. Sano reached inside. His fingers touched tatami, rolled into a loose bolt. He probed the bolt and thought he felt something at the center. Keeping his ears strained for footsteps, he unwound it. He hoped the guards couldn't hear the faint rustle of the matting from this distance.

The last fold opened. Two soft objects fell onto the ground beside Sano. He picked them up. Triumph flared within him.

In one hand he held a sandal, made of straw and heavily worn on the inner heel. His other hand tightened around a coil of rope. He'd seen the sandal's mate in Dr. Ito's dissection room: it belonged to Noriyoshi. He would swear on his life that the rope had once bound the matting around two bodies during transport between here and their watery grave. Mentally reconstructing the murders, Sano imagined Lord Niu bringing his victims to the villa—Noriyoshi with the promise of money, perhaps, and Yukiko with a simple brother-to-sister command. Stealing up behind them to deal the fatal blows. Carrying the unwieldy bundle by horseback to the river's edge, where the boat waited. Then having the boat and its contents retrieved at his leisure. Sano thrust both sandal and rope inside his cloak. The first real smile in days tugged at the corners of his mouth. This evidence he could take to the authorities—not Magistrate Ogyu, but higher, to the Council of Elders. They would have to listen to him now.

But instead of making straight for town, he hesitated. He still didn't know why Noriyoshi and Yukiko had died. The absence of a motive weakened his case against Lord Niu. He must find out what it was, even if he had to stick with Lord Niu all night.

Inspiration came when he saw that the corridors leading from the pavilions to the side houses were elevated, too. He could look straight down the narrow, stilt-framed tunnel beneath the one adjoining his pavilion and see daylight on the far side. Carefully he crawled toward the light. Halfway there, he heard the guards' voices from the veranda. Would they hear him? It was darker under the corridor than under the pavilion, and he swept the ground ahead of him with his hands as he advanced. One bump against an unexpected obstacle, one tumble into a hole would alert the guards.

Sano had just reached the large space beneath the side house when he heard hoofbeats coming from the direction of the gate.

He flattened himself against the ground, arms over his head. The floor above him creaked as someone inside walked across it. Footsteps crunched on the gravel path.

A man called, "Hail, brothers! What took you so long? His lordship is waiting."

Sano missed the reply. The guards had gone to meet the new arrivals, who had stopped just out of earshot. He scooted to the front of the house. Now he heard voices raised in argument and could make out broken phrases:

". . . meaning of this?"

". . . insisted on coming . . . wouldn't deliver the goods otherwise . . . know he won't like it, but . . ."

Peering out from between the house's stilts, Sano saw eight men clustered on the path. The two guards faced four mounted samurai and two bearers with a palanquin. The gray afternoon had begun to dissolve into a darker gray twilight, and he couldn't see the newcomers' faces clearly, or distinguish any crests on their garments. But the guard had greeted them as comrades: they, too, were Lord Niu's men. Sano wished they would come closer so he could hear better.

Suddenly a loud rapping came from within the palanquin. The bearers eased it to the ground. The door opened and a small, stooped man burst out.

"Take me to Lord Niu Masahito immediately!" he yelled, his voice carrying across the distance to Sano.

The guards grabbed at the man. He darted away and ran toward the house. The mounted samurai galloped forward, blocking the stairs to the door. Thwarted, the man skidded to a stop. The guards seized him. As they dragged him back to the palanquin, he stumbled and fell sideways, his face turning toward Sano.

Even from a distance of some thirty paces, Sano saw and recognized the stained mouth and chin. The man was Cherry Eater, *shunga* dealer and former employer of Noriyoshi.

Sano smiled again as he grasped the significance of Cherry Eater's presence. Whatever business had brought the *shunga* dealer here must have once included Noriyoshi. Now, if he could just learn what that business was! He didn't believe Cherry Eater would come all the way from Yoshiwara, uninvited, just to deliver artwork.

The guards flung Cherry Eater toward the palanquin. He fell in a heap on the ground beside it.

"Unload the goods and take this pest back to Yoshiwara," one of the guards ordered the bearers.

"I won't go until I've spoken to Lord Niu," Cherry Eater shouted. When the bearers tried to pick him up, he kicked and thrashed.

Sano heard a door open, then Lord Niu's voice demanding, "Just what is going on here?"

Cherry Eater scrambled to his feet. "My lord, what a pleasure to see you," he simpered, bowing. "And to receive such great hospitality is an honor indeed." Even under the circumstances, he didn't—or couldn't—curb his wit. He took a few steps toward the house and dropped to his knees before the guards could grab him again. "I apologize for the imposition, but there is something I must discuss with your lordship."

"What is it?"

Although trees blocked Sano's view of the veranda, he could imagine the annoyance on Lord Niu's face.

"I am afraid that the price of my services has increased," Cherry Eater said. "Perhaps you would like to discuss the matter inside, in private?"

Lord Niu ignored the suggestion. "We had an arrangement," he said. "I see no reason to change it."

Cherry Eater rubbed his hands together, an ingratiating smile opening within his red birthmark. "Noriyoshi's death has made change regrettably necessary."

Sano expected Lord Niu to protest. But the daimyo's son seemed to lose interest in the conversation. "All right," he said impatiently. "How much?"

Cherry Eater named a sum that sounded outrageous to Sano. Was the dealer taking over Noriyoshi's position as blackmailer, or just charging more because his employee's death made more work for him?

Lord Niu didn't ask; he just said, "Come to the *yashiki* tomorrow. The money will be waiting for you." To the bearers, he called, "Get him out of here, and bring me what he's brought. And hurry. Time is short." The door slammed.

Sano watched the bearers reach into the palanquin. A wave of shock hit him when they lifted out an inert body wrapped in a blanket. They carried it between them like a sack of meal, toward the house. The man's head lolled. Sano drew a sharp breath as he glimpsed closed eyes and pale cheeks.

"He's dead!" One of the mounted samurai voiced Sano's thought.

Cherry Eater waved his hands. "No, no. Just drugged, as his lordship ordered. He won't wake up for at least two hours."

The *shunga* dealer got inside the palanquin. Then he stuck his head out and called, "I'm sure that's more than long enough, heh, heh, heh!"

Sano left his lookout point and shot under the corridor that connected the side house to the *shinden*. He had to find out what Lord Niu intended to do with the man. Was he on the verge of learning what hold Noriyoshi had had on Lord Niu, and why the artist had died? A moment later, the corridor creaked above him as the bearers shuffled along it with their burden. He crawled after them, back to the side house he'd just left. They stopped near the rear corner, and he heard a thud as they set down the body. Should he climb up and try to see inside the room?

Not yet: a pair of trousered legs was approaching the house. Sano shrank back into the shadows. The man stooped at intervals to thrust torches into the ground and light them. Soon a line of dancing flames surrounded Sano's hiding place and lit the path to the gate. Hurrying footsteps came from the direction of the servants' quarters. Doors opened and closed. When Sano crept over to look toward the garden, he saw maids carrying laden trays up the stairs to the main house. What now? Lord Niu and his men must eat, of course, but the commotion suggested something more. A banquet? Sano's stomach growled, and he realized he was hungry. Reaching inside his cloak, he pulled out a cake of *mochi*. He bit off small pieces and swallowed them. The dense, nutrient-rich staple that fed samurai during long journeys would silence his stomach before it attracted someone's attention.

Gradually the commotion subsided. A hush fell over the villa as night encroached. From the house above him, Sano heard nothing. No one passed. He waited with growing impatience, longing for action as much to warm his cold, cramped muscles as to satisfy his curiosity. At last he crawled to the side of the house and put out his head and shoulders. Seeing no one lurking among the dark trees, he slid the rest of himself out and stood.

He staggered a little, his legs stiff from crouching and crawling. The air outside was colder, but fresher; he breathed it with relief. Cautiously he moved along the side of the house, stooping below window level. At the corner room, he slowly straightened to his full height—and halted in frustration. Behind the lattices, the windows were closed. He could distinguish only vague, dark silhouettes inside the lighted room. He put his ear to the wall. This time he heard a faint moan. He had to see!

Sano examined the wall for cracks or holes, but found none. He ran his hands over the smooth, weathered wood. His searching fingers found a rough, circular spot about the size of a human eye. A knot. Maybe . . .

He drew his dagger, stuck it into the knot's center, and wiggled it. The knot held firm. Sano tried again. Did he feel a slight movement this time? He pulled gently. Ah, there . . .

The knot came out with an almost inaudible scrape that neverthe-less sent Sano hurtling back under the house. Had Lord Niu heard? Sano lay still, clutching his dagger and expecting shouts and chaos. But nothing happened. He waited for what seemed like forever. The villa remained steeped in silence. He crept out again. Still holding his dagger, he looked around, then put his eye to the knothole.

A ring of candles lit the naked body stretched out on the floor. It was not a man after all, but an adolescent samurai with a shaved crown and the long forelock that signified he'd not yet had his manhood ceremony. He lay motionless, eyes closed. An unnatural redness, perhaps from the drug, colored his slack face. Lord Niu stood over him, also naked, his manhood erect. Sweat sheened his muscles. The scarred and withered right leg was a monstrous deformity grafted onto the perfection of the rest of his body. His feverish eyes shone; his parted lips glistened wetly. Chest heaving with rapid, shallow breaths, he dropped to his knees beside the boy. One hand grasped his own organ and began to stroke it.

Sano, clued by Cherry Eater's parting remark, had half expected something of the sort. Now both disgust and disappointment rose inside him. Child prostitution, even in a grotesque form like this, was legal, common, and socially acceptable. Lord Niu was guilty of nothing but indulging himself outside the Yoshiwara licensed quarter. Even a refined young lady like Yukiko would have known this. And Lord Niu would neither have paid Noriyoshi nor killed him to keep such a secret.

Then Lord Niu reached behind him with his free hand and picked up a knife. He held it aloft, pointed upward, so that the blade sparkled in the candlelight. He stared at it as if mesmerized. His tongue passed once over his lips. The hand on his organ moved faster. With a slow, deliberate motion, he lowered the knife. He held it to the sleeping boy's neck. Just as slowly, he drew it across the rosy flesh. A thin line of blood welled against the blade.

Rooted to the spot in awestruck horror, Sano realized too late that someone had come up behind him.

21

There stood a woman, her eyes wide with fear. She opened her mouth to scream.

Instinct took over. In a flash, Sano seized her and dragged her away from the house and into the woods. He pressed her against him with one hand clamped over her mouth, the other holding his dagger before her face. She squealed and kicked. Locked together, they struggled. He could feel her heart beating as she tried to twist free.

"I won't hurt you," Sano whispered urgently against her ear. "Please don't scream."

Merciful Buddha, he didn't want to kill her! But he couldn't let her raise the alarm. Belatedly he recognized her: the Nius' maid.

"O-hisa. You remember me—Sano Ichirō. I came to the *yashiki* and to Miss Yukiko's funeral. Will you be quiet if I let you go?"

A nod and a whimper. O-hisa stopped struggling. Sano released her cautiously, ready to grab her again, or to run.

O-hisa turned to face him. Hugging herself, she nodded toward the house.

"He's doing it again, isn't he?" she whispered. Her face bunched, as if she might cry.

"Again? He does this often, kills children for his own pleasure?" Sano experienced anew the shock of seeing Lord Niu cut the boy's throat. He had to save the boy—if it wasn't already too late. He took two steps toward the house, remembered the guards, and stopped. They would kill him before he got near Lord Niu. But he had to intervene, even if he died in the attempt. Clutching his dagger, he offered a silent prayer for courage and strength. Then, before he went to his confrontation with Lord Niu, he turned to O-hisa. There was one thing he must know before he faced death.

"Did Yukiko know about this?" He assumed that Noriyoshi, in league with Cherry Eater, had known.

"No, no!" O-hisa's hands fluttered in vehement denial, and at first Sano thought she meant Yukiko hadn't known. Then she said, "He never killed them before. He just cuts them a little, then sends them home."

Sano didn't believe her. He'd seen the blood, and Lord Niu's desire for it. He ran back to the house and looked through the hole.

Lord Niu knelt in the center of the room, his back to Sano, a white under-kimono draped over his body. Beside him, two guards were wrapping the boy in a blanket. The boy's eyes remained shut, but he groaned softly. The superficial cut, cleansed of blood, encircled his throat like a red thread.

Relief forced a long, shaky breath out of Sano. Neither he nor that boy would die tonight. Sheathing his dagger, he returned to O-hisa.

"I didn't understand, either," she babbled, her voice rising. "It's my fault Miss Yukiko is dead!"

"Shhhh!" Sano took O-hisa's arm and pulled her deeper into the woods. "What do you mean? You didn't kill her—did you?" He could not believe that this frail, weepy woman was a murderer.

O-hisa responded in characteristic fashion: she burst into tears. Sano wanted to comfort her, but they couldn't stand there indefinitely. The patrol might arrive at any moment. He grabbed her shoulders and shook her, hard.

"Tell me what you mean," he ordered.

Halted in mid-sob, O-hisa glared at him in bewildered outrage. Then she blurted out, "Miss Yukiko died because I thought the young master was killing boys." With pathetic bravado, she drew herself up, head high. "Honor demands that I take my own life as payment, but I am a coward. So arrest me, please."

Sano let go of O-hisa and cast a nervous glance at the house. "Why don't you tell me why you think you're responsible for Miss Yukiko's death," he whispered. Here, finally, was the person who could tell him why Lord Niu had killed Yukiko and Noriyoshi. But if she didn't start making sense soon, he would have to leave.

O-hisa let loose a torrent of words, as if eager to share the secrets she'd kept for too long. "I came to work for Lady Niu last autumn," she said. "After three weeks at the *yashiki,* the house-keeper sent me here to serve the young master, who comes when his health requires that he leave the city. The weather was warm. The young master's window was open, and I happened to look inside as I was passing by. I saw . . . what you saw.

"And two nights later, the same thing, with a different boy! I thought he'd killed them. All the blood, and they lay so still. Later, the young master's men would come and carry them away. At first I told no one. It's not my place to inform on my master. But after the third time, I couldn't let him kill more boys. So . . . so I told Miss Yukiko, who was always kind when she spoke to me." O-hisa's voice broke.

"What did she do?" Sano asked, hiding his impatience while she got herself under control.

"She didn't believe me. She loved her brother and could think no evil of him. But she must have wanted to see for herself. The next time the young master came here, she followed him. I was there"—she pointed to the window—"watching, when she arrived. She opened the door without knocking and came into the room." O-hisa gulped. Her hand went to her mouth.

Sano remembered Midori saying that Yukiko had gone out by herself one night. That fact had seemed unimportant at the time.

Now he knew she'd come here. He admired Yukiko's courage and her faith in Lord Niu, even as he regretted the dangerous innocence that made her breach her brother's privacy.

"Lord Niu was with a boy," he prompted.

A vigorous nod. "The boy had cuts on his throat and chest. The young master was dressing. When he saw Miss Yukiko, he was very angry. He scolded her for coming into his room without permission and slapped her face. Miss Yukiko began to cry. She asked him how he could kill innocent boys and begged him to stop. I cried too, I was so afraid. The young master shouted that the boys were drugged, not dead, and that he hadn't harmed them. Then the boy groaned and sat up. He saw Miss Yukiko and the young master, and saw the cuts on his body. He screamed, 'What have you done to me? Who are you? Where am I?'

"Miss Yukiko screamed, too. The young master ordered them both to be quiet. Oh, he was furious. And when the boy wouldn't stop screaming, he—he—"

O-hisa's voice dropped so low that Sano had to lean closer to hear. "The young master grabbed his sword and cut the boy's head off." She buried her face in her hands and dissolved into sobs.

Sano shook his head, mentally completing the story. The blood-spattered room; Yukiko's horror; O-hisa cowering outside the window. Lord Niu, his fury quenched by his impulsive act of violence, turning to the task of covering up the murder. Did he regret his preference for boys of his own class instead of *eta* or other commoners, whom he could kill with impunity?

"Miss Yukiko fainted. The young master shouted for his men, then picked up Miss Yukiko and carried her out of the room." O-hisa's trembling voice narrated the scene as Sano envisioned it. "Then the men came. They took away the body. After they left, I could hear Miss Yukiko crying in the corridor. And I heard the young master say to her, 'If you tell anyone about this, I will kill you!' "

So that was why Lord Niu had killed his sister. Yukiko's high morals wouldn't have let her keep silent forever, and Lord Niu had known it. And Noriyoshi must have discovered the murder, too, either by spying, or when Lord Niu failed to return the boy he'd procured.

"He knew Yukiko would tell someone, so he killed her," O-hisa said, confirming Sano's guess. "If only I had spoken! She would still be alive. It was my duty to sacrifice myself for her, and I failed." She threw herself at Sano, hands scrabbling against his chest. "Her spirit haunts my dreams. To put her to rest, I must die. So arrest me!"

Sano held her. "It isn't your fault, O-hisa," he said, deploring the ingrained loyalty that made her want to punish herself instead of Lord Niu. "If what you say is true, the young master is solely responsible for his sister's death. Will you help me see that he pays?"

O-hisa's mouth fell open in dismay. "I?" she whispered. "Oh, no."

"By doing so you can pacify Miss Yukiko's spirit," Sano pressed. "Please."

"But what can I do?" Hope lit O-hisa's eyes, eclipsing the dread.

"Come with me to the Council of Elders tomorrow," Sano said. "Tell them your story." And he would tell them his. "They will administer justice to young Lord Niu." Surely they couldn't do otherwise when they heard O-hisa's testimony. Daimyo's son or not, Lord Niu would be punished for a crime of this magnitude.

O-hisa's eyes unfocused, and Sano watched her turn the idea over in her mind. Then she pulled away from him and hung her head.

"No," she mumbled. "I cannot betray my master. For myself, I care nothing. But he might punish my family, too, and I cannot let him do that." She started to back away. "I must go now; I've been gone too long, they'll be looking for me."

Sano knew the risk he was asking her to take, but he understood her position better than she did. "Lord Niu probably suspects that you know about the murder," he said. "He knows who was here that night. For now, he's content to let you live, because the fewer servants who know of his habits, the better. But even if you continue to say nothing, he may decide it's safer to kill you anyway, just as he did Miss Yukiko. The only way to protect yourself and your family is to deliver him to the authorities before he can act. Don't you see?"

O-hisa's mouth worked silently. Her eyes darted from side to side as if trying to see an alternative to this scenario.

Finally she said, "Yes. All right. The young master returns to Edo tomorrow morning, I and the other servants as well. I will go with you to the Council of Elders then."

"Thank you, O-hisa." Sano hid his relief under a businesslike manner. "Shall we meet somewhere at noon?" Knowing it wouldn't be safe for either of them if he went to the *yashiki,* he cast about for another rendezvous place. "How about in front of Musashi the swordmaker's," he suggested, choosing a well-known business in Nihonbashi.

"Yes. All right. Good-bye." O-hisa bowed hastily, then turned and scurried off toward the servants' quarters.

Sano watched her go. Would she change her mind between now and tomorrow? Would she talk about their plan with the other servants, who might report it to Lord Niu? He had no time to worry about that now. So far he'd been lucky; the guards hadn't seen him. He should leave before they came. Besides, he was wet to the skin and so cold that his hands and feet had lost all feeling.

Still he hesitated, remembering the guards' conversation, Lord Niu's impatience, and the banquet preparations. What other sinister happenings might they foreshadow? More revelations about Lord Niu's motives?

Sano crept through the woods until he could see the front of the house. Crouching inside a triangle of thick tree trunks, he watched. Soon he heard hoofbeats on the road outside the wall.

The gate opened to admit two mounted samurai who cantered up the torchlit path, dismounted, and vanished inside the main house. A few moments later, another pair came, then a lone man. Then more, always singly or in pairs. Soon twenty horses stood outside the door. Sano wished he could see into the house. This gathering must have some secret purpose; otherwise, Lord Niu could have held it in greater comfort and convenience at the *yashiki*.

A sudden movement on the left edge of his field of vision made Sano turn his head. Two spots of light had appeared at the side of the house near where he'd met O-hisa. They began moving toward him. In another moment, he saw the guards' bulky figures illuminated by the lanterns they carried. A needle of fear pierced his chest as their voices reached him:

"The housekeeper said she heard a stranger's voice out here."

"Probably just imagining things, the stupid old hen."

"Can't take that chance."

A shrill whistle split the air. To Sano's dismay, one of the guards left the front entrance and hurried to meet the others. Twigs snapped as they converged on him. They were less than a hundred paces away.

Sano turned and ran, away from the house, into the dark woods. He tried to move silently, but he couldn't see where he was going. Invisible branches shot out to rasp against him; unseen puddles splashed under his feet.

"I think I hear something over there."

The guards came thrashing through the woods after him. An arrow sang past his ear to land in the ground somewhere beyond his sight. Another thunked into a tree he'd just passed. Sano lunged for cover, falling flat on his belly. He lay still as the guards' footsteps stopped, then began to approach again, cautiously, stealthily. Fighting panic, he half-crawled, half-slithered over grass and mud. He bit back a cry as he tumbled down a short but steep incline. His hands and knees struck stony ground. Nearby a small brook gleamed faintly, reflecting starlight from patches of clear sky between the fleeing rain clouds. Then Sano found sanctuary in the form of a great dead tree stump that stood at the top of the incline. Its gnarled roots made a cave at the water's edge. He scuttled into the cave, drawing as far back from the entrance as he could.

Quiet footfalls halted above him: all three guards, by the sound. Their lights flashed yellow over the brook. Sano held his breath, fearful that they would see its thin vapor rising from within the cave of roots. Then someone said, "I think he came this way."

"No," said the voice that had called the housekeeper a stupid hen. "He'd have jumped the wall."

The first voice: "We'll keep looking until we're sure. The young master's orders—no trespassers."

Their voices grew fainter as they moved off. Sano crept from his hiding place and peered over the incline. He saw the lights bobbing through the trees, one toward the front wall, the other deeper into the woods. He relaxed, safe for the moment, although he faced another problem. The guards' presence made his familiar escape route too risky. He had to find another way out, but he didn't know how far it was to the rear wall, if he could find his way to it through the woods, or where other guards might be stationed.

An idea came to him. With these three men out chasing him, the house was less heavily guarded. And they would expect him to run away from it, not toward it. He could pass under the buildings and head for the wall on the far side of the gate.

Sano began a slow advance on the house. He felt each step of the way with his hands and feet so he wouldn't make any noise. Finally he reached the edge of the clearing. Lying there, he scanned the house.

The front-door guard remained at his post, gazing after his companions. Another guard was patrolling the side of the villa. Sano watched the man complete two rounds of inspection to learn the pattern. Walk to front of house, pause, look around. Turn. Walk along side of house, all the way past covered corridor to pavilion, while scrutinizing woods. Turn, repeat. Sano waited until the guard had almost reached the turnaround point at the pavilion. Then he hurried across the open space in a crouching run and dived under the house.

He traversed the side house and its covered corridor. He'd reached the *shinden* when he heard muffled voices and creaking wood overhead. Lord Niu and his guests. Crawling to the *shinden*'s rear corner, Sano poked his head out from under the house. He saw no one on the back veranda or in the garden. Those guards must be the ones now searching the woods for him. He eased the rest of his body free. The voices grew louder, carrying through the flimsy paper panes between the lattice bars. The men sounded agitated, all talking at once, their words unintelligible. Tense in anticipation of more flying arrows, Sano knew he should go before the guards came. He reminded himself that he had the sandal and the rope and O-hisa's testimony. What more could he expect?

Instead of running, Sano drew his dagger. He'd come too far and risked too much to leave without learning all he could. Emboldened by the noise in the house, he cut a hole in the window. Cautiously he put his eye to it.

Oil lamps and charcoal braziers filled the vast room with an eerie, flickering light and a smoky haze. In the center, twenty young men sat in a semicircle, arguing, oblivious to anything outside. Sano recognized some of them as men Lord Niu had met at the swordmaker's shop and the martial arts academy. So Lord Niu's movements hadn't been as aimless as they'd seemed. He'd arranged the "chance" encounters to summon the men to this meeting. Now they faced him as he knelt upon a platform, a painted screen at his back. An uneasy quiet, punctuated by throat clearings, fell over the group, as if they feared his response.

Although the remains of a meal lay on trays scattered among the men, Sano found the scene more suggestive of a haphazard picnic than of a banquet. Their serious expressions and the almost palpable tension in the room told him this was no ordinary social occasion. Also, the men were armed, as they normally wouldn't be in a private house. Sano pursed his lips in surprise when he recognized the crests on their kimonos: those of the Maeda, Date, and Hosokawa families among them. Lord Niu had assembled representatives from every major daimyo clan except for the Tokugawas.

The Maeda man spoke. "I think the plan is too risky," he said. "It won't work. I propose we reconsider the alternatives."

Immediately the others joined their voices again in furious dissent.

"He's right!" "No! It will work!" "There's no time to lose, we have to act!" "I don't like it, either."

"That's enough." Lord Niu, who had watched with a thin smile as his companions argued, now silenced them with one peremptory command.

They turned to him, faces reflecting various degrees of fear, respect, and admiration. Sano could understand how Lord Niu inspired such emotions. The daimyo's son fairly shimmered with a passion that lit his eyes and made his small body seem larger. Even his skin, flushed perhaps by his recent sexual release, suggested an inner fire that drew the men to its warmth. For what scheme had he recruited them? Sano wondered whether it had any bearing on the murders, or if he was risking his life needlessly by eavesdropping.

"There will be no more discussion of the plan," Lord Niu said, disappointing Sano. He stood, a slight jerkiness of movement the only sign of his deformity. "But in case you have forgotten, let me remind you why our action is necessary, and what we stand to gain from it."

His voice rose in both pitch and volume; he dominated the room, holding the other men motionless as he paced the platform. "Are we not sick unto death of the repression and humiliation that our oppressors have perpetrated upon us? Have our fathers and grandfathers not been stripped of their ancestral fiefs and moved to lesser ones at the ends of the earth? Have they not suffered the indignities of alternate attendance in Edo and imprisonment on their estates? Are they not unable to come and go freely?''

An angry rumble passed through the men. Backs straightened; fists clenched.

''Must we continue to let the Tokugawas drain our wealth away by forcing us to subsidize the maintenance of their castles, their roads, their waterworks?'' Lord Niu shouted, eyes blazing. ''Why should we finance the government while the shogun wastes his own money on his harem of boy actors and peasants? Why should we let him dictate how we should furnish our homes, and even how we should dress? Should we endure his spying upon us? Or the abominable harassment by his inspectors when we travel on the Tōkaido?''

The rumble became a roar. ''We won't stand for it any longer!'' someone shouted. Other men took up the cry, quieting only when Lord Niu raised his voice over theirs.

''Tokugawa Tsunayoshi is a weak fool who lets his army and his chamberlain, the despicable Yanagisawa, run the government while he sports with the wives and daughters of his ministers. And with his enforced peace, he would drag us down to his own level of moral depravity. Do we let him deprive us of our rightful occupation—that of serving our honor by making war?''

''No! No! Down with the Tokugawas!''

Sano had to choke back a gasp of surprise. He found himself trembling with excitement. The meeting's isolated setting, the secretive arrival of the participants, and Lord Niu's incendiary speech could mean only one thing. The risky plan constituted a plot against the Tokugawa government. Treason. For which Lord Niu, if caught, would be executed and disgraced more certainly than if convicted for the murder of a samurai child. And for which his family would share his punishment. Now Sano wondered whether Yukiko had died not because she'd witnessed the murder, but because she'd discovered the plot. And what about Noriyoshi? Had he learned of it too?

"Do we let Tsunayoshi rob us of our samurai heritage and values as well, by turning us into simpering bureaucrats who protect dogs, or vulgar oafs who brawl in the streets for want of anything better to do?" Lord Niu asked.

"No!" all twenty voices shouted in unison.

"Then we must act without delay. We must fight as we were born to do. We will restore to our names the honor and glory that has been denied them for too long!"

Now that he'd recovered from his initial shock, Sano sensed an underlying false note in Lord Niu's performance. His pacing, his hand gestures, and the anger in his voice and expression seemed overly theatrical. Lord Niu was playing to his audience as an actor would, exploiting their legitimate anger toward the Tokugawas. Did he really care about the shogun's mistreatment of his or the other daimyo clans?

But the men responded with great enthusiasm to his theatrics. "Yes! Yes!" The floor shuddered as they leaped to their feet. Metal rasped as they unsheathed their swords and held them high.

Lord Niu reached behind the painted screen. He held two objects high: an open scroll half covered with characters, and a writing brush. "Then it is time to pledge our oath," he announced.

Kneeling, he laid the scroll and brush on the platform. He drew his dagger. A hush fell over the room as he gashed his palm. Dipping the brush into his blood, he wrote the characters of his name on the scroll below the text. His face betrayed no sign of the pain he must have felt, but some of the other young men winced. One by one, they mounted the platform, cut their palms, added their signatures to the scroll, and returned to their places.

Sano's own palms tingled as he watched. These men, although foolhardy, were serious. A blood oath was a solemn one. He would have given anything to know what the text on the scroll said.

When they finished, Lord Niu stood. "A poem to commemorate this occasion,'' he announced, a sly smile lifting the corner of his mouth. Gesturing with the rolled scroll, he recited:

"The sun sets over the plain—
Good luck as the New Year approaches.''

The poem was not familiar to Sano, nor did it seem a very good one. And its significance escaped him. But the conspirators greeted it with wild cheers and laughter that broke the tension which had accompanied their oath. Then Lord Niu began shouting more epithets against the Tokugawas, inciting his men to greater fury. The house thundered with their shouts.

"Soon we will show our fathers that we are true samurai!'' Lord Niu cried. "We will make them proud to call us their sons!''

For the first time, Sano heard real passion behind Lord Niu's words. Now he understood that while the other young men sought power and glory for their generation, Lord Niu was doing this for his father. The knowledge gave Sano an unexpected and unwilling sense of identification with Lord Niu. Filial duty compelled them both. Except in Lord Niu, some warped form of love drove him to expose the daimyo to the dubious benefits and certain dangers of having a traitor in the family. But Sano began to despair of learning the details of the plot. Even if he didn't need them to complete his case against Lord Niu, duty required that he report them to the authorities. He looked over his shoulder for the guards. How long could he stay without getting caught?

A sudden drop in the noise level inside recalled his attention to the window. He brought his eye to the hole again. He saw the men turn toward a guard who had entered the room.

Lord Niu said, "What is it?'' Breathless from his efforts, he wiped the sweat from his brow with his sleeve.

The guard bowed. "I am sorry to interrupt you, master, but I must warn you that there is a trespasser on the grounds. We almost caught him in the west woods, but he got away.''

262 / Laura Joh Rowland

First Sano froze. Then he felt an instinctive desire to flee. Only his compelling need to hear more kept him where he was.

"A spy!" a Hosokawa man gasped.

The others let loose a volley of panicky questions and laments. "Oh, no! Are we discovered? Who betrayed us? What will we do now?" They seemed so young, so excitable, and so easily frightened that Sano wondered how they would manage to carry out whatever plan they'd concocted.

Lord Niu strode to the front of his platform. He alone showed no fear. "Fools!" he said with a sardonic laugh. "Why do you waste time talking and worrying? Go out and kill him, and he won't trouble us any longer."

"He's right! Come on!" Swords drawn, the men stampeded from the room.

"And don't just look in the west woods—search the whole estate," Lord Niu called after them. He remained on his platform, arms folded, face stern and immobile.

Sano didn't wait for the bloodthirsty horde to spill out of the *shinden.* Turning, he ran into the woods, making straight for the wall. He scaled it and jumped into the darkness and safety that lay outside.

22

The swordmaker, dressed like a Shinto priest in white ceremonial robes, pulled a glowing bar of red-hot steel from the outdoor furnace with his tongs. His assistant grabbed the other end, bending the pliant metal double. Then, chanting prayers, the two men began to beat the bar with heavy mallets, the first step in the process of folding and refolding the steel into a million layers that would give the finished blade flexibility as well as strength. Each blow rang sharply in the clear morning air. Apprentices dashed about, fetching water for the final quenching, stoking the furnace with coal. Heat poured from the furnace into the lane that separated the swordmaker's shop from a row of foundries where craftsmen shaped metal into horseshoes and other more mundane forms.

Sano leaned against the low wooden fence, alternately watching the swordmakers and scanning the lane. Laborers pushed past him, carrying raw materials and finished wares to and from the workshops. Whenever a woman approached, he straightened in anticipation, then leaned back again when he saw it was not O-hisa. But he wasn't worried. He'd arrived a little ahead of the appointed hour, and besides, a short wait couldn't spoil his mood.

Lord Niu's men hadn't caught him last night. A hot bath and a few hours of sleep at an inn had eased the effects of the long walk back to Edo and an equally long stay at a disreputable teahouse on the edge of town, where he'd waited for dawn and the opening of the gates. In clothes dried over the brazier, and with both swords at his waist, Sano felt confident that he could meet the day's challenges with success. The crisp, bright weather reflected his renewed optimism. Only the constant worry over his father gnawed at the edges of his thoughts. Patience, he counseled himself. He had Noriyoshi's sandal and the rope tucked in his cloak, ready to bring to the Council of Elders. And soon he would have O-hisa, his witness.

He would regain his former status as *yoriki,* thereby positioning himself to investigate and thwart the plot against the government. He would reclaim his honor. His father would live.

Noon came and went. The street quieted as the craftsmen had their meals, then clamored with activity again when they returned to work. Still no O-hisa. Sano's optimism waned. He began fabricating excuses for her. Lord Niu had decided to stay longer at the villa and had kept the servants with him. Lady Niu or one of the other women had detained her with some task, and O-hisa would sneak away as soon as she could. Finally, though, he had to entertain the worst of all possibilities: she'd changed her mind. Or been found out by the Nius and silenced. She wasn't coming. He'd lost his chance to salvage his family's honor, and all hope of his father's recovery.

Panic made Sano reckless. He rushed through Nihonbashi to the daimyo district. Just as he reached the Nius' gate, it opened. Hope swelled, then died again when he saw not O-hisa, but a mounted samurai come charging through the portals. One look at the man's face sent him running for cover. It was Lord Niu.

In an instant, Sano had to weigh his choices. He could wait for O-hisa, who might never appear, or he could follow Lord Niu and perhaps learn more about the plot. His commitment to O-hisa and their earlier plan warred with his curiosity. He took a step in Lord Niu's direction, then paused, looking back at the estate. Finally a desire for positive action swayed his decision. He hurried after Lord Niu.

Following the daimyo's son proved harder than it had yesterday, but not because he was on foot while Lord Niu rode. Although *Setsubun* wouldn't officially start until dark, the streets of Nihonbashi were filling with rowdy townspeople who had begun their celebrations early. Young men dressed in women's clothes assailed Lord Niu with mock come-ons, persisting until he waved his sword at them. His horse shied when children threw firecrackers that popped near its hooves. Housewives hurried to and fro with bundles of last-minute purchases for their New Year's Day feasts. In such confusion, a mounted man could travel no faster than one who walked. But without his disguise, Sano had to lag far behind Lord Niu to avoid being seen and recognized. The crowds got in his way and distracted him. What if he confused Lord Niu with some other rider dressed in plain dark clothing? A drunken old man accosted Sano, urging sake upon him. A group of adolescent boys blocked his way with a mock sword battle. With relief he emerged from the suffocating residential district into a wide, relatively uncrowded street of fine shops and rich merchants' dwellings. He was just in time to see the back of Lord Niu's horse disappear down an alley on the other side. He hurried forward, but a roaring wave of sound, comprised of shouts, hoofbeats, and the tramp of countless marching feet, bore down on him.

A horde of mounted samurai rounded the corner, bearing banners emblazoned with the cross-within-a-square Asano crest. Ahead of them, runners dashed back and forth across the street.

"Out of the way!" they yelled. "Bow down! Bow down!"

All around Sano, people hastened to comply. Dropping their bundles, they fell to their knees in the gutters, arms extended before them, foreheads pressed to the ground. Everyone knew that the samurai wouldn't hesitate to exercise *kirisute*—their legal right to cut down and kill any peasant not quick enough to bow before a daimyo's procession. Sano leaped forward, hoping to cross the street ahead of the procession. But rows of kneeling bodies blocked his way.

The procession thundered past. First the horsemen, haughty and upright, then hundreds of servants carrying baskets of provisions and treasure. Foot soldiers came next, wearing big, circular wicker hats, shoulders moving in their characteristic, bold "cutting the air" manner. Finally the daimyo's gaudy palanquin appeared, followed by endless regiments of more samurai and servants.

Sano ran sideways, hoping to cross the street behind them. He couldn't bear to lose Lord Niu. But he couldn't get around the corner; there, the marchers filled the street from wall to wall. Fairly hopping with impatience, he was forced to wait until the whole procession passed.

Finally the street cleared. The peasants picked themselves up and went about their business. Sano dashed across the street and into the alley, only to find that Lord Niu had vanished without a trace.

Cursing his bad luck, Sano raced through the streets, asking shopowners and pedestrians, "Did you see a young samurai on horseback pass this way?"

No one had. Either the procession had claimed all their attention, or else the sight of one ordinary rider was too unremarkable to remember.

Sano refused to give up. He climbed a rickety ladder to a vacant fire-watch tower and looked down over the rooftops to the seething streets. In the distance he saw several horsemen, but he couldn't tell which, if any, of them, was Lord Niu. Then, just as he was descending the ladder, he saw a familiar figure emerge from an inn down the block.

Cherry Eater, hand over his eyes to shield them from the sun, craned his neck as if looking for someone. He carried a large cloth bundle slung over his shoulder; it thumped against his back as he broke into a run.

Jumping the last few rungs, Sano landed with a jolt and hurried after Cherry Eater. He remembered Lord Niu ordering the *shunga* dealer to pick up his money today. Perhaps the two of them had arranged to meet again somewhere away from the Niu estate afterward. If Cherry Eater didn't lead him to Lord Niu, Sano would return to the swordmaker's shop to look for O-hisa again.

The *shunga* dealer seemed afraid of being followed. He kept looking back over his shoulder. He would suddenly veer around corners or hide behind notice boards. He ducked into shops and teahouses, waited awhile, then cautiously poked his ugly face out to look both ways before emerging again. Once he stayed so long that Sano wondered whether whatever misfortune he feared had befallen him inside. Then, realizing what had happened, Sano ran around the block just in time to see Cherry Eater come out the teahouse's rear door and hurry away.

He almost lost Cherry Eater again at the fish market, which sprawled over the banks of the canal beside the Nihonbashi Bridge. Cherry Eater plunged into the vast, noisy building, threading his way through the crowds that choked the narrow pathways between row upon row of stalls. Sano dodged around barrels of live mackerel and tuna and baskets of clams and scallops. The reek of rotting fish filled his nostrils. A cluster of customers haggling over the price of three huge sharks suspended from a horizontal pole blocked his way. By the time he'd elbowed past them, Cherry Eater was far ahead of him, leaning over a table laden with seaweed to talk to the proprietor.

Catching up, Sano heard Cherry Eater shout, "I need my money now! Give it to me!"

"But I don't have it," the man protested.

Cherry Eater gave a howl of pure despair. He turned and ran, darting out through one of the arched doorways and into the sunshine. Sano lunged forward. His feet slipped in the fish scales and entrails that befouled the ground, and he almost fell. Why, he wondered, did Cherry Eater need money so badly after extorting a fortune from Lord Niu? He thought of questioning the seaweed vendor, but he mustn't lose Cherry Eater.

Outside, Cherry Eater made straight for the canal, where fishermen had drawn their boats up to the bank to auction off their catches. Sano hurried after him as he picked his way through the shouting bidders. Cherry Eater squinted at each boat. Then he paused, his drooping posture making it obvious that he hadn't found the one he sought. He spoke to a few fishermen, and Sano caught a few phrases:

"Have you seen . . . the boat was supposed to be waiting . . ."

Getting only shakes of the head in answer, Cherry Eater headed back toward the market. But instead of going inside, he cut across an alley and entered one of a long line of establishments in a dingy building whose once-white plaster walls had turned a scabrous gray.

Sano hesitated about twenty paces from the doorway. FRESH-CATCH SUSHI, the sign read. Teahouses filled with fishermen and laborers occupied the rooms on either side. When Cherry Eater didn't reappear immediately, Sano wondered whether to look for him at the back door, or wait in one of the teahouses. Was Cherry Eater meeting Lord Niu now, or just trying to shake pursuers? Sano risked a walk past the sushi restaurant and glanced inside.

A chest-high counter ran along the right side of the long, narrow room, stopping just short of the back wall, where a curtained doorway led to the kitchen. Behind the counter the chef, wearing a blue headband over bushy eyebrows, sliced raw fish, encased it in rolls of vinegared rice and seaweed, and distributed it to his seven customers with remarkable speed and precision. Cherry Eater stood near the end of the counter, his back to the door. Oblivious to the full plate before him, he was speaking in urgent tones to the man beside him.

The room was dim, and hazy with smoke from the customers' pipes. Sano took another chance. Entering the restaurant, he stood at the counter two places away from Cherry Eater. His neighbors, both ripe-smelling dockworkers, scowled their greetings and reluctantly moved aside to make room for him.

"What will you have, master?" the chef called to Sano, not looking up from his flashing knife.

"Anything that's good," Sano answered absentmindedly. Keeping his face averted, he listened to Cherry Eater's conversation.

The *shunga* dealer had dropped his bundle. Wringing his insectile hands, he moaned, "Yes, I know it's a lot of money, and more than we agreed on." For once he did not offer a wisecrack or veiled insult; anxiety had stifled his wit. "But I need it, and I need it now."

His companion was not Lord Niu, but a gray-haired, shabbily dressed fat man who answered in a gruff mumble that Sano strained to understand. Was he a moneylender? Or another of Cherry Eater's blackmail victims? Unfortunately, the chef chose that moment to interrupt.

"Dancing sushi, best in town," he barked, zinging a plate down the counter toward Sano. "Eat up now."

"Thank you." Sano picked up a still-wriggling prawn with his chopsticks and ate it, wishing the chef would keep quiet. He'd missed Fat Man's entire reply.

"Easy for you to say do not worry," Cherry Eater railed. "You are not running for your life!"

Sano ate the rest of his prawns without tasting them. Now he grasped the significance of Cherry Eater's bulky bundle, his panicky flight, his need for money, and the boat. Something or someone had frightened him into an abrupt departure from Edo. Was it Lord Niu? Maybe Cherry Eater hadn't gotten money from him, but a death threat.

Mumble mumble was all Sano heard from Fat Man.

"I must leave immediately," Cherry Eater said. "Now where is the money you owe me?"

The chef slid Sano two more plates, announcing loudly, "Tuna and sea bream."

Sano raised a hand to signal that he wanted nothing more. He saw Fat Man take a pouch from inside his baggy cloak and give it to Cherry Eater. Then he frowned as Fat Man's hands caught his attention. Too white and slender and graceful to belong to such a gross person, they also looked familiar. Sano had a sudden image of them holding a fan instead of a pouch. He took a closer look at Fat Man—and froze with his chopsticks held halfway to his mouth.

The gray wig and padded clothing effectively changed the man's age and shape. He'd plumped his face, probably by stuffing cloth in his cheeks and nostrils. But he couldn't disguise the hands, which tipped Sano off to his real identity.

Fat Man was none other than Kikunojo, the great Kabuki actor—in male attire for another secret rendezvous.

Sano looked away before Kikunojo could recognize him. He'd more or less dismissed Kikunojo as a suspect, but the actor's sudden reappearance raised strong questions in his mind. Kikunojo had evidently lied about refusing to pay blackmail, and perhaps about other things as well. Had his forbidden affair been with a married woman—or Yukiko? Could he have killed her and Noriyoshi because he feared that either might reveal the affair to the Nius, who would have destroyed him if they'd learned of it? Had he worn a disguise to follow Sano along the Tōkaido and kill Tsunehiko?

These questions went unanswered as Cherry Eater dominated the conversation, apparently out of a reckless desire to confide.

". . . shouldn't have asked him for more money . . . didn't know how dangerous . . . he'll have my head if I don't get away fast. . . ."

Cherry Eater's voice had dropped to a fretful mutter, but Sano understood his meaning. Lord Niu had refused to tolerate more extortion. Did Cherry Eater believe—as Sano still did, despite Kikunojo's reemergence as a suspect—that Lord Niu had killed Noriyoshi, Yukiko, and the samurai child and would not hesitate to kill again to protect himself? The *shunga* dealer's fear suggested that he did. But then why had he risked blackmail? Sano felt a certain admiration for Cherry Eater's nerve and enterprising spirit. The ugly little man was quick to seize opportunities to make money wherever he found them.

Kikunojo mumbled something else.

"But it did not seem like a bad idea at first!" In his agitation, Cherry Eater forgot to keep his voice low. "Do you think I am so stupid as to follow in my miserable employee's footsteps?" He gave a shrill, hysterical laugh. "No. I merely suggested that an increase in my commission was called for. Because of that boy who died. I had to pay his family a fortune not to tell the police. How was I supposed to know that Lord—" He caught himself. "That a certain person would misunderstand my intentions and assume that I, too, am a *metsuke* informer who wants money in exchange for not telling the authorities about his conspiracy?"

Sano nearly choked on a mouthful of sea bream. It didn't surprise him that Noriyoshi had learned about the conspiracy, or that he'd attempted to use his knowledge for personal gain. But never had he guessed that Noriyoshi was an informer for the Tokugawa spies. This unexpected piece of information strengthened Lord Niu's motive immeasurably. How much more dangerous was the knowledge in an informer's hands than in those of a simple blackmailer! Sano conjectured that the self-serving Noriyoshi had first used the secrets he learned for his own benefit, reporting them to his employers only after he'd wrung enough money out of his victims. This time, however, it appeared that Lord Niu had made sure Noriyoshi didn't live long enough to report the conspiracy.

"The Conspiracy of Twenty-One . . . all twenty-one years old." Increasingly hysterical, Cherry Eater released a flood of babble. "All younger sons of daimyo. Noriyoshi said they want to restore their clans to the glory of the old days. Dangerous, yes, because Lord Niu is crazy and will stop at nothing to reach his goal." Cherry Eater paused. "Do you mind?" he asked Kikunojo, pointing to a bottle of sake on the counter.

At Kikunojo's nod, he picked it up, drained it, coughed, wiped his mouth. "Noriyoshi said that, impossible as it seems, they might even succeed! He said . . ."

Come on, come on, Sano urged silently. You've told me who they are, and I might have guessed, anyway, because of the crests. I already know what they want. Now tell me what they're going to do!

Cherry Eater said, "They truly intend to commit this murder— the ultimate treason!"

The impact of his words sent a spasm of horror through Sano's body. His hand locked convulsively around his chopsticks. If he interpreted Cherry Eater's meaning correctly, then the Conspiracy of Twenty-One planned to assassinate the shogun! And to what terrible end? At best, to bring down the wrath of the Tokugawas upon their clans. At worst, to usher in a new era of civil war, if the great daimyo each tried to claim the vacant post of supreme military dictator. Madness! Then, before Sano could think or hear anything else, a hand clapped his shoulder.

"Sano-*san*!"

Sano dropped his chopsticks, wincing at the sound of his own name. As he turned toward the speaker, he saw Cherry Eater's head snap around.

"And what brings you here, master?" It was the cheerful, wizened peddler who sold fish in Sano's parents' neighborhood. "I thought you worked for the magistrate now. A *yoriki*, aren't you?"

"Shhh!" Sano waved his hands to silence the peddler, at the same time throwing a backward glance at Cherry Eater and Kikunojo. With dismay, he saw that the damage had been done.

Cherry Eater and Kikunojo were both looking straight at him, alarmed recognition written on their faces. Then, simultaneously, they bolted in opposite directions. Kikunojo shot past Sano and out the front door. He threw off his cumbersome cloak as he ran, leaving it on the floor along with the cushions that had made him look fat. Cherry Eater snatched up his bundle, scurried around the counter, and disappeared beyond the curtain hanging over the kitchen door.

"Talked to your mother yesterday," the peddler went on, looking bewildered by Sano's peculiar greeting. "Your father's not feeling too good, eh? That's too bad. I'll bring him some whale liver next time I come. . . . Sano-*san,* where are you going in such a hurry?"

Sano flung some money on the counter to pay for his food. He hated to let Kikunojo get away; he had questions for the actor. But he had to go after Cherry Eater and learn more about Lord Niu's plot against the shogun, to whom he owed his first duty and loyalty. He beat aside the curtain and burst into the kitchen. A woman stood at a table, gutting fish. She screamed as Sano collided with her on his way to the back door.

"Sorry, excuse me!" he shouted.

Outside, he found himself in a fetid alley. He saw Cherry Eater's hurrying figure heading toward the canal.

"Wait!" he called. "I just want to talk to you!"

Cherry Eater kept running, hampered by his bundle. Sano quickly gained on him, but lost the advantage when some men came out of a door and blocked his way. He cleared the alley just in time to see Cherry Eater splash through the water and climb into a fishing boat.

"Wait, Cherry Eater!" he shouted, panting as he dodged around people, stray dogs, and piles of fishing net.

"Hurry, hurry!" Cherry Eater urged, his frantic hops and gestures almost upsetting the boat.

With a shrug, the boatman poled his craft away from the shore and guided it east, toward the Sumida River.

Sano waded knee-deep into the cold, filthy canal. He grabbed the boat. "Please," he begged Cherry Eater. "You must tell me more about the conspiracy's plans. When are they going to kill the shogun? Where? How? They must be stopped, don't you understand? Please!"

Cherry Eater kicked at Sano's hands, shrieking, "Go away! Leave me alone!"

The boat rocked, then tipped over. Cherry Eater and the boatman landed in the canal amid splashes and curses. Sano seized the thrashing *shunga* dealer by the collar. He dunked Cherry Eater's head under the water again and again.

"Tell me!" he ordered. Cherry Eater gasped and moaned each time he surfaced, but shook his head, refusing to speak. Sano pushed him underwater and held him there as long as he dared without actually drowning him. Cherry Eater's struggles weakened. Sano pulled him up. "When? Where? How?" he demanded.

His face red and his bug eyes filled with terror, the *shunga* dealer coughed and choked. He spewed water from his stained mouth. But he continued to shake his head.

"Kill me if you must, master," he wailed, "but it will do you no good. Because I don't know when or where or how Lord Niu plans to assassinate the shogun!"

O-hisa did not want to be sitting in the sewing room of the Niu mansion. She did not want to be making doll clothes for the daimyo's daughters, under the supervision of Yasue, the head seamstress. As the appointed hour for her meeting with Sano slipped past, her mind yearned toward the swordmaker's shop where he waited to take her to the Council of Elders. But she had no choice except to sit and sew and wish herself away.

"When you finish that," Yasue said, pointing to the tiny kimono that O-hisa was hemming, "there are plenty more." She waved a hand at the brightly colored silks strewn over the floor. "The Doll Festival is but a month away, and we have two hundred dolls to dress. We must not bring bad luck upon the house by failing to have them ready on time." Her eyes never left O-hisa.

O-hisa sighed. "Yes, Yasue-*san.*"

Once O-hisa would have loved this task, which reminded her of home and the happiness of childhood. Her mother and grandmother were both widows; they made a meager living by sewing. But they'd always given her a Doll Festival, the annual celebration for young girls. Late at night, after their day's work was done, they would sit around the stove in their one-room house in the poorest section of Nihonbashi and sew the dolls' clothes by lamplight. O-hisa could picture them now. Her mother, face tired, still kindly and patiently teaching her small daughter how to cut and stitch. Her blind grandmother, smiling encouragement as her deft hands miraculously fashioned garments she couldn't see. For all of them, O-hisa's tenth and last festival, just before she left home to take her first job, had held a particular poignancy.

"Don't cry, O-hisa," her grandmother had said. "You'll come back for visits on New Year's Day, when all servants are allowed to go home."

"Be a brave, obedient girl," her mother had said, bowing her head to hide her own tears.

Now O-hisa felt a stab of homesickness. She sighed, saddened by the comparison between past and present. The fabric in her hands was silk, instead of the cotton scraps her mother had saved from various sewing jobs. The dolls would be fine porcelain, not wood or straw. But they were for the daimyo's daughters, not her. And her present companions robbed the familiar ritual of all pleasure.

Yasue's gnarled, arthritic fingers could no longer hold a needle. She kept her position because she had once served Lady Niu's family and had come to Edo when her mistress married. O-hisa knew that her real job now was making sure Lady Niu knew everything that went on in the women's quarters.

Beside Yasue sat the maid O-aki. Stout, unsmiling, with large hands that looked strong enough to wring an ox's neck. Shunned by the other servants as an informer who would report their mistakes, gossip, petty thefts, and bad attitudes to Lady Niu. Once she'd caught a cook's helper stealing rice from the pantry. She'd broken the man's arm before taking him to Lady Niu.

"Your stitches are much, much too long." Yasue scowled in fierce disapproval at O-hisa's work. "Make them smaller. What a worthless girl! Did your mother teach you nothing?"

"So sorry, Yasue-*san*."

The room where they sat was an oasis of quiet in the bustling mansion. Although Miss Yukiko's death and the customary mourning period lent restraint to the holiday atmosphere, *Setsubun* preparations were well under way. O-hisa had returned from the villa to find the household in a state of subdued chaos.

She could still hear the other servants rushing to finish the pre–New Year housecleaning. Overexcited children shouted as they chased one another up and down the corridors. Twittery laughter came from the women's quarters, where the daimyo's daughters and concubines, and their ladies-in-waiting, tried on the clothes they would wear to parties at the other lords' houses tonight. Harried maids dashed about attending to their needs: heating baths, arranging hair, bringing still more clothes from storerooms, administering massages, serving tea and snacks. Good smells wafted from the kitchens as the cooks prepared enough food to feed the household tomorrow. O-hisa had thought that, in the general confusion, she could sneak out to keep her rendezvous with Sano. Now, though, it appeared that she was to have no share in the *Setsubun* preparations, and no chance to leave anytime soon. How long would he wait for her? How would she find him if he didn't? If only she had spoken to him sooner!

But when and how could she have done so? Although Lord Niu had never spoken to her or given any sign that he knew she'd witnessed the murder, a careful watch had been kept over her since Miss Yukiko's death. Many times she'd walked down the mansion's corridors and heard doors open and close behind her as unseen observers noted her progress. She'd gone on errands alone, only to have one of the other maids catch up with and accompany her. O-aki had moved into the room O-hisa shared with three other maids. And as soon as she'd returned from the villa, the net of surveillance had tightened. Yasue and O-aki had greeted her at the door, and they wouldn't let her out of their sight.

O-hisa cast a nervous glance at them. What would happen if she got up and ran? Would O-aki break her arm? Or would Yasue simply notify Lord Niu? Maybe he would have her killed. She was almost tempted to give up and let him. After all, she deserved to die. But she'd dreamed of Miss Yukiko again last night. Dark, beseeching eyes in a dead white face. Thin fingers, already nibbled by scavengers, reaching out in entreaty. Long black hair swirling in the turbulent water. If Sano thought she could lay that sorrowful ghost to rest by helping him bring young Lord Niu to justice, then she was willing to try. And he'd convinced her that this was the only way to protect her family from Lord Niu's wrath. The part of her that wanted to live hoped Sano was right, and that she could think of some way to escape her jailers.

"O-hisa!" Yasue's harsh voice broke into her thoughts. "You have just sewed that sleeve shut. In the future, watch what you are doing."

"Yes, Yasue-*san*. So sorry." O-hisa meekly bent her head to the task of ripping out the stitches. When she began to sew again, her hands trembled so badly that the needle slipped and jabbed her finger. The pain brought tears to her eyes; they spilled over as her despair increased. Sucking the blood from her fingertip, she mourned her lost childhood. She imagined Sano walking away from the swordmaker's shop.

From the corridor came the voices of two passing maids:

"Did you clean the north garden pavilion?"

"No. I thought you were going to."

"Well, we'd better do it now. Lady Niu will be angry otherwise."

The north garden wasn't far from the back gate. "Maybe I should go and help," O-hisa suggested timidly.

Yasue frowned. "You will stay here."

Catching O-aki's smug nod, O-hisa felt her spirits plummet. Then a brilliant idea came to her. Standing, she bowed and arranged her face in an innocent, apologetic smile.

"Where do you think you're going?" Yasue demanded.

"To the place of relief, please," O-hisa said, referring to the privy with the polite term used by the household.

Yasue pursed her lips, obviously annoyed and not wanting to

disobey orders, but unable to deny such a request. "Well, see that you do not take longer than necessary. O-aki, go with her."

Shadowed by her grim escort, O-hisa walked to the maids' privy, a tiny building set tastefully apart from the rest of the house, reached by way of a narrow corridor and a flight of steps. Once inside the windowless room, she shut the door and offered a brief, silent prayer. Then, her stomach churning with disgust at what she must do, she hiked up her skirts and tied them around her waist so they wouldn't get in her way. If only she had her shoes! But it was better to escape barefoot than not at all. Steeling herself, she knelt before the privy slot.

Despite frequent cleaning and the liberal use of fragrant herbs, the wide slot emitted a strong odor of feces and urine. O-hisa, peering into the dim compartment below the privy's raised floor, could see the partially full catch basin. She fought nausea as she sat down and gingerly lowered her legs into the slot.

The space between the slot and the floor of the compartment was less than her own height. Arms braced against the rim of the slot, O-hisa held her breath as she felt with her toe for the basin. She found it, then swung backward as she dropped, to avoid stepping in it. But she misjudged. When she landed, her foot struck and tipped the basin. Warm, slimy filth splattered her legs and drenched her socks. At the same time, her need for air forced her to breathe. The stench assailed her, and she retched. Crouching in the cramped, fetid compartment, she clapped a hand over her mouth, praying that O-aki hadn't heard and wouldn't open the door. The darkness disoriented her. Where was the hatch that the servants used to remove and clean the basin?

Her groping hands found the small trap door and pushed it open. Sickness and panic overcame caution, and she squeezed through it without remembering to make sure no one was watching. Free! She lay on the ground for a moment and gulped the clean, fresh air with relief. Then she struggled to her feet, letting down her kimono as she ran. Fear weakened her muscles and made her heart flutter in her chest. But O-hisa found strength and courage in the thought of her mother and grandmother. After she and Sano had seen the Council of Elders, she would go home for good. She would never return to the Nius.

Each of the mansion's many wings held potential dangers. O-hisa avoided the busy women's quarters and kitchens. Instead she scurried through the gate leading to the vacant men's apartments, where the daimyo, his elder sons, and their closest advisers lived when they were in Edo. There she would be safe from young Lord Niu, who had rooms in a separate wing, and from the watchful eyes of the servants.

She paused to get her bearings. She'd never been in this part of the *yashiki* before, and the unfamiliar complex of shuttered buildings and deserted gardens confused her. Which way to the back gate?

O-hisa struck off in a likely direction. She had no time to lose. At any moment O-aki would open the privy door, find her missing, and tell Yasue. They would send out a party to search the estate for her.

As she hurried down a narrow path between two buildings, O-hisa heard a raspy sound. A door opening? She let out a shriek before she could stop herself. She spun around, then her panic receded a little when she identified the source of the sound: a branch scraping against a wall. O-hisa almost longed to be caught and released from fear and uncertainty, but the memory of her family fueled her determination. In just a few hours, she would be home. She imagined her mother's and grandmother's pleased surprise at her arrival, a day early, for her New Year visit. She would bury her face against her mother's bosom and forget the murder she'd seen, and the terror she'd experienced since. She would not think beyond that moment of exquisite relief and joy. She would not think of how alarmed and unhappy they would be when they learned why she'd given up her post, or how the Nius might punish them all.

O-hisa dashed the rest of the way down the path to emerge into a garden where huge, craggy boulders dotted an expanse of white gravel. Her running feet left prints in its carefully raked pattern of parallel lines.

She'd almost made it to the gate at the other end of the garden when she heard footsteps coming across the gravel behind her. Without stopping, she half turned. Her mouth opened to scream when she recognized her pursuer and met his merciless gaze. But the scream never had time to leave her.

A cord slipped over her head. It tightened around her neck. Red darkness exploded in her brain as she coughed and choked, fighting for air. In desperation, she clawed at the cord. Her fingernails gouged her own flesh. Blood roared in her ears. Her teeth locked her tongue in an agonizing grip. Blindly she grabbed for her attacker's hands; her twitching fingers closed upon air.

"Uh, uh!" she gurgled, trying to call for help.

None came. Red turned to dense black. O-hisa felt herself begin to spin in dizzying, ever-faster circles. As consciousness ebbed away from her, she saw again the blessed golden image of her home, and her mother and grandmother sitting by the stove. Their loving smiles beckoned her. O-hisa's heart yearned toward them. With the last of her strength, she fought for life. She must survive to see them again. But the vision quickly darkened, then disappeared as another took its place.

Miss Yukiko. Radiant, smiling in infinite compassion. Holding out a hand to welcome O-hisa into death.

E do Castle dominated its wooded hilltop, a great fortified city-within-a-city that housed the shogun Tokugawa Tsunayoshi, his family, his closest allies, and a veritable army of soldiers, officials, and servants within its massive stone walls.

Sano walked up to the shimmering moat, gazing at the castle with the awe that this symbol of Tokugawa supremacy always inspired in him. For the first time, he grasped the full extent of Lord Niu's madness. Who in his right mind would dare challenge this? The castle had stood for almost a hundred years, and it looked ready to stand for at least as many more, judging from the strength of its defenses. Countless samurai stood inside guardhouses that topped the walls, and more occupied lookout towers. Above the walls, the keep soared five stories high, a square white tower composed of many smaller towers. Its gables and barred windows provided lines of fire to archers and gunners; its plastered walls and tile roofs could resist both fire arrows and bullets. At ground level, a battalion of guards manned the iron-plated main gate. Armed with muskets as well as swords, they controlled the heavy flow of traffic in and out of the castle.

Watching the visitors, mostly samurai who presumably had legitimate business inside, Sano felt more than a little intimidated. He'd never been inside the castle; his family was too unimportant and his rank too low for him to have enjoyed the honor. But he knew that somewhere, deep inside the palace, were the headquarters of the Tokugawa spy network. There the *metsuke* collated and interpreted information gathered by agents and informers all over the country and distributed it to the shogun and his advisers. To them he must bring the news of the treasonous Conspiracy of Twenty-One.

Still he hesitated, reluctant to cross the bridge. Except for Cherry Eater's word, he had no evidence that the conspiracy planned to kill the shogun. He didn't know how, when, or where the assassination attempt would take place. His own conviction that the plot gave Lord Niu a motive for the murders wouldn't influence the authorities. After all, Raiden had been executed for Yukiko's and Noriyoshi's murders, and Tsunehiko's death officially ruled a highway killing. He would just have to tell his story from the beginning, present his conclusions, and hope that the *metsuke* would draw similar ones. Taking a deep breath, he squared his shoulders and marched across the bridge.

"I would like an audience with the *metsuke*," he told the guards, after identifying himself.

They looked him over in a bored fashion. One of them said, "Show me your pass."

"I don't have one. But I've come on a matter of extreme urgency." Sano had anticipated difficulty in getting past the castle's security, which protected its occupants not only from physical threats but also from callers who might waste their time. "I bring news of vital importance to the shogun," he added. "Please allow me to convey it to the *metsuke*."

" 'Vital importance,' eh?" The spokesman leaned on his spear. "Suppose you tell me what it is. I'll see that it gets to the right people."

Imagining how his story would be distorted as it passed through the castle's bureaucratic channels—possibly never reaching the *metsuke* at all—Sano shook his head. "I must speak with them personally."

"Well, you can't." The guard shed his veneer of courtesy, his voice turning sharp. He was a Tokugawa foot soldier, one of a breed known for their arrogance and rudeness. "Either leave a message, and if the *metsuke* want to see you, they'll send a summons. Or else get lost. We're busy." He turned to question an arriving party of samurai.

Sano had managed to extract one more piece of information from Cherry Eater before freeing the drenched and indignant *shunga* dealer: the identity of the *metsuke* to whom Noriyoshi had reported. But Cherry Eater wasn't sure whether the exact name was Jodo Ikkyu or Toda Ikkyu.

Taking a chance, he said, "Toda Ikkyu will have your heads if you don't bring me to him at once."

The guard's head snapped around. "You're Toda's creature?" His face relaxed from a scowl to a knowing smirk. "Why didn't you say so in the first place?" Banging on the gate with his spear, he shouted to someone inside. Another guard came out. "Take this man to Toda Ikkyu."

The other guard gestured for Sano to follow him. Sano realized that they thought he was one of Toda's informers. Well, he was, in a way. And he'd learned that this was how the government bureaucracy worked: by manipulation of men through their fear of their superiors.

Inside the gate, more walls formed a square enclosure designed as a trap for invading enemies who managed to penetrate the castle's outer defense. At least twenty more guards stood watch, rigid and stern. They took away Sano's swords and searched him for hidden weapons. Then they swung open another gate that stood at right angles to the first.

This opened into a large courtyard bordered by long wooden sheds hung with red curtains. Inside them, Sano could see row upon row of weapons: swords, bows, spears, muskets. Hundreds of armored samurai stood in or in front of the sheds. Others, mounted on horses caparisoned with battle regalia, paced the courtyard. The odor of horses sharpened the air; the tramp of restless feet and the rumble of voices echoed off the walls. Beyond a second moat and bridge stood another wall. The keep towered above it, looking grimmer and more solid than from a distance. Sano felt tiny and insignificant in the presence of such military might. Lord Niu's madness must give him superhuman courage.

Once past another set of sentries and across the bridge, Sano entered another enclosure, with more guards and yet another gate. This gate led to a narrow, gradually ascending passageway full of turns and angles. Gun holes and arrow slits pierced the white plaster walls of enclosed corridors that ran along the high stone walls. At regular intervals, larger square openings in the corridors allowed the defenders to dump stones on anyone who tried to climb the walls. Sano spied more guards behind the openings. The other visitors he saw all had their own military escorts. Only samurai wearing the Tokugawa crest walked proudly alone and armed. Sano soon lost count of the number of checkpoints and gates he passed. Tokugawa Ieyasu had built his fortress to withstand a siege, but were his descendants safe from treachery? Remembering the fanatical gleam in Lord Niu's eyes, Sano wondered. Perhaps the Conspiracy of Twenty-One planned to somehow ambush the shogun outside the castle walls, away from his legions of soldiers.

The final gate brought them at last to the castle's inner precinct. There bands of guards patrolled a formal garden landscaped with plane trees, pines, and boulders. A wide gravel path led to the palace.

Sano stopped involuntarily to take in this sight he'd never expected to see. The low, vast palace had white plaster walls with dark cypress beams, shutters, and doors. Its heavy dark tile roof peaked in many high and low gables, each crowned with a gilt dragon. Serene and elegant, it drowsed in an oasis of tranquillity, far removed from the teeming streets of Edo. Only the faint strains of music and the muffled report of firecrackers disturbed its peace:

Setsubun celebrations were going on within its walls and court-yards, or in daimyo mansions elsewhere on the castle grounds. Sano thought of Lord Niu's speech. He reflected that the Niu and other daimyo clans had indeed purchased a fine home for the Tokugawas.

The guard interrupted Sano's thoughts. "Hurry up," he ordered.

They crossed the garden and gained admittance from the guards at the palace's carved door. As he removed his shoes in the spacious, echoing entry hall, Sano marveled that he should visit the castle at all, let alone for such a purpose.

Inside the palace, a labyrinth of corridors unwound before Sano, angling their way through the outer portion of the building, which served as government offices. Sunlight from the barred windows fell in bright lines across polished cypress floors. Wide halls led past airy reception rooms with daises, coffered ceilings, and lavish landscape murals. The narrower ones were lined with small chambers. There a few doors stood open to reveal an official dictating to his secretary, or a meeting in session. Twice Sano's escort saluted pairs of patrolling guards; once they both bowed to an official in flowing robes. Otherwise the palace seemed virtually deserted. An unnatural quiet pervaded the great complex that must normally buzz with the sound of officialdom in motion. The creak of the floor beneath their feet echoed through the empty corridors. Other soft creaks came infrequently from deeper within the building. Already quivering inside with tension, Sano started at each one.

"*Setsubun,*" the guard grumbled. "Those office layabouts have all quit for the holiday already."

He led the way down a very narrow, dim passage and through the only open door in it. Inside, paper-and-wood screens divided a long, thin room into many small compartments, each with its own window. As Sano passed each one, he saw desks and shelves stacked with books, scrolls, message containers, and writing implements. Maps hung on the walls, some stuck with colored pins. So this was the castle's intelligence center. A heavy odor of tobacco smoke underlay the scent of the herbs used to freshen the room for New Year. But the *metsuke* whose pipes had permanently tainted the woodwork were not here now. The room was cold and silent and dim, with most of the windows shuttered. No lamps burned, save in the very last compartment.

There a man dressed in black stood before a wall of shelves. At the sound of their footsteps, he paused in the act of straightening a row of books and turned.

"What is it?" he asked the guard. "Who is this man?"

"One of your informers, Toda-*san*," the guard answered, looking surprised.

Sano gazed with curiosity at Toda Ikkyu, the first *metsuke* he'd ever encountered. Seldom had he seen anyone so nondescript. Toda was neither tall nor short, fat nor thin. Of indeterminate age, he had thick black hair that might have given him a youthful appearance, if not for the weary expression in his eyes. His regular features, without particular flaws or beauty, could have belonged to any of a thousand men. Although Sano studied Toda's face carefully, he doubted whether he would remember it when he left. Perhaps this utter lack of distinction was an advantage for someone in Toda's profession.

"He is not one of my informers," Toda was saying in a voice as tired as his expression, "and I have never seen him before in my life."

"But—but he said—"

Toda broke into the guard's blustering defense. "I don't care what he said. Take him away. And see that I receive no more callers today. Can you manage that, or must I speak with your superior?"

The guard's face darkened. "Come on, you," he said, shoving Sano toward the door. "I'll deal with you outside."

"Wait," Sano said. "Toda-*san*." He bowed. "Please allow me

a moment of your time. I have important information for you. It concerns a plot against the shogun.'' Seeing the skepticism on Toda's face, he added, ''And it involves your informer, the late Noriyoshi.''

A glimmer of interest enlivened Toda's eyes. ''All right,'' he said. ''But one moment only.'' To the guard: ''Wait outside.''

When they were alone, Toda knelt and gestured for Sano to do the same. ''First your name and antecedents,'' he said, ''in order that I may know with whom I am speaking.''

Or whether to believe me, Sano thought as he recited his name and lineage.

To his dismay, Toda frowned and said, ''Are you not the *yoriki* who was recently dismissed by Magistrate Ogyu?''

Bad news traveled fast; there went all his credibility. ''Yes,'' Sano admitted. ''But I ask that you suspend any prejudice against me until you hear what I have to say. Then you can decide whether I'm telling the truth, and whether or not to relay my information to the shogun.'' Without waiting for permission, he plunged into his story, beginning with his assignment to the *shinjū* case.

The nondescript Toda did have one distinctive mannerism. With the tip of his right forefinger, he absently stroked each nail on his left hand, one after the other. He did this in silence while Sano spoke and for a small eternity afterward, his unwavering stare fixed on Sano's face. From somewhere in the castle grounds came the rapid *pop-pop* of firecrackers and the more regular percussion of drums. Sano squirmed inwardly.

Finally Toda said, ''So. You say that Niu Masahito—not the executed wrestler Raiden—killed Noriyoshi, to prevent him from exposing the Conspiracy of Twenty-One.''

''That's correct.'' Was the *metsuke* convinced? His neutral tone conveyed nothing. Sano tried to draw hope from the fact that Toda had not thrown him out of the palace. Realizing that he'd forgotten the sandal and rope, he laid them on the floor for Toda's inspection, and explained their significance. ''Here is my proof.''

"You think that young Lord Niu also killed his own sister, either because she, too, had discovered the conspiracy, or because she witnessed a murder. And that the murder of your secretary was actually an unsuccessful attempt on your own life, also perpetrated by Lord Niu?"

"Yes."

Toda nodded slowly as he began stroking his fingernails again. "A most ingenious piece of fiction," he murmured.

Sano's heart sank. "You don't believe me." Silently he berated himself for his unrealistic hopes. High-ranking officials achieved their positions by flowing with the current, not resisting it. He should have expected this.

"My apologies if you think that I mean to question your veracity, Sano-*san*," Toda said. "I do not. I can see that you truly believe your story. But your motives are clear to me, if not to yourself. First, you seek revenge upon the Nius for what you see as their part in your ill fortune. Second, you wish to prove that you know better than your former superior how to solve a murder case. And third, you wish to assuage your guilt over your secretary's death. Given your position, how can you expect anyone to believe you?"

"No!" The protest burst from Sano. "I didn't make this up, and you're wrong about—"

He caught himself as he realized that Toda's mind had closed against him the moment he'd given his name. The injustice filled him with outrage. But he tempered his emotions, knowing that right now there were concerns more important than his hurt pride. He couldn't afford to alienate Toda further.

"Before you dismiss what I've said, at least investigate Lord Niu and his friends," he pleaded. "For the shogun's sake. If there's even a chance of an assassination attempt, shouldn't you tell him so he can protect himself?"

"The shogun is already well protected—against *real* threats. His military power is absolute, and a group of conspirators such as you describe—even if they do exist—could not hope to prevail. The days when uprisings like the Great Conspiracy had a chance of success are long past. Besides, I can assure you that the daimyo clans, Lord Niu's included, have a strong stake in maintaining the present regime. They command their provinces and a large proportion of the country's wealth. In a war against the Tokugawas, they could lose it all.''

With a sense of irony that almost made him want to laugh, Sano countered the arguments that he himself had used against Katsuragawa under different circumstances. ''The conspirators are rash, ambitious young men who lack their elders' instinct for self-preservation,'' he said. ''And from what I've seen of young Lord Niu, he is not one to let logic govern his behavior. Perhaps because of the madness that runs in his family.''

''We're well aware of young Lord Niu's tendencies. There is nothing you can tell us about him that we don't already know. He is not a threat to the shogun.''

In spite of Toda's condescending tone and unchanged expression, a sudden tenseness about the *metsuke* told Sano that he'd scored a point. Maybe he could win another.

He said, ''Perhaps you underestimate Lord Niu because he's a cripple.''

But Toda just looked even wearier and shook his head. Rising, he went to the shelf and took down a notebook. He knelt again, opening it upon his lap.

''Lord Niu Masahito.'' He ran his finger over the columns of characters as he read. ''Born with a deformed right leg, due to . . .'' He quoted the opinions of the doctors and astrologers who had attended the birth. ''Resides with his mother in Edo because his father hates the sight of him.''

Toda turned a few pages. ''At age fifteen, he killed a *rōnin* in a duel which he initiated. In the same year, he led a gang that raided an *eta* settlement and killed ten people. At age sixteen, he beat to death a boy prostitute and was banned from Yoshiwara.

Since then he has had boys brought to his family's summer villa in Ueno. Prefers masturbation and superficial mutilation of a drugged partner to actual coupling. At age seventeen . . .''

The list went on and on. Incident after shocking incident, interspersed with the most personal details of Lord Niu's life. Appalled by Lord Niu's excesses, Sano was nevertheless impressed by the wealth of information that the *metsuke* had gathered. Had they managed to plant spies even among the Nius' servants and retainers? Maybe they did know everything worth knowing about Lord Niu. Maybe the plot was nothing but a game of make-believe played by a group of idle young men.

''All of these incidents were suppressed with the Nius' money and influence,'' Toda finished. ''But that didn't keep us from learning of them. I think you can see that we have sufficient information by which to judge Lord Niu's character. We don't underestimate him—or overestimate him.''

Or maybe the *metsuke* assumed that, because Lord Niu hadn't yet injured anyone who mattered to them, he never would. That assumption, plus their faith in the Tokugawa omniscience, blinded them.

''Can you be sure that your spy network is functioning as it should?'' Sano asked. ''It seems to me that by hiring blackmailers as informers, you run the risk that they'll use the intelligence they collect for their own purposes instead of reporting it to you. As Noriyoshi did.''

''Noriyoshi was not an informer.'' In response to the surprise that must have shown on Sano's face, Toda explained, ''You said so; I never confirmed it. He was merely an individual who came to our attention from time to time. We kept a watch on him, as we do upon all Yoshiwara inhabitants who deal with high-ranking citizens. But he was never in my employ. As you pointed out, blackmailers don't make the most trustworthy informers.'' His lips turned up in a humorless, insincere smile that didn't reach his eyes.

Sano stared at Toda in confusion. He was sure the *metsuke* was lying. But why? To save face? To protect the network? With Noriyoshi dead, what did it matter if anyone knew he'd been an informer?

"You granted me an audience because I knew Noriyoshi worked for you," he reminded Toda. He couldn't have been mistaken about that. But now he had the eerie sensation he experienced during minor earthquakes, when the subtle shifting of once-solid earth cast doubt upon his notion of reality. Toda's bland denial shook his belief in his own story. Had he indeed fabricated it, for the reasons Toda gave? Was he such a self-deluding fool? Magistrate Ogyu and Katsuragawa Shundai would agree. As would the Council of Elders, if he went to them without O-hisa. A growing sense of despair provoked him to speak more sharply than he'd intended.

"You were willing enough to listen before you found out who I was. Do you serve the shogun by dismissing the news of a plot against him without even checking to see if it's true?" He stood over Toda as he gestured with the rope and sandal that his hands had somehow picked up from the floor. "How can you fulfill your duties when you reject information that comes your way?"

"I granted you an audience because it would have been negligent of me to overlook the possibility that you had something of value to us," Toda corrected him mildly. "Contrary to your opinion, we welcome factual information from all reliable sources. We run an efficient operation that has served the Tokugawas well and helped keep them in power for eighty-eight years. We investigate whatever warrants investigation.

"And now, Sano-*san,* I hope you will excuse me." He clapped his hands to summon the guard. "Your moment is up. Good day."

Cold, hungry, and almost ill with fatigue, Sano slowed his footsteps as he approached his parents' district. Not wanting to face his father again, he still found himself drawn to the comfort and security of home. He couldn't face the cheerless impersonality of an inn; besides, he lacked the energy to walk to one. The physical exhaustion that drained his strength brought with it a sense of defeat just as enervating.

He now had to admit that his own ambitions, for which he'd sacrificed his father's, had come to nothing. He'd learned the truth, but failed to elicit value from it. He had discovered that Lord Niu planned to kill the shogun, but how could he stop him? Further attempts to warn the authorities would likely turn out no better than today's. O-hisa's broken promise had destroyed his hopes for a successful end to the murder investigation. Without her testimony, the Council of Elders would never act against Lord Niu—not on the strength of unsubstantiated theories, with a shoe and a rope as the only evidence. Tsunehiko's death would go unavenged, as would Noriyoshi's and Yukiko's. Sano had already lost Katsuragawa's patronage for good. And today he'd lost his belief in his own power to realize his desires—to expose the truth, reclaim his status and self-respect, deliver the guilty to justice, and save his father's life. Standing outside the gate that led to the canal, bridge, and street he'd known forever, he faced the sum of his losses.

It can end here, he told himself. The danger, the frustration, the ambivalence, the uncertainty. All he had to do was go back to the life he'd lived before he'd become a *yoriki*. Let Magistrate Ogyu's version of justice suffice; the real victims—Noriyoshi, Yukiko, Tsunehiko, and Raiden—were beyond caring. Let Toda and his kind protect the shogun however they chose. Such things need no longer concern him. But these consoling thoughts only increased his misery. His spirit sickened at the thought of giving up, even as reason told him it was his only choice. Bleakly he reflected that this episode of his life might end, but he would live with its consequences for the rest of his years. Then, because he had nowhere else to go, he passed through the gate and continued homeward. Maybe tomorrow he would think of a way to salvage his honor and make amends to his father—and somehow prevent the old man's death.

As he crossed the bridge over the canal, a furious barking from below caught his attention. He looked beyond the railing. Sluggish brown water flowed between short, steep, brush-covered banks crowned with high wooden fences. Downstream, three dogs snapped and lunged at one another beneath a straggly willow tree. The largest, a sleek black hound, seemed to be guarding something partially hidden by the willow's branches. Behind the branches and the dog, Sano could see a pale, indistinct shape. He started to move on, thinking that the starving animals had killed one of their own kind and were fighting over the carcass. The Dog Protection Edicts forbade him to interfere. But there was always a chance that a child had drowned in the canal. If so, he should chase away the dogs before they ravaged the body. He should try to identify it and locate the family.

Sano ran to the end of the bridge and skidded down the bank. He picked his way over the strip of muddy earth between water and brush. Just short of the willow tree, he halted in his tracks. Horror and disbelief drove a shaft of ice down his spine. Exclaiming in dismay, he stood and stared.

The snarling black hound stood over the naked body of a small, thin woman with tangled black hair and round buttocks. She lay facedown, one arm against her side, the other extended and bent at the elbow so that her hand would have touched her head—except that she had no hands. Both arms ended in bloody stumps, cleanly severed at the wrists. Her legs had suffered even worse damage: feet, ankles, calves, and kneecaps were missing.

Sano swallowed past a dry mass in his throat as he took in the extent of the mutilation. Deep gashes on her limbs and torso exposed bone as well as bloody tissue. Dark bruises covered her buttocks. And, as the wind lifted her hair, he saw another bruise around her neck, this one imprinted with the twisted pattern of the cord her killer had used to strangle her.

"Merciful Buddha." His lips moved in automatic prayer.

The black dog barked and suddenly lunged at Sano, stopping just short of actual contact. At this signal, the other two began growling. Sharp teeth gleamed in their red mouths as they pressed close to him, driving him away from their prize.

Released from his horror-stricken paralysis, Sano found his voice. "Get away!" he yelled. He aimed a kick at them. "Go!"

Still growling, the dogs retreated. Sano knelt beside the corpse. After seeing Noriyoshi's dissection and finding Tsunehiko's body, he'd thought himself inured to further shock. But the dissection had had a purpose, and Tsunehiko's death, however terrible, had been caused by a single cut. This meaningless savagery shook him to the core. What kind of monster would do such a thing?

Sano looked back toward the bridge and the street. He should call the guard, and the police. But first he wanted to see the woman's face. If she was a neighbor, better that he should notify her family than some *doshin* or other official. Carefully positioning his hands on her hip and shoulder so as to avoid the worst gashes, he rolled her over onto her back. His stomach twisted when he saw that both her nipples had been cut off, leaving raw circular wounds. Nauseated, he looked at her face.

He saw bulging eyes that still held an expression of sheer terror. Swollen cheeks and nose. A trickle of dried blood at each corner of her mouth. Familiar features, altered by death, but not beyond recognition.

"O-hisa," he whispered.

25

The world receded from Sano's consciousness as he struggled to comprehend his terrible discovery. The dogs barked and growled on the bank of the canal; ravens shrieked overhead as they circled the kill. These sounds merely brushed against the surface of his mind. Who had killed O-hisa, and why?

The guilt and self-hatred Sano had felt after Tsunehiko's murder returned in full force. O-hisa had died because of him. Now he had another death on his hands, this one worse because he'd known the risks. But what was she doing here? She couldn't have been coming to see him; he hadn't told her where he lived. Sano quickly scanned the surrounding area. There was very little blood on the ground beside the body, and no sign of her severed hands or legs, or her clothing. The fences shielded the canal from view of the houses, but surely someone would have heard screams and rushed to see the murder taking place. They would have summoned the police, if not in time to stop the murder, then at at least to remove the corpse afterward. So she'd been killed elsewhere. But then why had her body been dumped here, not much more than a hundred paces from his home?

Footsteps clattered across the wooden bridge above and behind Sano. He turned. Realization struck him in a wave of chilling sickness when he saw the three men hurrying toward him: a *doshin* accompanied by two assistants, one carrying a coiled rope, both waving barbed staves. He understood now why Lord Niu had left O-hisa here for him to find.

The *doshin* reached the end of the bridge. A heavy, muscular man, he clambered awkwardly down the bank of the canal. "Murderer!" he shouted. "For this you will die like a common criminal, Sano Ichirō. We'll have your head on a pike beside the river by next dawn!"

It was a setup. Lord Niu, not satisfied with seeing him relieved of his position as *yoriki,* intended to stop his investigation by framing him for O-hisa's murder. No matter that there was no blood on his sword, no witness to his supposed crime, and no reason for him to kill her. The Nius' wealth and influence had already purchased his fate. Magistrate Ogyu would seal it. Although a samurai wouldn't normally be treated like a criminal for killing a peasant, the hideous mutilation of O-hisa's body made her otherwise unimportant murder an atrocity, a punishable offense. Not even his rank would save him from execution. Lord Niu need never worry about his interference again.

This awareness hit Sano in a flash of searing, inarticulate comprehension. While he stood immobilized by shock and horror, the *doshin*'s assistants slid down the slope ahead of their master. Sano knew that whatever he did, he couldn't let them catch him. In Edo Jail, he, like Raiden and countless others, would eventually confess under torture. His only hope of survival lay in remaining free long enough to prove that he hadn't killed O-hisa, and that Lord Niu was both murderer and traitor.

"Come along with us easy, now," the *doshin* called as he lumbered and panted behind his men. "No use fighting. There're three of us and only one of you. Accept your destiny like a true samurai."

The assistants ran toward Sano. One began to uncoil the rope. The other raised his staff. Sano backed away as he cast about wildly for a way to escape. Simply running—the obvious, cowardly solution—would do him no good. He knew his home terrain. Just a few steps behind him, the canal's banks grew steeper, almost vertical. Surfaced with smooth stone, they offered no footholds. He'd tried to climb them often enough in his youth, but had always failed and fallen into the water. The water itself was shallow at this time of year, no more than waist high, but with a muddy bottom that would grasp and hold his feet. And there was no use running upward. They would catch him before he could scale those high fences at the crest of the bank. Trapped, he did the only thing he could: He drew his sword.

Perhaps taking his initial hesitation as a sign that he didn't mean to fight, the nearest assistant rushed Sano, body wide open to attack. Too late he saw the sword; too late he skidded to a stop and lowered his staff to protect himself.

Sano's blade cut him diagonally from neck to waist. He screamed and sank to the ground, hands clutching the torn front of his kimono, which immediately darkened with blood.

The other men crashed into him. They fell back, uttering yells of outraged surprise. Before they could recover and set upon him with their weapons, Sano fled. As he swerved around them, he recognized the *doshin* whose arson investigation he'd commandeered, the day he'd heard of the *shinjū*. How long ago it seemed! Seeing the lust for revenge in the small, cruel eyes, he charged down the shoreline and up the steep bank toward the bridge. He wished he could look back to make sure that the man he'd cut was only superficially wounded, as he'd intended, and not dead. Had he misjudged the pressure of his stroke? But the others were already hot in pursuit.

"Stop! I order you to stop!" the *doshin* yelled.

His unhurt assistant, younger and quicker, bounded up behind Sano. Blows landed on Sano's shoulders. He gasped as the barbed staff bit his flesh, and kept running. He didn't want to fight and kill the man, but he refused to die for a crime he hadn't committed. The added trauma of his arrest, conviction, and execution would hasten his father's death. Nor could he let Noriyoshi's, Yukiko's,

Tsunehiko's, and O-hisa's murders go unavenged. And now he had another, even more critical reason to live. He was the only person who believed that Lord Niu meant to assassinate the shogun, and hence the only person capable of thwarting him.

His feet hit the bridge. There onlookers greeted him with shrieks of terror.

"It's Sano Shutarō's son!"

"What's he done?"

"Killed someone, it looks like."

That the people he'd known all his life should think him a murderer filled Sano's heart with shame. He wanted to stop and explain that he'd been framed, but he couldn't. He must run for his life, or forever lose the chance to prove his innocence.

"Someone stop him!" the assistant shouted, panting as he landed another blow to Sano's shoulder.

The *doshin,* falling far behind now, shouted, "You are a dead man, Sano Ichirō! You can't run forever!"

Sano waved his bloody sword. The crowd scattered. People shrank back against the bridge's railings to get out of his way. One man jumped over the rail and landed in the canal with a splash. Sano sped across the bridge. Desperation drove his legs to pump faster. The staff no longer battered him as he pulled ahead of his pursuers. But when he reached the gate, he saw trouble waiting for him: the two guards.

"That man is a murderer," the assistant yelled to them. "Catch him!"

Sano had hardly cleared the gate when the guards joined in the chase. His heart was pounding furiously now; his chest heaved with each frantic breath. He heard more shouts. Heard swords rasp free of their scabbards, and the stamp of four instead of two pairs of running feet behind him. As he plunged into the maze of narrow streets, a cramp shot across his left side. He could run no faster. A quick glance backward told him that the men were gaining on him. His breath came in sobs now. Though he forced himself to keep moving, he tasted defeat. His skin tingled in anticipation of a sword's swishing descent and the mortal agony as it gashed his back.

Then he spotted his salvation: one of his neighbors, an elderly samurai mounted on a brown horse, ambling toward him.

"I'm sorry, Wada-*san*," he cried. "Please forgive me, but I must borrow your horse."

The old man gave a startled grunt as Sano dragged him off his mount.

"I promise I'll return it," Sano shouted as he mounted the horse and slapped the reins. Would that he lived long enough!

Urging the horse to a gallop, he risked a backward glance. He saw the men still following, but falling rapidly behind him. The *doshin* waved his *jitte*, shouted something, then stopped, a hand pressed to his middle.

Triumph pulsed through Sano's veins. He was free! For how long, though, he didn't know. The *doshin* would alert his comrades across the city; soon they and their men would join the hunt for the murderer Sano Ichirō. And exactly how he would use his temporary freedom, he didn't know either.

The alley was dim, deserted, and forbidding. On either side, rows of ramshackle buildings leaned inward, blocking much of the sky to form a short tunnel of twilight. Three public privies sent forth a sharp stench and leaked dirty water onto the ground. But Sano welcomed the alley as a haven from the streets of this poor section of Nihonbashi, where the *Setsubun* festivities were rapidly escalating in fervor. After a quick look behind him to make sure no one was following, he guided Wada-*san*'s horse into it. Seeing two adjacent doorways screened with bamboo lattices, he dismounted and squeezed both himself and the horse into the small space between them so that no one entering the alley from either end would see them. Then he leaned against the wall and closed his eyes, trying to rest. To think.

His wild, directionless gallop through Edo had consumed the remainder of the afternoon. He'd had no time to think past his immediate aim of putting as much distance as possible between himself and the canal where he'd found O-hisa's body. He had no plan except to lose himself in the crowds and avoid the police. In this he'd succeeded, barely. The teeming *Setsubun* revelers offered plenty of cover, but he'd sensed a heightened watchfulness about the police he'd spotted. Unusually tolerant of the antics taking place around them, they'd scanned each face as if looking for someone.

For him. Already.

Sano passed a trembling hand over his face. He had to plan his next move now. He couldn't afford to waste a moment of his precious freedom. But the noise from the street clamored at his aching head; desolation paralyzed his mind. The wounds on his shoulders throbbed, and blood plastered them to his clothing. Already the underlying muscles had swelled and stiffened; he couldn't turn his head or move his arms without pain. Fear had solidified in him like an iron skeleton. His whole body sagged with fatigue, and he'd never felt more alone. Shivering in his cloak, he reflected with amazement upon the changes that a few hours had wrought in his life.

Before finding O-hisa's body, he'd had a choice whether to continue pursuing Lord Niu. Now he had none. He couldn't turn his back on the events of the past fourteen days and go home. The *doshin* would be waiting for him there, no doubt with a small army of reinforcements to help carry him off to jail or kill him on the spot. Compared to this reality, the past disgrace he'd brought upon his family seemed insignificant.

He couldn't sink back into comfortable obscurity. As a fugitive, he would spend the rest of his days on the run while the whole country hunted him. Even if he'd possessed the cash to provision himself and Wada-*san*'s horse for a journey, he knew that a flight to the provinces was futile. By now Magistrate Ogyu would have dispatched messengers to the highway checkpoint guards and village headmen, warning them to be on the watch for him. His quest for vengeance had merged with the simpler, more powerful desire for survival.

From deep inside himself, Sano summoned what strength he had left, a small but brave force now reduced to the bare samurai steel his father's training had given him. He had no choice but to prove his innocence, or die in the attempt. Otherwise, his life was over anyway. If he remained a fugitive, everyone and everything he cared about—his family and friends and his honor—would be lost to him forever. To flee for his own life and let Lord Niu assassinate the shogun would be to fail in his ultimate duty to the highest lord of the land. The greatest disgrace of all. Sano's mouth twisted in a bitter smile. If getting help from the authorities had seemed difficult before, it was impossible now. Anyone he approached would have him arrested before he could finish one sentence.

The sound of footsteps jarred Sano out of his gloomy contemplation. He laid a steadying hand on the horse's neck and peered around the lattice screen. To his relief, he saw coming toward him not a *doshin,* but a man dressed in a gaudy purple-and-gold cloak and a strange flat cap. Obviously drunk, he zigzagged down the alley to the privies. Sano saw that his cap wasn't one at all, but a mask, pushed up on his head out of the way. Selecting the middle of the identical wooden sheds, the man stumbled inside.

The sight of the man's *Setsubun* costume roused Sano to action. A disguise was absolutely essential to the plan beginning to take shape in his mind. Mounting his horse, he walked it over to the privies and waited.

The drunk staggered out of the privy. With two swipes, Sano plucked the mask off his head and tore the cloak from his shoulders.

"Hey, what—" The man spun around and fell on his buttocks.

Sano kicked the horse's sides as he stuffed the cloak under his arm and fastened the mask over his own face. It was, he saw, an armored face shield that must have once belonged to a general or other high-ranking officer. Made of black metal, it had slits cut out for the eyes and mouth, and a bristly black horsehair mustache.

"Filthy samurai!" the drunk bawled at him, shaking a fist. "Think you can just take whatever you want!"

Now doubly a thief, Sano started to gallop away with his stolen goods. How ironic that in his crusade to catch a criminal, he'd become one himself! Then he turned back. Taking some coins from his pouch, he threw them at the drunk. They clinked and scattered across the ground.

"Have these as payment," he called. He might die at any moment, and he didn't want his last act to be one of thievery, no matter how necessary. Besides, there was no use hoarding money now. If he survived this night—if his plan succeeded—he could earn more somehow. If not, then what little cash he carried wouldn't even pay for his funeral. Now he wished he'd thought to pay Wada-san for the horse that he might never return.

He swung the horse about and headed for the street. At the end of the alley he slowed to don the purple cloak printed with gold peonies. His long sword made an awkward bulge in it, and he hoped no one would notice and wonder why a samurai hid his weapons.

Out in the streets, the crowd swirled around him. Masked faces leered: dragons, monkeys, demons, tigers. Troupes of wandering musicians played drums, flutes, and clappers. A shower of pellets rained down on Sano as he passed a house where a group of women stood on the roof.

"Devils out! Fortune in!" they chanted, throwing roasted soybeans into the street for good luck.

Sano headed southwest out of Nihonbashi toward the daimyo district. With part of his attention, he watched for the *doshin;* with the rest, he concentrated on making his way without trampling anyone, and on searching the blocks of buildings for the one he wanted.

At the torii gate of a Shinto shrine located between two shops, he dismounted and secured his horse. He walked through the shrine's precinct, where the neighborhood's residents flocked around stalls that sold snacks and *amazake,* the sweet, gingery fermented New Year's rice brew. The inner gates bore a long, looping rope of twisted rice straw, denoting the sacred space, strands of plaited white paper, and ferns. Outside the small, thatch-roofed shrine festooned with pine and bamboo and draped with white banners printed with the Tokugawa crest, he paused at the stone water basin to rinse his lips. He dropped a coin into the offering box, pulled the rope to sound the gong, and clapped his hands twice in prayer. Then, after leaving his shoes beside others that stood outside the door, he went into the shrine.

As he looked for the priest, he saw a family—father, mother, and two children—standing before the altar. The mother was unwrapping a package of cakes to leave as an offering to the stone image of the harvest goddess Inari.

"We do this so that she will bless us with good luck in the New Year," the father explained to the children.

With his own chances for good fortune almost nonexistent, Sano felt very remote from them, as if an invisible screen separated him from the everyday world.

"Come, why so sad? Holidays are for celebrating."

Sano turned to see the priest standing beside him, an old man with a face like a dried apple. He wore a cylindrical black hat on his bald head, and a deep purple robe over his white kimono. Wrinkles creased the skin around his eyes and mouth when he smiled.

"Are you troubled?" he asked. His expression turned serious with compassion. "Is there some way in which I can help you?"

No one could help him. He was alone in his trouble. But he'd come to ask the priest for a small service that might help those who cared about him.

"Yes," he said. "Might I have a brush, some ink, and a piece of paper? And a place where I can sit and write?"

If the priest thought this request odd, or thought it strange that Sano didn't remove his mask, he gave no sign. He merely motioned for Sano to follow him outside, to a shed at the rear of the shrine precinct. There, in a small room that served as storeroom, kitchen, and office, he arranged writing materials on a desk. He nodded to Sano and withdrew.

Sano took off his mask so that he could see in the dim shed. He ground the ink, mixed it with water, and dipped his brush.

Setsubun, Genroku 1.
Otōsan and *Okāsan,*

he wrote, regretting that his need for haste allowed him no time for the formal expressions of respect with which he would normally begin a letter to his parents.

By the time you get this letter, I will probably be dead. That being the case, I wish now to give you my most solemn oath that I did not kill the woman who was found by the canal today, no matter what anyone would have you believe.

Rather than passively accept my fate and the disgrace that my conviction and execution would bring upon our family, I must prove my innocence and bring the real killer to justice. I intend to do so by first stealing, then delivering into the hands of the authorities a certain scroll now in the possession of Lord Niu Masahito. It proves that he is guilty of treason and supports my contention that he killed four people and made me a fugitive from the law in order to conceal his plot to assassinate the shogun.

By this action may I also fulfill my duty to our highest lord by saving him from death at the hands of Lord Niu and his fellow conspirators.

I must leave you now, knowing that I might never return.

Please forgive me for all the suffering I have brought upon you.
With eternal gratitude, devotion, and respect,

Ichirō

Sano read over his ill-composed message, hoping that it would give his parents some measure of comfort, or at least explain his actions to them. He blotted the ink dry, folded and sealed the letter. He wrote his parents' full names and the directions to their house on it. Then he donned his mask and went outside, where he found the priest waiting.

"Will you please see that this message is delivered today?" he asked. He handed it to the priest, along with the rest of his money. "It's very important."

The priest frowned as he nodded and took the letter, though not out of offense at a stranger's imposition. He seemed to have accepted the gravity of Sano's predicament without question, as his next words proved:

"Is there no turning back from this dangerous course of action upon which you have decided?"

Sano looked away from the priest, toward the shrine's outer precinct, where a troupe of amateur actors had set up a makeshift stage. The hero, dressed as a samurai, was singing a lament about a son killed in battle. An appreciative audience cheered his anguished cries and posturings.

"No," Sano said. His destiny was laid out for him, just as that of the characters in the play. "I cannot turn back."

26

When Sano arrived in Edo's daimyo district just after night-fall, he discovered that the wide boulevards had undergone a dramatic transformation. Here, as in Nihonbashi, *Setsubun* had worked its magic, although to a more glamorous effect. Round lanterns hung on the walls of each estate, their orange glow warming the cold night. Gates stood open to receive processions of lavishly decorated palanquins accompanied by multitudes of attendants. Samurai, dressed either in their finest silk robes, or garishly costumed as children or warrior women or legendary heroes, rode or strolled, calling boisterous greetings to one another. Somewhere a bonfire burned, sending up wood smoke to mix with the cloying scents of perfume and hair oil. Jugglers, actors, and musicians performed with gusto, hoping to wring a few coins from the rich; beggars shouted pleas; monks sold charms guaranteeing good luck in the coming year.

Still disguised in his cloak and mask, Sano rode up to the Niu *yashiki* at a gallop. His heart hammered a rapid, urgent cadence in time to the hoofbeats: hurry, hurry, hurry! He must find a way into the estate and get the scroll tonight, when his costume let him move freely among the crowds of other gaudily dressed men, while *Setsubun*'s activity and confusion distracted the police. Fear and excitement sent flares of alarm through his body. This was his only chance to stop Lord Niu and exonerate himself. He must succeed.

He'd had plenty of time to foresee the difficulties his plan presented. The first, that of breaking into the heavily guarded estate, had seemed insurmountable. Now, however, he noted that security in the district was unusually lax. Most of the guards had left their posts to mingle with the crowds, sometimes straying far from the gates they were supposed to protect. Laughter and song issued from the barracks just inside the walls: The lords' retainers were celebrating, not standing watch. This was a holiday in peacetime; no one expected an attack. Maybe he had a chance after all. But when he reached the gate, what he saw there made him jerk the reins so hard that his horse reared. Fresh anxiety shot through him.

Deep in conversation with the guards was the *doshin* who had almost arrested him at the canal. Nearby stood another *doshin* and five assistants. Weapons in hand, eyes narrow with suspicion, they watched the crowds.

Sano forced himself to ride nonchalantly past the police. His skin prickled under their sweeping gazes, but to cut and run would only focus their attention on him. Dread strained his nerves almost to the breaking point and set up a deep tremor in his cold, aching muscles. His wounds, feverish now, throbbed harder. He breathed deeply through the mouth slit of his mask. His body relaxed a little, only to tighten again when he heard a shout close behind him. The man who'd given it ran past him, but Sano's uneasiness persisted.

He made his way to the back of the *yashiki,* a trip that took most of an hour because of the crowds and the size of the estate. An alley divided the Nius' property from their neighbors'. Just inside it, Sano dismounted.

The alley was long and narrow, its darkness relieved only by scattered light from lanterns on the side street, and the fainter radiance of the stars. As Sano led his horse deeper into the alley, he watched and listened. He met no one. No sound came from inside the walls, or at least none that rose above the muted noise from the streets. The Nius' rear gate faced that of its neighbor. Neither was guarded. Here he might enter the *yashiki* undetected—if enter it he could.

Sano contemplated the wall. Its smooth plaster-and-tile surface offered no handholds. Above it, the barred windows of the barracks stood high out of his reach. The barracks themselves extended without interruption along the wall, except where they rose slightly to form a guardhouse above the heavy timber gate. Then Sano raised his eyes higher. Ah, yes . . .

Elaborate curved finials crowned the peaks at either end of the guardhouse roof. Sano took the rope out of his cloak. Uncoiling it, he made a loop at one end, which he secured with a slipknot. He looked both ways, saw no one, then tossed the loop at the right-hand finial.

On his first and second tries, the loop missed the finial altogether. Sano began to sweat. The metal mask grew clammy against his face. He tossed the rope again. This time the loop fell over its mark. He pulled on the rope. The knot tightened and held fast.

Sano hesitated, reins in hand. He couldn't leave his horse here for a patrolling *doshin* to see. The best thing to do would be to send it away, but he hated to give up his means of escape. Despite the grave risk, he had to bring it through the gate once he got inside.

He dropped the reins over a post. Grasping the rope, he began to climb the wall, bracing his feet against it. The effort made the pain in his shoulders flare. He squeezed his eyes half-shut against it, wincing. A warm trickle down his back told him that his wounds had begun to bleed again. The coarse rope burned his hands. Certainly the wall hadn't seemed so high from below! At last he reached the guardhouse roof. Panting, he lay there, unable to move. If someone caught him now, he would have to surrender without a fight. When he recovered enough strength to lift his head, he looked down into the estate.

Dark buildings lay beyond a wide, dark stretch of open ground. Nothing moved or made a sound. Everyone had either left for the evening, or else they were up in the front part of the estate. But for how long?

Quickly Sano untied the rope and stuffed it back inside his cloak. He didn't want to leave evidence of his clandestine entry, and he might need it again. Then he slid on his belly down the sloping roof. Gripping the eaves, he lowered himself backward into the estate.

He was about to drop when he heard quick footsteps and men's voices outside the wall. The Nius' guards! If they heard him land, they would investigate the noise. Hands locked on the eaves, he dangled high above the ground.

The footsteps drew closer. Sano's hands and arms began to ache, then to shudder with fatigue. Spasms of pain gripped them, traveling to his wounded shoulders. He clenched his teeth and hung on. Now he could make out the men's words.

"This place is quieter than a grave."

"Well, we'll just make a quick check, then go back out front."

Sano recognized the second voice. Not a stranger's, but worse: the *doshin*. The thought of his horse, standing in plain sight in front of the Nius' gate, gave him no comfort whatsoever. Trying to will away pain and fear, he prayed for his pursuers to leave.

Then the *doshin* said, "There's nobody here. Let's go."

The footsteps and voices faded. Sano silently thanked the gods for incompetent police. How lucky for him that this particular *doshin* was as careless when chasing fugitives as when investigating arson! He let go of the eaves.

Hard earth flew up and struck him. He flexed his knees and did a backward somersault to keep his legs from breaking. His deepest, most painful wound—the one on his left shoulder—took the full weight of his body. A scream of agony almost burst from him. He stifled it by biting the inside of his cheek so hard that he tasted blood. His eyes watered as he forced himself to stand.

Sliding back the gate's heavy iron beams, he opened it and brought his horse inside. He tied the horse to the gate. Then, hoping it would be there when—if—he returned, he started toward the house.

With the problems of entering the *yashiki* and hiding the horse dealt with, Sano faced a whole new set of difficulties. How would he find the scroll? Was it even in the house at all? Was he correct in assuming that Lord Niu, wanting to keep the prized secret document safe and near, would have brought it back to town with him? Even if he did manage to escape with the scroll, how would he reach the higher authorities without being caught and killed? He thrust the last daunting thought aside. He would deal with each problem as it arose. First he must find Lord Niu's quarters in the vast, unfamiliar mansion.

He hurried across the bare expanse of what appeared to be a riding ground. Feeling conspicuous and vulnerable in spite of the darkness, he skirted a pond where the daimyo's men practiced swimming and fighting in armor. The sudden sight of two figures looming at him out of the blackness made him skid to a stop, heart in his throat. Then he recognized them as man-shaped archery targets. He reached the buildings weak with relief, but already anticipating the dangers ahead.

The first came when he passed the stables. Along with the stamping and snorting of the horses, he heard laughter; lamps burned in the grooms' quarters. He also saw lights in what must be retainers' and servants' wings. Ducking beneath the windows, Sano stole between the buildings. He crossed a garden like the one he'd seen on his first visit to the estate, and came at last to the great sprawling bulk of the mansion.

Its white walls shone eerily in the starlight. Above them, multiple roofs rose and fell like dark waves. Sano could see that the mansion was not one building but many, connected by low walls or covered corridors. He realized that the estate's layout was vastly more complex than that of the Nius' summer villa. How would he ever find Lord Niu's quarters, let alone the scroll?

The nearest gate led him to a narrow path that ran between the blank, solid walls of fireproof storehouses. He followed this until it dead-ended, forcing him to turn left. A wider path took him between high wooden fences with tiled rooftops rising above them, angling again and again. Sano soon lost all sense of direction. He could only hope that he was moving toward the center of the mansion reserved for the daimyo's family. The walls muted and distorted sound. Was he getting closer to the boulevard, or farther away? Were those voices coming from outside the estate, or from someone on the path behind or ahead of him? At each subsequent corner he paused for a longer interval, listening, but not trusting his ears.

Then a gate appeared in the fence. Standing to one side, Sano pushed on it. It swung open with a shriek that made him cringe. He peered inside to see a spacious garden surrounded on three sides by buildings with wide, covered verandas. A single lantern over each doorway threw weak light onto the pond, bushes, and pavilion. No lights burned in any of the windows, and Sano could see nothing to indicate exactly who lived in these rooms. They might belong to family members, or to high-ranking attendants. But even if Lord Niu's chambers lay elsewhere, getting inside would give Sano access to the rest of the mansion.

The garden's trees and shrubs shielded him as he advanced on the nearest building. Reaching the veranda, he tried a door. Locked. He jiggled, then shoved it, knowing that locks in even expensive homes tended to be flimsy. Why waste money on locks when roving patrols usually did a much better job maintaining security? But the door held firm. His efforts to pry it open failed; the point of his short sword wouldn't fit into the hairline crack between door and frame. He tried the other doors with no better luck, then turned to the windows.

These were covered with thin, closely spaced wooden bars. He selected one farthest from the lighted doorways and used his sword to pry away the bars. They broke in a series of sharp snaps that he hoped anyone inside would mistake for firecrackers. He cut and tore away the paper windowpane and looked through the jagged hole.

An empty corridor led past a series of closed doors separated by long expanses of paper-and-wood wall. Still clutching his sword, Sano climbed through the window. Stealthily he crossed the corridor and slid open a door. This led to an inner corridor, darker and also empty, with more doors opening off it. As he entered it, his elation over getting into the house faded.

Flowery perfume scented the air. In the nearest room, he saw the dark shapes of furniture that looked to be chests and dressing tables. The faint light from the doorway lanterns reflected off a tall mirror and gleamed on the satiny folds of discarded kimonos scattered on the floor. He was in the women's quarters. On tiptoe, he crept sideways down the corridor, his back pressed against the wall, in search of a way into the rest of the house.

Darkness magnified sound; each faint creak of the floorboards under Sano's feet exploded in his hypersensitive ears. Other noises—the house settling, a shout from somewhere on the estate—made him flinch.

Then he froze. A wavery smear of light was moving toward him down the corridor. An oil lamp, carried by a girl who walked soundlessly on stockinged feet. As she drew nearer, Sano could see her face glowing above the flame. At any moment she would come upon him.

Sano turned to retreat. Then he heard a door slide open somewhere behind him, and footsteps approaching. His mouth went dry; his stomach tensed. Lady Niu? One of the other women? Or a guard investigating the broken window? The footsteps grew louder. He could hear the girl, too, humming a breathy tune as she neared him. His escape cut off from both directions, he slid open the door of the nearest room. He would hide there until the girl and the other unseen person left, and then resume his search for Lord Niu's quarters. To his disappointment, he found not a room but a large closet crammed full of chests and boxes, with no space left for him. He had to run—one way or the other. Rather than face an unknown and possibly greater threat, he hurtled down the corridor toward the girl.

She gave a startled cry as he tore past her. Then she began to scream in earnest:

"A thief! Help!"

Sano burst through the nearest door in the outside wall. Instead of an outer corridor with access to the grounds, he saw a long, narrow passage ahead of him. The girl kept screaming. He raced down the passage. The door at the end led into an adjoining section of the house. He fled along its maze of corridors. Walls streaked past him in long expanses of wood broken only by mullioned paper windows. The interior windows were dark. Through the outside ones, he could see faint light coming from the garden, but the shadows of heavy bars striped the panes. Where was the door? Much as he hated to leave before he could find the scroll, he had to get out. Now. Before the guards came.

He turned a corner. To his horror, the floor began to emit loud, chirpy creaks every time he stepped on it. He'd hit a nightingale walk, a specially constructed floor that compelled intruders to give audible warning of their approach. Monks, nobles, and warrior lords had made use of this alarm system throughout history; he should have expected the Nius to have it. He tried to run lightly, staying close to the wall. Still the nightingales sang.

The corridor angled into another. A cold draft hit Sano. It came from an open door that led to a patch of lantern-lit garden. But as he raced toward the door, a horizontal oblong of brightness appeared ahead of him in the paper wall as someone lit a lamp in one of the rooms. A door slid open. Light spilled into the corridor. A tall figure stepped into his path.

Sano didn't wait for the person to speak. He pushed past it and lunged for the door. His feet hit the garden running.

"Eii-*chan!*" From the corridor, a woman's voice spoke.

Too late Sano saw the dark shape emerge from the shadows on his right. He sidestepped, but not quickly enough. The full force of the man's weight knocked him to the ground. The impact jarred his bones. His mask flew off his face; he dropped his sword. Pain burst in his left hip, which took the brunt of his fall. He fought and struggled, grabbing for his sword. But his assailant's strong hands were turning him onto his stomach, pressing his face into the dirt. Heavy knees came down on the small of his back. Steel arms caught his chest and shoulders in a fierce hug. Slowly, relentlessly, they bent his back upward. Sano gave an involuntary cry as pain shot through his spine. The man was going to break it! Jaws clenched, sweat running down his face, he resisted the pressure. It continued. Back, back his spine arched. He could almost feel the snap . . .

"No!" The woman's voice rapped out the order.

To Sano's immense relief, his assailant let go of him. The weight lifted from his body. Weakly he flopped over onto his back—sore, but unbroken—to face his captors.

Lady Niu stood over him. Her hair hung loose around her shoulders, and her grim face, with its layer of white makeup, looked ghostly in the flickering lantern light. The shimmering folds of her dark, sashless kimono enhanced her eerie appearance. With both hands she held a wicked-looking spear poised over his chest.

Then she smiled, lips parting to reveal her gleaming black teeth. She withdrew the spear.

"Bring him into the house, Eii-*chan,*" she said to the hulking manservant who stood beside her. "We will not kill him . . . yet."

27

The cruel triumph Sano saw in Lady Niu's eyes obliterated the slight relief he'd felt at being caught by her instead of her son. Hope died within him. Then Lady Niu turned and walked away. Her dark garments rustled against the ground and trailed up the steps of the veranda after her as she entered the house.

Eii-*chan* was leaning over him, reaching for him. Sano fumbled for his long sword. He dug his heels into the ground, pushing himself backward in a frantic attempt to evade the manservant. But his sword was tangled in the folds of his cloak, and the worsening pain in his wounds made his movements clumsy. Finally he kicked out at Eii-*chan*. His feet hit legs as solid as wood and just as unyielding. Eii-*chan* grabbed him and yanked him to his feet so hard that his arm nearly left its socket. A brutal shove sent him reeling toward the house. His foot struck the bottom step, and he gave a yelp of pain as he crashed against the veranda. Then Eii-*chan* lifted him by the collar, almost off his feet. One strong hand pinioned both of his behind his back; an arm locked across his chest. Sano struggled, then went rigid when the cold edge of a steel blade touched his neck.

As Eii-*chan* propelled him up the steps and through the door, Sano tasted his own death. A wild, animal terror surged through him. He fought it by forcing himself to concentrate on the minute details of his surroundings. Wind-bells tinkling from the eaves.

The corridor, no longer dark, but brightened by lamplight from the translucent windowed walls of the room where Lady Niu waited. The manservant's musty odor, strange but oddly familiar, that provoked in him an urge to sneeze. A faint memory swam just beyond Sano's grasp. He lost it when Eii-*chan* thrust him into Lady Niu's room and pushed him onto his knees.

He formed a quick impression of the room: spacious, with a wall of painted murals and another of built-in cabinets; several lacquer chests; a vase of flowers in the alcove. Then he focused his attention on its occupant.

"Tie him," Lady Niu ordered. She knelt upon a silk cushion, with more cushions supporting her back and arms. In spite of the heat that rose from the sunken braziers, she had wrapped a thick quilt around her shoulders.

Sano hid his discomfort as Eii-*chan* bound his wrists and ankles, although the cords dug into his skin and almost immediately began to numb his hands and feet. He suppressed a cry of protest when the manservant took his long sword—symbol of his class and honor—and tossed it on the floor like a piece of trash. All the while he never took his eyes off Lady Niu. He saw that her face was white not with makeup, as he'd thought at first, but with the pallor of illness. Beside her was a steaming cup of liquid that smelled like the sour herb broth Sano's father took for headaches. How unlucky for him that Lady Niu should happen to be sick at home tonight instead of out celebrating *Setsubun*! His senses sharpened by fear, he studied her, seeking clues that would tell him how to convince her to release him unharmed.

Her face revealed nothing except the same impassive control she'd displayed during their first meeting. The only words he could think of sounded too much like begging, which would only humiliate him further. He tried to take courage from the fact that she'd brought him inside instead of having him killed at once. Was she open to negotiation? Or did she want to enjoy seeing him tortured?

"Eii-*chan*," Lady Niu said, lifting her chin.

After one last tug on Sano's bindings, the manservant stepped back. He crossed the room to stand at a point halfway between and to one side of Sano and Lady Niu. He shot Sano a brief but eloquent glance that warned of the punishment he would administer should Sano try to escape or harm his mistress. Then his face hardened to its usual stony blankness, as though he didn't care that he'd just almost killed a man, or that he soon would. Raising one hand to his chest, he lifted a small pouch that hung on a cord around his neck and held it briefly to his nose. Then he folded his arms and looked straight ahead, immobile but with a waiting tension, ready to spring into action at any moment.

"You interest me, Sano-*san*," Lady Niu said as blandly as if this were an ordinary social occasion. She sipped her broth, then continued. "Before Eii-*chan* disposes of you, I would like to know why you have continued to pursue a course of action that has already cost you your position and will now cost you your life. Why do you compound your troubles by breaking into my house like a common thief? You are not, I think, an unintelligent man. Please explain yourself."

Although the amount of time remaining to him might depend upon his answer, Sano resisted revealing his inner self to her. He didn't want to try to articulate the insatiable desire for the truth that he barely understood himself. Anger burned in him as he realized that she was toying with him. But he would have to play along with her and hope she gave him an opening that would allow him to bargain.

"I came here tonight to collect evidence that proves your son guilty of at least one of the crimes that I know he has committed," he said, ignoring her first question and keeping his voice even.

"Oh?" Lady Niu's eyebrows rose in polite surprise. "And what crimes are those?"

How much did she know? Could he throw her off guard by giving her unwelcome news about young Lord Niu?

"The murders of his sister Yukiko and the artist Noriyoshi. The murder of my secretary, Hamada Tsunehiko, whom he mistook for me. The murder of a certain samurai boy, and of your maid O-hisa. And . . ."

He stopped when he saw Lady Niu regarding him with a complacent smile on her unpainted lips. Her relaxed posture reflected a total lack of concern. She didn't seem the least bit shocked, or even dismayed.

"You know all this already," he said, unable to keep the amazement out of his voice. "You know what your son has done, and you don't care."

Lady Niu's smile deepened as she shook her head. "Really, Sano-*san*, I am disappointed in you. Perhaps I have overestimated your intelligence."

Then Sano experienced one of those great intuitive leaps that come so seldom and never fail to stun. His mind reeled with shock as minor facts that he'd overlooked came together to form a pattern entirely different from the one he'd assembled using only the major facts.

Lord Niu, although as strong as rigorous training and self-discipline could make him, nevertheless had a physical handicap. He could—and did—kill, but could he have disposed of Yukiko's and Noriyoshi's dead bodies alone? His men had helped him get rid of the boy he'd decapitated in a fit of anger, but would he have trusted them to assist in a double premeditated murder—especially when one of the victims was their lord's own daughter? Sano thought not.

Midori's stepmother, not her stepbrother, had sent her to Hakone. And Lady Niu had been the one to complain to Magistrate Ogyu about Sano. Then there was the manservant's strange odor. It came from the pouch that Eii-*chan* wore, which probably held medicinal herbs. Sano now recognized the smell from his room in Totsuka the night of Tsunehiko's murder. He noticed the unhealed scratches on Eii-*chan*'s hands—inflicted by O-hisa and the nightwatchman he'd strangled. Sano had believed that Lord Niu had committed the murders to protect himself. Now he realized that Lady Niu had ordered Eii-*chan* to kill Yukiko, Noriyoshi, and O-hisa. She had sent the manservant to kill him on the Tōkaido, then had him dismissed and framed for murder. All to protect Lord Niu. He'd assigned the right motive to the wrong person. Shaking his head in wonder, Sano beheld the miracle of finally arriving at the truth he'd sought, and finding it so different from what he'd expected.

"I can see that you have guessed the truth." Lady Niu laughed, a silvery trill that echoed in the hushed room. "Although unfortunately too late to do you any good."

Sano knew he must keep her talking, if only to postpone the inevitable. "You sent Yukiko to the villa in Ueno," he said. "You lured Noriyoshi there by promising him enough money to open his own shop. While you were enjoying music at Lord Kuroda's house, Eii-*chan* killed them and threw them in the river."

Lady Niu laughed again. "Things are easy to understand when the facts are known, are they not?" To Eii-*chan* she said, "Kill this trespassing fugitive and turn his body over to the *doshin*."

As Eii-*chan* pulled him to his feet, Sano said, "There's no use committing another murder for your son, Lady Niu. You can't protect him from himself, and you have nothing to gain from his treason. He will only die for it. You must know that."

Neither Lady Niu's expression nor her posture changed, but she stiffened perceptibly. "Treason?" she repeated. "Really, Sano-*san,* I must caution you against making such offensive and groundless accusations. Do you want me to have Eii-*chan* make your death a prolonged and agonizing one?"

Her voice remained calm, but an underlying tremor told Sano that he'd shaken her. She wasn't lying—why would she bother, since she planned to kill him anyway? She didn't know about her son's conspiracy! She'd arranged four deaths solely to cover the lesser of Lord Niu's crimes. But Sano's surprise at this discovery was nothing compared to that he experienced as he watched her eyes take on a haunted, inward-gazing look. She didn't want to believe her son guilty of treason—but she did believe. She knew what he was capable of doing.

Sano stumbled as Eii-*chan* dragged him toward the door. He continued quickly: "Your son and a group of other sons of daimyo plan to assassinate the shogun and overthrow the Tokugawa government."

They were out the door before Lady Niu spoke.

"Wait, Eii-*chan* . . . bring him back." She sounded both eager and reluctant, wanting and yet not wanting to hear. "How do you know this?" she asked Sano.

On his knees before her once again, Sano told her. When he finished, she didn't respond at once. She frowned, deep in thought, while he waited in suspense. What would she do? He sensed that he now had a chance to save his life, but he couldn't guess what his next step should be until she made hers.

Then Lady Niu's face cleared. "You have a most impressive imagination, Sano-*san,* to dream up such a tale," she said, her smile back in place. "It amazes me that you have even managed to convince yourself that this scroll exists, so completely that you would risk your life by coming here to steal it."

Sano's chest tightened as he saw that Lady Niu had conquered her doubts about her son. But he didn't let her see his dismay.

"How do you know the scroll doesn't exist?" he said. "Can you say for a fact that it isn't in your son's possession? What do you think he does when he goes to the summer villa in winter?"

Working against his natural inclination to address a daimyo's lady with deference, he hurled the questions at her. And was rewarded by a flicker of doubt in her eyes.

"Why don't we go to young Lord Niu's chambers and look for the scroll now? Wouldn't you like to prove I'm wrong—if you can?"

He'd gambled that Lady Niu couldn't resist a direct challenge. She didn't disappoint him.

"Very well," she said, haughty and disdainful now. "We shall go at once. And when this futile exercise is finished, Eii-*chan* will see that you suffer doubly for wasting my time and addressing me in such a rude manner." She rose, picking up a lamp.

Lord Niu's chambers were in a self-contained house across the garden from Lady Niu's. With Eii-*chan* close behind him holding on to his ropes, Sano followed Lady Niu inside. She slid open a door.

"Bring him in, Eii-*chan*," she called over her shoulder as she entered the room.

The room's mean proportions surprised Sano, as did the starkness of its undecorated white walls and bare-beamed ceiling. Entirely different from what he'd seen of the rest of the house, it looked like a monk's cell. Even in the dim glow of Lady Niu's lamp, he couldn't miss the cracked plaster, the worn spots in the tatami, and the patched windowpanes. The room was very cold, but he didn't see a single brazier. He would have expected a daimyo's son to live surrounded by lavish displays of wealth. But now he decided that the room suited Lord Niu perfectly. A visual statement against self-indulgence, its austerity reflected the stern warrior values that Lord Niu upheld.

"And now I will show you that you are wrong about my son," Lady Niu said. Her voice had a too-bright quality, as if she thought that by convincing him she could convince herself. Setting her lamp on the floor, she began opening the cabinets that covered one wall.

The cabinets held very little—cotton bedding, toilet articles, a few of the plain dark kimonos that Lord Niu favored, a chest of books and another of writing materials. Lady Niu smiled as she made an exaggerated show of examining everything, but her hands shook. When she sorted through the chests, she cringed like a woman expecting a snake to strike at her.

Sano watched her in silence. He realized he was holding his breath, and expelled it. What if she didn't find the scroll? What if she did? Getting her to help him look might not be the clever move it had seemed at first. Either way, she was bound to punish him. Cold sweat formed on his skin. He clenched his teeth to keep himself from shivering in the frigid air. The pain in his shoulders worsened.

Lady Niu stooped to investigate the last section of the cabinet, a shelf that held underclothes. She pulled out each item and replaced it, stroking the fabric absently. Finally she straightened and spread her empty hands.

"See?" she said with obvious relief and a genuine smile. "The scroll you described does not exist. There is no evidence of any conspiracy." She folded her arms as her smile vanished. "You will pay dearly for this insult to my son and me." Her eyes flashed a signal to her manservant. "Eii-*chan*. Proceed."

As Eii-*chan* yanked on the ropes and pulled him toward the door, Sano cast one last desperate glance at the cabinet. He saw something he hadn't noticed before, which gave him hope.

"Look, Lady Niu," he cried. "There—in the cabinet. A place you missed. Do you see it?"

Lady Niu frowned, but her eyes went to the cabinet. She opened her mouth to speak, then closed it. Eii-*chan* paused and turned toward his mistress for her orders.

Knowing this was his last chance, Sano hurried on: "Above the shelf of undergarments. That blank rectangular panel. There's a hidden compartment behind it!" Many cabinets had such compartments, for hiding money from thieves. Would that Lord Niu's did, too, and that he'd found it!

Hesitantly Lady Niu tapped the panel with her knuckle. A hollow sound resulted, and she quickly withdrew her hand.

"It is nothing," she said. "Just . . . just a design flaw. The cabinet is poorly made, my son won't have expensive furnishings in his chambers. . . ." Her voice trailed off, and she lifted troubled eyes to Sano.

Sano could see her need to deny her son's crime, and her need to know whether the compartment contained the scroll. With a shock he realized that he and Lady Niu had more in common than he'd ever thought possible. Out of a need to control the forces generated by her son's turbulent nature, she might scheme and kill and destroy. Hers was a dangerous, misplaced loyalty. But like himself, she would never rest until she knew the truth. The knowledge both disgusted and heartened Sano. He thought he knew what her decision would be now. He let her struggle with herself until she reached it.

"Eii-*chan,* remove this panel," Lady Niu ordered.

Dragging Sano with him, Eii-*chan* walked to the cabinet. Sano watched in an agony of anticipation as the manservant drew his short sword with his free hand and applied it to the panel. Lady Niu held the lamp close so that Eii-*chan* could see. The only sounds in the room were her rapid breaths, the scratch of metal against wood, and the distant bursts of firecrackers from the street.

Eii-*chan* inserted the blade beneath the panel. With a single quick movement, he bore down on the sword's handle. The panel came loose with a sharp crack that made them all start. As it fell to the floor, Sano felt a surge of triumph. He heard Lady Niu gasp.

There before them was a narrow, dark compartment just large enough to admit a man's two hands. Lady Niu reached inside it. The stricken look on her face told him what she'd found even before she pulled out the scroll.

Moving slowly like a woman in a trance, Lady Niu handed her lamp to Eii-*chan,* who let go of Sano to take it. Here, Sano thought, was his opportunity to escape. He let it pass, realizing as he did so that he'd already lost another when Eii-*chan* had relaxed his grip to work on the panel. The same yearning for knowledge and truth that had made him pursue his investigation kept him rooted to the spot. He had to see this moment through. Unless he could use what came out of it, his life was worth nothing anyway.

Lady Niu untied the silk cord that bound the scroll. Her face was devoid of all emotion now, but it had grown even paler. She let the scroll fall open. Her eyes moved up and down the columns of characters on the paper. Her colorless lips formed the words silently as she read. Then she sank to her knees, the scroll spread across her lap with her head bowed over it.

Sano took a step closer to Lady Niu. Eii-*chan,* perhaps uncertain what to do without orders from his mistress, didn't stop him. Looking down at the scroll he'd glimpsed only from a distance before, Sano read:

We whose names appear here, signed in our own blood, commit our lives to the overthrow of the Tokugawas. Death to Tokugawa Tsunayoshi. Victory and honor to our clans, the rightful rulers of the land.

        The Conspiracy of Twenty-One:

Niu Masahito

Maeda Yoshiaki	Date Takatora
Hosokawa Tadanao	Hosokawa Tadao
Kuroda Nagakira	Kuroda Nagamura
Asano Naokatsu	Mori Kagekatsu
Nabeshima Yorifusa	Todo Yoshinobu
Todo Yoshihiro	Ikeda Hirotaka
Hachisuka Sadao	Yamanouchi Hidenari
Satake Masatoshi	Arima Iyehisa
Uyesugi Tadateru	Uyesugi Tadasato
Ii Masanori	Torii Ōgami

Sano looked up from the scroll to see that Lady Niu had lifted her head. Her sorrowful eyes stared off into space, and he knew she had finally accepted the fact of her son's treason. She was picturing and weighing the dangers that he faced. Betrayal by one of his servants, retainers, or fellow conspirators: possible. Death at the hands of Tokugawa Tsunayoshi's bodyguards or the public executioner: likely. Or, if he somehow managed to kill the shogun and escape, a relentless manhunt that would leave no corner of the country safe for him. Young Lord Niu would die without glory, sooner rather than later, successful or not, by his enemies' hands—or by his own, as a last-resort attempt to avoid capture and dishonor. His mother understood this. Sano could see it in the way her face seemed to crumple, as if the bone structure were disintegrating. Then she spoke, in a small, hollow voice completely different from her usual one:

"He cannot succeed. He will only destroy himself."

Sano realized how much hinged on his handling of this moment. He might never make Lady Niu pay for the murders, but he could save the shogun and prevent much needless bloodshed. He chose his words carefully.

"You can save your son by preventing him from assassinating the shogun."

Tears shimmered in Lady Niu's eyes as she shook her head. "You do not understand. Ever since he was a child, my Masahito has had his own will. No one, nothing, could ever break his contrary spirit. And I, who have loved him and given him everything, have the least influence over him. I cannot stop him." Her voice broke in the ugly, tortured sob of one who rarely wept.

"You must try," Sano said softly. "Otherwise . . ." He paused, knowing he didn't have to finish the sentence. She knew as well as he that the standard punishment for treason was death not only for the traitor, but for his entire family as well. The Nius, with their power and influence, might be able to get their sentence reduced—to confiscation of their fief, and lifelong exile. But they would prefer death's lesser disgrace.

Lady Niu sat as still as a stone. Only her trembling lips betrayed her struggle for self-control. Then she said in a barely audible whisper, "It will do no good."

"At least talk to him," Sano coaxed. He wished he could put

his hand on hers; touch might persuade where words couldn't. Instead he leaned toward her until Eii-*chan* pulled him back. "Go to him. Now, while there's still time."

"No. He will not listen to me. And besides, I do not know where he is. He said he was meeting someone who is costuming himself as a princess from *The Tale of Genji* . . . they plan to celebrate *Setsubun* together. Masahito seemed very excited . . ." Obviously dazed, Lady Niu was rambling as though unaware of the irrelevance of what she said.

"Then what about his father?" Sano asked. "If you tell the daimyo, surely he could—"

"No!"

Lady Niu's composure shattered. Her eyes widened, darkening as if she beheld some horror visible only to her. Then she bowed her head. Tears dropped onto the scroll as she wept silently.

Sano felt an unexpected sympathy for her. How would his own mother feel upon learning that her son was doomed? As she soon might. He fought his sympathy by remembering Tsunehiko and that terrible night in Totsuka.

"Then you must report the conspiracy to the authorities," he continued mercilessly. "For your own sake, and the sake of your husband and your family. You know you cannot cover up an attack on the shogun as you did the murders of Noriyoshi and Miss Yukiko. The truth will come out for everyone to see. And when it does, you won't be able to shield your son from the consequences of his actions."

A sudden stiffening of Lady Niu's body told him that she'd been trying to think of a way to do exactly that. Her tremulous sigh marked her failure.

"We will go to the Council of Elders now, and show them the scroll. They will—" Sano started to say "have your son arrested," then rephrased it "—see that young Lord Niu hurts no one. Come. You know you have no other choice."

She continued to weep. Sano waited. And waited. Would she

agree? His own fate depended on her decision. He needed her company and that of her armed escorts to protect him from the police until he got to Edo Castle. Once there, he was almost sure he could make the devastated and distraught Lady Niu confess to the murders and exonerate him. Eii-*chan*'s hand tightened on the ropes, increasing both his physical distress and his impatience.

Then Lady Niu raised her head and blinked away her tears. She squared her shoulders and achieved a poor semblance of the proud daimyo's lady she'd once been.

"You are right," she said, her voice at once bleak and resolute. "I have no other choice. Eii-*chan,* untie our guest and give him back his weapons. Then come immediately to my chambers. Sano-*san,* please excuse me while I make myself ready."

"Of course." Sano heaved a huge breath of relief as Eii-*chan* cut the ropes from his wrists, and not just from the end to discomfort. Very soon he would deliver a murderer into the hands of the authorities, reaping his revenge and serving justice. He would be a free man. And soon Lord Niu and his coconspirators would be arrested; the shogun would be safe. Picturing himself vindicated, restored to his status as a *yoriki,* his father well again, Sano fought down a surge of premature joy.

"May I have the scroll?" he added. It had lost much importance now that he had Lady Niu's cooperation. He'd known all along how little chance he'd have of convincing the authorities to revoke the charges against him—rather than arresting or killing him at once—and act against Lord Niu instead, scroll or no scroll. But he'd risked his life for it and still didn't want to let it out of his sight.

Lady Niu rolled up the scroll and retied the cord. Rising, she proffered it to Sano with a bow, her tear-stained face tense with the effort of simulating its former serenity.

Sano found her behavior oddly formal at a moment when no amount of formality could minimize the seriousness of her situation. Maybe she found comfort in polite ritual. He gravely returned her bow and tucked the scroll inside his cloak with the rope and sandal he still carried.

Alone in Lord Niu's room after Eii-*chan* left, Sano fastened his swords at his waist. The now-useless mask, which the manservant had also returned, he absently toyed with as he paced the floor. Time passed; still Lady Niu didn't reappear. What was taking her so long? Had she changed her mind about going with him? What would he do if she had? He wondered how the knowledge that she'd killed to protect a son bent on self-destruction had really affected her. She deplored Lord Niu's wrongdoing, but he was her flesh and blood, and she loved him. Would she really betray him, even if the alternative meant her own and her family's downfall? But she'd seemed so resigned, Sano argued to himself. As if she'd fully accepted the rightness of her decision. . . .

Sano stopped pacing in mid-step. A sudden premonition stunned him.

"No," he whispered as he realized what Lady Niu's real choice had been.

Bolting through the door, he raced down the corridor. He sped across the dark garden and burst into the building that housed Lady Niu's chambers. As he neared her sitting room, he heard a loud, anguished moan. He was too late. A shout burst from him as he halted in the doorway and saw exactly what he'd dreaded seeing.

"No!"

Lady Niu knelt on the mat, gripping the handle of the dagger that protruded from her throat. Blood gushed from the vertical gash in her pale flesh and onto her kimono. Her mouth was open. A thick gurgle issued from it, then a gout of blood. Her eyes rolled back to show their whites. Eii-*chan* stood beside her. Holding his long sword in both outstretched hands, he swung it upward, behind and high above the nape of her neck.

"No!" Sano shouted again. Rushing into the room, he fell to his knees before them.

Eii-*chan*'s sword flashed down in a swift arc, cleanly severing

Lady Niu's head, which hit the floor with a sickening thump, then rolled to land face up right in front of Sano. A great fountain of blood spouted from the neck of her slumped body, drenching walls, floor, and ceiling in red. Warm droplets pelted Sano's face as he stared helplessly at the manservant who had helped Lady Niu commit *jigai,* the women's version of ritual suicide.

Eii-*chan* had acted as her second, ending her misery by cutting off her head after she stabbed herself. To the end, he'd carried out his mistress's orders with a complete and terrifying obedience. Sano couldn't hate this man who stood contemplating his blood-stained sword with an expression of sorrow, pain, and disbelief that made him seem for once fully human. Eii-*chan* was in many ways a better samurai than he. What tremendous inner strength must it require to kill the person one had sworn to serve!

Sano looked down at the mutilated thing that had been Lady Niu. Her body had fallen onto its side; her hands still clutched the dagger. With something akin to pity, he saw that she'd tied her ankles together so that her body would be found modestly composed, whatever her death agonies. He felt no satisfaction at witnessing the destruction of the murderer of four people. Instead he experienced an overwhelming rush of sorrow for this woman whose loyalty and love had destroyed her. His appetite for vengeance dissipated, leaving him empty and shaken. He'd never imagined regretting the death of the killer he'd sought, but now he wished with all his heart that he could bring Lady Niu back to life. For a week, a day, or even an hour longer.

Because without her, how could he stop Lord Niu and exonerate himself?

28

As Eii-*chan* watched the glistening rivulets of blood drip from his sword, an unbearable emptiness opened inside him. The room seemed to blur until he was barely conscious of his surroundings. He was alone now. Horribly, frighteningly alone, as he'd been before Lady Niu entered his life.

He remembered that long-ago day in the courtyard of her father's mansion. He had been ten years old, ugly and already huge, painfully shy and sensitive and awkward. A confused child in a man's body which he hadn't yet learned to control. An outcast, trying not to cry as the other young samurai attacked him with their wooden swords.

"Kill the ugly demon!" they shouted.

Just when he could no longer hold back the tears, she came. Beautiful and imperious even at age seven, she sent his tormenters fleeing with a single glance. He gaped at her, too stupid and surprised to think of anything to say.

But his silence seemed to please her; she smiled. Pointing a tiny finger straight at him, she said in her high, little-girl voice, "You shall be my servant."

He never understood why she'd chosen him from among her father's retainers, never questioned his good fortune. He only knew that his life had changed in a miraculous way. With her patronage, he gained standing and respect. No child ever dared tease him again; no adult ever scolded him for his stupidity. And he repaid his mistress. He perfected his fighting skills so that he could protect her. He obeyed her every order instantly. When she married, he helped her manage the daimyo's household, spying on its members for her, punishing them for her. He loved her, but asked nothing in return except the honor of serving her. His greatest fear was that he might disgrace himself by failing to please her. For Lady Niu, he'd gladly killed Noriyoshi, O-hisa, and even Miss Yukiko, whom he'd liked for her beauty and sweetness. Discovering that he had killed the boy Tsunehiko instead of Sano had seemed like the worst catastrophe of his life.

Until now. Never, before he'd taken his sword to Lady Niu, had he ever imagined feeling such pain over carrying out her orders.

And now she was gone. He had nothing, no one to live for. Grief swelled his throat; the pressure of unshed tears built until he thought his head would burst. He looked down at Lady Niu's body and saw instead the smiling face of a beautiful seven-year-old girl. . . .

Dimly he grew aware of someone shouting at him. He blinked, and the room sprang into focus. The man Sano, whom he'd forgotten, was standing in front of him. Locked in his private void, he couldn't make sense of the man's words, or understand his agitation. But Sano's presence reminded him that he had one final task to perform for Lady Niu.

"Eii-*chan*, can you hear me?" Sano shouted in increasing desperation. "Can you understand what I'm saying?"

Lady Niu's death had greatly diminished his chances of proving his innocence and saving his own life. But perhaps he could still save the shogun. At Lord Niu's secret meeting, he'd gotten the impression that the assassination attempt would happen soon. Possibly while he still had his freedom? Without much hope, he turned to the silent and unmoving Eii-*chan* for the information he needed because there was no one else left to ask.

"Do you know where young Lord Niu is, or when he plans to attack the shogun?"

He resisted the impulse to grab the manservant and shake him, instead keeping a respectful distance away. Eii-*chan* might still be dangerous even without Lady Niu to direct him.

"If you do know, tell me. If you can. Please!"

The manservant gave no sign that he heard or understood. Instead he laid his sword down beside his mistress's body. Careful not to step in her blood, he walked to a writing desk by the window. He pointed at the sheet of paper that lay there. The inked characters on it, still wet, shone in the lamplight.

Lady Niu's farewell letter! Sano snatched it up eagerly in the futile wish that her message would somehow help him. Disappointment crushed him as he scanned the page.

To my dear and only son Masahito,

Know from this, my last message, that I love you above anyone or anything else in this world. To protect you I had Yukiko, Noriyoshi, and O-hisa killed. I also ordered the death of Sano Ichirō, whose secretary died in his place. Accept these terrible deeds as proof of the devotion that you would never let me express directly in words or gestures.

Now, in spite of my duty to your father, our family, and our lord shogun, I cannot bear to betray you. Therefore I choose *jigai,* the only alternative left to me, in order that I may restore my honor after failing both you and the others to whom I owe the debt of loyalty.

My dying wishes are two. The first, that you honor my spirit by not committing this treasonous act which will only destroy you. I know that you would not grant me this request in life; please grant it now. Do not let me have died in vain.

My second wish is that Sano Ichirō will stop you—if you do not stop yourself—and thus rescue our family from death and disgrace as I cannot.

And now I take my farewell of you, my beloved son. The merciful Buddha willing, may we meet again someday in the hereafter.

Your Mother

Sano leaned wearily against the wall, letting the paper dangle from one hand. Here at last was proof of the murders—and of his own innocence—in the form of Lady Niu's confession. Little good might it do him now, with the police more likely to kill him than to listen to reason! And it wouldn't save the shogun. After what Lady Niu had told him, he doubted whether her plea would influence her willful son.

"Read. Letter. Me."

The sound of Eii-*chan*'s voice, rusty with disuse, made Sano's head snap up in surprise. Never having heard him speak, he'd assumed that the manservant was mute.

"Read," Eii-*chan* repeated, bowing his head and clasping his hands like a beggar.

Sano had no more time to waste at the *yashiki*. He must at least try to deliver the scroll and Lady Niu's letter to the authorities so they could arrest Lord Niu and prevent the assassination. He must try to exonerate himself before someone killed him. But he'd suspected all along that Eii-*chan* was intelligent; his stealthy pursuit of Sano and Tsunehiko on the highway meant he was good at spying, perhaps on his own household as well. And now he knew Eii-*chan* could talk. Perhaps doing as Eii-*chan* asked would make the manservant tell what, if anything, he knew about Lord Niu's plans. Sano read the letter aloud.

When he finished, Eii-*chan* waited in silence for a moment. Then he grunted, "Is. All?" His face reflected the surprise in his voice.

"Yes." Sano thought quickly. "Eii-*chan*, listen to me," he said, stepping closer and extending a hand in tentative entreaty. "Lady Niu wishes me to stop Lord Niu, but I may die before I can warn the right people about him." He forced himself to keep the impatience out of his voice. "And even if they do learn of the conspiracy, they may not act in time. So if you know where Lord Niu is now, please tell me. For her sake."

A shake of the head, a shrug, his hands spread to profess ignorance, was his only response.

"Do you know when and where he plans to attack the shogun?"

But Eii-*chan* only brushed him away with a sweep of his mighty arm. He crossed the room to kneel beside Lady Niu's body. Her blood soaked his garments, but he didn't seem to notice or care. Unresponsive to further pleas, he stared mournfully down at her severed head as if the world and everything else in it had ceased to exist.

In despair, Sano reviewed every fact he'd learned about Lord Niu. But none gave the slightest hint at where or when the plot would culminate. Sano opened the scroll, seeking some hidden message within its lines. Then he stopped in the act of replacing the scroll inside his cloak. As he gazed at it, his vision blurred; a forgotten memory surfaced. His breath caught.

He saw Lord Niu at the secret meeting, standing on the platform, waving the scroll as he recited a poem.

> "The sun sets over the plain—
> Good luck as the New Year approaches."

Now Sano belatedly recognized the poem's references. "Sunset, and the coming of the New Year—*Setsubun,*" he said aloud in a voice hushed with dawning enlightenment. " 'Luck' and 'plain': 'Lucky Plain!' "—the familiar euphemism for the Yoshiwara pleasure quarter.

The conspirators had cheered because their leader had alluded to the date and place of the attack on the shogun.

Sano released his breath in a rush as a previously irrelevant fact completed the picture. Elation dizzied him. Lady Niu had said her son—probably flirting with danger by hinting at the plot—was very excited about meeting someone costumed as a princess from *The Tale of Genji*.

The shogun, celebrating *Setsubun* in female disguise. In Yo-shiwara. Tonight.

Sano turned and ran out of the room. Shock, anxiety, and an urgent need for haste pumped fresh energy through his tired, aching body. The hour was late; he was far from Yoshiwara. He didn't know the exact time and location of the attack, or how it would take place. Still, he might yet have time to warn the shogun of the danger. What little information he had was better than nothing.

Was it also enough?

Alone now, Eii-*chan* bowed his head as he knelt beside Lady Niu, weak and drained from the effort of speaking. Although he could understand words and compose them in his thoughts, some deficiency of nature had always kept them locked inside him. He hadn't talked at all until his sixth year. The habit of silence, formed when the other boys mocked his slow, faltering speech, was deeply ingrained. Only because he couldn't read and wanted to know what Lady Niu's letter said had he broken it tonight. And now he wished he hadn't.

He still couldn't believe that Lady Niu had left no last message for him. No thanks for his years of service; no expression of concern about what would happen to him after her death. Not even a farewell! He thought he would die of disappointment. He realized now that to the woman who'd meant everything to him, he was nothing. All along she'd considered him just a servant—or worse, merely a tool. She'd spent her last moments writing to her precious Masahito—the wicked, unloving son who had destroyed her. Afterward, she couldn't even bother to convey her gratitude to the man who really loved her. Eii-*chan* heard a terrible sound, half-sob, half-bellow, come from his own mouth. Nothing for him! After all he'd done for her!

But even now, he couldn't stop loving her. He couldn't hate her. She was still his lady.

Eii-*chan* sighed. He let himself experience the full depth of his anguish. Then, with the sheer discipline born of his samurai training, he put aside sorrow and anger. His hands moved swiftly and efficiently, removing the medicine pouch from around his neck, untying his sash and shedding his kimono. Drawing his short sword, he took one last look at his mistress's head. It was just a meaningless lump of flesh. The real Lady Niu lived on in that netherworld region where he would soon join her.

Imagining the joy of their reunion, he didn't even cry out as he drove the sword deep into his vitals.

29

Yoshiwara loomed ahead of Sano as he galloped along the highway through the dark marshes. Fireworks erupted over the walled compound, fitfully illuminating its rooftops with red, blue, white, and green sparks. Soon he heard shouts and laughter and the rat-a-tat of firecrackers above the pounding of his horse's hoofbeats.

The horse's pace slackened. Sano could feel its sides heaving with exertion, but he urged the exhausted beast on. His own breath came and went in gasps through the mouth slit of his mask, as if he'd run the whole distance himself. The wild ride from the daimyo district had taken two hours; now midnight was drawing near. Had the Conspiracy of Twenty-One already begun their attack on the shogun? Did he still have time to find and stop them?

If only Lady and young Lord Niu had given him more details! And if only he dared risk asking for help. But he was still a fugitive. Lady Niu, who might have called off the manhunt, lay dead in the blood-spattered tableau that would forever haunt his memory. Even with her letter and the scroll in his possession, he couldn't approach the magistrate, the police, or the castle guards; he might be killed before he could convince them to send troops to protect Tokugawa Tsunayoshi. With yearning he thought of his father's students and his friend Koemon, all skilled, courageous fighters, and loyal to their teacher's family. Just the allies he needed, and

impossible for him to contact. He couldn't go near his neighborhood, where the *doshin* would be patrolling in case he returned.

As Sano neared Yoshiwara's gate, he saw that it stood wide open
and virtually unattended. A group of men lounged to one side of
it: the two guards leaning on their spears, and five or six other
samurai. All held cups or flasks. Sano slapped the reins and charged
past them through the gate.

"Stop!" he heard the guards call. He didn't look back to see if
they were following him.

The pleasure quarter exploded around him in a burst of light,
noise, and confusion. Thousands of lanterns blazed from the eaves
of the buildings along Naka-no-cho. Men on rooftops launched
rockets. Smoke from a huge, flaming bonfire down the block made
Sano's eyes smart as he tried to steer his mount through the
crowds. Yoshiwara seethed with *Setsubun* merrymakers of every
description: samurai in full battle dress, peasants wearing nothing
but loincloths and shoes, bands of musicians and drummers.
Masked faces bobbed below him. The music and shouts merged
into one deafening roar of sound. Drunks reeled from side to side,
spilling sake and adding more aroma to air already pungent with
liquor, urine, and vomit. Some of the *yūjo* had left their cages to
mingle with the crowds. Sano had to stop when a parade of them
cut across his path. Dressed in their gaudiest silks, the women
tittered shrilly as they made mock bows to him. Roasted soybeans
crunched under countless pairs of feet. Every establishment was
open and full to capacity. Shrieks of laughter issued from teahouses; gay parties sparkled behind the windows of the pleasure
houses.

Sano gritted his teeth as he edged around the *yūjo* parade, only
to come to a standstill again at a large audience gathered around
a juggler. Frantically he scanned the crowd. How in this inferno
would he ever find Tokugawa Tsunayoshi and Lord Niu? At least,
he consoled himself, the police would never catch him here.

He realized his mistake when he saw a *doshin* standing outside the teahouse that advertised women's wrestling. Conspicuous because of his everyday work clothes and his unsmiling demeanor, he accosted a samurai coming out of the teahouse and began yelling questions into the bewildered man's face. Nearby, the *doshin*'s assistants had detained a mounted samurai. As Sano watched, they dragged their victim from his horse and tore the tiger mask off his face. One held a spear to his neck. The other yanked open his cloak.

Sano turned his horse and forced his way to the opposite side of the street. Both samurai were roughly his own height, build, and age; the mounted one had a brown horse like his. The police were stopping and searching men who fit his description. Toda Ikkyu, doing the job of a good spy, must have reported his visit to the police and told them about the sandal and rope he carried—better proof of his identity than a possibly forged or stolen set of credentials. Sano knew he should get rid of these incriminating items, and the horse. Still, he couldn't throw away any of the evidence that tied the Nius to the murders, any more than he wanted to abandon Wada-*san*'s horse. He might yet have a chance to return the horse and use the evidence to clear his own and Raiden's names, to restore his honor, position, and consequently his father's health.

With difficulty, he maneuvered the horse through the crowd and resumed his search. Having read an illustrated version of *The Tale of Genji,* he had an idea of how the shogun would look tonight. The women of that period four hundred years past had worn layers of sashless kimonos—five or six, each a different color, with flowing skirts that dragged on the ground and sleeves that covered their hands. They'd worn their hair long and loose and parted in the middle. But where was the shogun? What was he doing?

Sano tried to put himself in Tokugawa Tsunayoshi's position. As a man eager to shed the burdens of power and fame for one night, where would he go? The elaborate costume suggested that he wanted to mingle with the revelers in the streets and teahouses, protected from enemies or suppliants by a disguise not as easily penetrated as a simple mask. He could be anywhere, although he wouldn't have come alone. He'd have brought bodyguards with him, possibly dressed in costumes of the same period. With that little to go on, Sano fought his way down the street. He only hoped Lord Niu had no more information about the shogun's plans than he did.

Where were Lord Niu and the other conspirators? In their place, Sano would ambush Tsunayoshi outside the quarter for a quick, neat kill away from all the confusion, and an easy getaway. Yet he dared not try to predict the mad Lord Niu's actions. Neither did he have any idea what disguises the conspirators might be wearing.

Realizing he couldn't cover the whole quarter with any speed, Sano began stopping people he met. He shouted, "Have you seen—" and then described the shogun's party the way he imagined it. The answers he got were varied—

"No. Yes. Maybe. I don't know!" from a drunken merchant.

"Don't be so serious. Come have a drink!" from some rowdy young samurai.

—and largely useless.

Then a pleasure house doorman said, "An old-fashioned lady, you say? Why are you looking for her, when there are so many pretty modern girls here?"

The mention of girls and the sight of the parading *yūjo* reminded Sano of Wisteria. She'd helped him once; maybe she would again. She must have many friends in Yoshiwara who could join in the search, and enough samurai admirers to stand against Lord Niu's men. He started toward the Garden of the Heavenly Palace. Then he spotted another procession of *yūjo* gathered outside a teahouse. Joy and concern flooded him in equal measures as his gaze found the woman at the end.

Except for her distinctive round eyes, he wouldn't have recognized Wisteria. Much thinner and paler, she wore a plain cotton kimono. Beside her swayed a very drunk man. As Sano watched, he flung an arm around Wisteria, hand groping for her breast. Wisteria's face was frozen in a grimace that barely resembled a smile.

Sano had no time to wonder what had caused the high-ranking beauty to sink to such depths. "Lady Wisteria!" he called.

Somehow he reached her side without trampling anyone. He called her name again.

"Wisteria!" he shouted, lifting his mask for a moment so she could see his face. "Wisteria, do you remember me?"

Her false smile vanished. "You!" she shouted, eyes ablaze with hatred. "I helped you. I gave myself to you. And look what's become of me!"

Her angry gesture encompassed her drab, haggard appearance, her oafish customer, her place at the end of the line. Sano's heart contracted. He had, he recalled now, reported their conversation to Magistrate Ogyu. Ogyu must have ordered her demoted to low-class prostitute and social nonentity so that no one would pay attention to any stories she might tell about Noriyoshi's murder. Another life ruined by his actions. But he couldn't let guilt or pity stop him from doing what he must.

"Lady Wisteria, forgive me. I need your help again. I have to find—"

"Stay away from me!" she shrilled. "You've done enough harm already!"

Shaking free of her customer, she turned and fled. Her small size let her squeeze through narrow openings in the crowd as Sano could not. He had no choice but to let her go.

He turned away hastily when he saw another *doshin* pushing through the crowd toward him. He dismounted and continued down the street, leading the horse. From ground level, he could no longer look down over the crowds, but his new vantage point hid him from his pursuers and let him peer into doorways and open windows. In the teahouses and restaurants he saw many tall, heavy women that had to be men in disguise, but no one matching the shogun's description.

He rounded a corner into a street barely wide enough for four men to walk side by side. The quarter's outer wall blocked its far end. Brilliant lanterns, strung across the street between the roofs of the houses, danced overhead. The dense crowd brought Sano to an abrupt halt. He stood on his toes and craned his neck. All around him, men celebrated with increasing abandon as the festivities neared their peak. Caged *yūjo* cried out encouragements and invitations. The ground under Sano's feet was slippery with sour-smelling mud. Then he saw a sleek dark head that reached above the others, about thirty paces away. A momentary gap in the crowd gave him a glimpse of a large, homely white face and long, flowing hair. The man-woman smiled and waved to someone. His billowy gold sleeve fell back to reveal layered kimonos underneath: red, green, blue, white.

At the same time as Sano recognized Tokugawa Tsunayoshi, the crowd pressed against him. Three samurai, masked but in ordinary clothes, were moving his way, clearing a path ahead of the shogun. Six more bodyguards, three mounted and three on foot, covered their master's back and sides. Sano pushed at the bodies that stood between him and the middle of the street. He had to intercept the shogun before he disappeared into the crowd.

"Stop pushing!" someone yelled, shoving Sano back against a railing.

"Out of the way, out of the way," called the shogun's bodyguards.

Sano knotted his horse's reins around the railing. Then he wedged himself between two men. The first bodyguard neared him. An elbow knocked his mask askew, and as he righted it, he saw the bodyguard pause and turn his head in response to a call.

A *doshin* appeared beside the guard. They began a conversation that the other two front-runners joined, shouting in one another's ears because of the crowd noise. Sano couldn't hear what they were saying, but he could guess. The *doshin* was asking or telling them about a certain dangerous fugitive.

Sano continued to work his way forward. At whatever risk to himself, he must use this opportunity to warn the shogun. The Conspiracy of Twenty-One might make their move at any instant.

Just then, a distant boom sounded. A hush fell over the crowd; men paused in the act of speaking, drinking, dancing, walking. Heads lifted in listening anticipation, among them those of the shogun and his party. Another boom followed, then another. Suddenly the night came alive with the clamor of a million gongs and bells, some high-pitched and sweet, others deep and sonorous. A cheer swept the quarter. It was midnight, and the priests in temples all over Edo had begun to exorcise the evil of the Old Year and ring in the good of the New. The peals and booms echoed off the distant hills and rocked the ground. The very air shuddered.

Sano listened with the rest of the crowd, momentarily spell-bound as they were by the awe-inspiring music. Then, on the high right edge of his field of vision, he saw a movement. He turned.

A samurai dressed in dark robes, leggings, and mask crept along a roof. As Sano watched, the man knelt and took an arrow from the quiver that hung from his shoulder. He fitted the arrow to his bow and drew back on the string, aiming straight at the shogun.

"Look out, Your Excellency!" Sano shouted, pointing. "There. On the roof!"

His voice was lost in the noise of the bells and gongs. Although he couldn't even hear himself, he kept shouting.

"Your Excellency!"

No one standing farther than three steps away could see him, either. Sano plunged toward his horse, untied the reins, and mounted. He drove the animal against the massed bodies. Standing in the stirrups, he waved and shouted. No one moved. They couldn't. Still the bells and gongs tolled. The shogun kept his rapt gaze on the sky. Now Sano saw with increasing panic that two more archers had taken up positions on other roofs.

"You! Up there! Stop!" he yelled.

His cry coincided with an instant's lull between peals. Two of the archers kept eyes and bows trained on their target, but the nearest turned toward him. No sooner had Sano guessed his intent than the archer swung his bow around and set free the arrow. It flew at Sano in a blur of speed. He had barely time for a quick intake of breath, and none to dodge. Then his horse screamed, rearing under him. He saw the arrow sticking out of its neck. Blood gushed around the shaft in rhythmic spurts. Sano cried out, trying to steady the squealing, thrashing beast. But the horse lurched and started to fall sideways. As Sano fell with it, he saw the archers on the roof release their arrows. The shogun disappeared as if jerked to the ground from below.

Sudden mass hysteria threw the street into a writhing turmoil. People shoved and kicked, trying to reach safety. Their screams rose over the noise of the bells. Sano landed on bodies already knocked to the ground by his horse's wild convulsions. Feet trampled his chest. He managed to fight his way out from under someone who fell across him, only to receive a jarring kick to his chin. He regained his footing just in time to see two of the shogun's bodyguards pull themselves onto a roof and take up pursuit of the fleeing archers. Others closed protectively around their fallen master, while the rest began fending off the crowds that surrounded them. Dread and a horrible sense of failure gripped Sano. Was the shogun dead?

"Clear the street!" the bodyguards shouted. "Go on, move! Everybody. Now!"

The *doshin* who'd approached them earlier reappeared, wielding his *jitte* as his two assistants swung their clubs. The crowd stampeded toward Naka-no-cho. Shouts and screams filled Sano's ears: "What is it? What happened? Help!"

Sano realized that he could hear them because the bells had stopped ringing. He resisted the buffeting tide of humanity and pushed forward. He had to see—

In a space cleared by the departing crowd, a man lay dead, an arrow through his chest. Sano expelled a long, shaky breath of relief when he saw that it was one of the bodyguards. Tokugawa Tsunayoshi stood amid his remaining men, unhurt but obviously shaken. He pointed at the corpse, then toward the roofs. He scowled. He struck his men with his fists. His feminine costume contrasted sharply with his unladylike fury as he berated his men in angry whispers, probably demanding to know who the assassins were, and how they'd learned of his presence in Yoshiwara. Hands spread in helpless confusion, the guards ventured answers that he cut off with more blows.

Suddenly Lord Niu's plan became glaringly apparent to Sano. Ignoring the *doshin,* who had fixed him with a suspicious stare, he hurried toward the shogun. He pushed past everyone who got in his way. The shooting had been just a ploy to scatter the crowd and divert the guards—a prelude to the real attack. He had to warn Tokugawa Tsunayoshi that there were eighteen more assassins yet to come.

"You, there," the *doshin* said. He elbowed aside a pair of stumbling drunks and strode up to Sano. "Come over here."

Oblivious to the danger, Sano looked beyond the shogun toward the far end of the street. Among the fleeing bystanders, he saw three samurai who didn't appear in any hurry at all. Dressed in plain dark kimonos, with straw hats that shadowed their faces, they hung back and let others pass them. They were separated by some ten paces, with the man in the middle of the street slightly in the lead and the others flanking him. As they neared the shogun's party, they let the distance between them close and quickened their pace as a unit. The lead man raised his head for a brief look at the rooftops. The lanterns lit his tense young face. Sano recognized Lord Maeda from the secret meeting.

"Your Excellency!" he shouted, hurtling forward. "Behind you. Look out!"

Instead of turning, the shogun and guards stared at him. Lord Maeda was within a few steps of the guard that stood between him and Tokugawa Tsunayoshi. His hand went to the hilt of his sword.

Then, whether because of Sano's warning or because he'd sensed danger, the guard whirled. Lord Maeda whipped his sword from its scabbard. He swung it sideways and over his head. Before he could bring it down on his victim, the guard had his own weapon unsheathed in his left hand. He sliced a brutal gash across Lord Maeda's chest. Lord Maeda screamed. His blade sank deep into the man's neck. Both fell to the ground, mortally wounded.

A new uproar broke loose as people who hadn't yet left the street ran for safety. Shrill screams came from the women in the pleasure houses. Sano dodged running men. The doshin grabbed his arm.

"Who are you?" he demanded. "What do you know about this?"

Sano ignored him. "Take cover!" he shouted at the shogun. "There are more of them!"

But the time for escape had passed. More dark-robed men appeared out of nowhere. They surrounded the shogun's party, thwarting the guards' efforts to hurry their master indoors. Suddenly the street swarmed with darting fighters and flashing blades. Steel rang upon steel. Hoarse cries filled the night. In the midst of the tumult stood Tokugawa Tsunayoshi, the military dictator who preferred the genteel arts to the martial, Confucian studies to affairs of state. Unarmed, he cowered behind the cover of his men, a pathetic figure in his rich robes and long wig. His white makeup gave a ghastly comic look to his confused, panic-stricken face.

The doshin let go of Sano and shouted for his assistants as he joined the battle. The guards fought with the brave and deadly expertise befitting top Tokugawa warriors, but the defense was outnumbered two to one. Sano drew his sword and plunged into the melee.

One of Lord Niu's men rushed at him, sword raised. Sano sidestepped and spun around. He slashed his attacker across the back. The man screamed and fell facedown, dead. Sano felt rather than heard another man coming at him from behind. Dropping to one knee, he pivoted, delivering a low cut that slit the man's belly and left him lying on the ground near the first. It happened so fast that Sano had no time to think. Years of training had prompted his actions. Now the knowledge that he'd killed for the first time roared through his soul like a hot, fierce wind.

He had done what he'd assumed he never would—fought in the service of his lord. He was a samurai in the truest sense. Fired with excitement and ardor, he leapt to his feet and turned to do battle again. He would save the shogun after all!

One glance around chastened him. The *doshin* and both assistants had fallen. The bodies of guards and Lord Niu's men lay crumpled in the street. A member of the conspiracy slashed and stabbed two outsiders who had taken up the fight. Then he joined his three remaining fellows in an advance on the four surviving guards who formed a protective cluster around the shogun. The cluster tightened as the conspirators steadily backed the defense against the stone wall. Blood stained the garments of all the combatants. The best against the best; evenly matched. Then, as Sano hurried to the aid of the Tokugawa forces, he saw a dark-robed figure slip out of a doorway and into the street. The man's face was turned away, but he walked with a familiar stiff gait.

Lord Niu.

With a cry of agony, one of the guards fell. His absence left a gap in the shogun's human shield. Before the other men could perceive and fill it, Lord Niu shot forward, unsheathing his sword.

"No!" Heedless of his own safety, Sano threw himself in front of Tokugawa Tsunayoshi. His blade checked Lord Niu's in a resounding clang.

The glee on Lord Niu's face turned to fury. His eyes blazed even brighter than usual. In a gesture so quick that Sano didn't see it, he whisked the mask off Sano's face with the tip of his blade. He bared his teeth in a savage smile.

"You," he said. "Still interfering in my affairs. Do you never learn your lesson?"

Paralyzed by sudden terror, Sano could only stare in silence. Lord Niu could have killed him in that same casual stroke. The knowledge destroyed the confidence that his first two victories had given him. Against his will he remembered Lord Niu's impressive performance in the practice hall. The upraised sword wavered in his hand. He wet his suddenly dry lips and forced himself to speak.

"I, Sano Ichirō, will not let you kill the shogun," he said in a voice that sounded timorous to his own ears.

Lord Niu laughed outright, a high, demonic cackle that made the hairs rise on Sano's nape. His nostrils flared as if he could smell Sano's fear. "You cannot stop me," he said. "You can only die in the effort. But if you choose, then so be it." Holding Sano's gaze, he crouched, poised to spring, sword ready.

As Sano faced Lord Niu, he focused a part of his mind inward, on his spiritual center. He sought the calmness, mental clarity, and inner harmony that directs and empowers a warrior during combat. But he found only chaos and turmoil from which no energy flowed. He couldn't banish pain, fear, or memory; he couldn't neutralize the power that these distractions held over him. That essential state of concentration eluded him. Without it, he was just a trained mechanism deprived of a guiding force. He was lost.

Lord Niu struck. His sword whipped across the space between them with an audible hiss.

Sano parried, an instant too late. The blade sliced his left shoulder. Only his instinctive turn sideways kept it from continuing downward across his chest to his heart. Searing pain tore a gasp from his throat. He launched a counterattack, cutting empty air as Lord Niu easily dodged. A spate of blood warmed his skin;

his life was pouring from him. The guards, still occupied with Lord Niu's men, couldn't help. They didn't understand that Lord Niu posed a greater threat to their master than all three of the others. But if Sano couldn't save the shogun, he would at least give him the means to save himself.

He ducked as Lord Niu's blade sang in a circle over his head. His grazed scalp burned and tingled. With his left hand, he pulled his short sword free of its scabbard. The movement worsened the pain in his shoulder; black dots stippled his vision. For an awful moment, he thought he would faint. Blindly he flung the sword backward, shouting, "Here, Your Excellency!"

He had no time to see if the shogun had caught it. The whistling arc of Lord Niu's blade cut at him again and again. It battered his own sword, making two strikes for every one of his. He escaped mortal injury only by letting Lord Niu drive him away from the man he must protect.

Out of desperation, he resorted to verbal attack. "Your mother is dead," he shouted at Lord Niu. "She killed herself tonight, when she learned you were a traitor!"

Lord Niu gave no sign that he'd heard. His burning eyes stared straight through Sano toward glory.

Sano tried another tack. "You won't get away with this. Even if you kill me and kill the shogun, you'll never get out of Edo alive!"

With Lord Niu everywhere around him at once, Sano never saw the stroke that knocked the sword out of his hand. He automatically grabbed for the short weapon he'd given to the shogun. His terror mounted when he realized his mistake. He dashed backward, casting quick glances at the ground. Where was his fallen sword?

Lord Niu sped after him. Only a slight limp betrayed his handicap as he jumped over bodies. His features had gone taut with determination; he flourished his sword with incredible power.

Too late Sano saw the *doshin*'s body sprawled in his path. His foot struck it. He fell, landing hard on top of the dead man. His hands scrambled in a futile effort to right himself and to grab the sword that lay just beyond his reach.

Lord Niu stood over him. "You're a formidable nuisance, Sano-*san*," he said between rapid breaths, "but one that I need worry about no longer. Farewell, my enemy." Slowly and deliberately, he raised his sword high.

Sano saw his death in Lord Niu's glowing eyes, in the shiny steel blade. Then, as he prepared to meet it with a samurai's stoic courage, his right hand grasped a hard metal wand. Two prongs protruded above its hilt. Not his sword, but a *jitte,* the parrying weapon of the police.

As soon as he recognized it, something happened inside him. Fear vanished; all distractions faded to insignificance. The *jitte:* symbol of law and order against anarchy and chaos; right against wrong; truth against deception; the good in him versus the evil in Lord Niu. These thoughts flicked through his mind with lightning speed. A sunburst of wordless comprehension lit him. Power rushed from the weapon and into his body. In aligning himself with all that was moral and righteous, he found strength and courage. His fragmented center coalesced and began to radiate energy. Now, in the space of an instant, he faced his destiny.

With an ear-splitting shriek, Lord Niu brought his sword slashing down in a diagonal arc. At the same moment, Sano swung the *jitte* across his body. It met Lord Niu's blow in a clash that sent pain shooting up his arm. The hook caught the blade just short of his throat. Sano thrust sideways, using Lord Niu's surprise and momentum to throw his opponent off balance. Lord Niu stumbled. Before he could recover and free his sword, Sano jerked the *jitte* away and brought it around full circle to crack against the side of Lord Niu's face. Lord Niu went down hard. Sano could tell that this great swordsman had no training in *jittejutsu.* His confidence soared as he realized that his own limited experience gave him a small advantage. This expertise, combined with his newfound power, could win him this battle. He leaped to his feet.

Then he saw he'd misjudged the angle of the blow, the force required to kill, or his opponent's determination. Lord Niu righted himself with great agility. His broken jaw distorting his face into a ferocious, lopsided leer, he glared at Sano with undiminished fury. He lunged, his flashing blade whitening the air.

Sano's left arm was virtually useless, and his right began to tire under the force of the repeated blows. Lord Niu gave him no time to recover his own sword. But his perception sharpened until he reached a state of extraordinary mental clarity that he'd never before attained.

He acted without conscious thought, anticipating and countering Lord Niu's moves with his own. Although he kept his attention riveted on his opponent, he was simultaneously aware of everything in and around him. The battles still raged. He saw—without watching—a guard slice the throats of two men in rapid succession. Pain existed; he couldn't forget O-hisa, Raiden, Tsunehiko, Wisteria, his father, or his loathing for this man who had driven his mother to murder and suicide. But memory, emotion, and physical sensation simply merged with the oneness of his inner self. They fed his strength, inspired his judgment.

Moving with increasing aggressiveness, he used the other edge he had over Lord Niu—mobility. First swooping near and then bounding away, he forced Lord Niu to follow him. He jabbed Lord Niu's torso again and again with the point of the *jitte*. He paid for his extra risks when Lord Niu's blade sliced his forearms and cheek, but the added pain became another source of power and knowledge. Suddenly he grasped the central truth about his opponent: Lord Niu wanted to kill, but he also wanted to die. The two desires balanced each other. That was the real reason why he wanted to assassinate the shogun, and the reason he'd chosen to attack in a place from which there was little chance for escape.

Backhanding a blow to his opponent's good leg, Sano knocked Lord Niu to his knees. He felt the balance between the young man's kill-wish and death-wish shift for an instant. His twisted face contorted further in agony, Lord Niu paused before rising—just long enough for Sano to shift the *jitte* to his left hand, crouch, and rise again with his long sword in his right. A heady surge of elation erupted inside him. He tasted victory.

Lord Niu swung again. Sano parried with the *jitte* and caught the blade. He gave the *jitte* a sharp wrench. Lord Niu's sword snapped at the hilt. The long blade whirled away. Lord Niu froze. He looked first at his broken sword, then at Sano. Their eyes met for a moment that lasted an eternity. Sano saw hatred, anger, and fear in Lord Niu's. Then resignation.

Flinging away the *jitte,* Sano gripped his sword in both hands. He swung it around and upward. Pain screamed in his left shoulder. He screamed, too, in triumph. With all his strength, he sliced downward at Lord Niu's head. Steel met flesh and bone as his blade cleaved Lord Niu's skull from crown to brow.

Sano stood motionless for a moment, his hands still locked around the hilt of his sword. His energy abruptly ceased to flow. Like a banked fire, it flickered in the depths of his center, then died. The heightened clarity of perception left him. His surroundings lost color and life. Only a moment after leaving his exalted spiritual state, he could hardly remember what it had felt like. He was empty, numb.

Then the world and its cares came rushing back to fill the void. He stared at his fallen enemy. Lord Niu lay on his back, legs bent, still clutching his sword. Blood and gore oozed around the blade embedded in his skull and pooled under his head. Death had extinguished the evil light in his eyes. His face looked strangely innocent and peaceful in its final repose.

Sano released the sword. He stumbled backward. Fully conscious now of the throbbing pain in his shoulder and a debilitating weakness in the rest of his body, he sank to his knees. He forced his eyes away from Lord Niu and looked around.

Corpses lay strewn over the blood-spattered ground. All of the Twenty-One, it appeared, and all of the police. A surprising number of other samurai who'd joined the battle, including the armored guards from the gate. Revelers trampled during the stampede. His horse, and another belonging to one of the Tokugawa men. But the shogun and two surviving bodyguards stood a short distance away, watching him. Except for the excited murmurs of spectators who watched from the windows, the street was silent.

Sano closed his eyes against the carnage. It's over, he thought as a weary sense of completion spread through his mind like a soporific drug. He collapsed to the ground. Through a thickening cloud of pain and dizziness, he was dimly aware of the shogun's men loading him onto a litter, covering him with a blanket; of the tramp of their feet as they conveyed him out of Yoshiwara and down a dark road; of the immense star-flecked sky above him. He fought to stay alert so that he could explain to the shogun all that had led up to the assassination attempt, and the reason for his own presence. But waves of blackness lapped at his mind. Half-conscious, he dreamed.

He was dead. Pallbearers were carrying his body to a blazing funeral pyre.

"Please," he whispered. He couldn't die without telling his story and finally having someone believe him.

"Rest now, talk later," a gruff voice ordered.

Jolted out of his nightmare, Sano looked down the steep road at what he'd mistaken for a funeral pyre. It was a boat, bobbing on the black river beside the Yoshiwara dock, its cabin decked with glowing lanterns and its masts flying a banner emblazoned with the Tokugawa crest. The litter tipped beneath Sano as the men carried him aboard. He groaned when they slid him onto soft cushions in a small, bright compartment. He saw Tokugawa Tsunayoshi's

anxious face hovering over him, heard a voice ordering the boatmen to cast off. Someone cut away his garments and dabbed his
wounds with something that burned and stung. He closed his eyes
again.

Merciful unconsciousness descended as the boat bore him down
the river toward Edo.

30

*S*etsubun was over. The first morning of the New Year en-
folded Edo in a hushed serenity. In the deserted streets, only a
sprinkling of litter missed by the sweepers—a dusting of crushed
soybeans, an abandoned mask, a few colored paper scraps—served
as silent reminders of the wild celebration that had ended so
recently. A rare late snow had fallen sometime during the night,
frosting the rooftops with a barely visible tracery of white. The sun
glinted brightly from an icy blue sky, giving the city a sharp-edged,
crystalline quality.

Sano rode slowly toward his parents' home. Last night, the
shogun had rescinded the order for his arrest, and he was now a
free man. Through eyes watery from the cold and aching with
fatigue, he gazed with wonder at a world that seemed strangely
altered. The shops were closed for the holiday. Later the streets
would fill with people making their New Year's visits, but for now
the houses lay still and silent, their pine-and-bamboo-decorated
doors closed tight against the chill. This was the city where he'd
lived his entire life. He realized that it looked no different than on
any past New Year's Day. Only he had changed.

The city streets faded from his awareness as he thought about
the night he'd spent at Edo Castle. There the doctors had treated
his superficial cuts and bruises, stitched the deep gash in his

shoulder, and applied herbal poultices to ease the pain and prevent festering. Servants had bathed him, arranged his hair, dressed him in clean warm garments, and given him tea. Then, with no warning and no time to wonder at the miracle of it, he'd found himself in private audience with the shogun, the chamberlain, and the Council of Elders.

Tokugawa Tsunayoshi occupied the dais of the huge reception room. He'd removed his costume and now wore formal black robes. His face looked drawn and anxious and older than his forty-three years. Chamberlain Yanagisawa and the five elders knelt at the foot of the dais; the shogun seemed to need their protection as much as he had that of his guards during the battle.

"You saved my life, Sano Ichirō," he said in a voice higher and milder than Sano would have expected of the nation's supreme military commander. "For that I would like to express my appreciation. But first, will you please explain how you came to learn of young Lord Niu's plot?"

Sano told his story. He presented the sandal and the rope—talismans he'd clung to long after they'd lost their practical value. He read aloud the scroll and Lady Niu's letter.

When he finished, everyone spoke at once.

"An outrage!"

"Lady Niu a murderer?"

"Niu Masahito must have been possessed by demons. Why else would he even attempt such a thing?"

"And can it be true that Magistrate Ogyu obstructed the investigation that led to the discovery of the plot?"

Chamberlain Yanagisawa raised his voice above the others'. "I suggest we let the honorable magistrate speak for himself."

He clapped his hands. At this signal, two guards escorted a stumbling Magistrate Ogyu into the room. Sano stared in astonishment. His former superior looked as though he'd been dragged from his bed. His face was dazed with sleep, and he wore a cloak thrown hastily over his nightclothes. When he saw Sano, he whimpered and backed toward the door. But the guards yanked him forward and shoved him to his knees before the shogun.

"Your Excellency, what an honor this is," Ogyu faltered, bowing.

The shogun fixed him with a stern look. "Did you try to prevent Sano Ichirō from investigating the murders of Niu Yukiko and Noriyoshi?"

"Why—why, no, Your Excellency," Ogyu stammered, obviously too befuddled to lie with conviction.

The shogun exchanged glances with Chamberlain Yanagisawa, who frowned. "Are you aware that Lady Niu ordered the murders for the purpose of protecting her son?" Tokugawa Tsunayoshi demanded. "If Sano Ichirō had not persisted in investigating them—against your orders—Lord Niu would have succeeded in his attempt to assassinate me tonight."

"No. Oh, no," Ogyu moaned. Body quaking, he prostrated himself before the shogun. Sano could almost see the waves of terror rising from him. "Your Excellency, please understand. I assure you that if I had known, I never would have—"

"Enough!" The shogun's command cut off his pleas. "For your gross negligence of your duty and your treasonous endangerment of my life, I relieve you of your duties as north magistrate of Edo and sentence you to permanent exile on Hachijo Island. You will be held at Edo Jail until the ship sails in three months." He nodded at the guards. "Take him away."

"No!" Ogyu screamed. "Please, Your Excellency, have mercy!"

The guards seized him. He kicked and fought, but they bore him swiftly from the room. Sano could hear his hysterical sobs echoing down the corridor. He lowered his own head, shaken by the sudden fall of a once formidable adversary. A spurt of horror and pity diluted his satisfaction at seeing Magistrate Ogyu punished.

When the room was silent once again, one of the elders said, "What shall we do about this sorry state of affairs?"

Chamberlain Yanagisawa spoke before the shogun could. "One thing is certain," he said. "As few people as possible must be allowed to know that His Excellency was almost killed tonight, or that a slipup in our security ever occurred. I will tell you why this is so and how we can accomplish that which must be done."

The elders and Tokugawa Tsunayoshi listened with respect. Sano could tell that the handsome Yanagisawa wielded much of the shogun's authority, just as the other *yoriki* had implied during that long-ago breakfast in the barracks.

"We cannot afford to have the daimyo think that the shogun is vulnerable to attack," Yanagisawa explained. "Not only would the Tokugawa clan lose face, but a large-scale insurrection might result."

There were murmurs of agreement.

"Therefore I propose that we disseminate the following story, which will also be entered into the official records: One band of outlaws attacked a rival band in Yoshiwara tonight. During the ensuing riot, many innocent bystanders, who rushed to the aid of the police, were killed. Young Lord Niu and twenty of his friends numbered among them. All the outlaws not killed on the spot were taken into custody by the police and later executed."

There was silence while everyone considered this. The shogun nodded, and the elders exchanged glances. Sano, although appalled by this distortion of the truth, could nevertheless see the advantages of the chamberlain's plan.

Then the senior elder said hesitantly, "It will work, yes. Besides us, very few people know that His Excellency was in Yoshiwara tonight—just his bodyguards, his family, and his most trusted servants. Young Lord Niu and all the members of the Conspiracy of Twenty-One are dead. My assistants have visited the Niu estate and have confirmed that Lady Niu and her manservant Eii-*chan* are

360 / Laura Joh Rowland

also dead. We can use . . . methods"—his tone implied "threats and bribes"—"to ensure that the witnesses do not spread rumors. And no one associated with the Niu or other daimyo clans will admit to being a party to treason. But the law states that relatives of traitors must be punished. Should we not comply?"

Sano's heart sank as he imagined Midori and her sisters, Lord Niu Masamune and his sons and grandchildren, the families of the other conspirators—hundreds of innocent people—being led to the execution ground to pay for a crime they hadn't committed. Relief overwhelmed him when the chamberlain spoke.

"As you have pointed out, the guilty parties are all dead," Yanagisawa said. "Further punishment . . ." He spread his hands in an eloquent gesture, his meaning obvious. Further punishment would satisfy the law, but not the government's need for secrecy or the country's need for order and peace.

Sano's poultices had numbed his pain; the drugged tea was making him drowsy. His eyelids drooped as the shogun and the elders agreed to Yanagisawa's plan and discussed the particulars of carrying it out. He snapped awake when the shogun spoke his name.

"Sano-*san,* forgive us for keeping you so long. You are tired. But it will only take a moment more to settle the matter of your reward."

With difficulty, Sano roused himself.

"In return for the valuable service you have rendered me, I will grant you a favor of your choosing," Tokugawa Tsunayoshi said.

Sano was overwhelmed by the enormity of this unexpected gift. "Thank you, Your Excellency," he stammered. But how to make the right choice? Finally he settled on the one that would eliminate his most recent source of guilt. "I ask that the courtesan Wisteria be freed from the pleasure quarter and given enough money to live as an independent citizen."

The shogun leaned forward, a thoughtful frown on his face. "Very well. But surely this is too trivial a favor. Ask another."

Emboldened, Sano said, "I ask that a monument commemorating the death of my secretary, Hamada Tsunehiko, in the line of duty, be erected in his family burial plot." The shogun's recognition would go far toward comforting the boy's family, and some way toward fulfilling his own need to make reparation to them. "And that Niu Midori be released from the nunnery at the Temple of Kannon and brought home to Edo."

"He asks nothing for himself," the shogun said to the others in surprised admiration. "Only for others." Turning to Sano, he said, "The things you ask will be done. But in recognition of your selfless generosity, I shall further reward you as I see fit."

Now Sano entered the gate to his neighborhood. As he crossed the canal, he looked at the splendid black steed that Tokugawa Tsunayoshi had given him to replace Wada-san's dead one. Its saddlebags bulged with New Year gifts—fine lacquerware and ceramics and silver, beautifully wrapped parcels of *mochi* and tangerines—for his family and friends. He looked down at himself. The rich padded cloak and silk robes he wore came from the shogun's own wardrobe; all bore the Tokugawa crest. He touched the magnificent swords his grateful benefactor had given him: the finest work of the master swordmaker, Yoshimitsu. He felt the weight of the pouch containing ten gold pieces—an advance on the real reward that he would collect after his visit home. All the finery seemed as if it belonged to someone else, that stranger he'd become. And he couldn't bear to think of the real reward just yet.

In front of his parents' house, Sano dismounted. He'd no sooner led the horse through the gate when the door opened. There stood his father, frail and stooping and looking more ill than ever. With one hand he supported himself against the door frame; in the other, he held the letter Sano had sent by way of the priest. His sunken eyes reflected a mixture of hope, uncertainty, suspicion, fear, and helpless love.

Guilt tore at Sano's heart. Whatever he'd accomplished last

night, he would never forgive himself for inflicting such pain on his father. He started to speak, but his throat closed. Tears of shame stung his eyes.

"Ichirō." His father extended the hand that held the letter, then dropped it as if unsure whether to invite Sano inside or bar the door. A cough wracked his body. Recovering, he said, "Are you home to stay?" The tentative query encompassed myriad other unspoken ones.

Sano cleared his throat. *"Otōsan,"* he said, bowing, "I've returned home for the holiday only. The shogun has appointed me his special investigator. When I leave here, I shall take up residence in the castle and begin my work—at ten times my former salary." There: he'd said it aloud. Telling someone gave the reward a reality it had lacked when the shogun had bestowed it and he'd accepted. The acknowledgment filled him with a formless dread that left no room for pleasure. "If you let me inside, I'll explain."

His father frowned in disbelief. Then his eyes, which hadn't left Sano's face, moved to the horse, the clothes, the swords. He paled, and the arm that supported him began to shake. He started to fall.

"Otōsan!"

Dropping the reins, Sano hurried forward and caught him. At the same time, his mother appeared in the doorway. Her joyful greeting turned to an exclamation of dismay when she saw her husband's ashen face. With her help, Sano got the old man into the house and settled under warm quilts beside the charcoal brazier. Then he went back outside to stable the horse.

"Ichirō-*chan,* we were so worried, what happened to you?" his mother cried when he returned. "Where have you been?" She gazed in awe at Sano's clothes and swords, and at the treasure-laden saddlebags that he held. "What can be the meaning of this?"

Sano knelt before his parents. Tokugawa Tsunayoshi had given him permission to tell them the truth. After swearing them to secrecy, he did. "If anyone asks, you must say only that the shogun

promoted me because of a service I did him while I was a *yoriki*,"
he added when he'd finished. That was the story that Yanagisawa
and the elders had concocted. How neatly they'd secured his
complicity in the deception.

His mother reacted to the news with delight. "Oh, Ichirō-*chan*,
you are a hero! And what a wonderful reward for your courage!"
Eyes teary, she beamed at him. "Everything has turned out for the
best."

Sano wished he could share her belief. He feared, without being
able to say exactly why, that his new appointment would prove to
be as much a punishment as a reward. Trying to push these
disturbing thoughts away, he managed a smile for his mother.
Then he turned to his father.

The old man only nodded and said, "You have brought honor
to our family name, my son." But he sat straighter, visibly gaining
color, strength, and vitality.

Laughing, Sano's mother rose. "With all this excitement, I've
forgotten all about our meal!" She hurried out to the kitchen.

During their New Year's Day feast, Sano made himself eat to
please his mother. Pain and fatigue robbed him of desire for the
red beans and cold soup, the sweet spiced wine and other holiday
treats, although he took great satisfaction from seeing his father eat
with an unusually good appetite that presaged an eventual return
to health. All he wanted was to be alone, so that he could begin
to make sense of all that had happened to him since he'd first heard
of the *shinjū*. He wanted to ponder the meaning of his alarming
change of fortune, to understand the emotions now starting to
surface through his initial shock and numbness.

Finally the long meal ended. Sano rose, bowing to his parents.
"I must go to Wada-*san*'s house and give him his new horse," he
explained. Taking along parcels of *mochi* and tangerines to distribute among his neighbors, he escaped into the quiet streets.

He delivered the horse to Wada-*san,* who accepted it with awe
and made him stay and celebrate his promotion with a drink. He

called on his neighbors, but did no more than wish them a pleasant New Year. News traveled fast; they would know of his dubious luck soon enough. Afterward, he wandered through the streets on foot, carrying his one remaining gift parcel, his thoughts in a turmoil. Mulling over the events that had brought him to this moment, he wondered what he could have done differently. Could he have prevented a great tragedy without causing the lesser ones? Did his ultimate victory outweigh his many defeats? And why did he dread beginning his new servitude?

He wasn't surprised when he found himself outside Edo Jail once again. What he wanted was not solitude after all, but the right sort of company.

This time Dr. Ito did look surprised when he welcomed Sano at the door of his cell. After accepting Sano's gift and exchanging New Year's greetings, he said, "I must admit that I wondered whether I would ever see you again, my friend. Strange rumors have been circulating. What brings you here, obviously safe and—" His eyebrows lifted as he saw the Tokugawa crests on Sano's garments. "And if not well, then at least with every appearance of being well off?"

Sano said nothing. He felt full to bursting with the need to bare his soul. But now that Dr. Ito stood waiting for him to explain the real purpose of his visit, he didn't know how to begin. How could he voice the complex fears, regrets, and doubts that tormented him?

Dr. Ito broke the silence. "I am glad you have come, Sano-*san*," he said. "You are just in time to participate in my special New Year's Day ritual. Come with me."

He led the way through a series of guarded doors and passages and into a courtyard where the guards' barracks stood at the base of the jail's outer wall. In one corner, a flight of stone steps led to the top of the wall and the western guard tower.

As they climbed the steps, Dr. Ito said, "This is the day on which I look outside these walls and enjoy the view of Edo and its environs.''

Concern for his friend made Sano forget his own problems for the moment. ''You mean you're allowed to see outside the prison only once a year?'' he asked in dismay. In comparison with lifelong incarceration, his own ordeal seemed trivial and the shogun's reward an unmitigated blessing.

''Oh, no,'' Dr. Ito said with a wry laugh. ''The guards would let me come up whenever I asked. I treat their ailments, and in return they grant me privileges that our illustrious government would not. No, I myself choose to ration my pleasures. It gives me something to look forward to. And permits me less chance to reflect upon how much I have lost.''

They reached the top of the stairway and walked along the broad, flat summit of the wall. The wind fluttered their robes as they looked out at the city.

''It is beautiful, is it not?'' Dr. Ito said softly. ''The beginning of the New Year is a time for hope, and my hope is that I will someday regain my freedom.'' He turned and fixed his penetrating gaze on Sano. ''But you did not come to hear about my troubles.''

Encouraged by his friend's attentive and bracing presence, Sano told Dr. Ito how he'd spent *Setsubun*. Dr. Ito listened in silence. When Sano finished and turned to see his reaction, he nodded.

''And so you are a hero,'' he said. ''But not, it would appear, in your own estimation.''

The astute remark unleashed the torrent of emotion that Sano had been holding back. ''Oh, yes, I'm a hero,'' he said bitterly. ''I saved the shogun's life; I killed a traitor. Maybe I even prevented the collapse of the Tokugawa regime and five more centuries of civil war. I found the murderer and brought about her death. But three innocent people died because of me. Tsunehiko. Raiden. O-hisa. All sacrifices to what I considered a necessary search for the truth. To my vanity.

"If I'd known this would happen, I might have acted differently. I could have let the *shinjū* remain a *shinjū*. I've been a fool—a proud, clumsy fool—and rewarded for it!" Driven by unhappiness and self-disgust, he began to pace the wall.

Dr. Ito laid a gentle, restraining hand on his arm. "I can see why you feel as you do," he said. "But such self-reproach is useless. You have fulfilled your duty to the lord who commands your highest allegiance. Perhaps the others were fated to die, just as you were fated to save the shogun. You cannot know otherwise."

Sano shook his head. The doctor's sympathy and understanding gave him little comfort and no sense of absolution. But he began to grasp the reason why the prospect of serving as Tokugawa Tsunayoshi's special investigator disturbed him so much.

"When I saved the shogun's life—when I killed Lord Niu—I thought my troubles were over," he said, groping for the words. "This constant having to choose between personal desire and duty, when neither way seems entirely right or wrong. Pursuing inquiries without knowing where they will lead, or who will be hurt. Doing work for which I have no training and only instinct to guide me. Risking not only death, but also disgrace."

He laughed, a forlorn sound that came from the depths of his soul. "And what is this prize position that I've achieved, except a chance for more of the same? Now my life will never be any different."

"Really?"

Sano met his friend's cynical gaze and understood at once what Dr. Ito meant. With the shogun's authority behind him, he would have enormous power over other people's lives. He would have even greater opportunity to cause tragedy, to face danger and expose dangerous secrets. And the conflict within him would grow stronger. His need for the truth was undiminished, but woe upon him if he should disobey his new master's orders! Things were the same, yet different in a frightening way.

Sano nodded and sighed. "I see."

He stopped pacing to gaze out over the city. Above the snow-frosted rooftops of Nihonbashi rose the white tower of Edo Castle, where he'd spent one night and would spend many more. He avoided the daimyo district, instead turning to look at the western hills, the network of canals that ran in all directions, and the thick, mud-colored vein of the Sumida River. He peered north toward Ueno and Yoshiwara, and south toward the theater district. He contemplated the tiny, foreshortened human figures moving through the streets. Finally he let his eyes follow the thin lines of the roads that led out of Edo to the distant provinces.

"Even now, something that is happening out there may require your investigation," Dr. Ito said, echoing Sano's thoughts.

"Yes." Sano walked to the edge of the wall. He felt himself hovering on the brink of an uncertain future. Perhaps an adversary more formidable than Lady or young Lord Niu awaited him.

"I do not envy you, Sano-*san*. You face a difficult challenge."

But unexpectedly, Sano's spirits lifted. The New Year was a season for hope, as Dr. Ito had said. It offered chances for him to atone for the deaths he'd caused. His wounds would heal. Time and experience would bring him wisdom that would aid him in his pursuit of the truth. He imagined saving lives, delivering more criminals to justice, conferring more honor upon his family name. A cautious optimism began to stir inside Sano, and with it, an eagerness to take up his new responsibilities as the shogun's special investigator.

"A challenge I accept," he said.

ACKNOWLEDGMENTS

I would like to thank the following people, each of whom helped make this book possible: George Alec Effinger, friend, mentor, and master science fiction writer. My agent, Pamela Gray Ahearn; my editor, David Rosenthal; my husband, Marty Rowland. And the members of my writer's workshop: Larry Barbe, Cary Bruton, Kim Campbell, O'Neil DeNoux, Debbie Hodgkinson, Jack Jernigan, Michael Keane, Mark McCandless, Marian Moore, John Webre, and Fritz Ziegler.

ABOUT THE AUTHOR

LAURA JOH ROWLAND is a graduate of the University of Michigan. She has worked as a chemist, microbiologist, sanitary inspector, freelance artist, and quality engineer. She lives in New Orleans with her husband and their two cats.

ABOUT THE TYPE

This book was set in Perpetua, a typeface designed by the English artist Eric Gill and cut by The Monotype Corporation between 1928 and 1930. Perpetua is a contemporary face of original design, without any direct historical antecedents. The shapes of the roman letters are derived from the techniques of stonecutting. The larger display sizes are extremely elegant and form a most distinguished series of inscriptional letters.

03 - 2